Reginald Hill

Reginald Hill is a native of Cumbria and a former resident of Yorkshire, the setting for his outstanding crime novels featuring Dalziel and Pascoe, 'the best detective duo on the scene bar none' (*Daily Telegraph*). His writing career began with the publication of *A Clubbable Woman* (1970), which introduced Chief Superintendent Andy Dalziel and DS Peter Pascoe. Their subsequent appearances, together with the adventures of Luton lathe operator turned PI Joe Sixsmith, have confirmed Hill's position as 'the best living male crime writer in the English speaking world' (*Independent*) and won numerous awards, including the Crime Writers' Association Cartier Diamond Dagger for his lifetime contribution to the genre.

The Dalziel and Pascoe novels have now been adapted into a successful BBC television series starring Warren Clarke and Colin Buchanan.

By the same author

Dalziel and Pascoe novels

A CLUBBABLE WOMAN

AN ADVANCEMENT OF LEARNING

RULING PASSION

A PINCH OF SNUFF

A KILLING KINDNESS

DEADHEADS

EXIT LINES

CHILD'S PLAY

UNDER WORLD

BONES AND SILENCE

ONE SMALL STEP

RECALLED TO LIFE

PICTURES OF PERFECTION

ASKING FOR THE MOON

THE WOOD BEYOND

ON BEULAH HEIGHT

ARMS AND THE WOMEN

DIALOGUES OF THE DEAD

DEATH'S JEST-BOOK

Joe Sixsmith novels

BLOOD SYMPATHY

BORN GUILTY

KILLING THE LAWYERS

SINGING THE SADNESS

FELL OF DARK

THE LONG KILL

DEATH OF A DORMOUSE

DREAM OF DARKNESS

THE ONLY GAME

REGINALD HILL

AN APRIL SHROUD
A CLUBBABLE WOMAN

Two Dalziel and Pascoe novels

HARPER

Harper
An imprint of HarperCollins*Publishers*
77–85 Fulham Palace Road,
Hammersmith, London W6 8JB

This omnibus edition 2008
Reprinted 2008

www.harpercollins.co.uk/crime

ISBN 978 0 00 783484 6

Typeset in Meridien by Palimpsest Book Production Limited,
Grangemouth, Stirlingshire

Printed and bound in Great Britain by
Clays Ltd, St Ives plc

AN APRIL SHROUD

Contents

... the melancholy fit shall fall
Sudden from heaven like a weeping cloud
That fosters the droop-headed flowers all
And hides the green hill in an April shroud

JOHN KEATS

De'il and Dalziel begin with ane letter
The de'il's nae guid and Dalziel's nae better.

Old Galloway Saying

1

Epithalamium

No one knew how it came about that Dalziel was making a speech. Pascoe had with great reluctance let himself be persuaded into a church wedding, partly by the argument sentimental (*Mum's looking forward to it*), partly by the argument economic (*Dad's paying for it*), but mainly by the suspicion, hotly denied but well supported by circumstantial evidence, that Ellie herself wanted it.

But they had been agreed about the reception. *A pint and a pie*, insisted Pascoe. *A glass of sherry and a sausage on a stick*, Ellie translated to her mother. In the event, they were drinking champagne and eating creamed chicken canapés, but at least they were on their feet, able to mingle freely, and no one was going to start reading telegrams and making speeches. Especially not Detective Superintendent Andrew Dalziel.

'I reckon I know Sergeant Pascoe, *Inspector* Pascoe, *Peter*, as well as anybody,' proclaimed Dalziel.

'It can't be the drink,' murmured Pascoe. 'He never gets drunk. Not so you'd notice.'

'That's on scotch. Dad says he's sunk two bottles of Champagne so far,' said Ellie.

'He's counting, is he?'

'*No!* He just noticed, mainly because merry Andrew there keeps calling it perry. Which hurts when you've paid for genuine non-vintage Champers.'

They giggled together and drew some reproving glances from a group of elderly relations who clearly believed that Dalziel's speech was the first reassuringly normal thing at a wedding where the bride had not worn white and there was no sit-down meal at the reception. *If you do it standing up, it doesn't count* was a maxim which could carry a decent body through nearly all of life's tribulations.

'He's a good policeman,' Dalziel assured the elderly relatives. 'He'll go far. Deserves every success. I've encouraged him from the start. And I don't flatter myself when I say I've managed to give him a bit of a leg-up . . .'

He paused and mopped his brow with a huge khaki handkerchief. The bald patch, uncompromisingly visible through the grey stubble of his hair, shone with sweat. He smiled now as he lumbered towards a dirty wedding joke, and with his shining face, broad smile, broader paunch, and the Champagne glass held perpetually at the ready a foot from his lips, he should have been a figure of

2

Pickwickian jollity. Instead, he looked as if he had just kicked the door down and was demanding that no one moved as he had the place surrounded.

'. . . a bit of a leg-up in his career,' he resumed. 'But he'll have to manage by himself tonight.'

'Oh Jesus,' breathed Pascoe.

The elderly relatives didn't much care for the joke but were still willing to give marks for effort.

'Ellie I don't know so well. But she'll do very well, I'm certain. My old Scottish grand-dad used to say, when you're picking a lassie, start at the bottom and work up. Broad hips for the bairns, broad shoulders for the housework, and a broad smile for good-nature and a peaceful life. Ellie, now . . .'

Some early-warning system must have told him that he was heading into troubled waters.

'Ellie,' he repeated. 'It's a hard job being a police-man's wife. Not every woman can do it. But if she can, and I'm sure Ellie can, then it's a grand and rewarding task. There's nothing better for a policeman than to be well looked after at home. Nothing. I can tell you . . . I've been looked after in my time . . . once . . .'

'In every Toby Belch there's an Andrew Ague-cheek trying to get out,' murmured Ellie. 'I think he'd have been better droning on about my big mouth and huge bum.'

'So I give you,' cried Dalziel, explosively recovering from his introspective lapse, 'the happy pair! May *their* lot be a happy one!'

3

'The happy pair!' echoed the assembled crowd of about forty relations, colleagues, friends, while Pascoe and Ellie looked at each other with love and speculation in their eyes.

Later as they ran across the car park of the Three Bells to Pascoe's ancient Riley, it was Dalziel who trotted alongside them, using a Martini table-parasol to fend off the rain which had been beating down unremittingly on Lincolnshire for twenty-four hours.

'Good luck,' mouthed Dalziel at the passenger window. To Ellie he was almost invisible through the running glass. She smiled and waved. Her parents and the other guests had not risked their wedding finery in the downpour, which meant that at least they were spared the usual primitive valedictory rites. It also meant that she couldn't see anyone to wave at except Dalziel and even he had moved out of their way round the back of the car.

'Let's go,' she said.

Looking back, she saw him standing in the middle of the car park, waving the umbrella in a gesture of farewell and (accidentally, she hoped) menace.

'You're sure he doesn't know where we're going?' she asked Pascoe anxiously.

'No one does,' he replied with confidence.

'Thank God for that. I wouldn't put it past him to decide to spend his holiday with us.' She relaxed with a deep sigh, then suddenly laughed. 'But he was funny, wasn't he? *Leg up!*'

Pascoe laughed with her and they even managed to laugh again five minutes later when they were stopped by a police Panda driver, curious to know why they were towing a police helmet, a police boot and a banner inscribed Hello! Hello!! Hello!!!

'I thought it went very well, George,' said Dalziel. 'Very well.'

He sounded self-congratulatory as though he had arranged the ceremony himself.

'I suppose it did,' said Detective Inspector George Headingley, glancing at his watch. He and Dalziel were the sole survivors of five policemen who had travelled down from Yorkshire for the wedding. In fact they were the sole survivors of the entire wedding group and it was only his awareness of their profession and status which prevented mine host of the Three Bells from pushing them out into the gloomy damp of a late spring afternoon in Lincolnshire.

'Stop looking at your watch, George,' said Dalziel. 'Have another drink.'

He had abandoned the pernicious 'perry' and obtained a bottle of the true Hippocrene, Glen Grant straight malt, two large doses of which had restored him to his customary dignity and composure.

'I really mustn't, sir,' said Headingley. 'It's all

5

right for you, but I've got to drive back this evening. God knows what's happened back there with all the best minds down here!'

'Mondays are always quiet,' pronounced Dalziel. 'One for the road. A small one.'

Headingley knew better than to resist when Dalziel insisted. He watched the broad strong hand pour another measure of scotch into his glass. There was no unsteadiness, no wastage. 'A small one,' to Dalziel was the precise equivalent of a Scottish pub double. Dalziel's ancestry had long been subsumed by his Yorkshire upbringing, but in some matters he was true to his heritage. He tended to become very sad at the sight of an English small whisky and very irritated when people mispronounced his name.

Headingley had known him, or known of him, all his working life. Dalziel had been a sergeant when Headingley joined the mid-Yorkshire force and his reputation was already established. *Thick as two short planks*, opined the scions of the uniformed branch. *But if you get hit by two short planks, it doesn't half hurt.*

His rise to his present rank of Detective Superintendent had not been meteoric, but it had been inevitable. When the hippo comes up for air, the lighter creatures of the surface impede the process at their peril. These lighter creatures had included his wife.

Headingley did not like the man, but in his own interests had developed a protective shield of long-suffering diffidence which passed for a relationship. He usually contrived to be on the move in Dalziel's vicinity and letting himself be pinned down like this was an error attributable to champagne and post-wedding sentimentality. And also, he suspected, to a reluctance on Dalziel's part to be left to himself.

'Do you think they'll make a go of it?' he asked suddenly.

'What?' said Dalziel.

'Pascoe and his missus.'

The fat man shifted his bulk, not visibly affected by several months of intermittent dieting, and fixed his wide, short-sighted gaze on Headingley.

'Why shouldn't they?' he asked aggressively.

He feels protective, thought Headingley. Mustn't say anything against his precious whizz-kid, must we?

Absurdly, he realized he felt jealous.

Downing his drink, he pushed himself out of the chair.

'No reason,' he said. 'Must be off now, sir. Quiet or not, some of us will be back at work tonight.'

'This is the first holiday I've taken in God knows how long,' answered Dalziel. 'I'll be back in a fortnight today.'

There was a plaintive note in his voice which alarmed Headingley more than aggression.

'Have you decided what you're doing yet?' he asked cautiously.

'No.' The grizzled head shook ponderously. 'I'll

just drive around a bit. Look at the countryside if I can see it for this bloody rain.'

'Oh.'

Headingley's voice was studiously neutral, but Dalziel shot him a malicious glance.

'Of course, if I get bored, I might just come back early. Take you all by surprise. Give you all your sticks of rock where you're not looking for them.'

'That would be nice,' said Headingley. 'Enjoy yourself, sir. See you the week after next.'

Dalziel slowly screwed the top back on his bottle after Headingley had gone. Next he rose, not unsteadily but with a slowness which in another man might easily have become unsteadiness. He had taken the precaution of booking in at Orburn's main hotel, the Lady Hamilton, situated only a couple of hundred yards from the Three Bells. A short brisk walk was just what he needed now. It would blow, or in this weather wash, the stuffiness out of his mind, set him up nicely for a good solid meal. These buffets were all right but they didn't give a man anything to get his teeth into, especially a man who had resolved to forget his diet while on holiday.

But at the hotel he met a set-back.

'The restaurant does not open for another hour, sir,' said the shiny under-manager who to Dalziel's jaundiced eye looked as if he had been anointed with Mansion Polish. 'It is, after all, barely five-thirty.'

8

'Is that so?' said Dalziel. He stepped close to the under-manager and bared his teeth in a humourless smile. 'In that case, there'll be time for me to take a good look round your kitchens, won't there?'

Despite this inauspicious start the meal turned out to be almost as good as had been promised by the hotel publicity. And afterwards in the bar just to add a little spice to the evening there was a scene.

A tall blonde girl, who had caught Dalziel's attention in the restaurant because she wore a deep plunging dress without showing the slightest evidence that she had breasts, punched one of her two male companions on the nose. It was no mere feminine slap, nor even a piece of robust horse-play, but a whole-hearted punch, starting from behind the girl's right ear, ending with a squelchy thump on the point of the man's nose. It was a good blow for such a skinny fighter and it drove the recipient backwards over his tall bar-stool, setting up an interesting chain reaction along the whole length of the bar.

Dalziel sitting at a table by the door grinned with delight. The girl, who looked nineteen or twenty at the most, now casually picked up her bag and walked away from the bar. Dalziel stood up and opened the door for her.

'Well done, lass,' he said, genially peering down her dress. 'I really enjoyed that.'

'Did you?' she said. 'Let me double the pleasure.'

Dalziel was on his feet and much more solidly built than her first antagonist. Nevertheless the blow drove him backwards on to his table, shattering his glass and spilling the ashtray to the floor.

'Jesus!' he said, gingerly feeling his nose and looking after the girl's disappearing back.

He glowered round the room, defying anyone to be amused by his discomfiture, but most eyes were focused on the attempts to restore order at the bar. The floored young man was bleeding slightly but looked more puzzled than pained. He was in his early twenties, fair-haired, tall, athletically slim, a type Dalziel associated with the three-quarter lines of fashionable rugby teams composed mainly of young men called Bingo and Noddy. His companion was of an age, but shorter and stouter, in fact far too stout for someone so young.

He seemed to be the only person at the bar who had preserved his drink intact and he surveyed the others with a faintly complacent grin.

'Charley,' he said. 'You really ought to buy all these people a drink.'

'You buy them a drink,' said Charley. 'She's your bloody sister.'

Someone came through the door behind Dalziel.

'What seems to be the trouble?' said a voice in his ear.

He turned and looked at a small middle-aged man wearing an old pin-stripe suit of such hideous cut that it could not even be said to have seen better days.

'Trouble?' said Dalziel.

'I was in the restaurant. One of the waiters said something about a fracas.'

'Did he?' said Dalziel. 'I saw nowt.'

He turned and left, pleased for once in his life to have been a sufferer of, rather than from, witness blindness. No one but a sadist or a newspaper reporter would have let a rumour of a fight drag him out of the Lady Hamilton's dining-room and Dalziel had no wish to start his holiday as a comic paragraph in some local paper. Come to think of it, he had pretty little wish to start his holiday at all. It was supposed to do him good, to rid him of the irritability and fatigue which had begun to dominate his working life in the last few months. But it was the time away from work, the time he spent by himself, which he feared most, and all a holiday would do was give him more of that. But it had to be tried, he recognized that. Otherwise . . . well, there was no otherwise he cared to contemplate.

Tomorrow he would set off like a good tourist to explore the highways and byways of the Lincolnshire countryside. Peace and quiet away from the mainstream of traffic, and in a fortnight he could return to work revitalized. Perhaps.

Meanwhile, as he had done for many nights now, he set about postponing the moment of switching off his bedroom light until he was on the very brink of sleep. He poured himself a carefully measured dose of scotch and put it on the bedside table. Next, clad in pyjamas suitable in pattern and size for the fitting of three or four deckchairs, he climbed into bed, placed his reading spectacles gingerly on his still throbbing nose and picked up his book. It was Bulwer Lytton's *Last Days of Pompeii*, which he had stolen from the hotel where he spent his honeymoon and had been reading and re-reading off and on now for thirty years.

2

A Bridge to Nowhere

The countryside was brimming. The rain had continued all night and he had woken several times to hear its monotonous pizzicato on the tiny metal balcony which some ironical builder had positioned outside his unopenable window. It had taken several medicinal malts to get him a couple of hours of dreamless sleep and he had been packed and ready for breakfast by eight o'clock.

He collected his bill at reception just as the under-manager passed without speaking. Dalziel, however, was not a man for childish grudges and he addressed the other cheerfully.

'Listen,' he said. 'Two things I don't do. I don't pay VAT on a service-charge and I don't pay a service-charge on VAT. You get it sorted.'

It took a little time to get it sorted but he was still on his way shortly after nine-thirty.

Orburn was a country town of about seven thousand souls and had been neglected by development and history alike. Nothing earth-shaking had ever happened here nor did it now seem likely that it would. Dalziel, in a conscientious rather than enthusiastic attempt to prepare himself for his touring holiday, had read in a Guide to Lincolnshire of the fine broach spire of the small Early English church in which Ellie and Pascoe had been married, but the thing itself hadn't done much for him. The Guide had found little else to say and the only choice left to Dalziel now was one of direction. The main road (if so it could be called) through the town ran east to west. His car was pointing west so that was the direction he chose. A few miles farther on he hit the north-south trunk road and was faced with another choice. North would take him to Lincoln which he ought to visit. But it was also the direction in which home and work lay and he had the feeling that once he started north he wouldn't stop till the anguished faces of Inspector George Headingley and his colleagues told him he was home.

He turned south, spent ten minutes crawling in the blinding wake of a convoy of huge lorries and angrily turned off the main road and began to work his way back east along a network of narrow country lanes. It was only now that he realized how wet it really was. His morning paper had talked of serious flooding in some parts of the country but in print this made as little impact as shooting in Ulster or air disasters in the Andes. Now, however, as more and more frequently he encountered troughs of brown water wherever the road dipped, he began to realize that the weather was likely to be a key factor in his plans. Finally he stopped, partly because the next trough looked suspiciously deep, and partly because a signpost indicated a road coming in from the left; or rather, where the road ought to be. A hump-backed bridge rose over the stream which, running parallel to the road he had been following, was the source of most of the overspill. But now it was a bridge to nowhere. The land must have dropped away on the far side, the stream had completely broken its banks and the bridge descended into water.

Dalziel got out of the car and looked at the signpost. Another mile in his direction lay High Fold while in better weather the bridge might have led him to Low Fold, two miles away, and (here he laughed humourlessly) Orburn only twelve miles away. He glanced at his watch. It had taken him more than an hour.

He strolled to the top of the hump and gazed out over the flooded fields. The rain he realized to his surprise had stopped, though the atmosphere was still very humid. It was quite warm and there was even a dirty orange glow behind one threadbare section of the low cloud cover where presumably the sun was self-destructively trying to suck back into the air some of the moisture of the recent downpour. Curls of mist and vapour were beginning to form *art nouveau* designs in the more regular pattern of trees and hedgerow breaking the surface of the level waters. Patches of high ground too rose serenely from the floods. On one of these about a quarter of a mile away it was possible to make out a house to which design and distance gave the outline of a story-book castle. Someone had been lucky or wise in his choice of site. Farther than this the damp air made it impossible to see, but the floods certainly stretched as far as the visible horizon.

There is something ineffably depressing about water where it shouldn't be. Dalziel peered down from the bridge and it seemed as if the brown depths were full of dead things. Leaves and branches drifting on the surface were all he could see. Presumably fish and other aquatic creatures survived below. Presumably also the floods had killed as they invaded the dry land, hopefully not humans, but livestock and wild animals certainly.

If, thought Dalziel staring down at the turgidly flowing water, if I saw a body floating by, what would I do? Ignore it and go on with my holiday?

He shook his huge head gloomily. He had been wise enough in his life not to bother trying to plumb the depths of his own motivations and make-up, but he knew too well he'd probably risk lumbago, beri-beri and God knows what wading about in this filthy muck to pull the cadaver out, and then he'd hang about to the embarrassment and annoyance of some local jack till he was satisfied of the cause of death. Floods would be a good chance to get rid of some unwanted relative, he thought sagaciously.

No! Sod it! This wouldn't do at all. The holiday was the thing. Fresh air, commune with nature, bathe in beauty, pay homage to history. An English holiday, tired policemen, for the revitalization of.

Any corpse comes floating this way, I'll say Hello sailor, and goodbye, avowed Dalziel and as an act of both symbol and necessity he descended to the water-lapped limit of the bridge, unzipped his flies and began to pee in the flood.

He had just finished when a noise made him look up. It was a long, creaking noise followed by a gentle splash. It came again from behind a wedge-shaped copse of beeches rising stoically from the water about fifty yards to his left. The mist seemed particularly thick here and he strained his eyes in an effort to penetrate the grey barrier. Then through the haze appeared a shape. The sound sequence was heard once more. And into full view glided a rowing-boat. Hastily Dalziel began to fasten his flies.

The boat pulled by him, the oarsman taking long, leisurely strokes. He had the look of an old countryman, weathered and fit, anything between fifty and a hundred but able to row for ever. In the bows, like a reverse figure-head, sat another old man of more determinate age, about seventy, with a profile fit for a Roman coin. But it wasn't either of the men who held Dalziel's eye.

Sitting on the thwart bench was a woman. She

was clad all in black, even to a black veil over her face. Her head did not move as she passed, but Dalziel had a feeling that the eyes moved and saw him from behind the veil. So riveting was the tableau in the boat that Dalziel did not instantly take in the most macabre detail of all.

The rowing-boat was towing something behind it, a small flat-bottomed boat.

On it was a coffin.

It was unmistakably a coffin. The brass handles gleamed against the dark mahogany sides and three wreaths splashed white and green along the lid. Even the oarsman's evident expertise could not keep the tow-rope perfectly taut and this strange piece of freight proceeded jerkily, its momentum almost bringing it up to the stern of the rowing-boat at the end of each stroke, as if it were in pursuit. But the woman never turned and Dalziel stood perfectly still, his attitude compounded of astonishment and the conventional deference of one who meets a cortège in the street.

But now a new sound came from behind the copse. Splashes again, but not the soft splashes of expertly wielded oars, and commingled with these were voices chattering and the occasional shout.

Another craft emerged through the mist but if the first could have been created by Lord Tennyson this one owed more to Jerome K. Jerome.

It was a large punt, the kind once used in duck-shooting with a stove-pipe gun mounted in the bows, rusty through neglect and non-use but still menacing for all that. Did they neglect the licence also? wondered Dalziel.

There were six people in the punt, which was perilously low in the water. The gunwale had no more than an inch of clearance at best, and water slopped over the sides with each thrust of the pole by the punter whom Dalziel recognized instantly as his companion in assault the previous evening. The breastless girl was seated in the punt alongside the fat young man, who still wore the same complacent expression. Opposite him was a boy of about sixteen, slim and pensive but with sufficient of the fat youth's features to look as if he had just got out of him. And by the boy's side was a young woman whose straight jet black hair and impassive, high-cheekboned face made Dalziel think of an Indian Maid (Pocahontas in the Board School history book rather than Little Red Wing in the rugby ballad, his only source-texts).

Finally, in the bows, resting nonchalantly against the gun, was a dark, ugly-looking man probably in his twenties, though it was difficult for Dalziel to be certain as the man's black hair seemed to be in a state of insurrection and only the high ground of his nose and the valley of his eyes were putting up any real show of resistance.

Despite the impious exchange of views taking place between the girl and the youth with the pole, it was clear that this vessel was in convoy with the rowing-boat. The nearest any of them got to full mourning was the black turtle-neck sweater worn

19

by the boy, but they had all made an effort. The fat youth wore a black armband around the sleeve of his tweed jacket, the hairy man had a black rosette pinned to his *University of Love* shirt, the Indian Maid wore a white blouse and slacks but looked as if she had been specially carved for a funeral, and the breastless girl had tied a length of black crape round her straw boater. Their only protection against the probable resumption of the rain consisted of two umbrellas and a parasol, carried at the slope by the men, except for the punter whose contribution to the solemnity of the occasion and his own dryness was a black plastic mackintosh under which he seemed to be dressed for cricket. Swimming would have been a sport more suitable, thought Dalziel, watching his efforts at propulsion. Basically, he had a not inelegant style, tossing the pole high and sliding it into the water with a casual flick of strong, supple wrists. The trouble was, deduced Dalziel, that the pole was then plunged two or three feet into sodden earth and his efforts to drag it out acted as a brake, so that the punt moved even more jerkily than the coffin.

The Indian Maid spotted Dalziel first and drew the attention of the others to him. The fat youth said something and they all laughed except the young boy. Dalziel was ready to admit that the sight of a portly gent apparently about to walk in to four feet of water was faintly comic, but none the less laughter in these circumstances struck him as a breach of decorum.

The rowing-boat was now out of sight and Dalziel watched the punt till it too disappeared. Then he walked back over the bridge and tested the depth of the water on the road. It was just within the limits of safety and he edged the car through it with great caution.

The road now rose again, following the skirts of the relatively high ground to his right which acted as a block to the flooded stream. From the crest of this small slope he could see for quite a way. The road dipped once more and about a hundred yards ahead it was flooded for a distance of thirty or forty feet. But presumably thereafter it rose steadily away from flood level, for just on the other side of the water stood a hearse and two funeral cars. The oarsman was in the water, pushing the coffin ashore where the top-hatted undertaker and his assistants were trying to grapple with it without getting their feet wet.

Dalziel halted and once more settled down to watch. Finally all was finished, the punt party reached shore safely, dividing themselves among the two cars, in the first of which the woman and the old man had presumably been seated all along, and the sad procession drove slowly away, leaving only the oarsman seated on the bows of his boat rolling a well-earned cigarette.

When the cortège was out of sight, Dalziel started his car once more and rolled gently down to the trough below, humming 'One More River

To Cross'. There was nothing like the sight of someone else's funeral for making life look a little brighter.

Half-way through the trough, he suddenly realized this was much deeper than he had anticipated. At the same moment the engine coughed once and died. Dalziel tried one turn of the starter, then switched off.

Opening the window, he addressed the uninterested oarsman with all the charm and diplomacy he could muster.

'Hey, you!' he shouted. 'Come and give us a push.'

The old boatman looked at him impassively for a moment before he slowly rose and approached. He was wearing gum-boots which came up to his knees but even so the water lapped perilously close to their tops.

When he reached the open window he stopped and looked at Dalziel enquiringly.

'Yes?' he said.

'Don't just stand there,' said Dalziel. 'Give us a push.'

'I hadn't come to push,' said the man. 'I've come to negotiate.'

He proved a hard bargainer, totally uninterested in payment by results. It wasn't till he had folded the pound note Dalziel gave him into a one-inch square and thrust it deep into some safe apparently subcutaneous place that he began to push. The effort was in vain. Finally Dalziel dragged his own

22

scene-of-crime gum-boots out of the chaos in the back of the car and joined him in the water. Slowly the car edged forward but once it reached the upslope its weight combined with the water resistance proved too much.

'Sod it,' said Dalziel.

They sat together on the rowing-boat and smoked. Dalziel had already had the one post-breakfast cigarette he allowed himself nowadays, but he felt the situation was special.

'They'll be coming back soon?' he asked between puffs.

'Half an hour,' said the boatman. 'Not long to put a man in the earth.'

'Good,' said Dalziel. 'I'll beg a lift from the undertaker. Who're they burying?'

'Mr Fielding,' said the boatman.

'Who's he?'

'Mrs Fielding's husband,' was the unhelpful reply.

'Mrs Fielding was in the boat with you?'

Dalziel reached into his pocket, produced the emergency half-bottle he always carried with him in the car, took a long draught and offered it to his companion.

'Ta,' he said, and drank.

'You didn't make that in your garden shed,' he added when he'd finished.

'No. Are you Mrs Fielding's . . . ?'

He let the question hang.

'I work up at the house. Most things that need

23

done and can't be done by lying around talking, I do.'

'I see. Not a bad job if you play your cards right,' said Dalziel with a knowing smirk. 'Have another drink. That was Mrs Fielding's family, was it?'

Why he should have been interested in anything but getting his car out of the flood and back into working order, he did not know. But time had to be passed and the habit of professional curiosity was as hard to change as the habits of smoking or drinking or taking three helpings of potatoes and steamed pudding.

'Most on 'em. The old man's her dad-in-law. Then there's the three children.'

'Which were they?' interrupted Dalziel.

'The two lads, Bertie, that's the older one, him with the gut. Then there's Nigel, the boy. And their sister, Louisa.'

'The thin girl?'

'You've got bloody good eyes, mister,' said the man, taking another drink. 'Must be this stuff.'

'What about the others?'

'Friends. Visitors,' he grunted.

'For the funeral?'

'Oh no. They were here when he snuffed it. Not that it made much difference to 'em, mark you. Not to any on 'em. No. They just carried on.'

'Oh, aye?' said Dalziel, thinking that the trio he had observed in the Lady Hamilton the previous night had hardly comported themselves like grief-stricken mourners.

'What made you take to the water?' he asked. 'Couldn't the funeral cars get round to the house?'

'It'd be a long way round. They checked first thing this morning after last night's rain. Couldn't afford the time. They've a lot of work on in this wet weather. So it was either the boats or wait. And they wanted shot of the coffin quick, you see.'

'Well, I suppose it's a bit deadly having it lying around the house,' said Dalziel charitably.

'Oh yes. Specially when it's on the billiard table,' said the other.

There was no answer to this and they finished their cigarettes in silence.

'What did he die of, anyway?' asked Dalziel, growing tired of the unrelenting lap of water.

'Some say his heart stopped,' said the boatman. 'And some say he was short of breath.'

With difficulty Dalziel restrained himself from bellowing *don't you get funny with me!*

'What do *you* say?' he asked instead.

'Me? What should I know about it?'

He relapsed into a silence which plainly rejected breaking by any conventional social means. Dalziel walked along the water's edge a short way and stood inspecting the punt gun. It had been a formidable weapon, but looked very long disused. While the metal had probably never been bright (why give the poor bloody ducks even a chance of a chance?), now it was rusty and dirty and a spider had spun a few hopeful strands across the muzzle.

It began to rain and after a few moments he returned to the shelter of the car. The boatman ignored his invitation to join him and remained where he was, even his cigarette appearing impervious to the downpour.

Nearly half an hour later the first of the funeral party returned. It was the blond youth, alone and on foot.

'Shit!' said Dalziel and clambered out of the car once more.

'Hello,' said the youth as he approached. 'You're stuck in the water?'

Dalziel smiled his congratulations.

'Yes,' he said. 'Where's the funeral cars?'

'I was just telling Pappy, there's a lot more water on the road about a quarter of a mile round the bend. They weren't very happy about taking their shiny limousines through it on our way to the church and now they reckon it's even deeper, so I was sent on to bring the boats a bit farther along.'

He grinned amiably, apparently unresentful of the task. Dalziel could guess who had elected him to it. Anyone who let a woman punch him on the nose without setting matters right between them very quickly was saddling himself up for a hag-ride.

The boatman was casting off already.

'Hang on,' said Dalziel. 'I'll get my stuff.'

The level of the water seemed perceptibly higher as he waded back to the car and unloaded his old cardboard suitcase. As he returned cautiously to the dry road, he saw to his chagrin that the rowing-boat was already on its way, leaving him to the uncertain mercies of the punt.

'He's in a hurry,' he grunted as he placed his case carefully on one of the seats. The floor looked as if a halfpenny dropped from three feet would blast a hole through it.

'A devoted retainer,' said the other with enough of mockery in his voice to give Dalziel some hope for him. 'I'm Charles Tillotson, by the way.'

'Andrew Dalziel.'

'Dee-Ell,' echoed Tillotson. 'Dee-Ell. Spelt D-A-L-?'

'Z-I-E-L,' finished Dalziel.

'How impressive to be pronounced differently from the way you are spelt,' said Tillotson, flourishing the pole. 'It's sort of a test for people, isn't it? Perhaps I should drop the ILL, Totson. What do you think?'

'How about Tit?' said Dalziel. 'Are we going to move or shall we sit here getting wet all bloody day?'

Gingerly he seated himself next to his case and closed his eyes as Tillotson thrust off stylishly, got the pole stuck instantly and almost dislodged himself in his efforts to pull it out.

By the time they had followed the bend of the road and got the rowing-boat back in sight, it had reached the new landing-point and the rest of the party were already embarking. To Dalziel's dismay the funeral car then began to move off.

'Hey!' he bellowed, drawing the attention of the mourners and frightening a small batch of teal who were exploring their new-found territory. But the black limousine purred disdainfully on its way and was soon out of sight.

'Sod the bastard!' said Dalziel savagely.

'Pappy must have forgotten,' surmised Tillotson.

'Sod him too.'

Some explanation of his presence must have been required and given on the rowing-boat for when they drew level, no one showed much curiosity about him.

The woman, Mrs Fielding he presumed, was sitting in the stern with the old man. The stout youth had taken an oar and was seated alongside Pappy who returned Dalziel's accusing gaze blankly. The boy was in the bows, curled up like the Copenhagen mermaid. And the other three were crowded in the flat-bottomed boat lately occupied by the coffin.

'I think some of you must go back with Charley,' said Mrs Fielding in a firm, rather deep voice. Her veil was lifted now, revealing a strong almost masculine face which grief and hard weather had only been able to sting to a healthy flush.

'Oh no,' protested the thin girl, Louisa. 'Bertie's rowing too, and we can't weigh much more than a coffin.'

'Nevertheless,' insisted her mother.

'I'll go,' said the dark hairy man who was taking some shots of the floods with an expensive-looking

28

camera. He stood up and stepped into the punt with the ungainly ease of a sailor.

This seemed to satisfy Mrs Fielding's distribution problems for the moment. She now addressed Dalziel.

'I'm sorry the car went before Pappy could speak with the driver. If you'd care to come to the house, you can phone from there. Alternatively, we can leave you here and phone on your behalf.'

The man called Pappy started rowing and Bertie quickly picked up the stroke as Dalziel considered the alternatives. The rain was coming down harder. The occupants of the rowing-boat were concealed almost completely by a carapace of umbrellas which brought to mind the shield-wall of a Viking ship.

Dalziel turned to Tillotson.

'Follow that boat,' he said.

3

A Nourishing Broth

The teal had dropped back to the surface and followed at a safe distance.

'I had a friend,' said the ugly man in a pseudo-American accent, 'got badly hurt trying to screw a duck.'

'Oh, yes?'

'Yeah. He had this thing, you know, about having relationships with the whole of creation. But the duck didn't see it that way. Took half his nose off. After that he changed his scheme, went for the spiritual communion thing more, you know.'

'Just as well perhaps,' said Dalziel. 'He might have had trouble with ants.'

The other laughed approvingly.

'That's true, man.'

He thinks he's tested me, thought Dalziel. Now I've passed his little shock test, he'll try to patronize me.

'Charley there, the boy with the wooden whanger, now he goes in more for this kind of kick.'

He squatted behind the punt gun and made firing noises more appropriate to a howitzer.

'No, Hank, you've got it wrong,' protested Tillotson amiably. 'I like a bit of sport, that's all. I say, these floods are rather jolly though. I bet a lot of birds will come back. It must have been fine fowling country, this, before they drained it.'

'See what I mean?' said the other. 'He's just aching to get this old phallic symbol jerking off again.'

At last Dalziel had penetrated through the pseudo-mid-Atlantic flip speech style to a couple of recognizable vowels. He liked to know where he was with people and basic information about background was a good place to start. It gave him something to occupy his mind, to keep out the greyness which threatened to seep in whenever he relaxed.

'Not many ducks in Liverpool,' he said. 'My name's Dalziel. Who're you?'

The dark man looked at him assessingly before replying, 'Hank Uniff.'

Dalziel laughed, a short sharp offensive bark which acknowledged that there hadn't been much chance of his interlocutor being called Jim Smith or Bill Jones.

'Pleased to meet you,' he said. 'How was the funeral?'

'Full of images, man,' said Uniff. 'Hey, Charley, great funeral, huh? I mean, when they dropped the coffin in the hole, well, it was just about waterlogged. Cheerist, what a splash!'

'Yes,' admitted Tillotson as he passed them in practice of his new technique which involved thrusting the pole into the water off the bows and walking the whole length of the punt. It was inevitable, thought Dalziel, that one so obviously born a victim would sooner or later step over the side.

'Yes,' repeated Tillotson, 'it *was* rather like a burial at sea. Full fathom five, Tom Bowling, all that. Did you get some good pictures, Hank?'

'I shot off a whole roll,' replied Uniff. 'But did I get the light right? It wasn't easy to judge and that creepy preacher man didn't help by complaining.'

He cradled his camera protectively as if an attempt were being made to wrest it from his hands.

'Didn't Mrs Fielding object?' queried Dalziel.

'Bonnie? Hell, no. I mean, why, man?'

'Hank's an artist,' explained Tillotson, passing them again at a smart trot. His new technique was certainly moving the punt along much faster, but at the expense of direction if one assumed that the rowing-boat was taking the shortest route home. It was now almost out of sight and several points to the nor'-east.

Dalziel pulled his coat collar more tightly round his neck and resisted the temptation to take charge of the vessel. He was the super-cargo, not the captain. But something of his feelings must have shown to Uniff who grinned maliciously at his discomfiture and began to whistle 'The Skye Boat Song'.

'What kind of artist are you, Mr Uniff?' asked Dalziel.

'What kinds of artist are there, man?' replied Uniff.

'Well,' replied Dalziel, irritated, 'there's con-artists, and there's shit-artists, and there's . . .'

But his catalogue of abuse was interrupted by the forecast disaster. Tillotson drove the punt forward into a half-submerged hedge, the bows rose in the air, Tillotson screamed and went over the side, Uniff and Dalziel fell together in a tangled heap from which Dalziel recovered just in time to see his suitcase slowly toppling into the water.

Furious, he rose and put his huge hand into the face of Tillotson who was trying to clamber back on board.

'My case!' he yelled. 'Get my bloody case!'

Recognizing that this was an essential condition of readmittance, Tillotson pursued the case which had floated only a few feet but was sinking fast. Dalziel took it out of his hands and tried to drain it as, unassisted, the blond youth dragged himself on board, his exertions freeing the punt from the hedge. Uniff all the while took pictures, including one of the pole which for once had not become embedded in the mud but was floating away at a distance of some twenty feet.

Dalziel banged his case down with a force that nearly brought on a new disaster.

'Mr Dalziel, sir,' said Uniff, still photographing. 'By the ancient laws of the sea, I elect you captain. What now, man? Are you going to run a tight ship?'

Dalziel swallowed the anger which he realized would not be particularly productive at the present time.

'I might just marry you to this goon,' he said, 'and see if you could fuck some sense into him.'

Instead he swung his wellingtoned foot at the narrow planks which formed the cross seat and his fierce onslaught quickly loosened one sufficiently for it to be torn free. Then, using this as a paddle, he sent the punt in pursuit of the pole.

Uniff now put away his camera and rescued the pole from the water. Tillotson with the natural gallantry of the aristocrat offered to resume his post, but Dalziel with the equally natural bluntness of the peasant told him to keep his hands on his knees and his bum on the floor and not to move on peril of his manhood.

Uniff stepped to the back of the punt and with a vigorous driving stroke, which more than made up in efficiency what it lost to Tillotson's in style, he sent the punt scudding over the surface at such a rate that they were only fifty yards behind the rowing-boat as it reached the farther boundary of the water.

There was a lake here, Dalziel surmised, which had overflowed its banks and joined its waters with those of the stream running parallel to the road more than a quarter of a mile behind them. A small landing-stage, waterlogged by the rise in the level of the lake, led to some steps set into a steep sloping garden which rose to a substantial nineteenth-century house in a state of dilapidation not wholly explained even by three days of incessant rain. It was the house he had noticed earlier from the bridge to nowhere and, though close to it lost most of its fairy-tale-castle quality, it still had a solid, fortified look about it.

The other party had disappeared into the house by the time the punt reached the landing-stage and Dalziel did not stand upon ceremony but, using Tillotson's head as a support, he stepped ashore, strode grimly up the garden steps and entered the house without waiting for an invitation. Now he paused, not because of any late revivings of social courtesy but because it was far from clear to him where everyone had disappeared to.

A large entrance hall stretched before him. What might have been elegant wood-panelling had been ruined by the application everywhere of dark brown paint. It was to Dalziel like a nightmarish blow-up of the narrow lobby of his grandmother's house which family loyalties had required must be visited every Sunday although the Presbyterian conscience forbade that anyone should gain pleasure from such a visit. Momentarily he felt like Alice, reduced in scale to a position of total vulnerability.

A door opened. Instead of a monstrous grand-mother, Mrs Fielding emerged and made for the staircase.

Dalziel coughed and she stopped.

'Yes?' she said. 'Oh, it's you. There's the telephone. Help yourself.'

She turned to go but Dalziel detained her with another thunderous cough.

'I'd like to dry my things,' he said. 'Get changed. A hot bath would be welcome too.'

She looked at him with puzzled, rather disdainful eyes.

'Look, we're *all* wet, but this isn't a hotel,' she said. 'You might find a towel in the kitchen.'

Again she turned.

'Hold on,' said Dalziel.

She ignored him and started climbing the stairs.

'Look!' he bellowed after her, losing his patience. 'I've been punched on the nose by your daughter, I've been stranded by your boatman, and I've had my case dumped in the water by that long streak of nowt you left in charge of the punt!'

She stopped four stairs up. He couldn't see her face in the shadows, but he got the impression that she was smiling.

'It was your choice to accept the lift,' she said reasonably.

'Lady,' he answered, 'I didn't know what I was doing. But you did. You must have known I'd have had more chance of getting here safely if I'd set out to walk across the blasted water.'

Now she laughed out loud.

'We're warned about turning away angels un-awares,' she said. 'I see how easy it could be. Come along, Mr . . . ?'

'Dalziel,' said Dalziel and followed her upstairs, his case leaving a trail of drips which ran parallel to that cast by his sodden coat.

On the landing she paused uncertainly.

'We're a bit crowded at the moment,' she explained. 'It's a big house, but half the bedrooms haven't been used for years. I wonder . . .'

She opened a door and went in. The room was in darkness but a couple of moments later she opened wide the curtains and beckoned Dalziel in from the threshold.

'You're not superstitious, are you?' she asked. 'This was my husband's room. Well, it's got to be used again, I suppose. You don't mind?'

The last question might have been ironical as Dalziel had already opened his suitcase and begun to empty its damp contents on to the bed.

'Not at all,' he said. 'Very kind.'

'There's a bathroom through that door. It communicates with my room, so if it's locked, it'll be because I'm in there.'

'Thanks,' he said, starting to remove his coat. But she did not leave immediately.

'You said something about being punched on the nose,' she prompted.

'It was nothing,' he said generously. 'A misunderstanding.'

'I see. Well, our children seem determined to be misunderstood, and usually it's someone else who gets hurt. Don't you agree, Mr Dalziel?'

'I'm not married,' said Dalziel, unpeeling his huge sports jacket and revealing broad khaki braces. 'And I've no kids.'

'Oh. The last of the line, Mr Dalziel?' she said.

'Aye. You could say. Or the end of the tether.'

With neat efficient movements she gathered the damp clothing from the bed, an act of conservation as well as kindness.

'I'll see to these,' she said. 'You look as though you could do with a hot bath straight away.'

Dalziel was touched by this concern with his health till he saw her gaze fixed on his right hand which had unconsciously unbuttoned his shirt and was presently engaged in scratching his navel.

'Thanks,' he said and began to take off his shirt.

The water in the antiquated bathroom was red hot both to the touch and to the sight. Having seen the brown peat water used in the manufacture of the best whisky, Dalziel did not anticipate harm from a little discoloration and wallowed sensuously in the huge marble tub, his feet resting on brass cherubim taps which time and neglect had verdigrised to a satyric green.

From what he had seen so far of the house, he surmised that the Fielding family had been going through bad times. You needed a lot of cash to keep up a place like this these days. This didn't necessarily mean they were poor, not by his standards. It did mean that probably they had been living beyond their means, or rather that as far as the house was concerned their means had lagged behind their rapidly growing expenditure. He was rather surprised to find himself being so charitable towards the idle rich but whatever the failings of the younger members of the household, Mrs Fielding had struck him as a pleasant intelligent woman. And handsome with it. Not a word much used of female attractiveness nowadays. You couldn't call loose-haired kids with consumptive eyes and no tits handsome. But Mrs Fielding was. Oh yes.

One of the cherubim seemed to leer at him with unnecessary salaciousness at this point. A trick of the steam. He got out and towelled himself vigorously.

Back in the bedroom he discovered that his tin of foot powder had become a runny blancmange, so he opened the bathroom cabinet in search of a substitute. There was a mixture of male and female cosmetics and a variety of pill bottles. Either Mrs Fielding or her late husband was a bit of a hypochondriac, thought Dalziel. It was difficult to tell from the scrawl on the labels. Even the printed words were difficult. Boots of Piccadilly he could manage. But Propananol . . . could that be for athlete's foot? Piles, more likely. There was a tap on the communicating door.

'Just finishing,' he called.

'Your trousers were soaking,' Mrs Fielding

answered, 'so I've put them with the rest to dry. You'll find some things in the wardrobe to wear for the time being if you like. There're hot drinks downstairs.'

'Ta,' he called. A kind and thoughtful woman, he decided. Once she had made up her mind to be welcoming she carried it through.

Mr Fielding had clearly not been as fat as Dalziel but he had been tall and broad-shouldered. The trousers wouldn't fasten at the waist, but a long nylon sweater stretched over the cabriole curve of his belly and covered the shameful schism. An old sports jacket, also unfastenable, and a pair of carpet slippers completed the robing and it was time to descend.

Downstairs no sounds offered him a clue to the location of the hot drinks, but after three false starts he at last opened a door into an inhabited room.

'Who the devil are you?' demanded the old man, glaring at him through the steam rising from a mug held at his thin bluish lips.

'Andrew Dalziel. I was given a lift. My car broke down. Can I have some of that?'

He advanced to the broad kitchen table on whose scrubbed wooden top stood a steaming jug.

'No. That's mine. You'll find some on the hob through there.'

There was the adjacent back kitchen where on a gas stove coeval almost with the house Dalziel found a pan of what his mother would have called 'nourishing broth'.

He plucked a large mug from a hook on the wall, filled it and tasted. It was good.

He returned to the other room. Probably nowadays an estate agent would call it a breakfast-room, but the plain wooden furniture pre-dated the studied pseudo-simplicities of modern Scandinavian pine. These chairs threatened real painful splinters to the unwary. Dalziel sat down cautiously.

'Those are my son's clothes you're wearing!' exclaimed the old man. 'I recognize them. Even the slippers. Ye gods, ye gods, how little time it takes!'

'My clothes were wet,' explained Dalziel, thinking that someone ought to have persuaded the old man also to a change of clothing. The raincoat and umbrella had not been able to protect the bottom of his trousers and his shoes from a soaking.

'I'm sorry about your son,' he said.

'Why? Did you know him?'

'No. How could I? I'm here by accident.'

'So you say. So you say. Men come, men go, and it's all put down to accident. Have you known Bonnie long?'

'Your daughter-in-law? I don't know her at all, Mr Fielding,' averred Dalziel. 'I don't know anyone here.'

'No?' The emphasis of Dalziel's answer seemed almost to convince the old man. But only for a moment.

'You're not from Gumbelow's, are you?' he suddenly demanded. 'Or television? I have positively interdicted television.'

Dalziel's patience was wearing thin, but now the door opened and the stout youth who must be Bertie Fielding came in. He ignored the inmates and passed straight through into the back kitchen, returning a moment later to stare accusingly at Dalziel.

'That's my mug. You've taken my mug.'

Dalziel blew on his soup till he set the little globules of fat into a panicky motion.

'Sorry,' he said.

Bertie turned once more and went back to the stove.

'My grandson is an ill-mannered lout,' said Mr Fielding sadly.

'Can't think where he gets it from,' answered Dalziel.

Bertie returned, drinking soup from what appeared to be an identical mug.

'I hear Charley sank your case,' he said, more amicably now. Like a baby who doesn't really mind what teat gets stuck in his mouth, thought Dalziel.

'Mr Tillotson? Aye, there was a spot of bother,' he answered.

'There would be,' said Bertie maliciously. 'Evidence of divine whimsy is Charley. Looks like a Greek god but things happen to him like Monsieur Hulot.'

'You haven't quite got the balance right,' mocked Mr Fielding, explaining to Dalziel, 'Bertie likes to rehearse his witty abuse till he's got the lines off pat.'

Bertie smiled angrily.

'Still can't bear a rival near the throne, Grandpa?'

'Rival?' exclaimed the old man, pushing himself upright. 'When has the eagle considered the boiling fowl a rival? Or the antelope the hog? Good day to you, Mr Dalziel. If you are as uninvolved in our affairs as you claim to be, it seems unlikely that we shall meet again. On the other hand . . .'

He walked stiffly from the room, his shoes squelching gently on the stone-flagged floor.

'Your grandfather seems a bit upset,' probed Dalziel, sucking in a noisy mouthful of broth.

'Yes, he usually does, these days. It's not surprising, I suppose, when you've lost your last surviving child. Especially as he thinks I killed him.'

The door opened again at this point and the arrival of Tillotson, Louisa Fielding, Uniff and the Indian Maid masked Dalziel's surprise and prevented him from following up Bertie's statement.

'Hello,' said Tillotson. 'I say, are your things all right? I hope there's no permanent damage.'

'If there is,' said Dalziel, 'I'll send you a bill.'

'That's right, captain,' said Uniff. 'Don't let him polite talk you out of your legal rights. I'm a witness. Hey, Mavis!'

The Indian Maid came over to them with two

mugs of soup. She was really a striking girl with much of Uniff's prominence of feature, but regularized into something approaching beauty. The likeness was confirmed when Uniff said, 'Mave, meet the captain. Assumed command in our hour of need. Captain, may I present my sister?'

'How do you do, Mr Dalziel,' said the girl. Her voice confirmed his assessment of Uniff's origins. It was unrepentantly Liverpudlian.

'Pleased to meet you,' said Dalziel.

'It was you we saw on the bridge, wasn't it? You looked as if you were going to walk into the water.'

'Or on it,' said Uniff. 'The second coming, nineteen-seventy style.'

'He hasn't had much luck stilling the waters this time,' said Bertie, peering out of the chintz-curtained window.

The door opened once more and Mrs Fielding came in.

'Everyone here? Good. Is there plenty of soup to go round? I can't see Herrie. Or Nigel.'

'Grandpa was here. But Nigel hasn't been down, has he?'

Bertie looked enquiringly at Dalziel who shook his head.

'I hope he's not moving around in his damp clothes,' said Mrs Fielding. 'Lou, darling, run upstairs and find him. Make him come down.'

'But I've not had my soup yet,' protested the blonde girl. 'Bertie can go. He's nearly finished.'

'He'll take no notice of Bertie,' her mother answered firmly. 'Or worse, even if he was on the point of coming Bertie would make him change his mind. You go.'

'Oh bugger,' said Louisa. But she went.

Mrs Fielding came over to the table now and smiled down at Dalziel.

'I just rang the garage,' she said.

'I'm sorry, you shouldn't have bothered, I was just going to,' answered Dalziel.

'No, it struck me you wouldn't know which was nearest or best for that matter. Anyway they were a bit worried when I told them where the car was. There's a great deal of water all along that road now and they aren't sure their breakdown truck can get along. Once it stops raining the water will go down pretty quickly, of course.'

'So I'm stuck,' said Dalziel. 'Well, that's life. Well, if I can use your phone, I'll try to find myself a hotel and a taxi. How close can a taxi get?'

'He's worried about another trip with Charley,' said Bertie Fielding. 'Be comforted, it's just on the south side that the water lies, Mr Dalziel. The road to the north is a bit damp, but passable. I'd say the Lady Hamilton in Orburn would be your best bet, wouldn't you, Mother?'

Dalziel groaned inwardly, visualizing the under-manager's mixture of dismay and triumph at his return.

'Nonsense, Bertie,' she replied. 'It's expensive, unhygienic, and nearly ten miles away. Mr Dalziel will stay with us until he can pick up his car. Please do, Mr Dalziel. We would all be delighted to have you.'

Dalziel looked slowly round the room and saw delight manifest itself in a variety of strange ways. It masqueraded as indifference on Mavis's face, amused knowingness on her brother's, vague uncertainty on Tillotson's and downright dislike of the idea on Bertie's. Only on Bonnie Fielding's did delight appear in anything approaching full frontal nudity.

'I'd be delighted to stay,' said Dalziel.

'Mother,' said Louisa from the door.

'Hello, darling. Did you find Nigel?'

'No, but I found this in his bedroom.' She held up a piece of paper.

'The little sod's taken off again.'

4

Premises, Premises

The general atmosphere of resigned annoyance told Dalziel he was in the middle of a routine upset rather than a major disaster. Nigel, it seemed, had left home to seek his fortune on several previous occasions. Looking at the flaking paint and faded wallpaper around him, Dalziel felt that perhaps the boy had a point. It would take a fool or a clairvoyant to seek a fortune here.

The current weather, however, added a new dimension of concern to this latest escape, for his mother at least. His brother and sister seemed completely unworried, though the Uniffs whether out of sympathy or politeness were much more helpful.

'He can't have gotten far,' said Hank. 'Poor kid. He'll soon have his bellyful of this rain.'

It was not the most diplomatic use of the idiom. Quickly Mavis stepped in.

'Hank, take a look outside. He might be sheltering quite close. If not, we'll take a run down the road in the car.'

Hank left, and Mrs Fielding sat down at the table. She appeared quite composed now.

'Lou, darling,' she said. 'How's the soup? Nigel will be freezing when he gets back.'

'There's oodles left,' said Bertie. 'We're hardly down below yesterday's tide mark.'

'I like it best when we reach that ox-tail we had at New Year,' said Louisa. 'That was my favourite.'

Indifferent to this family humour, Dalziel picked up the note which Mrs Fielding had dropped on the table.

I am leaving home because (1) my plans for the future don't coincide with yours (2) I have no desire to live off money coined by my father's death and (3) there are some people I don't care to have near me. Nigel. PS. I don't mean you. I'll write when I'm settled.

He turned it over. It was addressed to the boy's mother.

Hank returned.

'Any sign?' asked Mavis.

'No. But the rowing-boat's gone.'

'He always threatened to run away to sea,' said Louisa.

'Lou, shut up, will you?' said Mrs Fielding. 'Oh damn. I wish he hadn't taken the boat. I don't like the thought of him on the water.'

'Shall I go after him in the punt?' volunteered Tillotson, a suggestion which drew derisive groans from everyone except Mrs Fielding and Mavis. And Dalziel too, though he groaned internally.

'Thank you, Charles, but no,' said Mrs Fielding. 'Hank, did you see Pappy out there?'

'Not a sign,' said Uniff.

'See if you can find him and tell him Nigel's loose again. Then perhaps you'll join us in the study. It's time to talk.'

Uniff left and the other young people drifted out after him. When Mrs Fielding spoke, Dalziel noted approvingly, the others jumped. He liked a strong leader.

'I'm sorry to leave you alone, Mr Dalziel,' she said. 'But we have to have a business conference. Make yourself at home.'

'Thanks,' he said. 'I'll keep the soup hot for Nigel.'

'That boy. You must think us very odd.'

Dalziel did not deny it.

'He sounds a sensible lad,' he said, indicating the note.

'You think that's sensible?' she asked, surprised.

'Well, it's neatly laid out. One, two, three. I like that,' he said with the authority of one whose own official reports were infamous for their brevity. *I came, I saw, I arrested* was the Dalziel ideal according to Pascoe.

'It's possible to be methodical and still find trouble,' she answered. 'There's probably a cold joint in the pantry if you're hungry. We usually eat on our feet during the day and sit down for a meal about six-thirty.'

She left and Dalziel glanced at his watch. It was one o'clock. Five hours.

He went into the kitchen in search of food. There was a small deep freeze into which he peered hopefully. It contained very little and nothing of particular appeal. He shuffled the contents around in the hope of coming across one of his favourite frozen dinners-for-two, but there was no sign of such delights. One foil-wrapped package caught his eye. The remnants of a cold joint perhaps. He unwrapped it.

'Well bugger me!' said Dalziel.

Inside the foil, sealed in a transparent plastic bag, was a dead rat.

These sods might be hard up but there were limits, he told himself. Gingerly he re-interred the corpse in its icy tomb and closed the lid.

His appetite had left him for the moment so he lit a cigarette and sat down once more to muse upon this odd household.

Just how odd was it? he asked himself. Well, the atmosphere for a start. It didn't feel very funereal. Not that that signified much. He'd been at funerals where by the time the poor sod was planted, half the mourners were paralytic and the rest were lining up for the return to the loved one's house like homesteaders at the start of a land-race.

Anyway atmosphere was too vague. You could breakfast on atmosphere, but you'd better make your dinner out of facts.

Fact one was the age of the non-Fieldings. Coeval with Bertie and Louisa, they were hardly the mourners one would expect at the funeral of a man of Fielding's assumed age.

Fact two was this business conference going on. What were they doing – reading the will? Not likely these days. Then what?

Fact three was the lad, Nigel. His farewell note hinted at household relationships more turbulent than the usual teenage antipathies.

Fact four was the enigmatic remarks people kept dropping about Fielding's death.

And fact five was a freezer with a dead rat in it.

He stood up and dropped his fag end into Bertie's mug. When it came down to it, he distrusted facts almost as much as atmosphere. He knew at least three innocent men who would be bashing their bishops in Her Majesty's prisons for many years to come because of so-called *facts*. On the other hand, on other occasions other *facts* had saved all three from well-deserved sentences. We are in God's hands.

So he abandoned facts and set off on a walkabout of the house hoping to encounter truth.

He strolled along the brown horror of the entrance hall opening doors at random. One room contained a full-size billiard table, presumably the one on which the coffin had rested. There were two or three balls on the table and a cue leaned up against a pocket. Someone had not waited long to resume playing.

Dalziel moved on and reached the next door just as a telephone rang inside.

51

'Hello!' said old Fielding's reedy but still imperious voice. 'Yes. This is Hereward Fielding speaking.'

So that's what 'Herrie' was short for. Jesus wept!

He remained at the door. He was firmly of the conviction that if you didn't have enough sense to lower your voice, then you either wanted or deserved to be overheard.

'No, I will not change my mind,' said Fielding. 'And I am too old to be bribed, persuaded or flattered into doing so. Now please, leave me alone. I have just buried my son today, yes, my son. Spare me your sympathy. You may come tomorrow if you wish, but I make no promises about my availability. Good day.'

The phone was replaced with a loud click. Dalziel pushed open the door and entered.

The room was large and ugly, its furnishings and decoration old enough to be tatty without getting anywhere near the ever-shifting bourne of the antique. Fielding had turned from the telephone to a wall cabinet, the door of which seemed to be jammed. He glanced up at Dalziel.

'Oh, it's you,' he said, heaving. The door flew open and a glass unbalanced and fell to the threadbare carpet. He ignored it, but plucked another from inside and with it a bottle. Dalziel fixed his gaze on this. It took a strong man to stand with a bottle in one hand, a glass in the other, and not offer him a drink.

'Can I help you?' asked Fielding.

'No. The others seem to be in conference and I was just having a look around,' said Dalziel.

'Were you? Well, this room, by general consensus the coldest and draughtiest in this cold and draughty house, is sometimes regarded as my sitting-room. Though naturally should anyone else wish to eat, drink, sleep, play records, make love or merely take a walk in it, my selfish demands for privacy are not allowed to get in the way.'

'That's good of you,' said Dalziel heartily, closing the door behind him. 'Terrible, this weather. I pity all the poor sods on holiday.'

'I understood *you* were on holiday,' said Fielding, filling his glass.

'So I am,' said Dalziel, mildly surprised at the idea. 'Pity me then. Yes, it's still chucking it down. I hope your grandson's all right.'

'What?'

'Your grandson. He's run away, I believe. I'm sorry, didn't you know?'

The old man took a long swallow from his glass. What was it? wondered Dalziel. He couldn't see the label which was obscured by Fielding's long bony fingers, but the liquid was an attractive pale amber.

'It would be too optimistic to hope you might mean Bertie?' said Fielding.

'No. The lad. Nigel.'

'I feared so. It was ever thus. Wilde was wrong. You don't have to kill the things you love. Just wait long enough and they'll go away.'

'Who?' said Dalziel, pouncing on this further

reference to killing and wanting to get its prov-
enance right.

'Who? You mean, who . . . Oscar Wilde. *The
Ballad of Reading Gaol.*'

'Oh, the poof,' said Dalziel, his interest evap-
orating.

Unexpectedly Fielding laughed.

'That's the one,' he said. 'Will you have a drink,
Mr . . . ?'

'Dalziel. Yes, I will.' Here's another one who
thinks he's summed me up and can start patronizing me, thought Dalziel as his huge hand held the
glass he had retrieved from the floor steadfastly
under the bottle till the meniscus touched the rim
and Fielding said ironically, 'Say when.'

It was brandy, a cheap brand Dalziel suspected,
not from any connoisseurship of the liquor but by
simple taste-bud comparison with the smoothness
of his own favourite malt whisky. Something of his
reaction must have shown and he realized he had
inadvertently got back at Fielding for his suspected
condescension when the old man said, 'I'm sorry,
it's not good, but these days we all have to make
sacrifices.'

'It's fine. Just the job for this weather,' said
Dalziel, emptying his glass and proffering it for
a refill.

'The weather. Yes. That foolish boy. I hope he
will be all right. He never goes far, at least he
didn't when Conrad – that's his father, my son –
was alive.'

'Fond of his dad, was he?'

'Very,' said the old man firmly.

'But he still ran away, even then?'

'Certainly. It's in the family. Conrad was always taking off when he was a boy. I myself ran off to join the Army in 1914. I was sixteen at the time.'

'Did they take you?' asked Dalziel.

'Not then. I looked very young. We *were* younger then, you know. Balls dropping, menstruation, it all happened later in my generation. But now they seem to need jockstraps and brassieres in the cradle.'

Fielding laughed harshly.

'Anyway, it was a blessing I see now. I went legally and forcibly in 1916 and within six months I was ready to run away again, home this time.'

'It must have been terrible,' said Dalziel with spurious sympathy. 'All that mud.'

'Mud? Oh no. I didn't mean the trenches. I never really saw the trenches. It was just the sheer boredom of the whole thing that made me want to run away. Very unfashionable. I wrote a book about my experiences a few years after the war. A light, comic thing, it went down well enough with your general reader, but it put me in bad with the intelligentsia for the next decade. But then I did a bit of Eliot-bashing and that was a help. Even so, I still got the cold shoulder, more or less, until the fifties. After that it was just a question of survival. Hang on long enough and you're bound to become a Grand Old Man. Like the essays Paul Pennyfeather set in *Decline and Fall*. The reward is for length, regardless of merit.'

He laughed again, a series of glottally-stopped cracks, like a night-stick rattling along metal railings. Dalziel contemplated making him laboriously explain what he had just said, sentence by sentence, but decided against it on the grounds that the poor old sod probably couldn't help himself.

'So you're not too worried about the boy?'

'In the sense that he is too sensible to contribute willingly to his own harm, no. But as you say, the weather is appalling and, in addition, we live in troubled times, Mr Dalziel. The post-war period is an age of unbalance, of violence. Women and children cannot wander around with impunity as in my boyhood. Even the police seem more likely to be a source of molestation than a protection against it.'

'They've a hard job,' said Dalziel mildly.

'I dare say. They certainly make hard work of finding an answer to the crime wave.'

'Oh, the answer's simple,' said Dalziel. 'Charge two guineas a pint for petrol, have a dusk to dawn curfew, and deport regular offenders to Manchester.'

It was a Yorkshire joke. Fielding was not very amused.

'It's in man's mind, not his motorways, that the answer lies,' he said reprovingly. 'Has Bonnie organized a search for Nigel? No, you said they were in conference, didn't you? Conference! You see how this house is run, Mr Dalziel!'

Dalziel felt impelled to defend Bonnie Fielding.

'The man, Pappy, has been warned to keep look-out. The lad took the boat, it seems.'

'Worse and worse,' said the old man angrily. 'That fool Papworth is totally unreliable. Let's go and find him and you'll see.'

He drained his glass and led the way out at a pace which had Dalziel's borrowed carpet slippers flip-flopping on the uncarpeted floor.

Dalziel paused in the hallway as he heard the sound of raised voices drifting down the stairs. Someone, it sounded like Bertie, was shouting angrily and other voices mingled in the background.

'Come on!' commanded Fielding, irritated by the delay, and obediently Dalziel followed him through a door which led into a new complex of meaner corridors running through what presumably had once been the servants' quarters.

Fielding strode on ahead till he reached a door on which he rapped imperiously. Then without waiting for a reply, he flung it open with an aplomb which won Dalziel's professional admiration.

The room looked as if it had been furnished from an army surplus sale. The metal bed was made up with a neatness that invited inspection and the objects on the bedside locker – ashtray, alarm clock and a box of matches – were placed at the corners of an isosceles triangle.

Pappy was not there and in an almost unconscious reflex Dalziel stepped into the room and opened the metal wardrobe. It contained a couple of jackets and an old but well preserved black suit.

Glancing round, he realized that Fielding was regarding him strangely. Bursting into a servant's room was evidently OK, but searching it was something else.

'He's not here then,' said Dalziel.

'No. I doubt if he spends a great deal of time in the wardrobe.'

'Perhaps he's out looking.'

'Hah!' snorted Fielding, setting off again. Dalziel followed after glancing out of the window. It was still raining and the cobbled yard which lay outside was inches deep in water so that it looked like a sea of semolina. For the second time since coming into this house, Dalziel felt a sense of physical belittlement.

Fielding was knocking on another door now, more gently this time and without trying the handle. A woman's voice answered from within.

'Who is it?'

'Mr Fielding. Sorry to trouble you, Mrs Greave, but I'm looking for Papworth. Do you know where he is?'

After a short interval, the door was opened by a bright-eyed woman of about forty, whose magenta-tinted hair and green dressing-gown wound tight around her body gave her the look of a cornfield poppy. She was not unattractive in a bold and brassy kind of way.

'I was having a nap,' she said with more of accusation than explanation in her voice.

'I'm sorry,' said Fielding. 'Do you know where Papworth is?'

'No,' said the woman yawning, showing good teeth in a moist pink mouth. Her glance flickered towards Dalziel who looked her up and down from her bare feet to the untidy brightness of her hair and leered grotesquely at her. Dalziel's leer was so unambiguous that it was like a lesser man exposing himself. Mrs Greave screwed up her mouth in distaste and said, 'Sorry, I've no idea. I'd better start thinking about dinner, I suppose, so if you'll excuse me.'

She began to close the door but Dalziel leaned forward so that his belly curved into the doorway. It was more subtle than putting your foot in the jamb.

Sniffing noisily, he said, 'Is something burning?'

The woman half turned, then swung back again to prevent Dalziel from entering the room.

'No,' she said, and swung the door to so violently that he had to skip back to avoid a collision. But he smiled to himself as they moved on. He had penetrated far enough to see a man's suede shoe lying on the floor. It looked wet.

'So she's the cook, is she?' he asked.

'So rumour has it,' said Fielding drily. 'It was probably the dinner you smelt burning.'

Dalziel laughed. It was turning out to be a very interesting household, this. It had to be Papworth who was in the woman's room. Perhaps he was just taking evasive action. With this old fusspot on the prowl, who could blame him? Though, of course, you didn't need to take your shoes off to hide.

'Papworth's knocking her off, is he?' he said, voicing his thought.

'Who?'

'Mrs Greave. The cook.'

Fielding laughed again.

'I hope not,' he said. 'She's his daughter!'

'His daughter?' echoed Dalziel. 'You're sure?'

'No one can ever be sure of their father,' said Fielding. 'We believe what we're told, don't we? Come on. We might find him in the Hall.'

It seemed that this hunt for Papworth was becoming an obsession with the old man. Dalziel's own enthusiasm had waned, partly because he still had not discarded his theory about Papworth's whereabouts (a man could visit his daughter in her bedroom, couldn't he?) but mainly because Fielding now proposed that they should go out into the rain-filled yard.

'Hold on,' he said at the door. 'Where are we going?'

'Just over there,' said Fielding, pointing to a long high-roofed building which ran out from the main house. It looked as if it might once have been a stables, but surprisingly, in this neglected

house, this particular block looked as if someone had been working on it fairly recently, an
impression confirmed by the wording on a sign
propped against the wall. *Gibb and Fowler, Building
Contractors, Orburn.*

'It joins up with the house,' said Dalziel reasonably. 'Can't we get into it without going outside?'

'If you must,' said the old man crossly, shutting
the door.

Their route this time took them through a new
world in the form of a large room (or perhaps
two or three rooms knocked into one) where the
old stone walls had been plastered and painted a
brilliant blue. On one side were a pair of large
freezers and on the other, gleaming in silver and
white, a row of microwave ovens. It was like
stepping out of a bus shelter into a space ship.

'What's all this?' asked Dalziel in bewilderment.

'We drink a lot of soup,' said Fielding, not stopping to offer further explanation but pressing on
through the room with unflagging speed.

Dalziel followed down another short corridor,
then into the building which was the object of
Fielding's forced march.

Here he halted and let his eyes get used to
the dim light filtering through the narrow arched
windows. If the microwave ovens had been a step
forward out of the nineteenth century, what was
going on here was just as determined a step back.

The building had been a stables, he reckoned,
with an upper floor used perhaps as a hay-loft.

This floor had now been removed with the exception of a small section at the far end which had been transformed into a kind of minstrels' gallery. The joists supporting the arched roof had clearly lacked something in antiquity and they were being supplemented by a new fishbone pattern of age-blackened beams, standing out starkly against the white-washed interstices. Dalziel rapped his knuckles against one of these beams which was leaning against the wall, prior to elevation. It rang hollowly and felt smooth and cold to the touch. Dalziel was not repelled. He had nothing against plastic. He would as lief eat off colourful Formica as polished mahogany. Nor did it seem distasteful to him that the panes of stained 'glass' which were being fitted into the windows were plastic also. His reaction was one of simple puzzlement.

To what end would the Fieldings be transforming an old stables into something that looked like a set for a remake of *Robin Hood*?

Old Fielding, having peered into various recesses and through various doors, now abandoned his search for Papworth and returned to enjoy Dalziel's bewilderment.

'What do you think of this?' he asked, gesturing with a flamboyance more in keeping with his surroundings than his person. 'Is it not a fit monument for our times? What would Pope have had to say?'

'Monument?' said Dalziel, wondering momentarily if the old man was being literal and this place was indeed intended to be some sort of mausoleum, a kind of bourgeois Taj Mahal. But what about the ovens?

The answer was obvious.

'It's a café,' said Dalziel.

This solution sent the old man into paroxysms of laughter which modulated into a coughing bout from which it seemed unlikely he would recover. Dalziel watched for a moment coldly, then administered a slap between his shoulder-blades which brought the dust up out of the old man's jacket and sent him staggering against a section of stone reproduction wall which gave visibly.

'Thank you,' said Fielding. 'Though I fear the cure was more dangerous than the disease. Well now. A café. Yes, that's the word. Not the word that will be used, of course, should this sad enterprise ever come to fruition. No. Then this place will be called a *Banqueting Hall*. My daughter-in-law is too careful, I think, to risk the penalties prescribed under the Trades Descriptions Act by calling it a Medieval Banqueting Hall, but the word "medieval" will certainly appear somewhere on the prospectus.'

'People will eat here,' said Dalziel.

The prospect did not displease him. Eating was one of the Four Deadly Pleasures. Though he could not see the necessity for all these trappings. A meal was a meal.

'That's right. A dagger and a wooden platter. At a given signal, chicken legs will be thrown over the right shoulder. It's a pastime very popular I believe in the North-East where the past is still close and tribal memories are long. My foolish family believe the inhabitants of Orburn and district will be equally gullible. The dreadful thing is, they may be right.'

'There's still a bit of work to be done,' observed Dalziel. 'Where are the builders today?'

'They would not come today,' said the old man significantly.

'No? Oh, of course. Sorry. The funeral.'

Fielding laughed again, but this time, with a wary eye on Dalziel's hand, he kept it to a controlled barking.

'Builders are not noted for their delicacy, Mr Dalziel, not here, anyway.'

Dalziel ran his mind's eye down a list of building contractors working in his area and had to agree.

'What then? The weather?'

'Money, Mr Dalziel. When the head goose has been killed, you make damn sure someone else is going to start dropping the golden eggs.'

'Ah,' said Dalziel. 'Then this business conference . . . ?'

But his cross-examination was interrupted.

'You are looking for me, Mr Fielding?' said a voice from above.

They looked up. Leaning over the rail of the minstrels' gallery was Papworth.

'There you are,' said Fielding. 'About time too.

Have you seen anything of my grandson yet? Young Nigel?'

'No,' said Papworth. 'Should I have done?'

'Don't you know he's missing? Hasn't anyone told you?' demanded Fielding.

'No,' said Papworth. 'I've been busy. What's the fuss?'

'The boy's run off again. It seems he's taken the rowing-boat and naturally we are all very worried.'

'The rowing-boat,' said Papworth thoughtfully.

'That's right, man. Aren't you going to do anything? You can take the punt out and scout around, if you are not too busy, that is.'

You didn't have to be a detective to spot the dislike the old man felt for Papworth, thought Dalziel. If only all relationships were so clear!

'No. That's just what I was going to do when I heard you wanted me,' said Papworth.

'But you said you didn't know the boy was missing,' interjected Dalziel.

'No. But the boat is. Or was.'

'Was?'

'Yes. I can see it drifting out beyond the island. But one thing's certain. There's no one in it.'

5

A Pleasant Surprise

For the second time that day, the three men got soaking wet. Papworth seemed impervious to the rain as he propelled the gun-punt over the water with strong economical strokes, but Dalziel was concerned about the old man who had rejected all attempts to make him stay ashore. His clothes were clinging to his body, accentuating its frailty, and the skin of his face seemed to have shrunk in the downpour and be clinging almost transparently to his patrician skull.

Dalziel himself drew comfort from the thought that this time at least it was not his own clothes that were getting wet. There was a philosophy in there somewhere if he had the time or energy to winkle it out. Or a rule of life at least. He was dimly aware that his blacker moments were often survived only because he had certain usually unspecified and often arbitrary rules of life to cling on to, though whether these added up to the weight and dignity of something called a *philosophy* he did not know.

Duty was one of them, or at least the notion that a man got out of bed and went to his work no matter what he felt like, and saw the job through if he could manage it without collapsing. It had proved a useful and necessary rule in recent weeks.

The rowing-boat was drifting with one oar missing and the other trailing from the rowlock. The island referred to by Papworth was, Dalziel realized, a real island in the real lake, with water lapping shallowly at the roots of the trees growing there. It would be possible to land here still at the expense only of getting your feet wet, and he scanned the trees closely. They were willows mainly, packed tight together as though drawing back from the threatening waters, but the total area of the island couldn't have been more than a quarter-acre and he felt pretty certain that Nigel was not lurking there, watching them pass.

Nor was the boy in the boat. Papworth had asserted it was empty from the start, but Dalziel had not been so positive. You could lie in the bottom of a boat and not be seen from the shore, he suspected. But the boy was not in it and suddenly the dimensions of the problem had changed.

Papworth jumped lightly into the boat and pulled the trailing oar inboard. From the punt Dalziel examined the rowing-bench closely, looking for he did not know what.

'Where's it come from?' he demanded.

'God knows,' said Papworth with a shrug.

'Can't you tell?' said Dalziel.

'They don't leave tracks,' said Papworth. 'And there's no regular currents, tides, that sort of thing here. No, the wind'd move it most, and *you* tell *me* which quarter that's in.'

He was right. What wind there was gusted fitfully from no constant direction.

Old Fielding who had been uncharacteristically quiet ever since they had left the shore now said, 'There's an oar missing. Surely if we can find that, it will give us a clue.'

'Mebbe,' said Papworth laconically. 'But to what?'

'Listen,' said Dalziel, glowering at the impassive boatman. 'There's three things. The boat could have drifted back from wherever Nigel got off; or it could just have drifted away from the landing-stage in the first place and the boy's on the road; or if he did have a spot of trouble he could be stranded on a tree or on top of a hedge or something. He can swim, can't he?'

'Like a fish,' said Fielding.

'Right then,' said Dalziel, standing so that the punt rocked dangerously. He ignored the movement and scanned the waters. It was pretty obvious where the lake proper ended and the floods began. A line of trees and half-submerged undergrowth delineated the sweep of the farther bank and, beyond this, the geometric outlines of fields were marked where their hedges broke the surface of the water.

'OK,' said Dalziel. 'Shout.'

'What?'

'Shout,' he said. 'If he is stuck somewhere, he'll answer.'

They started to shout, sometimes separately and sometimes with Fielding's reedy tenor, Papworth's strong baritone and Dalziel's totally unmusical bellow blending into a single dreadful cry. The damp air absorbed all their effort with indifferent ease and returned nothing.

'Let's try a bit farther out,' said Dalziel finally, reaching for the punt pole. But as he did so, he realized their yellings had not gone entirely unheard. Standing in the garden near the flooded landing-stage were the rest of the Fieldings and Tillotson. He guessed what anxieties were swarming through Bonnie's mind and spoke to Papworth.

'We'd best let Mrs Fielding know what's going on,' he said. 'Can you scout a bit farther in that thing while I take the punt back?'

'If you like,' said Papworth. He removed the oar from the thole-pin and using it as a rather cumbersome paddle began to move away.

'Where's that fellow going?' demanded Fielding. He looked to be in the extremities of distress, both physical and mental. Even without his daughter-in-law's right to an explanation, it would have been necessary to get him back to the house soon.

'He's going to search,' said Dalziel, wielding the pole inexpertly and for the first time feeling some sympathy for Tillotson. 'We'd better get back to the house and organize things there.'

Mrs Fielding remained controlled when she heard what Dalziel had to say, but he sensed a strong underlying concern.

'Let's get inside,' she said. 'Herrie, you're soaking! What possessed you to go out in only your jacket?'

She gave a half-accusing glance at Dalziel. She had the kind of solid, bold-eyed face much admired by the Edwardians and which had still stared provocatively at an adolescent Dalziel from Scarborough What-the-Butler-Saw machines a couple of decades later. He felt an in the circumstances incongruous urge to wink invitingly.

Surprisingly in the light of her earlier indifference, Louisa was outwardly the most agitated.

'We can't just hang about, doing nothing,' she cried. 'Let's get something organized.'

Her urgency seemed to infect the others and her mother and brother began to move back to the house at an accelerated pace almost beyond the means of the old man who hung on to his daughter-in-law with the stoic look of one who is ready at a moment's notice to make his final exit.

Dalziel followed, eager to get out of the rain but without any feeling of urgency. He doubted whether speed was going to contribute much to Nigel Fielding's safety now. Either the lad was safe or his body was waiting to be grappled from the water by a boat-hook. But the illusion of great activity was a useful anodyne.

The Uniffs who had had enough sense to stay

out of the wet met them at the door and received explanations in the hall.

Mavis displayed the same calm competence as before and even Hank made conventional soothing noises, putting his arm round Louisa's thin shoulders and pressing his *University of Love* T-shirt (the same one? or did he have duplicates?) against her soaking sweater whose new skin-clinging properties managed the merest hint of a female figure.

'We must ring the police,' she said. Dalziel sighed and prepared to step forward to reveal himself. It would be unprofessional to let this short-tempered girl give her unstructured and semi-hysterical account of the situation to the local bobby when he could get things moving in half the time.

'Perhaps,' he began. And the telephone rang. For a moment they all froze. It was Bonnie Fielding who was quickest off the mark, heading for the room which old Fielding claimed as his own.

They heard her pick up the phone.

'Nigel!' she exclaimed.

'Yes,' she said, as the rest of them crowded into the room. 'Yes. Look, Nigel, where are . . . no . . . oh, damn!'

It was clear from her face that the boy had rung off.

'Where is he?' demanded Fielding.

'I'm sorry, Herrie,' said the woman. 'But he didn't say. Just that he wanted us to know he was

71

OK. He saw the boat go adrift after he'd abandoned it and thought I'd be worried. Anyway, thank God he's safe. Now, Herrie, let's see about you before you get pneumonia.'

She ushered the old man out of the room, and though the news of his grandson's safety revived him enough to snap a token protest at this unwanted solicitude, he let himself be led upstairs with no physical demur.

'End of crisis,' said Uniff cheerfully. 'All's well etcetera.'

The telephone rang again and the bearded man picked it up.

'Hi,' he said. 'Yeah. Look, man, you take that up with the Post Office, OK? No, she's not available right now. I mean, we just had the funeral so she may not want to talk insurance. OK. I'll tell her.'

He replaced the phone.

'Sphincter?' said Bertie.

'That's it. Seems to think we're trying to avoid him. The usual moans. He's a pain. I should have asked if we were insured against Nig's taking off!'

Louisa's sibling solicitude, recently overflowing, was now completely spilt.

'Little bastard,' she said. 'He should have been drowned at birth.'

'That's a bit strong,' protested Tillotson, but she ignored him and followed Uniff out of the room.

Tillotson caught Dalziel's eye and grinned sheepishly.

'Someone ought to tell Pappy,' said Bertie suddenly. He was right, thought Dalziel, but he obviously had no intention of doing anything about it himself.

'Yes, they should,' said Tillotson. 'I'll take the punt.'

He left, whistling cheerfully.

'Go with him,' said Dalziel.

'Do you mean *me*?' said Bertie incredulously.

'I'm not so old I see bloody spectres,' said Dalziel. 'Who else? You really want a drowning on your hands, then let the lad go punting by himself. Hurry up.'

'Why can't you go?' demanded Bertie.

'I'm older than you,' said Dalziel, patience draining away. 'And I'm colder than you, and I'm wetter than you, and I'm a guest in your fucking house, and I don't care a toss if yon silly bugger ends up in the south Pacific. But he's *your* friend. So get a bloody move on!'

Bertie moved, looking rather dazed. At the door he paused, opened his mouth goldfish-like, but left without speaking.

'You've had practice,' said Mavis admiringly. 'What was it? Army?'

Dalziel had lost sight of her presence and looked at her assessingly, working out if an apology were in order. He decided not.

'Not really,' he said. 'Natural leadership qualities. That one needs a bit of stirring.'

'Mebbe so,' said the girl. 'But don't be too certain

73

about Bertie. Some people develop that kind of complacency as a cover. The world's ruled by calm, smug, self-righteous pigs, and they've all been clever enough to get to the top of the dungheap.'

'Cocks,' said Dalziel.

'Eh?' said the girl warily.

'It's cocks on dunghills, not pigs,' he explained. 'I don't expect there's a lot of nature study in Liverpool.'

'You'd be surprised. Hank's right. You *are* wet. Better get into something dry or you might find yourself spending more time here than you plan.'

'I don't *plan* to spend any time here,' said Dalziel. 'What about you? Just down for the funeral, are you?'

She shook her head, her straight black hair moving with it and stopping when the negative movement stopped. It was heavy and wiry, perfectly natural and with none of the gloss and bounce the TV commercials projected as the most desirable qualities of the female – and male – coiffure.

'No,' she said. 'Business mainly.'

Dalziel sneezed.

'Business,' he echoed invitingly, but all she answered was, 'You're mad to hang around like that.'

'I suppose I am,' he said. 'I'd best go and see if I can borrow any more clothes from the late lamented. Hey, he didn't die of anything catching, I hope?'

'Not unless having a hole drilled through your chest's catching.'

'What?'

'He fell off a ladder in the Banqueting Hall,' said Mavis. 'You've seen the Banqueting Hall, have you? Well, when the builders stopped coming, Conrad decided to have a go at the do-it-yourself. He was up the ladder with an electric drill trying to fix one of the beams. The ladder slipped. Down he came. Unfortunately he fell on to the drill and it was locked on. Straight through his ribs into the heart. Goodbye, Conrad.'

'That's nasty,' commented Dalziel, more because he felt it was expected of him than because he felt any distress. But it was certainly an interesting way to go.

'Was he by himself?'

'Yes.'

'So no one saw it happen?'

'What do you want? Colour pictures?'

'No. I don't think so. Well, I'd best get dried. It's been nice talking to you, Miss Uniff.'

'Mavis will do. It makes me feel younger.'

'You want to feel younger?' he said, surprised.

'Oh yes,' she answered. 'When I see what age does to you, I want to feel as young as I can possibly get, Mr Dalziel.'

'And what does age do to you?'

'It makes you crazy for money, I think,' she said slowly. 'Like, in the end perhaps that's the only way left to keep on pretending you're young.'

'I've stopped pretending,' grinned Dalziel.

'That's what they all think. But you'll see. You're not rich are you, Mr Dalziel?'

'Does it matter?'

'It might do. If you've got money and you stay in this house much longer, you'll be offered a deal. You might not even notice but you will. Go and get dry now.'

Dalziel lay naked in the dead man's bed under half a dozen blankets. After stripping off his wet clothes and towelling himself down till his flabby and fat-corrugated skin glowed, suddenly a warm nap had seemed best of all things.

He had pondered a long time on the events of the day and decided that though there was enough in this household to make him curious, so far it was curiosity at a personal rather than professional level. There must have been an inquest on Fielding and the usual investigations. It wouldn't require much effort on his part to get an unofficial look at the finding. But he had no intention of doing so. Oh no. This was an interesting interlude, a bit damper but probably a bit more lively than following a guide round some mouldy cathedral or making conversation with some poofy hotel barman. But tomorrow he'd be on his way. If they couldn't do anything about his car, then sod it. He'd hire another and collect his own later.

Relaxed by his resolve, he fell asleep.

When he awoke it was quarter to six and he was

starving. He rubbed his eyes, yawned, scratched his groin sensuously and headed for the bathroom.

What kind of nosh did they dish up here? he wondered as he pushed open the door. Old Fielding had made some nasty crack about Mrs Greave, the cook. But it'd have to be very bad to blunt Dalziel's appetite tonight.

The bathroom was full of steam. He paused in the doorway. Someone moved among the wraith of vapour and he had no difficulty in recognizing Mrs Fielding though her head was half covered by a towel and the rest of her body was not covered by anything but a healthy post-hot-bath glow.

'Beg pardon,' he said, stepping back and closing the door. But he couldn't close out the mental picture of what he had seen and when he sat down on the bed, he realized he had the beginnings of an erection.

He whistled softly as he considered the phenomenon. He was far from being a sexual obsessive. Indeed, since his wife had left him, his sex life had been minimal. Not that opportunity was short. Like any society dedicated to money and male chauvinism, Yorkshire provided the kinds of relief strong men need from the pressures of the day. But a police officer had to be very careful. It was on the surface a very conventional society and scandals were easily kindled. As for paying for it, Dalziel refused on a point of pride rather than principle.

So generally he went without. It wasn't too difficult. With age, lust became an aesthetic tingle rather than a physical shock. It was a long time since desire had manifested itself to him so uncompromisingly as this!

He felt absurdly pleased with himself, as though something valuable had been proven. She was a fine-looking woman, mature, well-fleshed, without the flabbiness which his own once well-muscled body had declined to. He looked down at himself with distaste and his pleasure drained away at the thought that this ton of lard was all that she had had to look at in return. Not many women reacted to the pleasures of visual stimuli in the same way as men, but revulsion at ugliness must be a shared reaction.

There was a tap at the bathroom door and he jumped up, and dragged a blanket off the bed and wound it round him.

'May I come in?' she called.

'Yes,' he answered.

She entered, wearing a dressing-gown and carrying with her a coathanger festooned with his clothes.

'This lot's dry,' she said. 'I've been over them with an iron, so they should be fit to wear.'

'That's kind,' he said stiltedly.

'I brought them an hour ago, but the bedroom door was locked. You must be a distrustful soul, Mr Dalziel. Whereas me, I don't even remember to lock the bathroom.'

She laughed as she spoke, but he took it as a rebuke.

'I'm sorry, Mrs Fielding,' he began.

'For what?' she said. 'I'd be sorry if you were altogether sorry. We'll be eating soon. First come, first served, so I shouldn't hang about.'

She went back through the bathroom and Dalziel followed her a few moments later, making sure the door into the farther bedroom was locked before setting about his ablutions.

She was a kind woman, he thought, and she didn't shock easily. But that was hardly a basis to build erotic fantasies on. She didn't sleep with her husband, that was an interesting point. Could be good. Could be bad. He'd guessed at first it was because the poor sod was sick. But now it seemed he'd died from an accident.

Dalziel opened the cabinet again. One shelf was now entirely clear and all the pill bottles had gone. The process of clearing out in the wake of the departed had begun.

Or perhaps, some ridiculous and hitherto unsuspected romantic area of his imagination suggested, perhaps she had cleared the space for him, anticipating a longer than overnight stay . . .

These were mere hunger-fantasies, he told himself. He shook them out of his head and began to dress.

6

A Step into Summer

Dinner was served in the room in which they had taken their nourishing broth. The only alteration was the covering of the big kitchen table with a white cloth liberally spotted with the stains of previous meals and with one corner unravelling. Mrs Greave was present to start with, emerging from the back kitchen with a series of covered serving dishes which she deployed over the table with more panache than strategy. Dressed now in a pair of tight-fitting yellow slacks and a flowered blouse, with her red hair piled high in a precarious beehive, she looked less like a flower of the field and more like some exotically gaudy insect. Dalziel made no attempt to make contact with her, but he felt her eyes examining him from time to time as she came in and out.

'You all right now, Mrs Fielding?' she asked finally.

'Yes, thank you, Mrs Greave,' said Bonnie from the head of the table.

'Good night then.'

She left and there was a general uncovering of serving dishes as though no one had cared to delve beneath the china surface while the cook was still in the room.

'I can't believe it,' said Louisa.

'What?'

'Sausages. And some of them look only mildly burnt. First or second degree.'

'It must be because we've got a visitor.'

Pleased to be thought the cause of such a treat though unable to comprehend its particular nature, Dalziel, seated at Bonnie's right hand in the place of honour, piled bangers and mash on to his plate.

'Mr Fielding not coming down?' he asked, glancing round the table.

'No. He's a bit under the weather, I fear. He's well over seventy you know and today's been a great strain,' said Bonnie.

'I hope he doesn't snuff it before Gumbelow's cough up,' said Louisa.

'Would it make any difference? The award has been announced,' mumbled a fast-chewing Bertie whom Dalziel had picked out as his only serious rival in the race for a second dip into the depleted sausage dish.

'Children!' reproved Bonnie. 'This is no way to talk!'

She smiled apologetically at Dalziel. She was wearing a white sleeveless blouse, semi-transparent. Her right bra strap had slipped and was visible at her shoulder. Dalziel concentrated on his plate.

'What's Gumbelow's?' he asked.

'Oh, haven't you heard?' said Tillotson. 'Herrie's got an award.'

'What for?' asked Dalziel, meaning to be polite. But they all laughed.

'That would please him!' said Uniff. 'Where've you been, man? Herrie's a great poet. At least that's what Gumbelow's have decided. Yes, sir. Sixty years, but they get there in the end!'

'It's an American thing called the Gumbelow Foundation,' explained Bonnie, seeing Dalziel's puzzlement. 'They have various artistic prizes they dish out every so often. Herrie's will, of course, be for his poetry. He gets a silver plaque, I believe.'

'It should be a silver loo seat for the stuff he writes,' said Bertie viciously. 'Ouch!'

He started to rub his leg, glancing round the table as he did so. Plainly someone had kicked him beneath the table, but it was impossible to tell who. Dalziel put away two sausages and a substantial portion of mash while his rival was recovering and sent grateful vibrations out to the assailant.

'Of course there's the money too,' said Bonnie. 'Fifteen thousand.'

'Pounds?' asked Dalziel, amazed.

'Oh no. Dollars.'

But even *dollars*, he thought. Fifteen thousand. For *poetry*.

Uniff was grinning at him, openly amused.

'Are we getting to you now, Mr Dalziel? That old silvery, tinkly sound?'

'I'm a plain, poor man,' responded Dalziel. 'I know nowt about poetry, and I wouldn't recognize fifteen thousand dollars if it got into bed with me.'

'Well, you may have the chance to see it,' said Bonnie. 'These people want to have a little award ceremony. Herrie's too old to go wandering across the Atlantic so he's told them that if they want to give him anything, they have to come here. It's a marvellous bit of cheek really, but, as he says, he didn't ask them to make the award.'

'He also says he doubts he'll live long enough to enjoy the money,' said Uniff.

'What's that mean?' said Bertie, staring across the table at the bearded man.

'It means he's old, and he's sick, and what the hell is there down here you can spend fifteen grand on?' answered Uniff slowly and coldly.

There was a pause of complete silence, even Dalziel stilling his champing jaws for a moment.

'There's the restaurant,' said Louisa brightly.

Uniff roared with laughter.

'You know what your grandfather thinks of the restaurant, Lou,' said Bonnie reprovingly. 'We've been through all this before.'

'Now that'd be the place out back,' said Dalziel. 'The one that's being done up.'

'You've seen it?' said Bonnie, surprised.

'Mr Dalziel gets around quite a lot,' said Uniff with a malicious inflection Dalziel found it hard to understand.

'Your father-in-law took me in there this afternoon,' explained Dalziel. 'Looking for Papworth.'

'Ah. And what did you think?'

'It looked –' he searched for a word which would combine admiration and reservation – 'all right.'

Uniff and the young Fieldings laughed. Dalziel glared at them. They didn't know how lucky they were that he chose to pick his words carefully. Their amusement stung him to go on.

'Me,' he said, 'I don't much care where I eat. If the food's good and there's lots of it, the surroundings don't matter.'

He dug out a spoonful of sausages from under Bertie's questing hand.

'You're missing the point, Mr Dalziel, baby,' said Uniff.

'Oh aye?' grunted Dalziel.

'The thing with this medieval banquet kick is the food doesn't matter. Serve up this –' he held an impaled sausage – 'and call it King Henry's Banger and they'll shovel them down. What we're talking about is the cafeteria system with five-star prices. You dig?'

'I know nowt about the catering trade,' said Dalziel heavily, 'but that sounds fraudulent to me.'

'Hank's exaggerating as usual,' said Bonnie quickly. 'This is a simple business enterprise, Mr Dalziel. We've all got money in it.'

'Though whether we'll get anything out of it's a different matter,' said Louisa.

Tillotson spoke for the first time, with a reproving look at Louisa.

'I'm sure we'll all get a good return on our investment. The Hall's nearly finished and the kitchens are ready. With a bit of luck we could still open on time.'

He looked defiantly round the table.

Bertie shook his head.

'You don't listen, Charley. You *were* at the meeting, weren't you? Confucius he say, no pay, no play.'

'Everyone done? Right, pass your plates,' said Bonnie firmly. 'Mr Dalziel, how do you feel about apple crumble and custard?'

'Keen,' said Dalziel.

'You look like a crispy edge man to me,' said Bonnie, piling a substantial portion on to his plate. 'That do you for now? Good. Now, no more shop till we've finished. Understood? Hank, how's your film coming on?'

'Fine, man, fine. I showed Herrie some clips yesterday and he made a couple of suggestions.'

'Painful, no doubt,' said Bertie.

'No, no. Pertinent. Words are his scene. You should learn to give credit, Bertie boy. Bend a little.'

'You're making a film, Mr Uniff?' said Dalziel.

'That's right. Don't be surprised. I mean, do I look like a tycoon? I mean, do any of us look

85

like tycoons? Bertie there, perhaps. Yeah, Bertie's got some of the distinguishing marks of your lesser duck-billed tycoon. No, we've all been sweet-talked into this business in the hope and expectation of much bread, by which, verily, man might not live alone, but without which, verily, he surely can't live with anyone else.'

'We agreed, no shop,' said Bonnie warningly.

'Did we? You need to watch yourself in this house, Mr Dalziel. You can be lying in bed minding your own business and wham! you find you've made an agreement!'

He subsided behind his apple crumble and the rest of the meal passed in meteorological chitter-chatter, though Dalziel had to field a couple of invitations to reveal his own line of business. Never before could he recall himself concealing his profession – except for professional reasons. There were none that he could formulate, so why was he doing something which, when admitted by his colleagues, had always filled him with contempt?

After dinner they drank coffee whose bitterness resisted the addition of four teaspoons of sugar. The dinner dishes were then piled on a trolley to be wheeled down to the new kitchen where a huge dishwasher was the one positive benefit so far derived from the restaurant scheme.

'You know, it's stopped raining, for the moment at least,' said Bonnie, looking out of the window. 'I think I'll stroll out and post some letters. Anyone fancy a walk?'

'I'd like some fresh air,' said Tillotson, but Bonnie shook her head.

'Sorry, but I told Herrie you'd go up and read to him. There's nothing wrong with his eyesight,' she explained to Dalziel, 'but there are many things he prefers to hear read aloud. And Charley's got the best voice for it.'

'It's those upper class vowels,' said Bertie. 'Basically the old man's a simple snob.'

'Hush. So you run along, Charley. Mr Dalziel, what about you?'

'It'd be a pleasure,' said Dalziel. He thought he saw an ironic smile flicker across Mavis's face, but it was hard to be sure.

'Right. Gum-boots and wet kit, I think. Your stuff should all be dry now. I'll see you outside in five minutes.'

The rain had indeed stopped, but the atmosphere was damp to the point of saturation. What light there was seemed to glint dully from the surface of the water rather than come from above. There was at first an illusory silence which after a while fragmented into a myriad soft lapping, splashing, dripping noises and the gentle night wind was like a damp breath on Dalziel's face.

They walked without speaking along what he took to be the main drive of the house. It ran downhill but only reached the level of the floods at the gateway to the road and the light from Bonnie's torch showed that the water though extensive was easily fordable here. They splashed through it, turned away from the lake, and were soon back on dry tarmac as the road began to climb.

'It's a pity the drive didn't dip lower,' said Bonnie. 'It would have been rather nice to be quite cut off.'

'Why's that?' asked Dalziel.

'I don't know. Isolation. An interlude before the outside pressures started up again. As it is, well, everything's been going on at the same time. Business troubles, legalities, funeral arrangements.'

'It can't have been easy,' said Dalziel.

'No. You've heard how my husband died, have you, Mr Dalziel?'

Dalziel's professional instinct was to say no and get it from her own lips, but he had no difficulty in subjugating it.

'Yes,' he answered. 'Terrible.'

'Yes. And it couldn't have happened at a worse time.'

'Money?' asked Dalziel.

'That's right.' For a moment she sounded like Uniff in her inflection. 'We were scraping the bottom of the barrel. Conrad – my husband – was more enthusiastic than expert in business matters. He spent ten years in the Army – REME, nothing heroic – and came out convinced his gratuity was going to be the basis of a financial empire. Well, I always added fifty per cent on to his estimate of the cost of anything, but I think he must have started taking that into account! Anyway, we were well short and the contractor stopped work. That's why Conrad was trying the do-it-yourself thing.'

'Tragic,' said Dalziel. He felt he was doing well. Single words, the odd phrase here and there, a man could make quite a good impression if he watched his tongue. But when you hadn't cared to watch it for twenty years, it needed maximum alertness.

'Yes, it was tragic, I suppose. The inquest helped in an odd way. It made things official, gave us a bit of red tape to get tangled up with. In the end we were glad to get Conrad out of the house. Well, you saw yourself what a fetch we got up to. But I'm sorry. I must be boring you to tears. Your holiday's gone wrong enough without having other people's woes to contend with!'

'No, I'm interested,' said Dalziel. 'Well, you'll be all right now, are you? There must be some insurance.'

Everyone had insurance in Yorkshire. Even Dalziel had insurance though he did not know why as there was no sod living he particularly wanted to benefit from his death.

'Conrad wasn't a very provident man,' said Bonnie. 'The only insurance he had was the cover the finance company insisted he should take out when he got the loan to start the business moving. Naturally it would be fine to have that paid off, it's a lot of money. But the insurance company doesn't seem to be in a hurry to settle up.'

'Oh?' said Dalziel. His use of the monosyllable filled him with pride.

'Yes. I don't know what the trouble is. It's

straightforward enough, I should have thought. But they sent this man round. He asked a lot of questions. The police asked a lot of questions. *Everyone* asked a lot of questions. And the only question I wanted to ask was, how the hell are we going to be able to open a week on Saturday?'

You'll be bloody lucky! was the brutal answer that rose in Dalziel's mind but he held it back and said instead, 'You'll have to postpone, that's all.'

'Not quite,' said the woman. They had reached a railway bridge the arch of which curved so sharply it was almost a humpback. Bonnie stopped and leaned on the parapet staring down the line which, as far as the darkness permitted Dalziel to see, ran arrow-straight through a deep cutting. Dalziel presumed that there must have been a natural valley there, perhaps containing a stream diverted by the engineers, for even his untutored eye could tell that the stone work they leaned against predated the railway age. Bonnie spoke into the dark hollow.

'Conrad at his high moments was pretty much of an optimist. We decided on a provisional opening date when we started the scheme, just something to aim at. When I went through his desk after the accident, I discovered what I might have guessed. Nothing was provisional to Conrad. He'd been taking advance bookings for the opening night!'

'*Had* he? How many?'

'One hundred and twenty. Our full capacity.'

'Jesus wept!' said Dalziel. 'But you must have

known he was doing it! I mean, advertising, that kind of thing?'

'Oh, that I would have noticed, but Conrad didn't work that way. No, he told all his cronies in the local pubs and down at the Conservative Club in Orburn. People approached him, I suppose. I don't mean for a couple of tickets for a quiet anniversary dinner. Oh no. This is a togetherness thing, haunch to haunch on a hard bench. These are group bookings. A dozen from the Bowls Club, twenty Young Wives looking for Fellowship, forty Rotarians, six Pigeon Fanciers, the Townswomen's Guild. That's the way it went. None of them bodies that any of the rest of us were likely to have dealings with. I think Conrad realized he'd gone too far when the contractor refused to go on with the work. Hence his eagerness to do it himself. He just didn't dare tell us about the bookings.'

'It's a bad way to start,' agreed Dalziel. 'But not disastrous. Nice apology, a bit of creeping, special circumstances and all that, money back, first refusal next time.'

She turned round, leaned backwards against the parapet, and laughed. It was a good laugh, very infectious, so that Dalziel found himself beginning to smile even though his detective's mind had hopped ahead to the cause of the laughter.

'There's no money to give back,' he said.

'You're very sharp, Mr Dalziel. Conrad had no machinery for retaining money. I used to tell him to get his suits made without pockets. What did he need them for? I kept quiet about it till today, hoping that the insurance people might cough up enough to pay off the Young Wives at least. But they're still dragging their feet. My business partners were far from pleased when I told them.'

'I heard something,' said Dalziel. 'It sounded like Bertie, mainly.'

'Yes. The others are less committed,' she said. 'Or rather, he's the only one who understands enough about finance to know just how close to bankruptcy we really are. If Conrad had let Bertie look after the business side . . . but you know what fathers are like with their sons.'

'No,' said Dalziel. 'You're an odd lot though.'

'What?'

'For a board of directors, I mean.'

She laughed again.

'I suppose we are. We just happened, really. Bertie started it. He did a business studies course at Liverpool, then got a job up there with a big combine, Provincial Traders. They have a lot of interests and he sampled them all, including catering. But he didn't like company politics and wanted his own business. The house is mine, or rather mine and Lou's. It belonged to her father, my first husband. The boys are just her step-brothers, you must have spotted that, of course. When he died he left it to me, but entailed so that it couldn't be sold and would become hers when I died. Well, as you've seen, it's a white elephant. We tried letting it, but for what? We couldn't get anyone to pay enough to keep us somewhere else. There's no fish worth speaking of in the lake and the big marshes to the east where there used to be some good duck-shooting were drained over ten years ago. Now we've got to stop Charley Tillotson going out and blowing up the few poor survivors!

'Anyway Bertie suggested a restaurant, one of these medieval junket places. A licence to mint your own money, he said it was. The catering was done on a production line, no skill needed. And the discomforts were part of what the customer was paying for. So, the innocents abroad, we launched ourselves into it. It was either that or board up the house and apply for a council flat somewhere.'

'What about money?' asked Dalziel.

'Money?'

'You need cash. Nowt gets done without some cash.'

'You're right there,' Bonnie said. She turned once more and peered down at the railway line. Her movement brought her within a few inches of Dalziel who contemplated a brotherly arm around her shoulders but dismissed the idea on the grounds of indecency. A fraternal gesture would make what was happening beneath his mackintosh incestuous.

'We borrowed, mainly. Lou and myself raised a small mortgage on the house. They don't like lending money to women. Conrad was more successful. He didn't have much to offer as security, but he did have the gift of the gab. Bertie had no cash, but it was his idea and he knew something about the catering trade. Also he brought along Hank Uniff and his sister from Liverpool. Hank had just had a bit of a disaster. His studio had just been gutted by a fire, so he was desperate for somewhere to work. He's making a film and was delighted at the chance of being somewhere nice and quiet while the fire-insurance money worked for him in the business. He says he despises cash, really. Well, when we go bankrupt it'll be a test of his principles! His sister Mave's very artistic too, terrific with clothes. She's in charge of costumes.'

'What costumes?' interrupted Dalziel.

'Your retainers, court jesters, minstrels, serving wenches. Don't ask me what serving wenches. We're *all* serving wenches. Lou sings a lovely "Greensleeves". I can manage anything that stays within a four-note range. Hank plays the guitar – don't they *all*, these days? We were planning to hire *some* help, of course, but all of us in the business were going to be very actively involved.'

'You haven't mentioned Tillotson,' commented Dalziel.

'You notice *everything*, don't you?'

He glanced at her sharply. She was grinning slyly – there was no other word for it. It did not diminish her attractiveness one jot.

'Charley; well, Charley came along with Lou one weekend and he seems to have been around more or less ever since. He had a few hundred which he poured in almost uninvited and he'll make a lovely

Sir Philip Sidney or someone to direct traffic. So, there it is. Not a bad set-up. Money to be made. But we'll probably have to sell up to pay off our debts. We'll be lucky if we break even.'

There it was, thought Dalziel. If Mavis had been right, this was the gentle flick of the fly over the trout stream. No. Wrong picture. He was no trout. Carp, perhaps. Or shark. But even sharks could flounder in unfamiliar waters.

'What kind of money were you looking to make, Mrs Fielding?' he asked.

'I can't really say. Finance isn't my line. I wouldn't know which way up to hold the *Financial Times*. But the gross income's easy enough to work out. Five pounds a head; well that includes VAT, so we get four-fifty. Five hundred and forty from a full night. Bertie says other places like this in the north get six full nights a week *and* booked up for months ahead. So, six times five-forty.'

'Three thousand two hundred and forty a week,' Dalziel said, unimpressed. Income was nowt without expenditure. He didn't read Dickens but he'd heard of Mr Micawber.

'What do they get for a fiver?' he asked.

'Soup,' she said. 'Half a chicken. Spare rib. Cold pudding. Rye bread. Salad. Half a litre of red wine. Coffee. And a night's entertainment.'

'Uniff on guitar. Tillotson tripping over his codpiece,' he said. He didn't mean to be sarcastic nor did she take offence.

'You can pay more and get less,' she answered.

'Try to walk out of the Lady Hamilton's restaurant with a full belly and change from a fiver. And that's without any drink or floor show. We've got a bar too, of course.'

'Have you?' he said. That could double the profits. People come in groups, in a minibus, taxi, coach; someone else driving; one night when you could afford to let go without risking bother from the sodding police.

'Sounds a good proposition,' he said.

'It was,' she answered. 'Conrad will be sorry to have missed it, wherever he is.'

Dalziel glanced at her again. She was staring out into the night with a faintly puzzled look on her face.

'Or perhaps not,' she went on. 'You know, this is one of the straightest bits of track in the country. Look.'

She pointed. Dalziel stared into the blackness for a few seconds before spotting the light.

'Train,' she said. 'One of our rare expresses. Conrad and I often used to stop on this bridge if we'd been up to the village. Just about this time it must have been, because we'd watch this train coming nearer.'

The light was growing and now the sound of the wheels on the track was quite audible.

'It must touch a hundred or whatever it is that trains can travel at,' Bonnie continued. 'Conrad would stand here and watch it getting nearer. As if he couldn't take his eyes off it. And you know what he once said to me, one hard, frosty midwinter's night? "Bonnie," he said, "Bonnie, you realize it's just a step into summer".'

The diesel seemed to cover the last few hundred yards in a single leap, the horn blasted its three-note clarion call over the quiet countryside, and the upward blast of air as the train punched through the bridge made Dalziel take an involuntary pace backwards. Bonnie did not move.

'Some fucking step,' said Dalziel.

7

A Fried Egg Sandwich

Dalziel woke up early the following morning and lay in the darkness knowing it was full of menace. He forced himself to relax, and gradually the menace faded as the shapes and angles of the unfamiliar room began to emerge in gradations of grey, bringing with them something worse than fear, a sense of the grey hours, days, weeks, stretching ahead like a desert landscape of unrelieved, grinding, unsharable monotony.

Depression was a sickness, they told him. The previous year he had been worried enough by symptoms of physical illness to visit his doctor and had come away with a series of warnings and prohibitions concerning diet, alcohol, tobacco – the usual nonsense. But paradoxically his efforts to comply had led him inexorably to ask himself why he was bothering; what was so bloody marvellous about this life he was trying to preserve. Such metaphysical speculations were entirely foreign to his make-up and their formulation now was light years from being precise and intellectual. It was just a feeling of hollowness at the centre, a reluctance to awaken from the safe blackness of sleep, a sense of life like a hair floating on dirty bath water, sinking imperceptibly, moment by moment, till a final, spinning gurgling rush carried it away.

So he had taken a holiday. He had never cared much for holidays, but they were better than the happy-pills he knew many people took to preserve their truce with life. He was not one of those nuts who had to keep taking the tablets. A holiday would set *him* right. And this was it.

He forced himself to start thinking about this odd household he had fallen into. These people interested him. Professionally it might be a mistake to get involved, personally it might be a mistake not to. The previous evening had ended with no proposition of any kind from Bonnie. Most likely he had been entirely mistaken to expect one, but it had been a slight disappointment. Christ almighty, what did he expect? The bathroom door opening in the night and the shadowy figure in the diaphanous nightie stealing to his bedside? Kids' fantasies. No, he told himself grimly, if he had any attraction for the Fieldings it was what Mavis had hinted, as a potential investor, and they weren't going to start carving their roast beef for him till they knew what he was worth.

Not that he disapproved of this way of thinking, he told himself as he got out of bed. He liked people who trod carefully. And he liked people who took money seriously. That was what his job was about, mainly. The thought made him smile as he went into the bathroom and suddenly he realized that on this occasion at least his self-prescribed therapy was being successful.

He washed and shaved, making as little noise as possible, conscious of the sleeping woman behind the farther door. He wondered if it were locked, but did not feel able to try it.

He glanced at his watch as he got dressed and saw that it was six-thirty, later than he thought. The gloomy, overcast skies explained his error. Sunrise had been a secret ceremony that morning.

Guests should lie abed till they were certain the household was awake. This was a maxim he had learned long ago, but if he'd obeyed all the rules of polite behaviour he had ever known, he would still be a well-mannered constable. In any case, six-thirty was quite late enough.

He was not the only one stirring, he discovered. His nose told him there was someone in the kitchen making coffee. Uniff, he guessed. He looked a restless sod.

It was Mrs Greave.

'Morning,' he said.

She was wearing her green dressing-gown again and had obviously gone to bed without making any special provision for adjustment to her hair. The beehive now hung askew, giving her head a curious bent appearance as though seen through a funfair mirror.

She didn't reply. Dalziel helped himself to a mug (Bertie's again, he suspected) and poured coffee from the jug she had placed on a tray.

'You're an early bird,' he said after a scalding mouthful. 'And it's a long walk. What's wrong with them shiny new kitchens down there?'

'They're for cooking chickens, hunks of meat, a hundred portions at a time,' she said. 'Want a piece of toast?'

'Thanks,' he said, interested by this sudden thawing. Her dressing-gown was loosely belted and as she bent forward to butter the toast for him, he saw she was wearing nothing underneath.

He took another more careful sip of coffee and said, 'Careful you don't spill something.'

'You needn't look,' she said indifferently, passing him the toast.

'Why not? There's no charge, is there?' he said.

'What the hell do you mean?' she snapped angrily.

'Nothing. Nothing. How long have you been here with your father, Mrs Greave?'

She sat down opposite and watched him chew on his toast.

'Six months, maybe seven,' she said.

'Six, maybe seven. I see. This marmalade's good. Do you make it yourself, Mrs Greave?'

'No.'

'Pity. I like home-made stuff. But you've done a bit of cooking in your time. Those sausages last night. Grand! I bet you kept Mr Greave happy.'

'Pardon?'

'Mr Greave. Your husband,' said Dalziel. 'What happened? Died, did he?'

'Yes,' she said.

'I'm sorry. Poor fellow. What was it? Road accident? Coronary? Now Mrs Fielding did mention it last night, but I can't quite recall.'

He looked at her expectantly, his expression sympathetic but hopeful like a person's at a funeral.

'I'd rather not talk about it.'

'Of course not. Then after the unhappy event, Mr Papworth, your dad, found you a place here.'

'They needed a cook-housekeeper. And they'll need help when the restaurant opens.'

'True,' said Dalziel. 'Then you'll be able to use all that lovely shiny equipment. Mind you, things look a bit dicey just now.'

'I don't know anything of that,' she said, rising. 'I'm just the paid help. Excuse me. I'd better go and get dressed.'

She made for the door.

'Don't forget your tray,' called Dalziel.

She stopped, then slowly returned, picked up the tray and left. Someone spoke to her outside the door and a second later Louisa came into the room. She was wearing a short flowered tunic from which her thin white legs forked with, for Dalziel, all the provocative power of a couple of pipe-cleaners. But tastes differed, he was willing to concede, and he suspected she thought she was the sexiest thing since co-education.

'That was pretty nosy,' she said as she headed for the stove.

'You were listening,' he accused.

'I didn't like to butt in,' she said. 'All that about the way she was widowed. It was embarrassing.'

Dalziel laughed derisively.

'What's that mean?' she asked.

'It means I don't think either of you were embarrassed,' he answered.

She left the stove, came to the other side of the table, put her hands on it and leaned towards him.

She'd have to stand on her head and waggle her legs in the air to be interesting, thought Dalziel.

'Who the hell do you think you are to talk to me like that?' she demanded.

'I'm a man you punched on the nose without explanation or apology,' he retorted. 'That gives me rights.'

She decided to postpone confrontation and grinned.

'You want me to say I'm sorry? Well, I suppose I was later. Hitting a stranger's not like hitting someone you know. But since I've met you again, I'm not certain whether I'm sorry or not. And if you talk to me like you talked to Mrs Greave, I might just punch you again.'

'Mrs Greave didn't punch me,' said Dalziel. 'And your kettle's boiling.'

'It's easy to intimidate servants,' she called from the back kitchen. 'If she tells Pappy, you watch out. He's no respecter of persons.'

'Aye. I doubt if he respects Mrs Greave's person much,' grunted Dalziel.

'What do you mean?' said Louisa, returning with a mug of coffee.

'Come on, love,' said Dalziel. 'You're not *all* blind innocents here, are you? There were two cups on that tray. And a couple of doughnuts as well as toast.'

'So she's got a sweet tooth and she's giving her old dad his breakfast in bed. I like that,' said Louisa.

'It's not all she's giving him,' said Dalziel. 'It's plain as the nose on your face. I know a scrubber when I see one.'

'Clearly I haven't had your educational advantages,' said the girl. 'But if what you say is right, and she's Pappy's fancy bit, what's it matter? He's old enough and conventional enough to feel he needs a cover story, that's all. Your generation's made quite an art of hypocrisy.'

'What *are* you, Miss Fielding?' asked Dalziel suddenly. She was taken aback and looked at him in puzzlement.

'I mean, all the others seem to be something, to have done something. *You*, though. How old are you? Eighteen? Nineteen? Twenty? What do *you* do?'

'Haven't you heard?' she said, recovered. 'I've

got shares in a restaurant. You might say, I own it. Or will do.'

'What? Oh, the house. You're hoping to live off your inheritance, are you? It's always the way. What one generation makes, the next spends.'

'No one asks to be born, Mr Dalziel,' she said.

'Not many return the gift,' Dalziel said. He was trying to remember what it was like when he was nineteen. The girls he knew hadn't been like this but was that just a difference of class rather than of time? A bit of both. Time marched on, but you could always make allowances. The class thing was different. Dalziel liked a fairly rigid class structure. A sense of social level made people easier to deal with – to manipulate, if you spelled it out. That was also what his job was about. But more importantly it gave a man a sense of what he was, whereas these young sods didn't seem to worry about being anything in particular. And it was catching if you weren't careful. You could wake up and feel the numbness of self-doubt spreading to the heart.

He rose and went into the back kitchen to boil the kettle once more.

The girl sat still, inhaling the steam from her cup. She might have been twelve or thirteen, he thought, glancing at her narrow shoulders from behind.

Suddenly something about her age struck him, something so obvious he couldn't understand how he'd missed it before.

'How old's Bertie?' he asked, putting a spoonful of instant coffee into his mug.

'Twenty-four. Why?'

'And Nigel's fifteen. And they're your step-brothers?'

He made a business of pouring out the water and looking for the milk. From the outer room came a laugh.

'Oh, I see. You've just noticed. Yes, Bonnie had Bertie shortly after meeting Conrad for the first time. I think she fell for his Army uniform. She likes men in uniform, you know. She was bringing Bertie up herself when she met my father. They got married. Later I appeared. Then Daddy died and who should turn up again but Conrad. This time she was wise enough, or stupid enough, to get him to the altar. And after fifteen years of intermittent marriage, here we all are. Happy Family.'

'I see,' said Dalziel.

'It took you long enough,' she said, raising her voice. 'I thought everyone could see at a glance that Bertie was a bastard.'

When he rejoined her, he saw the reason for the change in tone. Bertie was standing in the doorway. Dalziel looked at his watch. It was still only seven o'clock. They really were early risers here; Bertie was fully clothed and, from the look of his shoes, he had been outside.

'Don't let me interrupt,' said the fat youth, walking through the kitchen. He shot a malignant

106

glance at Dalziel's mug as he passed but said nothing.

'Morning,' said Dalziel. 'What's it like out? Cold?'

'Why don't you try it?' said Bertie from the other room.

'Later. This restaurant was your idea, your mam says.'

Bertie returned with some coffee and looked insolently at Dalziel.

'What's it to you?' he asked.

'Nothing much,' said Dalziel. 'I was just hearing about your financial troubles. Wondering if it was worth pouring good money after bad, that's all.'

He was quite proud of that. The statement went no further than a general comment but obviously from the glance the other two exchanged it was the particular application that had been made.

Bertie's voice was definitely politer when he replied.

'I don't know what my mother's been saying, Mr Dalziel, but you mustn't get hold of the wrong end of the stick. The work's nearly finished as you can see. A token payment of a couple of thousand would get the contractors back in twenty-four hours. There's no question of long-term difficulty. Any finance house would be keen to advance money once they saw the state of the project. It's just a matter of time.'

107

'Oh. If that's all . . . well, I'm glad to hear it,' said Dalziel. 'I must have mistaken Mrs Fielding. Would anyone mind if I fried myself an egg?'

He didn't wait for an answer but set about the business with the expertise of a man long used to living alone. There was some bacon in the fridge, nice thick-cut rashers which looked as if the pig had seen the light of day in the recent past. He kept his mind off the contents of the foil-wrapped package which he had found here yesterday.

'Anyone else?' he called.

'I'll try one,' Louisa said, joining him at the stove. 'I can't cook for toffee.'

'I bet your mam can,' said Dalziel.

'When she wants,' said the girl. She lowered her voice. 'Don't take any notice of Bertie. He thinks all big businessmen talk like that.'

'Tell lies, you mean?' said Dalziel, cracking another egg one-handed and draining it through his fingers into the pan.

'Don't worry, love,' he went on. 'I know you can't even refund the Bowls Club their money. God knows what else I don't know about! No. If I was a finance house, I wouldn't lend you your bus-fare home.'

'Up you, then,' said Louisa angrily.

'But I am not a finance house. You know what? I'm going to have mine in a sandwich. It can be messy, but what's life without risks?'

There was no need for him to be talking like

this. The first hint that he might be interested in the project had been justifiable. Even then you had to pretend there was some kind of case and he was investigating it. But this was just economic prick-teasing. He tried to retrieve his position.

'If a couple of thousand's all that's needed, I can't see your problem,' he said, carefully organizing his montage of egg and bacon on a slice of thick-cut bread. 'Your grandfather's got this Gumboot thing coming; how much? Fifteen thousand dollars? Won't he chip in?'

'Not bloody likely,' said Louisa, eating her egg more conventionally, albeit straight from the pan. 'He's been against the project right from the start. He's got a little bit of money from his writing, enough to pay his way in the house, and there's not much he can do with the Gumbelow money at his age. But he'd rather flush it down the loo than let Bertie get his hands on it. That's how he sees the business, you see. Always has. Bertie's balls-up. They don't get on, you may have noticed. And now Herrie thinks Conrad would still be alive if it weren't for the business.'

'Is that right?' said Dalziel.

'So any knight in shining armour willing to take a small risk for a short time would be gratefully received and bounteously recompensed.'

She looked seriously at him and ran her tongue along the prongs of her fork.

'Is that right?' said Dalziel again. 'Short time.'

He bit into his sandwich. The egg burst, spread, overflowed faster than his mouth could take it in and ran down his chin.

'I said it could be messy,' said Dalziel.

8

Family History

As soon as it was a reasonable working hour, Dalziel rang the garage.

Yes, they remembered talking to Mrs Fielding. Yes, they hoped to send someone out for the car that day. No, they didn't think it would take long to put it right, just a drying-out job. In fact if they'd realized it was so urgent, they'd have brought it in yesterday afternoon. Of course (full of rural indignation) their breakdown truck could get through the floods if it had to.

Dalziel arranged to ring them later in the day and replaced the phone thoughtfully. At that rate, he could be on his way by tea-time. In fact it sounded as if he could have been on his way the previous day.

He was in Hereward Fielding's room and as he left the old man met him at the door.

'I was just using the phone,' Dalziel felt constrained to explain.

'There are other phones in the house,' snapped

the old man. 'But feel free. Feel free. It's Liberty Hall here.'

'Are you better?' asked Dalziel.

'Better than what? I was never unwell, if that's what you mean. I've been wet before, I'll be wet again before I go. You'll see.'

'There you are, Herrie. Why on earth have you got out of bed? You are being very silly.'

It was Bonnie, looking very stern and disciplinarian.

'You must allow me to judge what is best,' said Fielding. 'I am perfectly well. In any case those Gumbelow people are likely to turn up today and I've no intention of letting a lot of damned Americans find me in bed.'

'They may not come,' said Bonnie. 'Even if they do, you could have waited till they'd rung and said definitely.'

'The phones in this house are in such constant use that it may prove impossible for them to get through,' said Fielding, glowering at Dalziel.

'Well, sit down in here. I'll put the electric fire on and get Mrs Greave to bring you some breakfast.'

'Coffee only and a slice of toast,' said Fielding. 'That woman's not to be trusted with anything else. That meal last night. Vile!'

'The sausages weren't bad,' said Dalziel.

'You had sausages? I was given some nauseating stew of a kind hitherto undescribed in prose or poetry, unless on the occasion that Dr Henry

Spooner recited the opening lines of "The Burial of Sir John Moore".'

'It was chicken fricassée and it came out of a tin,' said Bonnie. 'Now go and sit down.'

She spoke in a stern schoolmistressy tone and Fielding obeyed. Dalziel felt he too might have obeyed if addressed in such a way, but her voice when she spoke to him after closing the door behind her father-in-law was humorously long-suffering.

'No wonder Herrie and Nigel got on so well! They're both at the awkward age.'

'Don't you think you ought to try to find where the boy went?' suggested Dalziel diffidently.

'I'll make some discreet enquiries round his friends,' she answered with an unworried smile. 'Boys of that age are very contrary. Any hint of a search would just make him burrow deeper. Did Herrie say you'd been telephoning?'

Dalziel considered.

'No. No, he didn't,' he said. 'But I have. I rang the garage.'

'What do they think?' she asked.

'They're not certain. I'm going to ring later.' The lie came easily.

'Well, you're welcome to stay as long as you need to,' said Bonnie. 'If you can stick us, that is.'

'I'll bear it,' said Dalziel. 'Tell you what. I'd like to go into Orburn if anyone's going that way. One or two things I'd like to get.'

113

'There's a shop in the village,' said the woman.

'Do they make up prescriptions?' asked Dalziel.

'No.'

'Well then. Perhaps I can phone a taxi if no one's going that way.'

'Don't be silly. I'll drive you myself. There's always some shopping to get.'

Any hopes Dalziel had of another solitary excursion with Bonnie disappeared when he met the car outside the house at the prearranged time of nine-thirty. It was an old Rover with what looked like the remnants of a nest in the radiator grille. In the front passenger seat was Tillotson and when Dalziel opened the rear door he found himself looking at Mavis Uniff.

Bonnie drove with considerable panache, passing through the flooded bottom end of the drive with an angel's wing of water arcing away on either side. Dalziel hoped the undercarriage was in better repair than the bodywork, but no harm seemed to be done. The suspension felt as if it had given its best and was now in decline, a state understandable if corners were always taken like this. The humped railway bridge where they had stood the previous night provided another interesting obstacle, but the Rover took it like a thoroughbred 'chaser which was more than Dalziel's stomach did.

They slowed to a sedate fifty to pass through Low Fold village, which was a cluster of cottages, a Post Office, a pub and a church. A thought occurred to Dalziel as they passed this last building.

'Why didn't they bury him there?' he asked Mavis *sotto voce*.

'I don't know,' she replied and, leaning forward to tap Bonnie on the shoulder, asked, 'He wants to know why you didn't bury Conrad in Low Fold?'

Dalziel shook his head reprovingly at the girl but Bonnie seemed happy to answer.

'Lake House dead have always been buried in High Fold churchyard. You see, Low Fold's high and High Fold's low, if you follow me. Mike my first husband's there as well, so it's convenient for all the family.'

Dalziel glanced surreptitiously at his companion but no one seemed to find the comment either amusing or odd. He scratched his left armpit thoughtfully and the rest of the journey was completed in silence.

Orburn appeared to him as a town he'd visited many years ago in his youth rather than one he had left just the previous morning. The main street widened into a kind of square, or rather an ovoid, as if someone had pressed his thumb on the narrow thoroughfares which ran out of it and the street had blebbed to four times its normal width. At one end of the bleb was the Lady Hamilton. Bonnie parked a little farther along, next to a marble statue which age or modesty seemed to have rendered anonymous.

'There's a chemist's over there,' said Bonnie. 'I'll

make for the supermarket first, I think. What are you two going to do? Labour for me or your own thing?'

Tillotson and Mavis seemed uncertain of their respective plans and in the end Bonnie said to Dalziel, 'See that baker's over the road? There's a little café behind it. We'll have a coffee there in about forty-five minutes. All right?'

She strode away, long firm strides stretching her simple denim skirt taut against her thighs. Tillotson hesitated a moment before following. One thing about your posh upbringing, thought Dalziel. Properly done, it instilled good manners. Their fatal weakness.

'What about you?' he said to Mavis.

'I never go into shops if I can help it,' she replied. 'Especially supermarkets. I'll show you the sights if you like.'

'That's kind,' said Dalziel, which it was. It was also a bloody nuisance. Time was short and he didn't want the girl hanging around.

'But it's shopping I'm after, too,' he went on. 'Just bits and pieces, but the sights'll have to wait till another time.'

'You *are* staying long enough for another time then?' she asked. 'Should I welcome you to the club?'

'We'll see. Thanks for your offer anyway.'

'That's all right. I'll go and brood on nature.'

She smiled at him and walked slowly away. He crossed the road and went into the chemist's where he watched Mavis out of sight while the assistant wrapped a bottle of aspirin.

'Anything else, sir?' asked the girl.

'Yes,' said Dalziel. 'Where's the police station?'

Fortunately it turned out to be in the direction opposite to that taken by Mavis and with the other two trapped in the canyons of the supermarket, Dalziel was able to enter the single-storeyed building which was the local station with minimum furtiveness.

'Yes, sir?' said the uniformed constable seated at a typewriter resting on a paper-littered desk.

'Always stand up for the public, son,' said Dalziel, producing his warrant card. 'Who's the boss here?'

'Inspector Grantley, but he's not in just now, sir,' said the constable, standing at a curious semi-attention occasioned by the fact that he had eased one foot out of its boot and was unable to fully re-insert it.

'CID?'

'That's Detective-Sergeant Cross. He's in his office. Shall I ring him?'

'No, it can't be far in a place this size. Which one? Second on the left. Thanks. You haven't got a rupture, have you, son?'

'No, sir!'

'If you stand like that much longer, you'll likely get one.'

Dalziel rapped sharply on the indicated door and entered.

The sole occupant of the room was not a pretty

sight. He looked as if in the best of circumstances he would have been unprepossessing; unshaven, haggard from fatigue, his shirt collar open, feet on his desk, a still steaming mug of coffee propped perilously on his belly, he was quite revolting. Dalziel regarded him with vast approval. This was how a hard-working Detective Sergeant ought to look at least once a day.

'Who the hell are you?' said the man with semi-somnolent irritation.

Dalziel reached forward and plucked the threatening mug from his lap.

'Embarrassing that,' he said. 'Scalded cock. Makes the nurses wonder about you. I'm Dalziel.'

His fame clearly had not penetrated to these dim recesses of the land and though the production of his warrant card set Cross struggling to his feet, it was a Pavlovian reaction to the rank rather than a spontaneous tribute to the reputation.

'Sit down,' ordered Dalziel, 'before you fall down. Hard night?'

'A bit,' said Cross, running his fingers through black spiky hair which might have been petrified for all the effect this had on it. 'Eight hours in a hen battery. God, the stink!'

'I thought there was something,' said Dalziel, sniffing. 'Anything to show for it?'

'No, sir,' said Cross gloomily. 'A waste of time. I've got my report here if you're interested.'

He proffered a sheaf of typewritten papers which Dalziel waved aside.

'No, thanks, Sergeant. I see enough of those on my own patch. This is unofficial. I'm on holiday in the district, so I thought I'd drop in and pay my respects.'

Cross looked at him with the utter disbelief of one who had seen enough of detective superintendents to know that courtesy calls on sergeants belonged with Father Christmas and the fairies.

'Thank you, sir,' he said. 'Nice to see you. Can I show you round?'

'I don't think so,' said Dalziel. 'Seen one, you've seen 'em all as the actress said. But you might be able to help me on another matter.'

He pulled up a chair and sat opposite Cross who smiled slightly. Dalziel decided this wasn't insubordinate and grinned back.

'Family by the name of Fielding,' he said. 'They live about ten miles out of town near a village called Low Fold.'

'I know them,' said Cross. 'A big house; Lake House it's called. They're converting part of it to a restaurant. Mr Fielding died recently. That the one?'

'That's it,' said Dalziel.

'Ah,' said Cross.

Dalziel watched and waited for a moment, scratching his left buttock vigorously, a luxury he had been consciously eschewing in the company of Bonnie Fielding.

'I'm a stranger here,' he said after a while. 'I

don't understand all the dialect. *Ah*. What does that mean? *Nice weather we've been having?* Or *hello cheeky, give us a kiss?* It's important I know.'

'Sorry, sir,' said Cross. 'I was just wondering; I mean, are you a friend, or what?'

'It makes a difference? That's a start. I never knew these people existed till yesterday when they helped me after my car broke down. Now I'm curious. That help you?'

'Thank you, sir,' said Cross, rising and going to a filing cabinet. 'They're well known in the locality, the Fieldings. They've been around for about eight years now, and, of course, Mrs Fielding was here before that when her first husband was alive. Here we are.'

He extracted a file and returned to the desk.

'The house belonged to Mr Percival, of course.'

'Who?'

'The first husband. The Percivals were very well known. Been around a long time. Not your aristocracy though they made some claims, but comfortably off. Their money came from trade, I believe.'

He said the word as though it still had a definite pejorative meaning in these parts.

'Trade?' echoed Dalziel.

'That's right, but distant enough to be all right. Too distant, perhaps. It was cotton mainly and the Percivals were worse hit than most during the slump. I don't know the ins-and-outs but, by the end of the war I get the impression they were pretty well finished financially. And as a family too. The war saw three of 'em off, two in action, one in the blitz. The older survivors dropped off pretty rapidly afterwards, and Michael Percival, your Mrs Fielding's first, got what little survived of the family fortune all concentrated in his own bank balance. It seems to have been enough for him to live modestly on – by his standards – and his wife too, when they got married in 1954. The girl, Louisa, was born the following year and a couple of years later, Percival died. Six months after that, Mrs Percival married Mr Fielding.'

'The father of her eldest son, you knew that?' said Dalziel.

'Oh yes. She made no secret of it. The local gentry didn't like it. They prefer to hide their bastards. But she didn't care. They weren't around much for a few years in any case. The house was let and the Fieldings, according to best report, were living it up in swinging London. But money doesn't last forever and they'd spent so little of it on maintaining the house that it became unlettable. Also the marshlands where the tenants used to go shooting were drained and reclaimed in the mid-sixties and no one was interested in the place any more. So they came back to live in it. By this time, they had had the youngest boy, of course, and they brought Mr Fielding's father along, to help pay the rates, I suppose. He's some kind of writer, they tell me.'

He spoke, Dalziel noted approvingly, as if to be

some kind of writer was the equivalent of being physically handicapped.

'You know a lot about these people, Sergeant,' he said.

'I did a bit of research when this last business occurred,' said Cross. 'You heard about it?'

'You tell me,' said Dalziel.

Cross opened his file.

'The deceased, Conrad Fielding, was discovered by his wife in what they're calling the Banqueting Hall at Lake House. Unfortunately by the time we became involved the body had been moved, but according to Mrs Fielding's statement the man was lying on the floor there –' he passed over a glossy half-plate print of the Hall floor on which an outline of a body had been chalked '– with his chest pierced by the bit of an electric drill. The drill was still switched on. There was a ladder lying alongside the body, and there were drill marks in the wall about twenty feet up. It seems that the building contractors had packed up work till they got paid and Mr Fielding had been trying to do it himself. The coroner decided that the ladder had slipped, he'd fallen down with the drill in his hand with the switch locked on, and unfortunately had fallen right on to the bit. Three-eighths doing two thousand four hundred revs. It makes a hole like that.'

'I'd have expected it neater,' said Dalziel, looking at the close-up of the naked chest on a mortuary slab.

'The bit stayed in the wound after death,' said Cross. 'The weight of the drill would force the bit sideways through the flesh till an equilibrium was reached. That's what the doctor said. Here's the p.m. report.'

Dalziel scanned it quickly, expertly. He usually left it to his subordinates to extract what was important from technical reports and relay it to him succinctly and accurately. But Cross had not been moulded on the master-potter's wheel.

'So,' he said. 'Accident. What's your interest?'

'We've a duty to investigate all sudden deaths, sir,' said Cross blandly.

'Get knotted,' said Dalziel amiably. 'If I fell off this chair and broke my neck, you wouldn't dig into my family history for the past thirty years. So?'

'There were a couple of things,' said Cross slowly. 'First, the way they all behaved. They're an odd lot up at Lake House, you may have noticed, but you'd have expected a bit of, well, respect. Instead they all chattered away, ten to the dozen, and seemed bent on carrying on just as normal, except that they were a bit annoyed at the disturbance. Mark you, I didn't see any of them till some time after the death, so I can't report on immediate reactions. Mrs Fielding seemed a bit distressed, but very much in control, and the boy, Nigel, seemed genuinely upset. But the others . . . well!'

'Even the old man?'

'Old Hereward? He was the oddest of all. No sign of grief but he said, "I told him no good would come of it. I told him," and that was all. Not another word.'

Dalziel glanced at his watch. He was running out of time.

'You said there were a couple of things which aroused your interest. What else besides the family reaction?'

'There was a phone call,' said Cross. 'Not to us, but to the insurance company carrying Fielding's policies. One of their investigators, Spinx they called him, came round to tell us. Co-operation, he called it. What he was after was for us to tell him they needn't pay up! Evidently someone rang up their office the day after the death and said they should look very closely at the circumstances before handing out any money. Well, we have to take notice.'

'Male or female?' demanded Dalziel.

'A woman, they think, though it could have been a male falsetto. Look, sir, can I ask if you're on to something? I mean, I don't want to sound as if I'm telling you your job, but it is *my* case.'

Cross stared at him defiantly. He's quite right, thought Dalziel. Being his superior gives me no right to act in a bullying, arrogant way.

'Just curiosity, lad,' he said with a disarming grin, showing teeth which were as perfect and as reassuring as a shark's. 'I might be spending a couple of days with these people and I wanted to know what I was getting into. From what you tell me, there's nothing to worry about. There's always someone ready to make nasty phone calls. And as for their reactions, well, we're all entitled to be different, aren't we? It'd be a grey place if all folks were the same.'

With these tolerant, liberal colours tacked to his masthead, Dalziel prepared to set sail through the door.

Cross reassembled his file and said casually, 'You don't happen to know if they are still going to open the restaurant a week on Saturday, sir?'

'No. I'm sure they'll do their best,' said Dalziel, never less sure of anything in a life of certainties.

'I hope so. I'm in the local Bowls Club and we've got a booking. There's ten quid of my hard-earned cash in that concern.'

'There's better things to do with your money,' said Dalziel reprovingly. 'But I'm sure Mrs Fielding will try to honour all commitments.'

He must have sounded a little defensive. Cross looked at him and said neutrally, 'She's a fine-looking woman, Mrs Fielding.'

Dalziel felt his tolerant, liberal colours slipping.

'What's that got to do with anything?' he said.

'Nothing at all, sir. Just thinking it's a pity her life should have been so full of tragedy. Two husbands, both lost in such nasty circumstances.'

It was a question he should have asked. Had he been in Cross's position investigating the business from scratch, it was one of the first things he would have looked to discover.

'How did Percival die?' he asked.

'An accident on the lake, sir,' said Cross. 'He fell out of a punt and was drowned.'

9

The Setting of Riddles

Dalziel moved swiftly once he had left the police station. There was one more call he had to make and he was short of time. Fortunately his destination was only round the corner from the station as he had ascertained in the chemist's.

He glanced quickly around when he reached the entrance to Gibb and Fowler's builders yard. The street was deserted except for a man entering a telephone-box about thirty yards behind him, and he pushed open the rickety wooden gates and went in.

It would have been simpler and more professional to get Sergeant Cross to do this, but for reasons he was still keeping obscure from himself, he did not wish to alert the local force more than he had done. Basically, he assured himself, it was just his own curiosity that was driving him on.

He was lucky to find the small, lop-sided and halitotic Mr Gibb in, or so the small, lop-sided and halitotic Mr Gibb assured him. Dalziel expressed his joy at such good fortune and tried to arrange Mr Gibb and himself in one of these curiously oblique conversational tableaux so favoured of television drama directors. Mr Gibb, however, would be satisfied with nothing less than confrontation so Dalziel produced his warrant card and came quickly to the point.

'Mr Gibb, why did your firm stop work on the job at Lake House?'

'It's not secret,' said Gibb. 'They'd got no money. We're not a charity, Superintendent. When I found out they couldn't pay for what we'd done so far (which was nearly the whole job, I might add), I saw no reason to chuck good money after bad.'

'I see that,' said Dalziel. 'But you were so near finished, why not complete the job and give them a chance to make some money? You must have known they were short of capital for a long while.'

'You're right, we did. And that's the way we *were* thinking until, well, we got information suggesting that even if the place was finished, they didn't have a cat in hell's chance of getting the business under way. It would just mean they had a better-looking concern to sell off when the official receiver got to them, and I saw no reason why I should spend more time and materials just so other creditors could get a better dividend! So I said, if you don't pay now, that's it.'

'I see,' said Dalziel, releasing his held breath. 'You say you got information. How did you get it?'

Gibb looked uncomfortable, then said aggressively, 'It was a phone call. Some woman, anonymous. I wouldn't take notice of such a thing normally, but we'd been worried about that Fielding fellow for some time. You know the type, good talker, very convincing, gets you full of confidence till you go away and think things out a bit later. Know what I mean? So I thought I'll put him to the test, ask for a payment on account. Well, he started his usual patter. Mind you, it wasn't up to his usual standard. I mean, normally he could have talked the pants off a nun, but this time he seemed stuck for words. Perhaps it was his conscience.'

'Perhaps,' said Dalziel thoughtfully. 'So you stopped work. Would you start again if there was some money forthcoming?'

'Yes,' said Gibb without hesitation. 'Like a shot. We're short of work just now. It's general. Six weeks ago, I was never in the office. Now, I'm never out of it.'

'You said I was lucky to catch you,' said Dalziel slyly.

'I thought you might be a customer then,' grinned Gibb through his ruined teeth. 'What's this all about anyway? Is there something up?'

'Not really,' assured Dalziel. 'Do me a favour, Mr Gibb, and don't let on I've been asking questions. You never know, you might be back on the Lake House job sooner than you think.'

That should keep him quiet, thought Dalziel as he left. The poor devil was probably down to his last Rolls-Royce. He strode back along the street, moving quickly for a man of his bulk.

I'm far too fat, he thought. I've let myself go. This belly's obscene. They'll need a domed lid on my coffin, like a casserole.

But it did have its uses sometimes. Like now, for instance, he thought, as he opened the door of the telephone-box and stepped inside, pinning the slightly built middle-aged man in the ill-fitting suit against the coin box.

'Right now,' said Dalziel. 'Who the hell are you?'

Even as he spoke he recognized the man. On the night he had been assaulted by Louisa in the Lady Hamilton it was this fellow who had come into the bar, asking about the disturbance. He had placed him then as a journalist. Whatever he was, it was probably this brief encounter which had made him familiar enough to stick out when Dalziel had got out of Bonnie's car in the square. Dalziel did not believe in coincidence and when the same man had been hanging around near the police station and subsequently near the builders yard, it bore investigation.

'What the blazes are you doing?' demanded the man. 'Let me out at once, or I'll call the police.'

'I *am* the police,' said Dalziel. 'So you needn't call too loud. Why're you following me? Come on, quick as you can!'

'The police? So it's you. I didn't realize. My name's Spinx. Hold on.'

Spinx tried to reach into his top pocket but

Dalziel never took chances and his great paw closed firmly on the man's wrist.

'What've you got there?'

'Just a card,' said Spinx, very frightened now.

Dalziel reached into the pocket, took out a business card and sighed. It was a sad business, this suspicion. But it might have been a razor.

Alfred Spinx said the card. *Claims Department. Anchor Insurance.*

'Come on, Alfred,' said Dalziel, stepping out of the box. 'Let's walk and talk.'

The open air seemed to make Spinx garrulous. He spoke in a strange not-quite-right accent and idiom as though he had learned English through a correspondence course with some minor public school in the thirties.

'I'm an insurance investigator,' he said. 'I used to be freelance, doing general work, you know. But the bottom's falling out of divorce now. Who needs evidence? Like a lot of dratted gypsies, break a pot and shout *I divorce thee* thrice, and that's it. I've thought seriously of emigrating, you know. By George, I have. To somewhere where they still have standards.'

'Flags, you mean?' said Dalziel, wondering whether to take this sodding little twerp for real. 'Try Russia. They like flags there, so they tell me. But before you buy your ticket, why were you following me, Alfred?'

Spinx stopped and stared with nervous resolution at Dalziel.

'Excuse me, Mr . . . er . . . ?'

'Dalziel. Superintendent.'

'Superintendent. I'd rather you didn't use my Christian name. I've studied a bit of criminology and I know it helps to establish a proper subordinate and familiar relationship with a suspect, but you know who I am now and I'd prefer to talk at the level of equals. We're colleagues in a sense after all, don't you know, you in the public, me in the private sector.'

The words came at a rush and Dalziel's first impulse was to laugh. But the man's attempt at dignity was not merely comic. In any case Dalziel wanted information and wanted it fast. He should be in the coffee shop now.

'I'm sorry, Mr Spinx. It is *Mister*? Good. But just a few questions if you'd be so kind. What precisely is the case you're working on at this moment.'

'The same as you, I imagine, Superintendent,' said Spinx. 'Mr Conrad Fielding's death.'

'Why should that interest you?'

'Any insurance company looks closely at any large claim on it, you must know that. We're probably even more suspicious than the police.' He spoke with pride.

'And there was the phone call,' prompted Dalziel.

'Yes. You'd know all about that, of course. Such things cannot be ignored, you understand.'

'Tell me about it again,' commanded Dalziel.

'Certainly. Wait a moment. Here we are. My book of words.'

He produced a plastic-covered notebook from his inside pocket, thumbed through it, his lips pattering together in time to the riffled pages, finally pursing in a reluctantly proffered kiss as he found his place.

'Here we are. It was a woman who phoned. Or so the oral evidence suggests. *Hello*.'

'What?' said Dalziel.

'That's me,' explained Spinx. 'I've got the whole conversation. *Hello!* Then she said, *You thinking of paying any insurance money on Conrad Fielding? Well, I wouldn't*. Then I said, *Hello!* I was playing for time, you understand. *Who's that speaking?* She said, *Never mind that. Just ask yourself what a man like that would be doing up a ladder in his condition*. I said *Hello!* and she rang off.'

He shut the book and looked hopefully at Dalziel like a dog waiting to be patted. The fat man reached forward and plucked the book from his hands.

'Let's have a look,' he said, opening it. 'Christ! What's this? Egyptian?'

'No,' said Spinx with pride, peering at the line of minute matchstick men which marched over the paper. 'My own shorthand code. A method I devised to preserve confidentiality, you understand.'

'It does that, right enough,' said Dalziel, returning the book. 'So you told the police like a good citizen and did a bit of looking round yourself.

That's what you were doing at the Lady Hamilton, was it? Keeping tabs on the family?'

'It was a last fling. I thought a little close observation might lead me to something,' admitted Spinx. 'It didn't and I'm having terrible trouble with my expenses. I only had an omelette, but the prices there are really shocking.'

'So you found nowt,' said Dalziel, impatiently glancing at his watch again. He was late. They were at the corner of the square in which the car was parked and he halted there, restraining Spinx with one brutish paw. 'The inquest said accident. So now you pay?'

'Well, we would have done,' said Spinx. 'Indeed the letter had been written and was ready for dispatch yesterday. Then I heard about you.'

'About me?' said Dalziel in surprise. He recalled Spinx's reaction in the phone-box. *So it's you* he had said when Dalziel identified himself. Which must mean . . .

'She phoned again, yesterday afternoon.'

The book was opened once more.

'*Hello!*' said Spinx.

'Just the gist,' growled Dalziel. 'Forget the witty interchange.'

'She said that if we were thinking of paying the money, we ought to know that the police were still looking into the business. There was one actually staying in the house at present. That was all. So we decided to bide our time again, you understand.'

'Well bloody well,' said Dalziel. 'It was the same woman?'

'I believe so.'

'Right,' said Dalziel. 'Listen, Mr Spinx, I've got to go now but I may want to talk to you again.'

'If you ring the number on my card, they'll find me,' said Spinx. 'Before you go, Superintendent, without breaching professional ethics, can you give me any hint of how your investigations are going?'

Dalziel examined the eager face before him. He didn't like small men and he didn't like private investigation and he didn't like the assumption that he had anything in common with this pathetic shadow. On the other hand Spinx wouldn't believe the truth and there was no point in antagonizing him by the rude rejoinder which was ever ready to leap from his tongue.

'Can't say,' said Dalziel. 'You understand?'

'Yes, of course.'

'Good. Now we mustn't be seen together. Cheerio!'

He stepped smartly into the square and strode towards the baker's shop. As he approached Bonnie emerged from the doorway with Tillotson and Mavis close behind.

'Hello,' said Bonnie. 'We thought you must have got lost, though God knows how in this place!'

'No, I just went a bit farther than I thought,' said Dalziel. 'Got your shopping?'

'Yes. We're ready for off, if you don't mind missing your coffee.'

They moved towards the car.

'Look,' said Tillotson. 'There's Sphincter.'

They followed his gaze. Standing at the corner of the street from which Dalziel hoped they had not seen him emerge was Spinx who stepped back furtively when he realized they were looking at him.

'Who?'

'His name's Spinx,' said Bonnie. 'He works for the insurance company that's being so bloody about coughing up for Conrad. The children call him Sphincter. Very apt.'

'He's just doing his job,' protested Mavis.

'He shouldn't have chosen such a nauseating job,' said Bonnie calmly. 'Strange, isn't it, Mr Dalziel, how little bankruptcy means to those with nothing to lose?'

It was hard to tell if she were getting at Spinx or at Mavis.

The drive home was silent, but when they reached the house they found plenty to talk about. The representatives of the Gumbelow Foundation had rung and confirmed they would be coming that afternoon, bringing with them a photographer, a freelance feature writer whom Dalziel had never heard of, and a couple of men from the BBC with sound-recording equipment. For a while it was touch and go whether Hereward Fielding would include this under the interdict he had placed upon television, but recollection of an unnamed kindness offered to him by a Third Programme producer in 1952 swayed the balance.

'But I will not recite for them,' Fielding averred fiercely. 'I never have done. Have you heard Eliot? Like an old man straining on a bedpan.'

Dalziel left them to their excitements and, pausing only to pick up a meat pie and a bottle of stout from the do-it-yourself lunch offering in the kitchen, he made his way towards the Banqueting Hall. When the investigatory mood was upon him he regarded open doors as invitations and closed doors as affronts and he peered into everywhere that wasn't locked. He found nothing of interest except a couple of rooms which looked as if some large and short-sighted squirrel had decided to use them as store houses. They were piled high with junk, old furniture, planks, tree branches even, and festooned with moth-eaten curtains and old clothes which would have been rejected by even the most desperate jumble sale.

The Banqueting Hall promised even less in the way of stimulation. He peered down at the patch of floor on which his memory of Cross's photograph told him Conrad Fielding had lain with an electric drill burrowing through his rib cage. A bit of gristly pork had got stuck in his teeth and he picked it out with a fingernail and burped. The floor had obviously been well scrubbed. Who by? he wondered as he placed his bottle and the remnants of the pie carefully on a wooden trestle and dragged a ladder from the shadows under the gallery. He was a careful man and after he had placed it against the wall, he wedged the trestle against the bottom rungs for extra stability before beginning his ascent. By the time he reached the level of the gallery he was wishing he hadn't bothered. The rungs felt far from secure under his bulk and the floor seemed a long way away. He reached across to the balustrade running across the gallery and felt somewhat reassured by the extra support.

The unfaced stone wall gave little away. There were a variety of scratch marks on it, some of which might have been made by a ladder scraping along the stone as it tumbled to one side.

About fifteen feet up the wall, the stone ended and was replaced by a band of white roughcast about three feet thick which reached the angle of the roof. There were signs of drilling here and Dalziel wondered if Conrad Fielding had intended to fit another beam in here, though it would have spoilt the symmetry of those already erected.

He climbed a little higher and craned his head sideways in an attempt to see how the next beam along was fixed. It was nearly three feet away and he had to lean out at a dangerous angle to get a decent view. The position suddenly made him feel very giddy, so much so that as he leaned forward and clung closely to the ladder it seemed as if it moved quite violently from side to side. He held on tight for a moment, then began to descend. Half-way down he felt able to look to the ground and he stopped abruptly when he saw a figure below, grasping the ladder and peering up at him. It was Papworth.

Quickly now Dalziel almost slid down the remaining few feet.

'You want to be careful,' observed Papworth. 'I thought you were going over just now.'

Dalziel did not reply at once but retrieved his beer bottle and emptied what remained in a single draught.

'Lucky you were here,' he said.

Papworth shrugged, an ambiguous gesture.

'I heard you,' he said. 'What were you doing?'

It was a blunt question, bluntly put, but justifiable from an employee of the house to a comparative stranger, thought Dalziel charitably.

'Morbid curiosity,' he answered. 'I just wanted to see where it happened. Was he much good at do-it-yourself?'

'Fielding?' said Papworth. 'I suppose so.'

'He didn't ask you to give him a hand in here then?'

'No,' said Papworth, turning away. 'I'm not paid to work at this.'

He began to walk towards the door.

'Just what are you paid to work at, Mr Papworth?' said Dalziel to his back.

'Maintenance,' said the man, pausing and glancing over his shoulder. 'House and garden. Not this.'

'I see,' said Dalziel. 'And Mrs Greave? She's in charge of cooking and cleaning. That right?'

'Right,' said Papworth.

'So neither of you would have much occasion

to come in here,' continued Dalziel. 'Strange, I've found you in here twice.'

'Wrong,' said Papworth, turning. 'I've found you in here twice. I don't know what right you think you've got questioning me, mister. You stick to the family. Do what you want there. You can get your leg across each of 'em in turn, and see if it bothers me. But don't try leaning on me.'

'Sorry,' said Dalziel with a smile. 'Like I said, just morbid curiosity.'

Papworth set off for the door once more but a man more acquainted with the sunshine of Dalziel's smile would have known matters were not at an end.

'What about Mrs Greave?' mused Dalziel.

'What about her?' demanded Papworth, halting.

'You still here? I'm sorry. I was just wondering if it was all right to get my leg across Mrs Greave. Or is she taken?'

'What do you mean?' said Papworth, his brown leathery face set in a mask of suspicion.

'I mean, what about you and Mrs Greave? Have you got full-time rights there?'

'She's my daughter,' said Papworth in a low voice.

Dalziel laughed.

'And I'm your long-lost sister Annie,' he mocked. 'Come on, Papworth. There's nothing to be ashamed of. We all need it now and then! It won't stay in the mind for ever.'

'With a gut like yours it's got to be in the mind,'

snapped Papworth. He looked for a moment as if he were going to say a great deal more, but his control was good and he left without another word.

Dalziel watched him go, then resumed his inspection of the hall and his ingestion of the meat pie. Afterwards he collected his raincoat without meeting any of the others and set off at a gentle walk along the road which led to the village. The pub was still open when he got there and it seemed silly to miss the chance. The landlord proved to be an amiable and forthcoming drinking companion, ready to talk knowledgeably and scandalously about everything in the neighbourhood. Fortified with drink and information, Dalziel next retired to the telephone-box outside the little post office. He spent an interesting half-hour in there too.

As he strode vigorously back towards Lake House he was passed by a total of three cars, each containing two men. None offered him a lift though one did slow down. Thirty minutes later, when with somewhat diminished vigour he finally splashed through the water by the gate and climbed up the drive, he saw the trio parked outside the house.

The Gumbelow deputation had arrived.

10

The Presentation of Awards

The house was full of noise, most of it emanating from Hereward Fielding's sitting-room. Dalziel met Bonnie in the hall. She looked exasperated but her face lit up when she saw him. He did not know what he had done to cause this reaction but felt himself basking in the glow.

'There you are!' she said.

'I went for a walk,' he explained.

'We'll have to do something about that surplus energy,' she said. 'These people have arrived; you know, the award people. But Herrie's throwing another tantrum. I used to think Conrad was the world champion, but he was minor country stuff compared with this. Do you think you could speak to him?'

'Me?' said Dalziel. 'You must be joking! I'm not even good with animals. Besides I don't know what the old bugg— fellow is talking about half the time.'

'That's part of your charm,' said Bonnie. 'He

142

mentioned you at lunch today, said it was nice to have someone safe and ordinary about the place for a change. I know it's a liberty, but if you could just let him know you think it's daft to turn down good money, he might take some notice.'

Dalziel let himself be led into the sitting-room, the whiles considering *safe* and *ordinary*. They were not adjectives many of his acquaintance would have applied to him, he thought. But *safe* in particular was an interesting choice for the old man to make.

The room seemed crowded with people, all gathered round the bay window in which, looking both defiant and trepid, stood Fielding. Dalziel's expert eye categorized the onlookers in a trice. The family and the other residents were there, of course. In addition there were two men in athletic middle age and well-cut grey suits, wearing such similarly cast serious expressions that differences of feature were eliminated and they might have been brothers. They also might have been gang leaders, astronauts, presidential aides or Mormon PR men, but they were unmistakably American. Alongside them, preserving the symmetry of the tableau, were two equally unmistakably English men (it's something about the eyes, decided Dalziel) who had had the misfortune to turn up, presumably without premeditation, in identical off-white corduroy suits. They looked as if they were part of an advertising campaign for spaghetti, thought Dalziel. One was balding rapidly but wore his hair so long at the back that it seemed as if the weight of it had merely pulled his forehead up over his crown. Associated with him was a pop-eyed girl, festooned with the impedimenta of photography and wearing a light green tunic which matched her chosen make-up. The other spaghetti man was presumably the radio interviewer for no one else could so impassively have ignored the comments and questions of a small Negro with hornrimmed spectacles who was fiddling apparently haphazardly with a large tape-recorder.

'Let's all have a drink, shall we?' said Bonnie in her best no-nonsense voice. No one, Dalziel noticed with approval, attempted to breach Herrie's well-fortified drink cupboard, but Tillotson disappeared and returned almost immediately with a laden tray, which must have been prepared for just such an emergency. Pausing only to seize two large glasses of scotch, Dalziel joined the old man.

'You drinking?' he asked, glancing at the almost empty brandy balloon which stood on the window sill. 'Well, sup up and try this.'

'You're *still* here,' stated Fielding with a scornful surprise. But he took the drink.

'Aye,' said Dalziel. 'I only start enjoying parties when I've outstayed my welcome.'

'I'm sorry. I had no right to be rude,' said Fielding, suddenly contrite.

'Don't apologize for Christ's sake,' said Dalziel. 'Once you start that game, you never can stop. I've no right to tell you to take this sodding money, but I'm going to. Why don't you want it?'

'It's not the money, it's the principle of the thing,' protested Fielding, raising his voice so that the others could hear him. 'All these people can talk about is *Westminster Bridge* which I published in 1938. They seem to imagine I've written nothing since then.'

'Keep your voice down,' said Dalziel grimly. 'All you want to worry about writing now is cheques. Don't give me this point of principle crap. What's the matter with the money?'

Hereward Fielding glared at him with an air of indignation approaching the apoplectic. Dalziel began to feel that his excursion into diplomacy was going to be as unsuccessful as it had been unchar-acteristic. But now the old man's face paled to a less hectic hue and he said in a low conversational tone, 'Money's not everything.'

Dalziel sensed that this banal assertion was not a mere continuation of the hurt pride debate.

'A thousand quid's two hundred bottles of good brandy,' he said reasonably. 'That's a lot of drink-ing.'

'Which needs a lot of time,' mused Fielding. 'It's your considered opinion, is it, Dalziel, that I would have this time?'

It was an odd question, but Dalziel took it in his stride.

'I can't guarantee it,' he said. 'But it's worth a try.'

'Mr Fielding, sir,' murmured a low, flat, American voice.

One of the Americans had approached with an expression of deferential determination, like an undertaker who is not going to let you buy pine.

'Sir,' he said, 'let me assure you that the Gumbelow Foundation is aware of and wishes to honour the totality of your achievement. My colleague, Mr Flower, mentioned *Westminster Bridge* merely as a volume of radical interest to the student of your mature work. Volumes such as *Victory Again, Indian Summer* and *A Kiss on the Other Cheek* are, of course, equally well known to us and equally admired also. It would be a grave disappointment . . .'

'Oh come on,' snapped Fielding impatiently. 'Let's get on with it.'

Long-winded the American may have been, but he could move at great speed when the circumstances demanded. Fielding was led to an armchair by a low table on which copies of what Dalziel presumed to be his books were strewn. There were five or six, about the size and thickness of police promotion manuals. The photographer, who answered to Nikki (the spelling formed itself unbidden in Dalziel's mind), took a stream of pictures, not seeming to care much who she got in the frame. Her camera appeared to require as little reloading as one of those guns the good cowboys used to have in the pre-psychological westerns. The tape-recorder was switched on and the Negro placed a microphone on the table and invited Fielding to say a few words.

'Must we have this sodding thing cluttering up the place?' he demanded. He referred to the microphone, but each of the visitors looked perturbed for a moment.

'We'd like to get the moment permanently recorded for posterity,' said the second spaghetti man.

'Who are you?'

'I'm Alex Penitent, BBC. I shall be interviewing you after the presentation.'

'Shall you? We'll see.'

'Gentlemen, gentlemen, may we commence?' said the American. 'Mr Flower.'

'Thank you, Mr Bergmann.'

Flower sat on a hard chair opposite Fielding while Bergmann stood alongside his colleague and put one hand inside his jacket. They looked as if they were about to make the old man an offer he couldn't refuse.

'Gentlemen, gentlemen,' said Bergmann. 'Right, Mr Flower.'

Flower began to speak in the deep vibrant tones of the travelogue commentator.

'For fifty years and more the Gumbelow Foundation of America has been seeking out and acknowledging rare examples of merit in the Arts. The Gumbelow Foundation does not make annual awards, for so high is the standard set that in some years no work attains this standard. Past recipients of awards have included . . .'

Here followed a list which might have been

an extract from a telephone directory to Dalziel except that it contained the name of a British artist whose talents had burgeoned during a gaol sentence for armed robbery. Dalziel did not know him through his paintings but through the more personal contact of having kneed him in the crutch when he resisted arrest. As far as he could make out, the Gumbelow Foundation had not given any money to a policeman.

Flower proceeded with his potted history of the Foundation and after a while Dalziel was pleased to note most of the others were beginning to look as impatient as he felt. Someone squeezed his arm. It was Bonnie who smiled at him and mouthed 'Thanks.'

Fielding brought matters to a head by turning away from the table and waving his empty glass at Tillotson who nodded understandingly, came forward with a bottle and tripped over the microphone wire.

When the confusion had been sorted out, Flower looked enquiringly at the tape-recorder man and said, 'Shall I start again?'

'Oh no, oh no,' cried the Negro. 'We can tidy it up. Oh yes.'

Flower seemed to sense the mood of the gathering for the first time and when he resumed his speech, his voice rose half an octave and accelerated by about fifty words a minute.

'In conclusion,' he concluded, 'may I say that few occasions have given me personally greater

148

pleasure than this meeting with you, Hereward Fielding. On behalf of the Gumbelow Foundation of America, I ask you to accept this award for services to literature. It comes with the admiration, awe and sincere respect of lovers of beauty the whole world over.'

He held up his left hand. Bergmann withdrew his right from inside his jacket and slapped a large white envelope into Flower's palm. The envelope was then thrust aggressively towards Fielding and Nikki's camera began clicking like a Geiger-counter in a uranium mine.

'Keep it there, keep it there, good, good, super, super,' she said. Flower held the pose, smiling fixedly at Fielding who, it gradually began to dawn on the spectators, was staring at the outstretched hand as if it were holding a dead rat. Even Nikki eventually became aware that all was not quite right and the clickings became intermittent, finally dying away into a silence which for a moment was complete.

'Oh Herrie!' breathed Bonnie.

The old man spoke. His voice was light, meditative.

'It is interesting to me that you only make your awards in those years which see the production of work of rare merit, particularly as I have published nothing for more than five years now. Still, better late than never, they say. Though I am not sure I agree with that either. I have been writing for over fifty years now and half a century is very late indeed. I am, of course – I *have* to be, I suppose – grateful for your offer. But fifty years . . . !'

He shook his head and sighed.

'If you'd given me this when I was twenty, I might have bought myself a big meal, a floppy hat like Roy Campbell's and one of those delicious little tarts who used to hang around the Café Royal.

'If you'd given it to me when I was thirty, I might have bought my kids some new clothes and my wife a sunnier disposition.

'Even if you had given it to me when I was forty or fifty, I'd have found a use for it. A more comfortable car, for instance. Or a cruise round the Greek islands to see the cradle of civilization.

'But now I am old and I am ill. I have little appetite for food or women. My children have grown up and gone their ways. Or died. I no longer care to travel by car. And civilization is dying where it began.

'So you might say that in a fashion not untypically American you have come too bloody late.'

He paused. No one spoke. The envelope remained in Flower's outstretched hand. The American's expression never deviated from respectful admiration, and the expressions of the others varied from amusement via distaste and indifference to Bonnie's evident anxiety.

'Bravo.'

It was Bertie who broke the silence, uttering the word with overstressed irony.

'Shut it, Bertie,' said Mavis warningly.

Bergmann shrugged, a massive Central European bewildered shrug which crumbled his streamlined New York façade as an earth tremor might destroy a skyscraper. Flower seemed to take a cue and relaxed in his chair, dropping his hand to the table. The old man's arm shot out as the envelope moved and he pulled it rudely from Flower's grasp.

'However,' he said, very Churchillian, 'I will not refuse your gift, late though it is. For I recall that I never did get a hat like Roy Campbell's. But now I shall. And I shall wear it slightly askew as I walk through the village in the hope that the tedious inmates will shun me as a man unbalanced and in the even vainer hope that this reputation might somehow distress my neglectful friends and ungrateful descendants. Bonnie, my glass is empty.'

After that somehow a party began. The BBC man tried for a while to get his intimate interview but in the end recognized that his efforts were losing him ground in the drinks race and set about catching up. The feature writer, aptly named Butt, was well in the lead, though Bergmann would have been neck and neck if his new flamboyancy of gesture had not been joined by a matching volubility of speech. Flower on the other hand was a recidivist and his speech got lower and slower and more and more slurred till he sounded like a second-rate English mimic doing James Stewart. Nikki had stopped clicking and was gurgling merrily through glass after nauseating glass of port and brandy.

Even Arkwright, the tape-recorder man, found time from his task of preventing others resting their glasses and persons on his equipment to down mouthfuls from a half-pint glass of gin.

Nor were the residents of Lake House far behind and Dalziel, ever a pragmatist, put all care for the past or the future out of his mind and set to with a will.

After a while for a relatively small gathering the noise became deafening. He found himself next to Fielding who was still holding the envelope tight to his chest as though fearing it would be taken from him. His words to Dalziel seemed to confirm this impression.

'It will be all right, you assure me of that?' he cried in what was relatively a whisper.

Dalziel nodded wisely, winked and turned away in search of Bonnie. Behind him the conversation between Fielding and the Americans resumed.

'I don't care for Updike. Overwrought, over-blown and overpraised,' cried Bergmann.

'Yeah,' drawled Flower. 'Updike's a shit.'

Bonnie was in the window bay being leaned over confidentially by Butt who seemed to fancy himself as the great poke as well as the great soak, but Dalziel's rescue mission was hindered by Penitent who grasped him by the arm, peered closely into his face and said something like, 'What are you doing after the show?'

'What?' bellowed Dalziel.

'Haven't we met somewhere before?'

His voice had the controlled flatness with which ambitious public school men in the BBC attempted to conceal their origins.

'I doubt it,' said Dalziel.

Someone grasped his other arm and he felt a surge of panic as if at any moment blows might be hurled at his unprotected gut.

It was Bertie. There was no physical danger but he was bent on being nasty.

'Enjoying yourself, Dalziel?' he asked. 'Enjoying your free booze, are you? And your bed and breakfast? Pity you'll have to be leaving us.'

'What's up, sonny?' snarled Dalziel. 'You putting me out?'

'No, no. It's just that once your car's ready, you'll be on your way, won't you? Well, I rang the garage after lunch and they say they've got it and it'll be ready for you in the morning. At a pinch, you could go tonight. Not that we want to lose you, of course.'

'Mensa!' said Penitent.

'What?'

'That's where we met, I think. Mensa.'

Ensa, thought Dalziel. He thinks I'm a sort of performer. Which I am.

'Not likely,' he bellowed. 'Nearest I got was seeing Tommy Handley at Catterick when I was in the MPs.'

'I'll say cheerio now in case we miss each other in the morning,' said Bertie. Dalziel shook his arm free and succeeded in slopping some of his drink over the youth's shirt which was some consolation for not being able to punch his fat, smiling mouth.

'MPs,' said Penitent, puzzled. 'Did Handley have something in the Eden administration?'

Dalziel smiled at him uncomprehendingly.

'You work at it, lad,' he said in a sympathetic voice. 'You can end up having as many "O" levels as Jimmy Young.'

'Charley!' He heard Bonnie's voice cut clearly through the din. 'We need some more booze. Pop along to the store and bring up a couple of bottles of everything, there's a love. Oh, and while you're down there, tell Mrs Greave I'd like a word. I suppose everyone will want to be fed eventually.'

She seemed quite unperturbed by the prospect. Dalziel recalled that his own wife had required five days' notice if he was bringing a mate round for a glass of beer.

There was a click in his ear and he thought that Nikki must have started up again but when he looked it was Uniff.

'One not enough?' he asked, nodding towards the green tunic which he now spotted alongside Louisa by the door.

'Her?' said Uniff scornfully. 'She's one of the creative accident mob. You shoot enough film, something's bound to be OK.'

'While you use your genius?'

'Right,' grinned Uniff. 'Besides I'm not so rich. Like big John Wayne says, you gotta make every shot count.'

'How's your picture going?' asked Dalziel.

'Up and down, you know how it is, man. You want to see it sometime?'

'If you want to show it,' said Dalziel.

'Why not? Hell, there's got to come a time for every artist when he exposes himself to the average bum in the street.'

'You try exposing yourself to me,' said Dalziel, 'you'll make a pretty picture yourself.'

Uniff laughed heartily.

'I like you, Andy baby,' he said. 'Christ, man, how do you stick it in here with this load of phoneys?'

His gesture seemed pretty well all-inclusive.

'Are they phoneys?' asked Dalziel.

'Can't you tell?'

'I don't know what the real thing looks like, so it's a bit hard,' said Dalziel.

Nor could he see any reason why anyone should want to *pretend* to be what he saw around him. In particular, you'd have to be bloody revolting to make it worthwhile *pretending* to be a conceited, blubber-lipped, purple-cheeked, perfumed ponce in a corrugated suit.

'Andrew,' said Bonnie. 'Have you met Eric Butt?'

His pleasure at hearing her use his Christian name almost overcame his distaste for Butt. The journalist smiled briefly at him and returned his attention to Bonnie.

'Next time you're in town,' he said, 'give me a ring. We can lunch together. Fellow I know has

155

just taken over a little French place in Hampstead. Not for the *hoi polloi*, you know, but you'd love it.'

'How sweet,' said Bonnie. 'I was thinking of taking all the children up next week. Perhaps we could meet there. Would Tuesday suit you?'

Butt emptied his glass and came up smiling.

'Sorry,' he said. 'Better to ring. I'm off to Brazil tomorrow and I'll be there over a week. It's a great thing, did you read about it? There was a bit in the *Observer* supplement last week. I'm doing a piece on the Brazilian football team and they've agreed for me to stay and train with them. It's a bit unique, actually. The Brazilian Ambassador fixed it, likes my stuff, felt I would do a good job. I wouldn't miss it for worlds. Ever been to Brazil, darling?'

'No,' said Bonnie. 'Andrew though has been around a lot, perhaps he could give you a few traveller's tips.'

She turned away to greet Tillotson who had returned with an armful of bottles.

Dalziel moved close to Butt and sniffed.

'The trouble with corduroy,' he said, 'is that it doesn't half smell if you piss on it.'

'Oh damn the woman,' said Bonnie crossly. 'It's not her night off. I'd better go and look in the larder myself. Andrew, see that everyone's got plenty to drink, will you?'

'What's up?' asked Dalziel.

'I couldn't find Mrs Greave anywhere,' said Tillotson. 'Her door was locked.'

'Did you look in Pappy's room?'

'No. Why should I?' said Tillotson.

Dalziel smiled and plucked a couple of spirit bottles out of the box. The smile died on his face and was replaced by an exasperated grimace. One of the bottles was quite empty. Was there nothing Charley could do without making a balls-up? He checked through the box and found three other empties. That still left eight which was plenty to be going on with, even for this lot.

He looked around the room. Arkwright was asleep on his tape-recorder. Nikki was trying to take a self-portrait with her camera, at the same time as, unawares, she was being photographed by Uniff. Bertie and Mavis were in close confabulation in a corner. They looked at him as he stared towards them, then hastily looked away. Penitent was talking to Louisa, probably offering to make her a star on *The Archers*. And the trio of Hereward and the two Americans still held the centre of the stage. Bergmann was gabbling away at a pace just short of incomprehensibility while Flower nodded his head sagely and drawled, 'Melville's a shit. Mailer's a shit. Hawthorne's a shit. Longfellow . . . well, Longfellow . . . well, Longfellow's a shit also.'

Seizing one of the full bottles of scotch, Dalziel went to help Bonnie.

He found her in the kitchen looking in disgust at a table covered with sausages.

'That's all there is,' she said. 'I thought we ate enough sausages last night to deplete local stocks for fifty miles around.'

'Perhaps she got them in a sale,' said Dalziel. 'Have a drink.'

He poured a tumblerful which she sipped like cold tea.

'What shall I do?' she asked.

It was a comfort to be consulted. A woman could be too competent.

'Stick 'em between two slices of bread and call 'em frankfurters,' said Dalziel. 'These Americans eat nothing else.'

'Fine,' said Bonnie. 'What about cooking them? It'll take hours.'

'Not,' said Dalziel, 'if you use one of those nice new ovens you've got out back.'

'You're a genius,' said Bonnie seriously. 'And we might even unearth Mrs Greave while we're out there.'

They had another large scotch apiece to celebrate the decision. Then the sausages were swept off the table into a large round basket and they set off for the Banqueting Hall kitchens like Red Riding Hood and the Wolf. The image put Dalziel in mind of Butt.

'That fellow Butt,' he said. 'You handled him nicely.'

'Thank you kindly,' she said. 'Though I reckon I lacked your finesse.'

'What? Oh you heard that,' said Dalziel sheepishly.

She laughed.

'You don't exactly whisper, Andy. May I call

you Andy? No, I've met your Butts before. Always off to Brazil, meeting exciting people, but usually ready to fit you in for a quick roll between jets.'

'I hope he gets a football up his . . . nose,' said Dalziel.

'Poor man! How's he harmed you?' she asked, then added thoughtfully, 'But if he really trains with them, it could be chancy. He looked a bit hearty to me.'

Dalziel mused upon this as they reached the kitchens where the ovens proved a complete failure. Dalziel, seated on an old wooden chair, watched with amusement as Bonnie, festooned with sausages, moved around trying to get them to work.

'Useless things!' she exploded.

'Is the power switched through?' asked Dalziel.

'Yes. I think so. At least, Bertie said it was. The dishwasher certainly works.'

'Shall I take a look?' asked Dalziel, heaving himself upright.

'No. Never bother. I'll tell Bertie. He's the only one who understands these things. God, I'm whacked!'

She slumped into the chair vacated by Dalziel who turned from his examination of the first oven with a comment on his lips which died when he saw her. Her head was bowed forward and her arms rested slackly over her knees as though they had been carelessly deposited there for collection later. One leg was crooked under the chair, the other stretched straight out. The whole composition was ugly, awkward, a study in defeat.

When Dalziel approached and she looked up, the pores of her face seemed to have opened; the fine Edwardian strength he had admired before was eroded by an admission of age and weariness into a puffy substanceless outline. She was, Dalziel realized, more his contemporary than he had imagined.

And at the same time he realized she was letting him see her like this out of choice. There was strength enough there still to have taken her back to the party and set wildly coursing whatever passes for blood beneath a corduroy suit.

'I don't think these sausages are going to get cooked,' he said.

'No, I don't think they are,' she said.

It had been the beginning of an explanation but he let it rest as the oblique comment she obviously took it for.

'Why don't you lie down?' he said.

'I should like that,' she answered. 'Will you lie down with me?'

'Aye, will I,' he said.

They lay together fully dressed for nearly an hour while Bonnie dozed and Dalziel counted the chrysanthemums on her William Morris wallpaper, wondering if this was going to be one of those queer Platonic relationships he heartily disbelieved in. Finally he gave her a bit of a shake and set about confirming his disbelief.

Bonnie was agreeable enough, her body and

mind soft and yielding in a half sleep. But Dalziel was no subtle wooer with diplomas in the arts of pleasure. The only prelude to penetration he had ever bothered with in his married life was four or five pints of bitter and now the brutal directness of his approach shocked Bonnie wide awake.

'Why not take a run to get up a bit of speed?' she demanded.

'What's the matter?' asked Dalziel.

'Well, for a start, get your clothes off. All your clothes.'

Grimly he undressed at one side of the bed while Bonnie stripped at the other.

'Now let's begin at the beginning,' said Bonnie.

Five minutes later she pinched his flabby left buttock viciously and said, 'For God's sake, don't be so impatient. There's two of us to consider.'

'We'll have to take turn about,' gasped Dalziel.

Bonnie shook with laughter and the movement removed any chance of restraint on Dalziel's part. When he'd done and recognized that there was no mockery in her laughter he joined in.

'I've never laughed on the job before,' he said finally.

'Why not? It's a funny business,' said Bonnie. 'What was that you said about turn about?'

Evening was well advanced when they rose and the house was quiet.

'Perhaps they've all gone,' said Dalziel.

'They're more likely to be too drunk to speak,' said Bonnie. 'Or they're in the kitchen guzzling sausages.'

Dalziel felt guilty. After the welter of confused emotion which had immersed him during the past couple of hours, it was almost a relief to isolate and recognize a simple reaction. It was a conditioned reflex rather than an emotion; policemen were bred to put the investigation of crime before their personal pleasure and he had been false to his breeding.

'I doubt they'll have cooked those sausages,' he said.

'Why's that?' she asked, tugging a comb through her thick brown hair which, unfastened, had tumbled in surprising profusion over her shoulders.

'Come downstairs and I'll show you,' he said grimly.

Puzzled, Bonnie finished her tidying up and let herself be led to the kitchens once more. They met no one en route and the basket of sausages remained untouched where they had left it.

'It's a bit like the *Mary Celeste*,' said Bonnie.

'No mystery,' grunted Dalziel. 'They'll all be stoned out of their minds.'

He took a coin from his pocket and rapidly unscrewed the control panel of one of the ovens.

'Take a look in here,' he invited. 'What do you see?'

Bonnie peered in cautiously.

'Nothing much,' she admitted.

162

'Right,' said Dalziel. 'Now what you should see is what makes these things work. Magnetrons, they're called. Don't ask me how I know.'

'Where are they?' wondered Bonnie, making her way round the kitchen inspecting every oven. 'What a stupid thing! You'd think Bertie would have checked when they installed them.'

'He probably did,' said Dalziel. 'I think you've been robbed.'

'Robbed?' She laughed. 'Don't be silly. Why should anyone steal whatever you said?'

'Some people'd steal owt for a bob or two,' said Dalziel. 'Don't mistake. Everything's sellable. But I'm feared this is just an extra.'

'Extra?'

'Aye. Where's the drink store?'

'Oh Jesus!' she cried, catching his drift now. 'There's a cellar ... we've got all our opening stock in there. Conrad got it in just before our credit gave up the ghost completely.'

They clattered down a narrow flight of stairs which led to an open door.

'Damn Charley!' snapped the woman. 'He had strict instructions to lock up behind him.'

'Don't blame the lad,' said Dalziel. 'I doubt if it's worth locking.'

At first glance all looked well. The crates of spirits, apéritifs, wine and liqueurs were all stacked in militarily neat array. But a few moments' investigation revealed the worst. Only the nearest bottles were full. Behind the front rank, all the liquor had been decanted, and in the nether crates there were no bottles at all.

'Charley got some of the empties in his mixed dozen,' said Dalziel. 'I thought it was just another bit of daftness then.'

Bonnie who, after an explosion of blasphemous obscenity, had got hold of herself very well demanded, 'What made you think differently. The ovens?'

'Aye. And one other thing.'

They went back up the stairs, Dalziel leading now. He strode belligerently to Mrs Greave's room and, without knocking, kicked the door open so that it rattled against the wall, and went inside. When Bonnie caught up, he had opened every cupboard door and drawer in the place. They were uniformly empty.

'You mean you think that Mrs Greave . . .' said Bonnie incredulously. 'But why? She's Pappy's daughter.'

Dalziel laughed, a short humourless bark very different from the deep guffaws he had emitted in the intimacy of the bedroom.

'If you believe that, you'll believe anything.'

'But how do you know? How can you be sure it's her?'

'I know a slag when I see one,' said Dalziel brutally. 'When her type and your property go missing at the same time, then don't waste your time praying for guidance.'

'If you worked this out before, you haven't

exactly struck while the iron was hot,' said Bonnie reprovingly.

'No. Well, something got in the way,' muttered Dalziel. 'I'm sorry.'

'Don't be,' she said, smiling. 'Well, what now? I suppose I'd better phone the police.'

Dalziel scratched the back of his neck and looked at her assessingly. The thought had already occurred to him that she might know he was a policeman. If so, she was playing it very cool for reasons which were far from clear (and, his constabulary mind whispered to him, perhaps just as far from virtuous). Those same reasons, the brutal whisper continued, may have got him into her bed. He'd been a detective too long to be surprised by what some women would do in the cause of injustice. No, it wouldn't surprise him. But what *was* surprising him was the realization of just how much it would hurt him.

'That'd be best,' he said. 'Though I doubt you've had your booze. It's probably been long gone.'

And someone had thought it worthwhile postponing the moment of discovery by first of all ringing the builders and telling them that Fielding was near on bankrupt, then ringing Spinx and telling him not to pay out the insurance money. And, he recalled, the anonymous caller had known there was a policeman in the house. That put it even more firmly at Mrs Greave's door. This kind of sixth sense was two-way traffic.

By the time they re-entered the main entrance

hall, he'd decided that it was worth trying to remain anonymous for as long as possible.

'I'll ring the cops,' he said. 'You go and see if you can find Papworth and see what light he can throw.'

But his ruse to get a quiet word with Sergeant Cross was unsuccessful. A door opened and Bertie appeared, flushed violet with drink. Surprisingly this seemed to have made him more affable.

'Dalziel!' he said. 'Come in and have a drink. On me. You mustn't take my words to heart, mustn't sulk. You're too big for sulking. Your *hulk* has too much *bulk* for you to *sulk*. How's that? Herrie'd get fifty dollars for that and you know how much the old sod would give us? Bugger all. *That's* all. What's your poison?'

'I shouldn't bother,' said Bonnie sharply. 'There's likely to be quite a drink shortage round here shortly.'

'What do you mean?' demanded her son, swaying.

'I mean we've been robbed. Mrs Greave, it appears, has been steadily removing all our drink stock and anything else she could lay her hands on. Including the working parts of your precious ovens. And now she's taken off.'

Bertie stood amazed. His colour remained the same, perhaps deepened slightly, but affability drained visibly from his face.

'Oh, the cow, the stupid cow! I'll kill the bitch!'

He smashed the fist of his right hand into his left

palm. Dalziel caught Bonnie's eye and raised his eyebrows. She did not respond but looked away.

'All right, Dalziel,' said Bertie. 'What now?'

'There's only one thing to do,' interrupted his mother firmly. 'We must ring the police.'

'We must ring the police,' echoed Bertie mockingly. 'What's the matter, Mother dear? Have his hidden charms enthralled you? I'll ring the police, never fear.'

He approached close enough for Dalziel to smell the gin on his breath.

'Dring dring,' he said. 'Dring dring. Is anyone there? I'd like to speak to a big, fat, ugly Detective Superintendent, please. You recognize the description? Good. Well, what happens next, please sir, Mr Dalziel?'

Dalziel looked from the youth to his mother. She made no effort to look surprised but shrugged her shoulders minutely. He took in a deep breath and let it out slowly, carefully, like a man decanting a rare wine against the light of a candle.

'What happens next?' he repeated, stepping forward so that Bertie had to move back quickly to avoid being knocked over. 'Well, first of all, sonny, you start talking polite to me or I might just level off your spotty ugly face so that it'd take emulsion. Then next after that, we'll start really digging into just what makes this place tick, shall we?'

11

Hello Sailor

Dalziel sat in the old man's sitting-room and drank brandy. He had no authority to investigate crime on this patch, he assured Fielding. But the truth was he had been so discomfited and irritated by Sergeant Cross's reproachful expression that the choice had been between escape and expulsion. The sergeant had not openly said that Dalziel had withheld information, but his suspicions – clearly roused by the fat man's visit to Orburn that day – must have seemed confirmed when Dalziel told him that Annie Greave (or *Annie Grimshaw*, or *Open Annie*) was well known to Liverpool CID.

'I telephoned them just on the off-chance she was using her proper name,' he explained. 'Not much imagination, these pros.'

'Ah,' said Cross.

The only immediate potential source of information about Mrs Greave was Papworth and he too had disappeared. His room, however, showed no signs of a hurried or permanent leave-taking and it seemed safe to assume he would return.

'You mustn't blame Bonnie,' said Fielding suddenly. He occupied the same chair in which he had received the Gumbelow award and Dalziel wondered if he had moved out of it since then.

Apart from the debris of glasses and bottles which littered the room, the only other sign of the afternoon's junketings was Arkwright, the sound engineer, who slept with his head pillowed on and his arms still clasped protectively around his recorder. From time to time a bubbly and rather musical baritone snore emerged from his mouth.

Whether the others had gone or were also to be found unconscious round the premises, Dalziel did not know.

'Blame her for what?' he grunted.

'Going through your pockets,' said Fielding. 'It is after all a sensible thing to do when hanging up a suit to dry.'

'What was she doing in my wallet?' demanded Dalziel. 'Ironing my money? And why didn't you lot say you knew I was a policeman?'

Fielding shrugged.

'Why didn't you tell us?'

'Why should I?'

'Why indeed? But it doesn't create an atmosphere of confidence having someone in your house under false pretence.'

Dalziel refilled his glass with a brusqueness

which in another man might have resulted in spillage.

'I pretended nowt.'

'Come, come,' said Fielding mildly. 'This morning Bertie and Lou went to Bonnie with some story about the possibility of your putting money into the restaurant. They were very put out when she told them who you were.'

'Oh. They didn't know till then?' said Dalziel thoughtfully.'

'No.'

'And you?'

'Bonnie told me this morning too. She's a very discreet woman.'

Dalziel considered the implications. It was a comfort to know there hadn't been a general conspiracy, with everyone watching the big thick policeman blundering around. It was also good to know that whatever asexual motives Bonnie might have had for going to bed with him, the hope of more money for the business wasn't one of them. But this still left some disturbing possibilities. A detective grew accustomed to attempts to use sex either as a means of buying him off or compromising him. It didn't happen every night or every week or even every month. But it happened. Dalziel didn't want this to be the truth, but his self-image argued against him. He had never considered himself a lady's man, but he had had his moments, and until a few months ago would have been complacent enough to accept that a big, burly, balding middle-aged detective superintendent might set some female hearts astir. Now there was too much darkness in his nights for the overspill not to cloud all but the brightest day, and his diminished concept of what he was hardly admitted the generation of love at first sight, or even enthusiastic lust.

Which left one more question. Why? What was he being bought off from, or more simply perhaps, distracted from.

He leaned forward and peered at the old man.

'Got your envelope safe?' he asked.

Hereward winked and tapped his stomach indicating, Dalziel surmised, either that he had stuffed it down his undervest or else eaten it.

'Why were you so bothered about taking it?' continued Dalziel.

Fielding looked at him cunningly.

'Pride,' he said. 'Literary pride.'

'Piss off,' said Dalziel easily. 'You wouldn't let pride get between you and all that brandy.'

'All right,' said Fielding. 'Ambition then.'

'Ambition?'

'Yes. This year I shall equal Browning. Another three will take me up to Wordsworth. And if I can hang on another three, I'll be past Tennyson.'

Dalziel laughed.

'Good-living bastards these poets, were they? So you want to be a hundred? Hey, you know what the Queen's Telegram says?'

'No. What?'

'Drop dead you silly old bugger.'

Fielding found this so amusing that he choked on his drink and for a moment Dalziel thought he was going to anticipate his sovereign's alleged command. But the cause of the upset also proved a remedy and after a moment he returned to his line of questioning.

'So what were the magic words I uttered that made you change your mind?'

'Nothing really,' said Fielding. 'I just wanted to be reassured that you would make your presence felt, which you have done with admirable timing. To be worth several thousand pounds in a household of relative paupers is no comfortable thing, Dalziel. You understand?'

'No,' said Dalziel. 'Not unless you're implying one of this lot'd try to knock you off. You're not saying that, are you?'

'Of course I'm saying that,' snapped Fielding. 'What do you want – a bibliography and index?'

'When people start talking about murder threats I want owt that'll stand up as evidence,' retorted Dalziel. 'Come on now. This is a serious allegation. What do you know?'

'I know that I am an old man,' said Fielding slowly, 'and in the eyes of many I have lived my life and run my race. I know that an old man is susceptible to heat and cold, to accidents, heart attacks, broken limbs, dizziness and dyspepsia. I shall not die, I think, from daggers or bullets or strange exotic poisonings. But die I shall and, as with many of the old, I suspect, I fear that a less than divine shoehorn will be used to ease me into my grave.'

Dalziel drank his brandy, shaking his head and marvelling inwardly at this strange and loving submission to the monstrous tyranny of words.

'Well,' he grunted, 'no bugger in this house'll kill you now, not while I'm around.'

'A champion!' said Bertie from the doorway. 'Sound the trumpet three times and Dalziel will gallop to the rescue!'

'What's happening out there, Bertie?' demanded Fielding. 'And spare us your tedious wit in the telling.'

'Nothing much,' said the stout youth, flopping into a chair. He seemed to have recovered both his sobriety and his temper. From the paleness round his eyes Dalziel judged that he had been sick.

'Sergeant Cross has been asking everyone questions,' said Tillotson, who had followed Bertie into the room. 'But he seems to have finished now. Is it true that you're a policeman too, Mr Dalziel?'

Dalziel regarded him kindly. Here was the last person anyone ever told anything. Tillotson and his kind would be carrying on normally days after the Last Trump had summoned everyone else to the Judgment Throne.

'That's right,' he said.

'Really? Sir George Cheesman who used to be Chief Constable of Worcester is my godfather. Do you know him?'

'No,' said Dalziel. 'But I used to have a budgie

that whistled the "Eton Boating Song". What are you lot going to do now?'

'What do you mean?'

'I mean you were in bad enough trouble with this restaurant business before. Now with your booze gone and your ovens knackered, you are right up the creek.'

'Which pleases you, does it?' asked Bertie.

'No. Not at all,' said Dalziel.

'We're covered against theft by insurance, surely?' said Tillotson.

Dalziel and Bertie laughed in unison.

'What's so funny?' asked Tillotson.

'After you,' said Bertie to Dalziel.

'Well, firstly no insurance company's going to rush to pay out on any claim coming from this household at the moment. Especially not if it's Anchor.'

'And secondly,' said Bertie, 'I doubt if my late lamented father ever bothered to insure the new equipment and so on. I asked him about it once, but got told in no uncertain terms that financial arrangements were his pigeon.'

'Oh,' said Tillotson. He looked very taken aback.

'Worried about your investment?' asked Bertie. 'Don't be, Charley. Just stiffen that upper lip and wave goodbye.'

There was a tap on the door and Cross came in.

'I'm finished now,' he said. 'May I have a word, sir, before I go?'

Dalziel rose.

'What are the chances of getting the stuff back, Sergeant?' asked Tillotson.

'Pretty low, I'm afraid,' said Cross. 'Do you think you'll be able to sort things out for the opening night?'

Bertie, to whom the question was addressed, yawned rudely.

'Who knows, Sergeant? But don't you worry about our business, just work hard at yours, will you?'

Dalziel put his arm over Cross's shoulder and ushered him through the door. He himself turned just before he closed it and said, 'Sergeant Cross has paid ten quid for two first-night tickets. So think on; the customer is always right, eh?'

'Puffed-up young git!' said Cross savagely in the hallway. 'I'll sort the bugger before I'm through.'

Inwardly Dalziel applauded the attitude but he put on his best impartial-guardian-of-the-law look and shook his head disapprovingly.

'That's no way to talk,' he said. 'You want to watch yourself, Sergeant.'

'I'm too busy watching other people, sir,' said Cross sulkily. 'I've had three hours' sleep today, and when I leave here I'm going back to those bloody chickens again.'

'It's a full life,' agreed Dalziel. 'What did you want to see me about?'

'Nothing really, sir. Just to ask, really, if there was any other way you could help me; I mean, you staying in the house, and everything . . .'

This was the closest he dared come to a spoken reproach, realized Dalziel.

'I don't think so,' he answered.

'How long will you be staying here, sir?'

'Not long. Just till tomorrow probably. I don't know.'

It was true. He didn't. Everything pointed the way to a quick exit. But there were questions still to be answered if he cared to, or dared to, go on asking them.

'I see. The man Papworth hasn't come back yet, sir. I wonder if you'd mind keeping an eye open and letting us know when he returns. I'd like a word with him as soon as possible and we don't really have the establishment to spare a man to hang around here half the night.'

'A super in the house is worth a d.c. in the bush?' said Dalziel. 'Aye, I'll watch out for him. Is anything known about him, by the way?'

'Not by us, officially. But he's well known in the district. He's been around for twenty or thirty years, most of them working for the Percivals. His reputation's not so good. A rough, tough character, keeps himself to himself, hard to beat in a deal or in a fight.'

'Women?'

'What?'

'Is he known as a womanizer? I don't suppose he had Open Annie down here to cut his toenails.'

Cross considered.

'No. I've never heard of anything out of the way

in that line. But I'll ask around if you think it's important.'

Dalziel shrugged indifferently.

'Your case, Sergeant. You ask what you want to know. Me, I'm just a tourist. Well, I won't keep you from your chickens. A tip-off, is it?'

Cross nodded.

'There's been a lot about and I've been told this battery's to be cleared out this week. I'll give it one more night.'

'It'll be tomorrow,' said Dalziel maliciously. 'Good hunting.'

He returned to the sitting-room. Louisa and Mavis had joined the others, but there was no sign of Bonnie. The two girls were looking down at Arkwright.

'Is he the sole survivor?' asked Dalziel.

Louisa nodded.

'The others left shortly before you and Bonnie reappeared,' she said. 'I think they got hungry. Also Herrie made it clear that he was fed up of listening to Abbott and Costello.'

'It wasn't very kind of Penitent to abandon *him*,' said Dalziel, indicating the snoring Negro.

'What shall we do with him?' asked Tillotson. 'We can't just let him lie there all night.'

'Are you going to give him your bed then?' mocked Bertie.

'Stick him in Mrs Greave's room,' said Dalziel. 'She won't be back.'

'And of course the servants' quarters are the

proper place for a black man,' said Bertie. He looked healthier now and his nastiness was returning.

'A bed's a bed,' said Dalziel, refusing to be drawn.

'A liberal policeman! But suppose it was your sister's bed, Dalziel. What then?'

'Personally,' said Dalziel, 'I wouldn't envy a randy billy goat getting into my sister's bed. Come on, sunshine. Charley boy, give us a hand.'

Together he and Tillotson lifted Arkwright from his tape-recorder and carried him, feet trailing, down the corridor to Mrs Greave's room where they dumped him on the bed, removed his tie and shoes and covered him with a patchwork quilt. Then at Tillotson's suggestion, they retired to the kitchen where the young man brewed a pot of coffee at the expense of only one cup and a few minor burns.

Dalziel glanced at his watch. It was still early, just a quarter past nine, but he found himself yawning.

'Tired?' said Tillotson sympathetically, pouring the coffee.

'A bit,' said Dalziel. 'It's been a hard day. Or a day of surprises, and that's always hard. You don't care much for surprises when you're getting on.'

'I don't like surprises either,' said Tillotson sadly.

'No? Well, you're young enough to take things in your stride anyway. How much cash have you got in this business?'

'A few hundred,' said Tillotson. 'Not much, but all I possess.'

'That's enough. All you possess is quite enough,' said Dalziel. 'What's your standing?'

'I'm sorry?'

'I mean, what's the deal? Is it shares? Or a partnership agreement? What kind of investment have you made?'

'Does it matter?' asked Tillotson.

Dalziel rolled his eyes and scratched the skin around his Adam's apple.

'Look,' he said, 'love's one thing but business is another. Of course it matters. One way you can just lose your investment if the thing folds. Another way, though, you can be held partly responsible if the thing goes bankrupt which might mean you having to find more cash. You follow? It depends what you signed.'

'Oh, I didn't sign anything,' said Tillotson. 'I just made out a cheque to Conrad, Mr Fielding that is.'

'That was,' said Dalziel. 'Well, so much for the fatherly advice. If you're ever in the market for a used car, give us a ring.'

Shaking his bull-like head, he drank his coffee. It was truly awful but something in Tillotson touched off a non-habitual response of kindness and he said nothing. They talked in a desultory fashion for nearly half an hour before Dalziel yawned again and said he would take a turn in the fresh air before heading for bed.

After checking that Papworth had still not

179

returned he left the house and strolled down to the water's edge to smoke a cigarette and think. The flood level had perceptibly dropped, for the wooden slats of the landing-stage were now quite clear of the surface. He took a couple of tentative paces along the stage, then halted, for the treads were not only still greasy from their long submersion, but in addition he felt them give under his considerable bulk. Indeed, at the end of the landing-stage there was a gap, just perceptible in the dim light, where the treads seemed to have fallen away altogether.

The waters of the swollen lake stretched away before him, stirred by a light wind so that small waves slapped against the recovered row-boat and the duck punt. They were moored together by the landing-stage, and occasionally in their rising and falling touched with a dull noise like distant artillery. Above, the cloud cover was broken now and the clustered stars shone through the uneven rents. Dalziel regarded them for a while, then looked away. There was something too much of the tribunal about the unblinking clarity of their regard to ease his mind. He had once promised a recalcitrant suspect justice if he co-operated. *Any cunt can get justice*, the man had answered. *Me. I want mercy*. He had got seven years. If, speculated Dalziel, instead of putting 'em away in prison, they could transfer the years from the criminal's life to the arresting officer's, I'd be nigh on bloody immortal!

All those years, his mind ran on. All those years for all those men. And for all those men guarding them. And for all those men chasing them and catching them and prosecuting them and condemning them. There were more stars, so they said, than could be counted. And in the end unless something strange and unbelievable happened to mankind, all those years too would add up beyond the reckoning of any human mind.

His mind was running on like a tuppenny novel. Such speculations were not for detective superintendents of the old school no matter how many sleepless nights they had had and no matter how many women proved to be as unreliable as the first. Eyes to the ground finds you sixpences. Cautiously but steadfastly he advanced along the landing-stage till he reached the gap left by the missing treads. In fact they weren't missing, but broken, their jagged edges sunk into the water.

Dalziel didn't move but stood quite still peering through the gap. There was just enough light to make out the surface of the water, dully shining and touched with little swirls of rainbow. The wind gusted, the small waves slapped, the boats came together. And rising to the surface as though drawn by a line from Dalziel's unblinking stare came a face.

Dalziel regarded it without surprise. Ever since he first looked on these floods he had been waiting for a body. The face began to sink again but he thrust his hands quickly into the chill water,

181

grasped the sodden collar and hauled the upper part of the torso clear of the lake.

The features had not been long enough immersed for identification to be difficult. It was Spinx, the insurance investigator.

'Hello sailor,' said Dalziel.

12

A View in the Morning

'All right, so it's accidental death!' said Cross.

'I didn't say that,' said Dalziel.

'Well, what do you say, sir?'

'You've had as good a look at the scene as I have. Those boards *were* rotten; there's a mark on his head where he *could* have banged it against the main support as he fell and there's traces of what *might* be blood on the edge of the support. You'll just have to wait for the p.m. and the lab reports.'

'I know all that,' said Cross. 'But it's a question of what I *do now*. I mean, there's all these other features . . .'

'Such as?'

'Well, the Greave woman for instance. And Mr Fielding's death so recently. Lots of odd things, sir. I'm asking for your advice.'

'My advice,' said Dalziel, 'is to do what you would have done if I hadn't been here. Personally, and this isn't advice, just me thinking out loud, I'd put a tarpaulin over one end of that landing-stage and a copper at the other and bugger off back to my chickens.'

Cross looked at him undecided, then the telephone rang inside the house. A moment later Bonnie appeared at the front door and said, 'Sergeant Cross, it's for you.'

Cross went inside. Dalziel lit a cigarette absently. It was about the twentieth he had lit absently in the past couple of hours. He was becoming quite adept at doing absently those things which he ought not to be doing at all.

'It's been a hell of a day,' said Bonnie wearily.

'Yes,' he answered.

'We could stop the best bit being spoiled,' she said after a pause.

'Oh. How's that?'

'I don't know, just by not letting it, I suppose. I saw your face earlier, Andy. You seem to think that for some reason I went to bed with you because you're a policeman. I mean, just think about it! What kind of reason would that be?'

'Not much of a reason,' he agreed.

'Well then.'

'Listen, love,' he said brutally. 'You put your husband in the earth yesterday. That's it, *yesterday*. And you met me yesterday. And you climbed into bed with me today. Now, whether you did it to keep yourself warm or whether you did it to stop me getting warm, I don't know. But I'm old enough, and wise enough, and I'm fat enough to know you didn't do it for my bonny blue eyes and my fascinating conversation.'

He hadn't meant to get angry but by the time he finished he felt anger creeping into his speech.

He threw his unfinished cigarette to the ground and screwed his heel viciously on the red cinder. When he looked at Bonnie again, to his surprise she was regarding him with a half smile on her face.

'I don't know why I did it,' she said. 'But one thing I do know. All my men have started by being able to make me laugh.'

'Mebbe so,' said Dalziel. 'But none of 'em found much to laugh about at the finish, did they?'

The front door opened and Cross reappeared.

'Bugger it!' he said.

'*Sergeant*,' said Dalziel sternly in his best low church voice.

'Sorry, Mrs Fielding,' apologized Cross to Bonnie whose smile broadened. 'Well, sir. I needn't worry about those chickens any longer. They've gone. The whole bloody lot! Sorry.'

'I'll leave you to swear in peace,' said Bonnie. 'Herrie's gone to bed so if you want to use the sitting-room, you won't be assaulted.'

She went inside.

'Nice woman,' said Cross diffidently. 'Pity about all this.'

'Yes,' said Dalziel. 'Well, what's it to be?'

Cross shrugged.

'It looks like an accident and I hope it's an

accident. Either way, it'll keep till morning.' He yawned prodigiously. 'One thing, with those chickens gone, I might get some sleep this night.'

'I'll fix you up with something to give you sweet dreams,' said Dalziel, ushering Cross into the house. 'I could do with a nightcap myself.'

It wasn't true. He had drunk enough that day and there was nothing more drink could do for him. But anything which put another activity between now and bed was welcome.

It was nearly two hours before Cross managed to drag himself away. After he had gone Dalziel sat alone in the half-lit room and whistled an idio-syncratic version of Sousa's 'Washington Post' as, for the want of anything better to do, he thumbed through the books on Fielding's table. They were the old man's works.

Dalziel ignored the poetry but examined the fly-leaf and the prelims. First editions with autograph, they might be worth a few quid. He was as far from being a bibliophile as a man can get who has received the corrosive imprint of a Western European education, but it was his business to know what was worth stealing, what not. He weighed the books in his broad palm. Little enough for a life's work, he thought. Some uncharacteristic dramatic impulse made him hold out his other palm, empty.

Carefully he replaced the books. They held no attraction for him, either as objects or vehicles.

Pascoe would care for them, he thought. Or Ellie. His new wife. With whom he was now cosily cocooned in some hotel bed. Inspector Peter Pascoe with a new wife by his side and all before him. Pascoe, who was as different from himself as chalk from cheese, who would go further than Dalziel's daftest dreams had even taken him, but who could also come to this, sitting alone in a darkling room full of drink and fear.

'Bugger this!' said Dalziel, standing up. 'I'm going weird!'

He switched off the reading lamp which dropped a cone of light on to the table and stood for a moment to let his eyes grow accustomed to the dark. As he opened the door into the hall he heard the noise of a car on the gravel drive outside and froze. A moment later the front door clicked open and someone entered. Dalziel retreated into the sitting-room and waited. The hall light went on and through the still open door Dalziel saw Uniff, wearing a belted suede jacket and carrying a black briefcase. His beard and his manner, controlled but stealthy, added to the overall impression he gave of a Balkan anarchist, up to no good. He closed and bolted the front door, looked round as though to get his bearings, switched off the light and began a careful ascent of the stairs.

Dalziel gave him five minutes, during which time he turned his formidably experienced detective's brain to the puzzles of this household and advanced not a jot. Then he too tiptoed cautiously up the stairs. As he opened his bedroom door with equal care, he suddenly realized that there existed in his mind a hitherto unformulated expectation that Bonnie would be waiting for him. But the room was empty and he was able to smile cynically at his own ambivalence. Quickly he undressed and went into the bathroom. He did not switch on the light but looked in some perplexity at the door to Bonnie's room. Was it open or locked? Which did he want, and either way what would he do?

Nothing was the answer. He would of course do nothing. But still he wondered, and his hand was actually on the door knob when he heard the voices. They were speaking so low that even with an ear pressed hard against the woodwork, there was no chance of picking out words. But he could make out that there were two voices – a man's and a woman's.

As carefully as he had approached he retreated from the door. If he had prayed before sleeping he might have said, 'Thank you, Lord, for changing nothing.' But he didn't. He just climbed into bed and fell into the deepest, soundest sleep he had known for months.

At seven-thirty the following morning he was down at the lakeside examining the scene of Spinx's death by daylight. There had been no rain that night and the water-level had dropped another six inches. Having dispatched the constable left by Cross in search of breakfast, Dalziel peered at the gap left by the broken treads with considerable uninterest. His attitude to physical clues was rather like that of the modern Christian to miracles. They could happen, but probably not just at the moment. Nevertheless the possibility could not be ignored and he jumped down into the duck punt to get a duck's eye look at the landing-stage.

The three broken treads trailed in the water like old fishbones. Carefully Dalziel poked at them with the blade of an antique penknife whose possession by a long-haired youth at a football match would have got him three months. The outermost two treads were soft but reasonably solid; the third was rotten almost right through. This it must have been that triggered things off. If Spinx had come down on this with his full weight, it could well have snapped, sending him plunging forward so that his head cracked against the timber uprights supporting the end of the stage and his body hit the other two treads with sufficient force to smash through them.

Unconscious from the blow, he would quickly have drowned and floated there, held between the submerged sections of the support baulks, till Dalziel found him.

That's how it could have happened, thought Dalziel, lighting a cigarette and relaxing in the gently jogging punt. If the post mortem showed death to be due to drowning and the head injury to be consistent with a crack against the upright, that would be that. Another Lake House inquest with a verdict of accidental death. And any journalistic interest thus engendered would mean merely so much free advertising for the restaurant. If it opened.

The odds against were now enormous. Dalziel was no businessman but it seemed fairly certain to him that unless they opened on time, the outcry from the disappointed (and uncompensated) customers would be so great that any remaining semblance of creditworthiness would be torn to shreds. His own discovery of the missing drink and the disembowelled ovens had probably been the scheme's death blow. Herrie's dollars might have made a difference but he was so obsessively against the venture that it would need another death to prise the money free. If it had been the old man's face that had peered up through the water the previous night, that would have been quite a different kettle of fish! Not all the rotten wood in the world would have bridged the doubts in Dalziel's mind.

Something clicked close by and he looked up to see Uniff towering above him with a smile on his face and a camera in his hand.

'What a shot!' he said. 'The great detective at work! What were you thinking of, man? A single-handed trip round the world?'

'I thought you were short of film,' said Dalziel, stepping up on to the landing-stage.

'There are some things too good to miss,' said Uniff. 'Say, that could be dangerous.'

He pointed to the broken treads and Dalziel recalled his late return the previous night. Presumably he had not yet met anyone who had told him about Spinx.

'It was,' said Dalziel. 'Oh shit!' He was looking at the sleeve of his jacket which was smeared with oil. He traced its source very quickly to the punt. Someone had been trying to clean up the duck gun.

'Tillotson!' he groaned. 'I'll kill him!'

'If he tries to fire that antique, he'll kill himself,' observed Uniff. 'What were you doing down there, anyway, man?'

As they walked back to the house, Dalziel filled him in on the discovery of Spinx's body.

Uniff was incredulous.

'That little creep? I can't believe it! His kind live for ever.'

'You didn't like him?' said Dalziel.

'What? No, I didn't say that. Some of my best friends are insurance creeps. Anyway, I wasn't around last night, not after nine. So it's no use grilling me.'

His Americanisms were sometimes venerably antique and, in his initial surprise at Dalziel's news, he had sounded very like his sister. But the fat detective's mind had seized upon points of other than linguistic interest.

'I'm not grilling you, Mr Uniff,' he said. 'But I'd be interested to know why you think I might be.'

'Well, hell, sudden death, the fuzz start asking questions all round. I *know*; we've had some, remember?'

'I remember,' said Dalziel. 'Point two, why should nine strike you as being a significant time? There's nothing yet that says Spinx didn't take his bath earlier.'

'It wasn't meant to be significant,' said Uniff. 'It was just the time I left, that's all.'

The uniformed constable came out of the front door as they reached it. He had a half-eaten bacon sandwich in his saluting hand and treated Dalziel to a distant and fatty wave.

'Which brings us to where you went last night, Mr Uniff,' said Dalziel heavily.

Uniff laughed as he ushered Dalziel into the house ahead of him.

'Now you *are* grilling me,' said Uniff.

The door which led to the kitchen opened at the other end of the hallway and Mavis appeared.

'OK,' said Uniff. 'If that's how it's gotta be, come on up to my pad. I got the equipment there.'

He steered Dalziel up the stairs at a speed which left him short of breath by the time they reached the first landing. Looking back, he saw Mavis standing at the foot of the stairs watching their ascent with the impassive intensity of a totem mask.

The room Uniff led him to was huge. The design of the faded and torn wallpaper suggested it had once been a nursery, though no other evidence survived. There were no broken rocking-horses, no disfigured Teddy-bears, just a huge table littered with paper and film equipment, and at the farthermost end of the room surrounded by spot lamps a rostrum camera set-up.

'Here we are,' said Uniff proudly. 'What do you think, man?'

'They must have had bloody huge families in them days,' said Dalziel.

'What? Oh, yeah. It was probably those long winter nights when the magic lantern broke down.'

Uniff wandered across to the camera, turned one of the lamps so that it pointed full in his face and switched it on.

'OK, captain. But I tell you again, I don't know nothing.'

'This your film then?' asked Dalziel, peering without comprehension at a huge sheet of card pinned to the wall. On it were pasted a series of drawings, about fifty in all, like a strip cartoon except that the sequence of events escaped Dalziel.

'I thought you'd never ask,' said Uniff, switching off his light. 'Yeah, that's my story board. I've got some rushes here. You want to see them?'

Like all obsessives, he could not doubt the answer but quickly drew down the black-out blinds and set the projector rolling. On the screen appeared the letter O. It turned into a man's head. A stone age club appeared and hammered down on the skull. The mouth opened and out came a strip cartoon balloon containing the letter O which in its turn became a breast. A hand caressed it. The response again was O; and in sequence every part of the human body was represented by the letter, then assaulted or stimulated in some fashion more or less appropriate, always with the same response. The animation was clever, often wittily obscene, though Dalziel doubted if in these blatant days it was actionable.

'It's about language,' explained Uniff. 'Mave does the animations. Not bad, eh? No sound yet. That's a problem. What do you think? Do we need those O's vocalized?'

The film ran on. Eventually a stone age doctor presented his stone age patient with a bill. The mouth rounded to an O, the eyes to two more, then they all expanded and exploded into a torrent of letters.

'How'd you like that?' asked Uniff as the film ran to an end. 'Commerce is the mother of language. Not love, hate, religion, sex. But money.'

'Well,' said Dalziel. 'It's not very long is it?'

'Hell, man, that's just the opening sequence. Next we go on to a historical survey. The letters and words are the characters, you dig? All languages, all literatures. It's very funny, Mave's done marvels. All the time there's a struggle between the different functions of language. Finally figures start coming in until at the end we get nuclear physics formulae dominating, then the whole thing goes bang and we're back to O.'

'Interesting,' said Dalziel. 'I like a good cartoon. Cheaper to make than a real film, I suppose?'

He was just fishing for some indication of where the finance for the project came from, but Uniff pulled up the blinds angrily, seized a large envelope from a shelf and spilled a dozen or more glossy half-plate prints into Dalziel's lap.

'Those more in your line, Superintendent?'

Dalziel studied them gravely. He was not one of those who found the vagina in close-up a particularly appealing sight, not even when its owner appeared to have a traffic no entry sign tattooed on the inner thigh.

'In a way,' he said. 'Professionally speaking.'

Uniff retrieved the photographs hastily and returned them to their envelope. His anger had quickly vanished.

'They're harmless,' he said. 'I was just showing them to you, not asking you to buy them.'

'No need to get legalistic, Mr Uniff,' said Dalziel. 'Though you ought to know that under the Obscene Publication Acts, publication (that is, simply *showing* someone your dirty pictures) is an offence, whether done for gain or not. But you're in luck. I doubt if anything you've got here is liable to deprave or corrupt me. So let's forget I ever saw them, shall we, and try to remember where you went last night.'

According to Uniff he had simply gone into Orburn for a drink and stayed on after hours as a guest of the landlord. He coyly refused to give the name of the pub on the grounds that he didn't want to risk spoiling a good drinking place. Dalziel found this quite reasonable and, in any case, he had no real authority for, or purpose in, questioning the man, so he didn't press matters.

He went downstairs again and as he reached the hallway, the door to the servants' quarters opened and Arkwright emerged. Dalziel had never seen a pale Negro before and the sight touched him.

'Morning, Mr Arkwright,' said Dalziel with the jovial sympathy of one hard-drinking man for another. 'How are you feeling?'

'Terrible,' said Arkwright. 'Listen. I'm very sorry about all this, I don't know what happened.'

'Something you ate I should think,' said Dalziel, but, observing that the man seemed genuinely distressed at what had passed, he put on his avuncular air and added, 'Think nowt of it. They're all silly buggers here, you wouldn't be noticed.'

A little comforted by this, Arkwright let himself be led to coffee which comforted him even more.

'Penitent left, I suppose?'

'Yes, I think so.'

'Shithead,' said Arkwright. 'I hate that bloody man. He always wants me on a job with him. I'm his liberal credential.'

'I think he'll be after a divorce this morning,' said Dalziel.

Arkwright laughed, regretted it, suddenly sat upright as though at a memory returned and said, 'You put me to bed? Whose bed was I in?'

'Why?' asked Dalziel. 'Have you spewed or something?'

'No. It's just, I remember now, some time in the night, I was woken up. Some guy was pulling at the blankets and saying, "Annie, Annie." So I sat up and said, "Sir, you are mistaken," and this guy shrieked like he was wetting his pants and ran.'

Dalziel thought about it for a moment, then as the image of Arkwright's coal black face emerging from the blankets sharpened in his mind he began to laugh. After a while with great care, Arkwright began to laugh too.

'This man,' said Dalziel finally, wiping his eyes with the khaki awning he used as a handkerchief. 'Did you recognize him? Was he one of the men you met yesterday afternoon?'

'I can't say,' said Arkwright. 'Might be. But it was dark and I was still very drunk. It must have been pretty early. He sounded urgent. I suppose I was lucky he didn't just climb in and get on with it.'

Dalziel smiled and nodded. The obvious interpretation of the intrusion would do for Arkwright, but he was by no means sure that the intruder's purpose had been sexual.

But the more interesting question was, who in this house had not heard last night of the discovered theft and Annie Greave's disappearance?

13

An Intimate Deodorant

Cross arrived shortly before ten bearing with him a preliminary autopsy report which indicated that Spinx had died from drowning and that the injury on his head was consistent with his having struck the wooden support as he fell. With grim amusement Dalziel recognized in Cross the mixture of relief and disappointment an overworked, middle-aged but still ambitious detective sergeant ought to feel.

'Never mind, lad,' he said. 'Perhaps there'll be an outbreak of double parking in the town square. No sign of Mrs Greave?'

'No, sir. Nor of Papworth either. Do you reckon they might have gone off together?'

'Without his clothes?' said Dalziel. 'I doubt it. And I can't see 'em as the great lovers somehow. Where'd they go anyway? He'd be as out of place in the middle of Liverpool as she was in the country.'

'That's what I thought,' said Cross. 'Makes you wonder how they met.'

'It does that,' agreed Dalziel who had been wondering this same thing for two days.

'I wonder if Mrs Fielding could help us there,' said Cross diffidently. 'She'd be the one who hired her, I suppose. What do you think, sir, knowing her as you do?'

Dalziel shot him a sharp glance. Christ! he thought. Could the rustic tom-toms work this quick? What did they do round here? Hide seismographs in the mattress?

'Why not ask her, Sergeant,' he said. 'And less of the *us*. I'm on holiday, remember?'

'Yes, sir,' said Cross.

Dalziel left him and strolled out of the room trying to look like a man whose only care in the world was whether to have one or two double scotches before lunch.

He met Bonnie in the hallway.

'Can we have a word together, Andy?' she asked. She looked very attractive in pea-green slacks and a tight silk blouse which would have gone seven times round Louisa and left enough to blow your nose on.

'Sergeant Cross is in there,' said Dalziel with a jerk of his head. 'I think his need's greater than mine.'

Again his rudeness only seemed to amuse her.

'I didn't realize you were a once-a-month man,' she said. 'Later then. Say in an hour? In my room.'

She brushed by him. The brief contact disturbed him more than he would have thought possible.

He wandered into the back of the house and looked in Papworth's room. Still empty, but now it bore signs of having been searched. Cross obviously didn't mind leaving traces of his passage.

Dalziel mused on Cross as he continued his stroll. He looked a good competent man, perhaps a bit long in the tooth for a sergeant but not yet hopeless of promotion. Perhaps he himself might put in a word . . .

Christalmighty! he suddenly laughed at himself. Lord sodding Dalziel dispensing bounty to the plebs! No. Cross could find another fairy godmother. Middle-aged superintendents needed belated christening gifts just as much as sergeants, though the one Dalziel wanted most of all just now had in fact been bountifully bestowed all those grey years ago and was only now beginning to run short.

Clarity of purpose.

Out in the yard he lit a cigarette and walked slowly past the so-called Banqueting Hall. It felt derelict. A white elephant, a folly. Unless someone coughed up some cash. He thought of his own deposit account. Not insubstantial. He hardly gave it a thought till he wanted cash for something special. Like the set of crystal decanters and glasses he'd given Pascoe and Ellie. *Looking after your own interests*, she'd mocked. But she'd been pleased. So she should have been too, it cost a bloody fortune even with the big discount his cash in hand and his bonny blue eyes got him.

Still, there was plenty left. Last night as he lay on Bonnie's bed, he'd even thought about suggesting an investment, but had put it off. At that moment it might have looked a bit like tucking a fiver behind the clock. Besides there was still the business of the missing gear to resolve. Risking your money was one thing, chucking it away quite another. And after Bertie's revelation . . . no, she'd have to find another fool.

The sound of a vehicle approaching interrupted his thoughts. He reached the end of the hall, stepped out and was almost knocked down by a large truck which rattled past him into the cobbled yard. He turned to harangue the driver, and saw the legend on the opening door. *Gibb and Fowler, Builders.*

Little Mr Gibb jumped out and the men on the back began to disembark.

'Hang around, lads. Have a smoke till I see what's what,' commanded Gibb.

He looked around as if in search of somebody and showed his teeth in a gothic smile when he spotted Dalziel.

'Hello there,' he said. 'You were right then.'

'Was I?' said Dalziel. 'What about?'

'Me being back on the job sooner than I expected. You drop into my place before you go. There's a big bottle there for my friends.'

He winked knowingly. Dalziel looked at him bewildered. Could he actually have *spoken* his thoughts about putting money into the venture last night? And if he had, could Bonnie have taken him seriously after what happened?

He didn't believe it. Anyway, one thing was clear. Gibb wasn't going to start work just on a promise.

'Mr Gibb!' a voice called imperiously.

They turned. Standing in the doorway of the main house was Hereward Fielding.

'Would you step inside for a moment, please.'

'Right. See you around,' said Gibb happily to Dalziel.

So, thought Dalziel. Mystery solved. But a bigger one put in its place. What had produced this complete turnabout by the old man?

He approached the men sitting on the tail-board of the truck who looked at him incuriously.

'What do you think of it then?' he asked, jerking his head at the Banqueting Hall.

'Think?' said a venerable grey head, wearing overalls overlaid with paint to the consistency of armour. 'There'll be fancy prices, no doubt.'

The others grunted with the sagacity of men who knew better than to be caught by fancy prices.

'Sad about the accident,' said Dalziel.

Grey-head nodded agreement but another rounder, jollier man piped up, 'Silly bugger shouldn't have been up there. Not his job.'

'Whose job was it?' asked Dalziel.

This flummoxed them for a moment.

'Depends what he were doing,' said grey-head cautiously.

'Come and have a look,' invited Dalziel.

Ghoulish curiosity proved stronger than Gibb's command and they followed him into the Banqueting Hall, dropping their voices to the hushed murmurs of a stately-home-tours party.

'He was up a ladder, there,' said Dalziel. 'With a drill. They thought he was fixing a beam.'

'Nothing to fix,' said grey-head. 'We put that beam up ourselves, last thing we did before knocking off. That won't come down in a hurry.'

'So what could he have been fixing? Up there along the wall a bit. You can see where he was drilling.'

They peered into the shadowy arch of the high roof.

'Christ knows,' said grey-head. 'There's nothing there. I plastered right along this wall after they finished the wiring.'

Suddenly everything was illuminated.

Gibb stood by the door with his hand on the light panel.

'So here you are then,' he said. 'Right, lads, let's get the gear in. We're in business.'

The men streamed out of the hall with no signs of over-enthusiasm.

'So the old man's coughing up,' pried Dalziel.

'Don't let on you didn't know,' said Gibb. 'I'll have cash in my hand before the day's out. That's the deal.'

'And how long will it take you to finish the job?'

'Working hard at it? With lots of overtime, two or three days.'

'That's not bad.'

'No. Well, frankly, Mr Dalziel, with things the way they are, I'd prefer to take it easy, give the lads a week, ten days even. But the old man's a tough nut. He's made it quite clear that he's no party to the original agreement. If I go to law, there's no way I can get my hands on his cash. So he's calling the tune. And that says, three days at the outside. So we're dancing the quickstep. Excuse me.'

Dalziel followed him out, musing on what had been said, but especially on the flash of illumination which had come to him as Gibb switched on the lights.

Hereward Fielding was standing in the doorway of the main house once more. He beckoned imperiously.

'Come in, come in,' he said impatiently. 'I've a great deal to do and it won't get done hanging around here, waiting for you.'

'You're expecting me then,' said Dalziel.

'Of course. When I saw you out in the yard with that man, I knew you'd be here in a short time.'

'Well,' said Dalziel. 'That saves the bother of being subtle.'

'Really,' said Fielding. 'A pity. *That* I should have liked to observe. To business then. I've changed my mind. I've decided after all to invest my newly acquired wealth in the family business. A foolish decision, you may think, but freely made. Blood after all is thicker than water.'

'Your blood than lake water, mebbe,' grunted Dalziel. 'That's got shot of the crap. Now tell me what really changed your mind.'

Fielding shook his head in reluctant admiration.

'If I could have written poetry of such simple directness,' he said, 'I would have been a set-book by now. No, Dalziel. That's all I have to say. Pry no further; or else.'

'Or else what?'

'Or else I shall command my daughter-in-law to forbid you the house.'

His eyes twinkled and an ironic smile tugged at his thin lips.

'You see, I am a man of influence now.'

Dalziel was unimpressed.

'Think on,' he said. 'You might think it's bad having me here privately, but that's nowt to having me officially.'

'I believe it,' said Fielding. 'But come now, there's no cause for us to quarrel. In your younger, greener days you must have been trained to help old gents cross the street. Now you may drive me into Orburn if you would be so kind. I must visit my bank and make arrangements for the malodorous Gibb.'

'And buy a big hat,' added Dalziel.

'Perhaps not today,' laughed Fielding. 'But I shall certainly be laying in a stock of decent brandy. They can use this stuff for flaming Christmas puddings.

We could do a little sampling at the Lady Hamilton after lunch. On me, of course.'

'I haven't got a car,' said Dalziel.

'We'll take the Rover. I have the keys.' He held them up as evidence.

'Five minutes then,' said Dalziel, turning away.

Fielding's manner interested him. His speech style was normally what Dalziel designated as 'clever poofy' but there was an element of strain behind it today which had nothing to do with intellectual affectation. Nor did he much care for the quick production of the Rover's keys. Fielding must have got them from Bonnie. And the house was full of young drivers. Indeed there was no apparent bar to the old man's driving himself.

Well, if they wanted him out of the way, he'd go. It suited him to go to Orburn anyway. But he'd go on his own terms.

He headed for the kitchen fast. Tillotson and Louisa were drinking coffee together. They weren't speaking to each other but the atmosphere between them was manifestly more cordial than ever before in Dalziel's limited experience. When he had a moment, he must find out why she'd punched the poor sod on the nose that night.

'Morning,' he said brightly.

'Hi,' said Louisa. 'Fancy a cup?'

This was real cordiality.

'No time, thanks all the same. I'm running Herrie to town. Like to come?'

They exchanged glances.

'No thanks,' said Louisa.

'Things to do,' said Tillotson.

'Great news about the restaurant,' said Dalziel.

'Yes, isn't it,' said Tillotson brightly. 'With a bit of luck we can still open on time. I always knew it would be all right.'

Unimpressed by this unlikely claim to clairvoyance, Louisa said nothing but pulled her lower lip forward so that the moist inner flesh showed. It was quite sexy, thought Dalziel. If you were as skinny as she was, he supposed you had to do your best with whatever protuberances you could lay your hands on.

'Grand,' said Dalziel. 'Excuse me.'

He went into the back kitchen and returned a moment later with something in a plastic carrier bag.

'Taking a picnic?' asked Louisa.

'Just a nibble,' said Dalziel. 'Sure you won't come?'

'Sure. Any news about Mrs Greave?' asked Louisa.

'No. You'll have to do your own dinner,' said Dalziel. 'Perhaps the great white hunter here will shoot a couple of flying fish. You owe me for a cleaning job, Charley.'

Tillotson was full of apologies when he finally grasped Dalziel's meaning. Louisa was unsympathetic.

'Messing about in boats is messy,' she said firmly.

'It seemed safer than the landing-stage,' commented Dalziel.

'Poor old Sphincter,' sighed Tillotson.

'Yes?' nodded Dalziel.

'Nothing,' said Tillotson, puzzled. 'Just poor old Sphincter.'

'A sad loss,' said Dalziel. 'Especially to Anchor Insurance. They'll have to send someone else to investigate you.'

He left on this good line. As he approached Herrie's sitting-room he thought he heard the noise of the door clicking to but when he peered in, the room was empty. Cross must have finished, which meant Bonnie would be ready for her talk.

On an impulse he pushed open the door of the next room in the corridor and stepped inside. It was the billiards-room, still heavily curtained, perhaps (though he doubted it) in recognition that Fielding's coffin had lain in here.

He found a light switch and clicked it on. A tent of light fell over the green baize, but enough spilled sideways to reveal a figure standing in the shadows of the old marble fireplace.

Another switch turned on the main light.

'Well, well,' said Dalziel genially. 'The wanderer returns.'

Standing before him with an ancient rucksack slung over one shoulder was Nigel Fielding.

He looked very pale and in need of a good night's sleep.

'Just got back?' enquired Dalziel.

The boy nodded.

'And you thought you'd like a bit of peace and quiet before showing your face? Well, it always takes a bit of nerve to come home. Take the piss a bit, do they, Bertie and Lou?'

'A bit,' said the boy.

'Pay no heed. Look, I'm just off upstairs to see your mam for a moment. I'll tell her you're here if you like. OK?'

'Thanks very much, Mr Dalziel,' said the boy.

A polite lad, thought Dalziel as he went up the stairs. But he didn't look well and it boded no good that he should shut himself up in the darkened billiards-room as soon as he got back.

Bonnie was sitting at her dressing-table applying with great care a rich damask lipstick to her lower lip. It must be sex zone of the day, thought Dalziel.

'Cross gone?' he asked.

'Yes. Did you want to see him?'

'No sweat. I can see him in town. I'm driving your father-in-law to the bank.'

'That's kind of you. What about our talk?'

'It'll keep, won't it? Anyway there's someone more important than me for you to see.'

'Who's that?'

'Nigel,' he said. 'He's just got back. He's in the billiards-room.'

It is always good to see that one's exit lines are effective and before he left he allowed himself the indulgence of watching the surprise round her lips to a roseate O, reminding him of Uniff's cartoon.

He thought of mentioning Nigel's return to the old man, but decided he would certainly have wanted to go straight in and see the boy. Bonnie was entitled to some time alone with him. He'd only been away a couple of days, true, but in Dalziel's estimation it wouldn't be long before he went away and didn't come back for much, much longer. So he drove the ancient Rover down the rutted and pot-holed drive without mentioning the boy.

Fielding was very quiet on the short journey and Dalziel made no attempt to break the silence. In Orburn he parked the car in the ovoid square once more and watched Herrie step smartly through the dignified portals of the bank. For a poet, he had a surprisingly stiff and military bearing, or perhaps it was just his contact with commerce which had effected the change.

Dalziel's first call was the same as on the previous day, the chemist's shop. The girl assistant smiled knowingly when he asked to see the chemist himself. She thinks I want a packet of rubbers, thought Dalziel, and he leered so grossly at her that the smile vanished and she retreated quickly into the dispensary.

'Yes, sir,' said the chemist, a man with a Douglas Fairbanks profile and what looked like a duelling scar down his left cheek. He might have been Rupert of Hentzau in retirement.

Dalziel took him to one side and presented him with a piece of paper. On it he had written PROPANANNAL(?).

'What kind of condition would you take this for? I'm not sure of the spelling.'

'Well,' said the chemist dubiously. 'May I ask why you want to know?'

Dalziel sighed. The less he had to use his police authority at this stage, the better he'd be pleased.

'My old mother,' he said. 'She's very independent but we're desperately worried. You understand?'

'I see,' said the chemist, weakening.

'She's not local,' urged Dalziel.

'In that case,' said the chemist.

It turned out that the chemist was not a romantic hero in retirement but rather a physician manqué. Once he started, even Dalziel, famed throughout Yorkshire for his ability to halt the most garrulous of witnesses in mid-syllable, found it hard to drive home the plug. In the end he plucked a packet at random from the nearest shelf, pulled out his wallet and escaped in the caesura produced by the reckoning of change.

But it had been a profitable visit none the less, though he felt no very great sense of triumph as he made his way to the police station.

There was another man closeted with Sergeant Cross this morning. Something about the way in which Cross introduced him as Detective Chief Inspector Balderstone made Dalziel feel that they had just been talking about him prior to his arrival. He wasn't surprised. It would have been strange if Cross's report on the presence in Lake House of a senior police officer had not produced some reactions from above.

Balderstone's attitude was very correct but, to start with at least, very reserved. He can't make his mind up if I'm a biased witness, impartial observer, or fifth column, thought Dalziel. And he wasn't altogether sure he knew himself.

After ten minutes or so, the atmosphere had thawed considerably.

'Look,' Dalziel had said. 'I'm just there by accident. It's Sergeant Cross's case, for what it is. And what is it? Well, there's two accidental deaths. Curious, but not criminal as far as we can see. A woman and a man have disappeared. It happens all the time. Christ, I'm not where I was planning to be three days ago, so in a sense I've disappeared. And lastly there's been a theft. That's the only crime. Simple theft. And, I tell you straight, it wouldn't surprise me if that didn't get quietly brushed under the carpet soon.'

'I don't understand,' said Balderstone. He was about forty, with the squashed face of a bulldog.

'A mistake,' said Dalziel. 'The booze not ordered, or stored elsewhere. A misunderstanding about the kitchen equipment. Mrs Greave exonerated.'

'Why do you say this, sir?' asked Balderstone.

'It's just a theory,' said Dalziel. 'That's why I came here this morning. Like I said, it's the sergeant's case. Any information or ideas I've got, well, it's my duty to pass them on. So here I am.'

He looked for a moment staunchly dutiful, like the centrepiece of a First World War music-hall tableau depicting patriotic pride.

A few moments later, after hearing what Dalziel had to say, Cross began to feel that it wasn't so much his rights as the officer in charge of the case that Dalziel was interested in as the facilities at his disposal. This was confirmed when Dalziel delved into his plastic carrier, produced a paper bag and handed it over with the instructions, 'And get your labs to take a look at that.'

Cross opened the bag and peered in.

'Any special instructions, sir?' he asked.

'What do you think?'

Out of the box in the paper bag, Cross lifted a large aerosol can of what was coyly described as an intimate deodorant.

'I don't know what to think, sir.'

Angrily Dalziel snatched it back and put it on the desk top. From the carrier he produced another bag, took from it a cake box, opened it and showed its contents to Balderstone and Cross. It was a dead rat.

'I'd like to know how it died,' said Dalziel.

'That's very interesting,' said Balderstone after listening to Dalziel for some moments after Cross had left the office. 'But what do we have if it all turns out to be true?'

'Bugger all,' said Dalziel. He glanced at his watch. It was nearly eleven-thirty.

'Are you in a hurry, sir?' asked Balderstone.

'No. I've arranged to meet the old boy at twelve in the Lady Hamilton. He's buying me my dinner. I should think we'll be there till two or later. So if anything turns up by then, you know where to get in touch.'

They talked a little more, exchanging gossip about mutual acquaintances till Cross returned with the news that Dalziel's enquiries had all been set in motion and the rat was on its way to the forensic laboratories.

'Grand,' said Dalziel. 'Well, I'd best be on my way. I'll hear from you later, I hope.'

He got up to go.

'Oh sir,' said Cross.

'Yes?'

'Don't forget . . . this.'

He handed over the deodorant can.

Dalziel examined him carefully for signs of amusement, but the sergeant's face remained expressionless. He took the top off the can and pressed the button. A thin liquid haze filled the air for a moment then disappeared, leaving behind a faint lemony scent. Dalziel sniffed.

'That's what the world's coming to,' he said, tossing the can into Cross's waste-paper basket.

It was his third good exit line of the morning but he felt strangely hypocritical as he left the police station. He had withheld nothing which had any direct bearing on the case as it stood at present, he assured himself. Should the scope of Cross's investigations widen, then of course he would reveal *everything* he had surmised.

But his mind, though not much given to symbolism, told him that his reassurances smelt of lemon.

14

When We Dead Awake

Lunch at the Lady Hamilton was an expensive and alcoholic occasion. Only the best would do for Hereward Fielding and though the Lady Hamilton's best had won it no stars in the posher eating guides, the food was hot and plentiful and· swam around very pleasantly in the three bottles of criminally costly claret that the old man insisted they drank with it. All this he regarded merely as a base for the brandy which followed and by two-thirty he was ready to tell the story of his life.

Dalziel whose caution and capacity had both proved larger was willing enough to listen to this personal history as long as it came fairly swiftly to the past twenty-four hours.

'My life has been tragic. Tragic,' Hereward assured him.

'It's been very sad lately,' agreed Dalziel.

'*Sad* is no fit word for it,' reproved Fielding. 'Sad is . . . sad. What I feel is despair. A despair all the

216

stronger because I half believe in futurity. We may survive, Dalziel.'

'That's hopeful,' said Dalziel. Surprisingly, he realized he meant it. That bloody wine must have got to him after all.

'No. Oh no. Think of it. When we dead awake it will be to each as if but a second ago he had felt the pangs of dying, the explosion in the head, the drowning of the lungs, the fingers tightening round the throat. What a noise of screaming and wailing there will be at that moment! Followed by what a moment of silence and amazement as we realize the pain is no more.'

'Well, that is hopeful,' asserted Dalziel. 'These dead people, did you have anyone special in mind?'

But the old man was not listening to him.

'But this in turn will be followed by the onset of such a fear at the strangeness and uncertainty of this awakening that all we remember of that forever unattainable past – sunlight, sea-smells, the pleasures of mind and appetite, and even the pains of dying – will seem more desirable to us than all the fabled joys of immortality. Even *your* lonely, frightened and unhappy existence will beckon you backward with siren song, Dalziel. Even that. Even that.'

He nodded emphatically, and set his brandy balloon like a specimen case over his nose as he sought the last few drops.

'I'll tell you what you are,' said Dalziel, irritated

by this unmannerly comment on his own state of being, 'you're pissed. We'd best be on our way home.'

Before I'm finished, he told himself grimly, I'll give these bastards something else to be sorry for.

The old man seemed to read his thoughts.

'Don't be offended, Dalziel. It's not pity I offer. Nor is it pity I ask for. It's merely an audience. And in return, I offer an audience. This is the best we can do for each other, be audiences. Shall we in good music-hall tradition exit with a song?'

He struck his brandy glass with a coffee spoon, took up the resultant note with remarkable accuracy and began to sing.

'Oh, the life of the spirit's a very fine thing
But you can't be a monk without flogging
    your ring
And strangely enough I believe you will find
You can't be a tart without flogging your
    mind.'

The waiters gathered in a concerned but uncertain posse by the kitchen door. The large bill had already been paid with a lavish tip, but it wasn't just gratitude or hope of future largesse that immobilized them, Dalziel felt; it was disbelief that this patrician figure could be the source of the disturbance. Then they were joined by the shiny under-manager whose face set in horror and indignation as he recognized Dalziel.

'Come on, Herrie,' said Dalziel grimly. 'Let's go home.'

He stood up, put his hand under the old man's arm and eased him up.

Outside he deposited the now almost comatose Fielding in the Rover and, puffing from the exertion, he closed the door with his buttocks, leaned against it and began to scratch himself against the handle. Chief Inspector Balderstone who turned up a few moments later was reminded of a brown bear he once saw up against a tree in a Disney nature film.

'Glad I've caught you, sir,' he said.

'Hello, lad,' said Dalziel genially. 'You've been quick. What've you found out? Was I right?'

'Mainly, sir. But we'll come to that in a minute. More important is, they've found Mrs Greave.'

'And you think that's more important?' said Dalziel scornfully. 'You've still a lot to learn, Inspector. Where'd they pick her up? Liverpool.'

'Not quite,' said Balderstone. 'Epping Forest.'

'Christ,' said Dalziel. 'She must have taken a wrong turning!'

'She did that all right,' said Balderstone. 'She'd been bashed over the head and then strangled.'

Annie Greave's body had been discovered at nine o'clock that morning by a man riding through Epping Forest. His horse had been reluctant to pass close to a pile of loose branches and leaf mould which looked as if it had been heaped hastily into a shallow ditch. The man dismounted, pulled aside a branch and saw shining through in all its unnatural glory the red hair of Annie Greave.

With her in the ditch had been a suitcase and handbag, so identification had not been difficult. When the Liverpool police were contacted to be told of the woman's death and asked if anything were known, they recalled that Cross had rung them the previous evening asking for a watch to be kept for the woman.

'Time of death?' asked Dalziel, screwing up his face at the temperature of his beer.

After ensuring that Herrie was comfortable and not in any immediate danger of choking himself, he had escorted Balderstone back into the Lady Hamilton with the assurance that professional ethics forbade him to discuss so serious a matter in the street.

'Not known yet, but I doubt if it'll be much help. You rarely get better than give-or-take three hours. But they reckon she was dumped before three o'clock this morning.'

'How's that?'

'There was a thunderstorm which started just about then. Very heavy rain for an hour. The body had obviously been out in it.'

'Who've they got down there?' asked Dalziel. 'Sherlock bloody Holmes? Anything else?'

'Well, she hadn't been robbed and she hadn't been raped. At least, not so you'd notice.'

'What's that mean?'

'She'd had intercourse not all that long before death. But no signs of force. Also a meal.'

'They're on the ball, these bloody cockneys,' admitted Dalziel grudgingly. 'Our police surgeon wants two weeks' notice to take a blood sample.'

'Their pathologist just happened to be handy when they brought her in.'

'What had she eaten?' asked Dalziel.

'Sausages.'

'That figures,' Dalziel laughed. 'Sausages, eh? What about her case?'

'Sorry?'

'Did it look as if she'd packed it herself? Had anyone been through it?'

'No, sir. Neatly packed, they said. Everything nicely folded. Woman's packing. Oh, and there were a couple of bottles of gin.'

'Souvenirs,' said Dalziel, thinking that it all fitted. Annie Greave hadn't rushed off in a hurry. No, she'd made up her mind to go, got ready, then slipped away when everyone else was too busy to notice. The last time she'd been seen at Lake House was mid-afternoon, as far as Cross's questioning had been able to discover. But Dalziel felt that she had probably delayed her departure till the post-presentation party was well under way.

What had happened then? Had someone come to collect her. A taxi, perhaps. Doubtless this was being checked. Or had she arranged with someone in the house to drive her to a bus or railway station?

He tried to arrange in his mind the inmates of the house during the period of hard drinking after the presentation, but found it almost impossible. Bonnie had looked for and been unable to find Mrs Greave round about five, but all that meant, of course, was that she'd vacated her room by then. She might still have been close by, waiting for her lift.

'The question is,' said Balderstone, 'did she mean to head south? And if she did, did she know who she was going with or did she just get herself picked up and come unstuck?'

'You mean some fellow who had his fun and then started arguing about the price? Possible,' said Dalziel, adding diffidently, 'You'll be covering transport cafés, that kind of thing? And local taxi services.'

'Yes, sir, thank you,' said Balderstone politely. 'Er, look, sir, what do you think? Could this have anything to do with what's going on in Lake House?'

'You tell me,' said Dalziel. 'What *is* going on in Lake House?'

'Well, those points you asked us to check. You were right in just about every respect.'

Dalziel showed no surprise, but sipped his beer cautiously to see if it had reached a drinkable temperature.

'First we checked on Henry Uniff. Liverpool fire

service had a record of his fire and someone had made a note of his insurers. A company called Royal Oak.'

'Oh,' said Dalziel, disappointed.

'Who are a subsidiary of Provincial Traders.'

'Ah,' said Dalziel. 'Get on with it, man. It's not a Book at sodding Bedtime.'

'Who,' continued Balderstone, unperturbed, 'as you know, were for a time Mr Bertie Fielding's employers. His ambitions, it seems, were managerial to start with, but the parent company found him unsatisfactory. It was thought his peculiar talents might be better suited to the more outward-going atmosphere of an insurance office and he was offered a transfer to Royal Oak. He dealt personally with the Uniff fire. There was a medium-sized amount involved. A few thousand all told, most of it on film equipment. They dictated us a list. Not much help except that this item, the rostrum camera, has a serial number.'

'Useful,' said Dalziel. 'I'll take that. Thanks.'

'Lastly, we've contacted Anchor Insurance. It seems that Mrs Fielding has already been on to them, expressing sympathy for Spinx's accident but great indignation that it should have taken place while he was unlawfully trespassing on her property – especially as it seems likely that he was there on Anchor's behalf. I think she's got them worried. It could be a bit embarrassing. As for what you asked, yes, there's a whacking great fire insurance. The building, I mean the restaurant and kitchens not the main house, plus contents is covered for fifty thousand pounds.'

'Jesus wept!' said Dalziel. 'It's nowt but a ruined stables!'

'Yes indeed. The thing is, it's not just intrinsic value that's covered, but potential loss of revenue, you follow? But there's no theft insurance at all. They felt that until the place was completed and properly covered by alarms, it was too easy a target. Premiums would have been very high, so the Fieldings put all their eggs in one basket.'

'Big bloody basket,' said Dalziel. 'And the rat?'

'Just as you thought, sir,' said Balderstone. 'I had to pass all this on to my superiors, you understand, sir.'

'I wouldn't understand if you hadn't,' answered Dalziel. 'What do they say?'

'Well, the way things stand, we've got no kind of case at all. In fact, we've not really got any crime. This woman's death belongs to the Met, the man Spinx will almost certainly get a verdict of accident, and that just leaves the theft . . .'

'Which I lay odds you won't have for long.'

'No, sir. And that's all. Isn't it, sir?'

'As far as I know,' said Dalziel, looking him straight in the eyes.

'Good. Well, sir, we'll be asking more questions up at Lake House, of course. And we're keener than ever to get hold of this man Papworth. But I can see us coming out of the other end of all this with nothing but a lot of time wasted. I just wondered, well, my super wondered, how long you intend staying at the house.'

'Why?' asked Dalziel.

'Well, it might be useful having someone on the inside, so to speak. Till we see how things go.'

'Jesus wept!' said Dalziel. 'I bet he didn't mention expenses! And I'm supposed to be on holiday.'

It didn't sound very convincing. He didn't even really try.

'All right, I can spare another day or so,' he said finally. 'But I'll have to tell them what I think. It's got to be stopped. I think it has been, but they've got to know we know, just in case.'

Balderstone looked dubious.

'I'm not sure, sir . . .' he began.

'Look,' said Dalziel. 'What're you hoping for? Conspiracy? Christ, there's no hope. I know 'em. No. Frighten the bastards, that's what. I'll do that, but I'll leave it to you to tell them about Open Annie. I'll have another chat with 'em first. Once they know she's dead, they'll clam up. Form a defensive ring! But I'll be inside and if anyone knows more than they should, I'll see they get an arrow up the arse!'

Feeling very pleased with his metaphor, Dalziel tipped the remnants of his beer into a pot holding a tired-looking rubber plant. The assistant manager stood in the doorway, looking disapproving. Dalziel addressed him as they passed.

'The reason the best barmaids have big tits,'

he said, 'is for warming up pots of cold tasteless beer.'

The man's expression did not alter but Dalziel was entertained to notice that Balderstone looked distinctly embarrassed.

Hereward Fielding had slumped across the driving seat in their absence so Dalziel pulled him upright and wound the seat-belt round him with all the ferocity of a devout executioner strapping a heretic to the stake.

'That should hold the old sod,' he grunted to Balderstone through the open window. 'Oh, by the way. You won't forget there were six, no five, other people who left Lake House last night, probably heading for London. All pissed and two at least horny with it.'

Balderstone looked nonplussed. Dalziel hoped he was pretending.

'Butt, the feature writer and his dolly photographer, Penitent the BBC man, and the two Yanks. I'd try Penitent first, he had a car to himself. His side-kick was too stoned to travel. Which, as it turns out, may have been lucky for someone.'

'How's that?'

'Well, someone tried to get into bed with him, thinking he was Annie. Which means that whoever it was thought that Annie was alive and well and ready for fun.'

The thought of Arkwright's black face rising from the pillow made Dalziel laugh again and it kept him amused all the way home. Or rather all the way to Lake House, which is not my home, he reminded himself. Though the sight of his own car parked at the head of the drive made him feel pleasantly lord-of-the-manorish as he halted the Rover alongside.

The garage had delivered it at lunch-time, Tillotson informed him. Bonnie had paid the bill, so would he please settle up with her?

Dalziel nodded his approval of this young gentleman's protection of a lady's interests. It was good to know that there were still young men who recognized that a lady of breeding should find it impossible to ask for money. Not that he approved of the elitism implicit in the recognition (as an elite of one, he felt that most other elites were puffed-up crap) but he disapproved even more of women being like men.

'I hope the sods haven't charged for cleaning it,' he said, looking disapprovingly at the tide-mark left round the paintwork by its recent immersion.

'I wouldn't be surprised,' said Tillotson cheerfully. 'Still, drop Pappy fifty pence and he'll give it a polish for you. Does it quite nicely too.'

'If he was here, I might do that,' said Dalziel.

'Oh, he's here,' said Tillotson casually. 'Turned up shortly after you left.'

'What!' bellowed Dalziel. 'Has anyone told Sergeant Cross?'

'No, I don't think so. Should they have done?'

Could he really be so thick? wondered Dalziel, looking darkly at Tillotson across whose face signs of uneasiness were passing like the movement of a field of wheat at the first breath of the approaching storm.

'Would you like to see him? Shall I fetch him?' offered Tillotson, eager to be somewhere else.

'No,' growled Dalziel who had paused in his efforts to ease the still-sleeping Fielding out of the car. 'You look after the old man.'

'Oh. Is he ill?' said Tillotson, concerned.

'No,' said Dalziel. 'He's unconscious. Which means he doesn't know he's back in this bloody nut house. Which means, for my money, he's very well indeed. Here, get hold.'

He found Papworth in his room, stretched out on his bed apparently asleep. He was fully clothed except for his boots which lay on the floor as though they had been kicked off and dropped over the bed end. The room smelled of tobacco, sweat and something else rather unpleasant which Dalziel couldn't place.

'On your feet, Papworth,' commanded Dalziel.

The man didn't move, but Dalziel sensed that he was awake. He lifted his right foot, placed it against the bed end and thrust with all his weight. The bed moved a couple of inches and crashed against the wall.

Papworth jerked upright, his face taut with anger.

'You stupid fat bastard!' he said.

'Temper,' said Dalziel mildly. 'You look as if you'd like to kill me.'

'Don't give me ideas,' said Papworth, swinging his legs off the bed.

'You think you could kill a man just because he woke you up?' asked Dalziel. 'That's interesting.'

'Your words, not mine. Why don't you sod off?'

Dalziel grinned horribly.

'I ought to warn you, Mr Papworth, that I am a police officer.'

'Don't bother. I know,' said Papworth. 'It's not hard to smell 'em out.'

'In here it would be bloody miraculous,' said Dalziel, sniffing. 'What else do you know, Mr Papworth?'

'What do you mean?'

'Come on!' snapped Dalziel. 'Don't play the thick ploughboy with me. That tube of tool-grease you've been passing off as your daughter, she took off last night. Where'd she go?'

'Mrs Greave? I don't know. She's a free agent. What's up? Didn't she give her notice?'

'It's not what she gave. It's what she took.'

Briefly Dalziel listed the missing items. Papworth, fully in control of himself now, was unimpressed.

'All that? She must have had a big bag.'

'Oh no,' said Dalziel who had also settled down. 'This lot's been going for a long while. And you never noticed?'

'I'm the outdoor man,' said Papworth. 'If she'd taken any trees, I'd have noticed.'

Dalziel smiled inwardly. There was nothing he loved better than a joker. In his experience of interrogation, wit was the last defence of the guilty and generally it sprang from deep uncertainties rather than the confidence it claimed to demonstrate.

'Look,' he said in a voice unctuous with reasonableness. 'Look. There's nothing for you to worry about. Don't take any notice of me if I shout a bit. It's my upbringing. I'm like you. Good solid working-class stock. I've no time for these fancy fal-da-rils. Look. This woman, Annie Greave, now we know what she's not. She's not your daughter. And we know what she is. She's a Liverpool whore. What we don't know is *where* she is. And it might help us to find her if you told us how you came to meet her in the first place.'

'If she's a pro,' said Papworth, 'I'd have thought that were obvious.'

'True,' said Dalziel, looking pleasantly surprised as though the thought hadn't struck him. 'So you picked her up. Where was this – Liverpool?'

'That's it,' said Papworth.

'I thought so. What were you doing in Liverpool? It's a good way. Not the kind of place you go for a holiday.' Dalziel laughed as he spoke, inviting Papworth to share the absurdity of the thought.

'I went there a few times with young Master Bertie,' said Papworth. The feudal phrase came awkwardly from his lips.

'Did you? As his valet?' said Dalziel, unable to restrain the sarcasm. But it appeared to pass unnoticed.

'He worked up there. Didn't have a car, so when he was going back after a stay at Lake House, I'd sometimes drive him in the Rover and bring it back the next day.'

'And spend the night screwing Annie,' said Dalziel with a wink.

'That's it.'

'And you got to enjoy this so much that when the chance came to install her here in Lake House, you thought, *why not*? But for decency's sake, and to save the bother of testimonials, you said she was your daughter?'

'Right again,' said Papworth. 'You needn't have woken me up, seeing you've managed to work it all out by yourself.'

'I like a nice chat,' said Dalziel genially. 'So. Let me see. Bertie was how long in Liverpool? Just over a year, I think. Fifteen months, say. And he came back here to start the restaurant project early this year. How often did he come home while he was away? Every weekend? Once a month? Twice a year?'

'Once a month, six weeks at the outside,' said Papworth cautiously.

'And you drove him back and screwed Mrs Greave. That'd make between eight and twelve jumps you had with her last year. Enough to give you a taste for it?'

231

'I didn't count,' said Papworth. 'Does it give you a thrill, these questions?'

'No. No,' said Dalziel thoughtfully. 'I was just thinking how advanced the prison service in Liverpool must be. Nowt like it in Yorkshire, I tell you, else there's some would be queuing up.'

'What do you mean?'

'I mean Annie Greave spent eight months last year in gaol, that's what I mean. And if you were getting on board each time you drove bouncing Bertie back home, then you must have real influence. Yes indeed.'

It was, of course, a lie. Criminals lied all the time and Dalziel saw no reason why this useful privilege should be reserved for them alone.

Of course, all Papworth had to do was say *you must be daft!* and indeed the man was looking at him with what might be honest puzzlement as he rolled another of his revolting cigarettes.

'Well?' prompted Dalziel.

The door burst open and Bertie Fielding entered.

'Hello, Pappy,' he said. 'I've been looking for you. Ah, you're here, Dalziel. That's useful. It'll save ringing up Cross.'

'We're having a private conversation,' growled Dalziel. 'Do you mind?'

'In *your* house with *your* employees, you can have all the private conversations you wish,' said Bertie. He was feeling confident enough to say it as a joke rather than make it as nasty as he was capable of, observed Dalziel.

'Pappy, now the water's going down, we really ought to start cleaning up the bottom bit of the lawn. The flood's left an awful mess. I've got Hank out there earning his keep, but we need your expertise.'

'Right,' said Papworth. 'I'll come now.'

'Hold on!' said Dalziel. 'I'm not finished with you yet.'

'Is this some kind of official interrogation?' enquired Bertie. 'What's it all about, Pappy?'

'He's asking me about Mrs Greave. Something about some missing stuff.'

Bertie laughed. The sight of his soft fleshiness gently shaking filled Dalziel with revulsion. At least at his age I was nothing but bone and muscle, he thought.

'Is that it? Well, consider your constabulary duty done, Mr Dalziel, sir. That's what I was going to ring Sergeant Cross about. It's all been a mistake.'

'What?'

'A mistake. Look, it's a bit complicated, but what it boils down to is this. There's nothing missing.'

'What?'

'That's the long and short of it, I'm afraid. I've done a careful check this morning and in fact all the missing stuff can be accounted for. The booze has been stored elsewhere. It's silly, really.'

'And you didn't know?' demanded Dalziel.

'Not in the least. Not till this morning.'

'And who was it that altered your arrangements without letting you know? And why didn't he or she speak up last night?'

'Well, that would have been a bit difficult,' said Bertie, grinning broadly. 'It was my late father, God bless him. Who else?'

'So now you've tracked the drink down? And the ovens? Had he fiddled with them too?'

'Oh yes,' said Bertie. 'Security. Very distrustful man was my father.'

It was of course unanswerable. And even though Dalziel had forecast this turn of events to Balderstone that morning, he felt angrily frustrated.

'You can see for yourself if you like,' offered Bertie.

'No thanks,' said Dalziel to whom another thought had occurred. Was this why he had been steered away from the house that morning?

'So come on, Pappy,' said Bertie. 'Mr Dalziel doesn't need to question you any more. Do you, Superintendent?'

Dalziel hesitated. Now would be a dramatic time to reveal that Annie Greave was dead. If he were in charge of the case and could have followed up his revelation by getting Papworth and Bertie into a nice neutral interview room for the next couple of hours, he wouldn't have hesitated. But it wasn't up to him. In any case, as he had stated to Balderstone, his ambiguous position in this house was a positive advantage. Once launched into a full-scale interrogation he would have stepped outside the wagon ring and joined the other red-skins whooping around in the darkness.

He decided to compromise.

'Don't forget,' he said to Bertie. 'It wasn't just a nonexistent theft we had here last night. A man got drowned.'

'What's that to do with me?' demanded Papworth.

'Depends what time you left the house last night and where you went,' said Dalziel. 'You might have seen him on the road.'

Papworth considered for a moment.

'No,' he said. 'I saw nothing. I've no time to gawp at passers-by.'

'That's a little bit vague,' said Dalziel. 'Let's see if we can help you. What time did you leave the house?'

'Latish. I'm not a man for clocks,' said Papworth.

'All right,' said Dalziel understandingly. 'Let's try the other end. Where'd you go and what time did you get there?'

'Well,' said Papworth. 'I had a wet in the village.'

'In the Green Man?' said Dalziel. 'But you were away all night, Mr Papworth. Don't the pubs around here ever close?'

'Not so you'd notice,' said Papworth, standing up and making for the door. 'I'd best be getting to work.'

Bertie stood aside to let him by, but Dalziel blocked his path.

'You're not telling me you were boozing all night,' he said incredulously.

Pappy grinned slyly.

'Not *all* night,' he said. 'These are long nights for a country woman if her man's away. They like a bit of company. You ought to try it, Mr Dalziel. Have another look round my room if you want to.'

He squeezed past Dalziel and went out. Bertie followed and closed the door behind him, leaving Dalziel in the fuggy room.

Dalziel wrinkled his nose in distaste as he considered what the man had said. With typical economy he found a word to cover both experiences.

'Chickenshit,' he said.

15

Pictures of Innocence

As Dalziel began to climb the stairs, Tillotson appeared on the landing and stood there looking down at him like a young hero ready to oppose the rising of the Creature from the Black Lagoon.

'You got him to bed?' asked Dalziel.

'Yes. He woke up a bit and started to sing.'

'That's bad. Has he got a bucket?'

'Sorry?'

'A jerry. A piss pot. Something to spew into. When they wake up and start singing it usually means they'll be honking their rings eventually.'

'You're jolly expert,' said Tillotson.

'I should be. I've bedded plenty of drunks in my time.'

'An interesting taste,' said Tillotson. 'Mrs Fielding was asking whether you were back. She's in her room and would like to see you.'

'Right,' said Dalziel. 'I won't be a moment. You going out to help tidy up?'

'What for?'

'Well, after the flood. Make the place look nice and please the customers. You ought to be protecting your investment, son. How are the builders getting on?'

'Oh, pretty well, I suppose.'

'Good. It looks as if you were right after all,' said Dalziel heartily. 'The place'll open on time.'

Tillotson shrugged.

'I suppose so,' he said and made his way downstairs looking disconsolate.

What's up with him? wondered Dalziel. Another row with Louisa or is he just unhappy about all those lovely birds they won't let him shoot?

He put the youth out of his mind and proceeded quietly upstairs. The interview with Bonnie would have to wait a while longer. There was something else to do first. While everything he knew pointed in one direction, it was always best to cross check thoroughly.

Uniff's studio was in darkness and it took him a moment or two to find the light switch. The blinds were down over the windows, double and tight-fitting to exclude all daylight. Uniff must have been working in here recently.

Dalziel moved lightly across the room to the rostrum camera. He examined it as closely as possible without touching it. If he respected anything it was expertise and he had no desire to do anything which might spoil the set-up. In the end, however, he had to undo a couple of clamps and twist the camera upwards to see what he was looking for.

A line of polished brightness in the dull metal of the base-plate.

He made no attempt to return the camera to its former position but wandered around the room whistling tunelessly to himself. He stopped before the old fireplace and knelt down. Something had been burnt here recently. He let the ashes flutter through his fingers, then with a grunt of effort pushed himself upright.

Next he made for the open shelf unit which stood between the windows. There were four large buff envelopes on one of the shelves, three with photographs in them, the fourth empty. He examined the prints in each envelope with interest. Most of the pictures in the first seemed to have been taken in and around Lake House. In some of them a man appeared whom he did not know, but there were sufficient of Hereward Fielding's features in the smiling self-confident face to make him sure this was the dear departed Conrad.

The second envelope contained shots of the funeral, the coffin being mounted on the punt, the watery cortège, misty and ghostlike in the rain-soaked atmosphere; and then one of a solid but sinister figure standing at the end of a half-submerged bridge and gazing impassively over a waste of waters. It was quite a shock to recognize himself.

Pictures taken at the funeral came next. No wonder the poor sodding vicar had got annoyed! The variety of shots and angles indicated that Uniff must have been hopping around like a blue-arsed flea. Dalziel laughed quietly at the thought and looked in the next envelope.

The mood changed though the sequence was maintained. Tillotson falling into the water; Dalziel, full of wrath, preventing him from getting back into the punt; Dalziel examining his dripping suitcase. The man had a flair, there was no denying it, thought Dalziel sourly. Then came the shots taken at the Gumbelow presentation. As a record of the progressive effects of alcohol, they were superb. But their interest to Dalziel was of another kind. He examined them closely and when he had finished was still not quite sure what he had seen.

Finally he picked up the fourth envelope and checked to make sure it was empty. It was. But when he turned to go, the room no longer was.

Mavis Uniff stood by the door watching him curiously. She was so still that she gave the impression that she might have been there all along and Dalziel had to re-run his actions on first entering to convince himself she hadn't been.

'Hello,' he said. 'I was looking for your brother.'

'He's down by the lake,' she said. 'Can I help?'

'No. Nothing really. He showed me some photographs this morning.' He held up the empty envelope.

'Yes. The ones of me.'

'Oh no,' said Dalziel. 'These were – well . . .'

'Me,' she said calmly. 'In close-up.'

'Jesus Christ,' said Dalziel. 'You mean you've got a tattoo?'

'No. But we use transfers. The skin-mags like a gimmick. That's all it is, Mr Dalziel. A commercial proposition. Nothing incestuous.'

Dalziel looked at her and shook his head.

'Shocked, Mr Dalziel?' she said. She was as impassive as ever, but observing him very closely.

'Hardly. Surprised a bit. Where are the photos?'

'Burnt,' she said, pointing to the fireplace.

'Why's that?'

'Hank got worried, thought you might remember your civic duty and speak to the local police. It didn't seem worth having a confrontation about a few pictures, not when he can replace them any time. So to be safe, he burnt them.'

'I told him they didn't bother me,' said Dalziel.

'Yes, I know. Seems you changed your mind.'

She turned and left. By the time Dalziel reached the door, turned out the light and stepped into the corridor, she had disappeared.

Quickly he ran downstairs and into Herrie's sitting-room where the telephone was. Balderstone and Cross were planning to leave for Lake House in another fifteen minutes.

'Make it a bit longer,' suggested Dalziel. 'I've got things to do. Oh, and there's something else you can find out for me.'

Before he went back upstairs he looked out of the window. Bertie, Uniff, Papworth and Mavis were standing in a little group, talking earnestly together.

Tillotson was sitting alone in the duck punt gazing over the still-swollen waters of the lake.

Grinning broadly, Dalziel climbed the stairs once more and knocked on Bonnie's door. There was a long pause, then, 'Come in,' she called.

She was sitting in front of her dressing-table as if she had not moved since he left her there that morning.

'Sorry I'm late,' he said.

She smiled at him, a cautious tentative smile, not the full beam.

'All alone?' he said.

'Till we get some things sorted,' she said.

'I'm all for that.'

He took his jacket off and laid it on the bed.

'Do you mind?' he asked.

She looked at his broad khaki braces with wry amusement and shook her head.

'Right,' he said, sitting on the bed and beginning a complicated two-handed scratch down the line of his braces. 'Sort away.'

'Andy,' she said. 'There's something going on here I don't know about.'

Dalziel grunted in disbelief.

'They must be doing it underground then,' he said. She ignored him.

'I'll tell you what I know if you tell me what you know.'

'Do we spin a coin for first off?' he asked.

'No. If you agree, I'll trust you,' she answered. 'I'll start.'

Dalziel held two fingers up, like a gun.

'On your mark,' he said. 'Bang.'

'It's hard to know where to begin,' she said. 'It's all so mixed up. Listen. This theft business. I suppose you know all the stuff's been accounted for? Well, they wanted you out of the way this morning to sort things out.'

'Who's *they*?'

'I'm not sure. Bertie certainly. Herrie said he wanted to go into town to arrange about the money and naturally I offered to take him. But Bertie said no. It had to be you. He rang the garage later, you know, and asked them to deliver your car. He wants rid of you altogether.'

'I'd noticed,' said Dalziel. He arranged the pillows as a back rest and stretched himself out on the bed. The brandy fumes were rubbing like a cat against the inside of his eyeballs and sleep would be easy.

'But why, Andy? I can't get any sense out of him.'

'Perhaps he doesn't like my after-shave lotion,' yawned Dalziel.

'No! I mean what's going on? Has there or has there not been a robbery? Where's Mrs Greave?'

'Questions, questions,' murmured Dalziel, his eyes half closed. 'You've told me nowt and already you're asking questions. Tell me this, why'd the old man change his mind?'

'I don't know. Family loyalty; God knows. Herrie's mind doesn't work like other people's.'

'Oh aye. He's a poet. Some folk used to think that was a defence in law. Like being daft. It's a lot like being daft, isn't it? I mean, if you're wise enough not to put cash into a half-baked business scheme when it's got some faint chance of succeeding, you've got to be daft to put it in just after a robbery's removed most of the visible assets. Don't you agree?'

'Why the hell didn't you ask Herrie yourself?' demanded Bonnie. 'You're his big mate at the moment.'

'Oh, I did, I did,' said Dalziel. 'But he's very close. Talks a lot but says nowt. That's what comes of being a poet. Tell you what I think, though.'

'What?'

'Come and sit beside me,' said Dalziel, patting the bed. 'Don't want to risk being overheard.'

Bonnie glanced uneasily round the room then brought her chair close to the bedside.

'This'll do,' she said in a low voice. 'You ought to get one thing straight in your mind, Andy. I bed down for pleasure, nothing else.'

'Me too,' said Dalziel. 'Here's what I think. I think Herrie must have known that the stolen stuff was going to be returned. And he must have known because someone told him last night. You had a long chat with someone in here last night.'

'So you listen at bedroom doors too!' she said scornfully.

'Only for pleasure,' he said. 'Nothing else. Anyway I heard nowt, just voices. *Did* you tell him?'

'How could I tell him what I didn't know?' she demanded.

'All right. So Herrie came to tell you he'd changed his mind, which means someone else had been talking to him already. What made him change his mind? Two things, I think. One selfish. The poor old sod's shit-scared of dying. He wraps it up in words, but that's the bottom of it. Which is interesting, eh? He thinks there's someone in this house capable of knocking him off.'

'And the other thing?'

Dalziel's eyes were fully closed now. Repose did nothing for his face.

'Unselfish. I've got this lad works for me in Yorkshire. Bright. Got degrees and things. I listen to what he says, pick the pearls out of the pig-crap. He'd say that most people doing something selfish like to find some unselfish reason for doing it. Not that you're going to change your crime figures much by saying things like that! No, but sometimes . . . anyway, what's old Hereward got to be unselfish about? I tell you; one thing only that I've observed.'

'What's that?'

'Nigel.'

Dalziel opened one eye and squinted at Bonnie. 'Why don't you fetch him in?'

He closed his eye again, heard Bonnie rise and

walk across the room, heard the bathroom door open.

When he opened his eyes again, Nigel was standing at the foot of the bed.

'Where's the grapes, son?' asked Dalziel.

'What?'

'You're standing there like a reluctant relative on a sick visit. For Christ's sake, make yourself comfortable.'

The boy came round the bed and sat in the chair vacated by his mother. Bonnie pushed Dalziel's feet aside and sat at the foot of the bed. She opened her mouth to speak but Dalziel shushed her.

'I'll do the talking,' he said. 'You listen. Both of you. I'll be brief. Don't interrupt. This whole project was never a serious attempt to get a restaurant going. At least not on your dad's part, Nigel. I mean, think about it! A medieval Banqueting Hall! Did you ever hear of owt so daft! So what was going on? I'll tell you. Bertie came home from Liverpool one fine day with a bright scheme for burning this place down and picking up the insurance. Only, it had to be a bit more complicated than that. To really collect you need something worth insuring, not just a tatty old house.

'He'd got a taste for this when he was in Liverpool and he was dealing with Uniff's bit of fire trouble. They recognized fellow spirits and came to an arrangement by which Uniff claimed for ten times more stuff than got damaged. It was so easy, they reckoned they could make a good living out of it.

'So they work out this scheme. It's ingenious. Launch what looks like a genuine business venture, so you're insuring not only a building which has rocketed in value since it got refurbished, but also the business itself. I haven't seen the policy yet, but I gather they're covered for six months' loss of estimated profits. Plus, of course, a little bonus. You're covered for all fittings, furnishings, stock etc. But why burn it? Why can't it, like Uniff's equipment, just be moved elsewhere? Resold later? I wondered why anyone should want to store all that junk I found. But I soon caught on. If you're going to claim for expensive reproduction furniture and hangings, not to mention costumes, you need lots of ash of the right kind. It's a grand scheme. Really grand.'

Dalziel shook his head in reluctant admiration. Bonnie let out an incredulous sigh.

'I don't believe it,' she said. 'I don't believe it.'

Dalziel put on his favourite-uncle look and reached across to pat her knee with one hand while with the other he squeezed Nigel's arm reassuringly.

'I know it's hard,' he said. 'I'm sorry. They didn't tell you; knew it would be no good. You wouldn't have gone for anything like that. Aye, the criminal mind recognizes honesty when it sees it.'

Bonnie looked at him sharply but his expression matched his tone of vibrant sincerity.

'No, I reckon that in on the deal were Bertie and his father, the Uniffs, and Mrs Greave and Papworth, of course.'

'Why Mrs Greave?'

'Obvious. You wanted to take on someone who'd look after the skivvying behind the scenes. They couldn't risk you getting hold of some nice ordinary kitchen manager who'd spot something funny was going on right off. So they brought in Mrs Greave. As Papworth's recently widowed daughter, she wouldn't be asked for references, that kind of thing. And she was very useful to have around. No doubt she and Papworth were going to start things burning while the rest of you were giving each other nice alibis a good distance away. A big fire like this, you see, they'd look very closely at it. That's where your husband came in.'

'How?'

'Well the REME's one branch of the Army where they let officers know things. With his electrical know-how, it must have seemed a good idea to have some kind of electrical fault causing the fire. Now in an old place like that, especially an old stables, you must have had a lot of rats. Stands to reason. Right then. A big hungry rat comes along, sees some nice new wire, decides to have a chew. What happens? It sinks its teeth in, gets electrocuted and sets up a short. I won't get technical, because I know bugger all about it, but it's possible. It has happened. A little glow becomes a big fire. When the fire-investigation officer has a

248

look, what does he find? Well, the charred remains of a rat for one thing. And if there's enough left to do any tests on, he finds it's been electrocuted. Problem solved. Insurance coughs up. Everyone's happy.'

'How do you know all this, Andy?' asked Bonnie quietly.

'I'm guessing. But it seems likely unless Mrs Greave kept frozen rats in your fridge to make pies with. Frozen *electrocuted* rats.'

'What happened to Mrs Greave.'

'Simple,' said Dalziel cheerfully. 'She spotted me right off. Didn't need to search my pockets. Her kind know a bobby when they see one. So she got cold feet in the end and took off. She was scared that Bertie and Uniff might still go ahead even with me around. She wanted no part of it, so off she went to sell her wares down Lime Street again.'

Nigel shifted in his chair and Dalziel looked at him thoughtfully.

'Of course, if you suspected some of this, it might explain why you decided to run away, lad,' he said. 'You're a puzzle to me, I must admit.'

'I just wanted to be by myself,' said the boy unconvincingly.

'Like Garbo,' guffawed Dalziel. The boy flushed and began to stand but the big hand caught hold of his arm again, not reassuringly this time, but like a clamp.

'Sit still, lad. Visiting time's not up yet. I've not finished my story. You see, everything was fixed

249

to go ahead. All that was needed was to get at the wiring and plant the rat. So first they got the workmen out of the way. Someone, the Uniff girl I think, rang Gibb and said there was no money in the kitty. Gibb remarked how badly Conrad conducted the interview, not his usual persuasive self at all. You see, he wanted the workmen out of the way so he could work at his leisure. And also having Gibb off the job gave him the excuse for carrying on himself so that no one, i.e. you, or Herrie, or Louisa or even Charley Tillotson, would be surprised to find him up a ladder with a drill. But then he did something very silly which spoilt everything.'

'Yes,' said Bonnie.

'He had his accident and got killed. Jesus! I bet that upset everybody. Careful, son!'

He spoke sharply to Nigel who had forced himself upright and glowered threateningly down at the recumbent policeman.

'Never hit a man when he's down,' advised Dalziel. 'Not unless you can hit him so hard, he'll stay down. Stand if you want, but don't go away.'

'Why are you doing this, Andy?' asked Bonnie.

'Because he's got as much right as you have to know what his dad was up to. Frankly I don't think either of you find it too hard to believe. He sounds a likely lad, does old Conrad. But it's better you hear about it now, straight, than that you get it through some roundabout questioning later on.'

'Questioning? Who from?' asked Bonnie. 'You

mean that the police can still do something about it, even though nothing happened?'

'Mebbe,' said Dalziel grimly. 'There's a thing called conspiracy. Hard to prove if people keep their mouths shut. Me, I reckon that Bertie's got sense enough to try to cut his losses and actually make a go of the business. I think that's the other reason Herrie has decided to invest his money. I don't know how much he knew, but he must have had a shrewd idea of what his son was like. But then so must you.'

He eyed Bonnie thoughtfully for a moment before going on.

'Anyway, now the only way of protecting the investment and protecting your and Nigel's interests is to make a go of things. I don't know if it's possible but it looks as if they're going to have a try. I just want to be sure there aren't any fires around here in a couple of months' time when everybody's forgotten I ever existed. Well, that's it.'

He made to rise from the bed, but Bonnie restrained him.

'You run along, Nigel,' she said to her son. 'There are one or two things Mr Dalziel and I have to talk about.'

The boy rose and left without speaking.

'He looks as if he could do with two good nights' sleep,' commented Dalziel.

'Couldn't we all?' said Bonnie. 'Andy, why are you doing this?'

'Doing what? I'm doing nowt except having a private chat.'

'Private chat nothing! You know damn well Bertie will screw everything you've said out of Nigel in ten minutes flat. And if he didn't talk, well, I'd have to.'

'That's honest,' said Dalziel. He eased his braces off his shoulders, settled back on the pillow and inserting his hand into his shirt began to scratch his belly. Impatiently she snatched his hand away. He opened one eye and looked at her. With a sigh she leaned forward so that her head rested on his chest, pulled his shirt out of his waistband and began to scratch for him.

'Oh Andy,' she said. 'What are you up to?'

'What do you mean?'

'Well, you're a policeman, and I think you believe in it. But you seem to be giving us a warning.'

'I'm on holiday,' he said. 'A little bit to the left. That's grand.'

'Well,' she said dubiously. 'I suppose there's a bit of the Sydney Cartons even in the nastiest, most cynical of us.'

'Of the what?'

'Oh, do stop pretending to be pig-ignorant! Yes, I suppose one generous, unselfish act might squeeze even you into heaven.'

'I'm at it all the time,' protested Dalziel. 'Farther down please. Ah!'

She kneaded away at his flesh with strong fingers.

'Oh Andy,' she said. 'I need someone to trust and rely on. I really do. I'm tired of trying to hold things together single-handed.'

Dalziel reached over her shoulder and cupped her right breast in his broad palm.

'Why don't you take two hands to it?' he asked.

Forty-five minutes later after a perfunctory tap on the door, Tillotson burst in and halted, red with embarrassment, when he saw the two heads on the pillow.

'What is it, Charley?' asked Bonnie in an exasperated tone.

'I'm sorry,' said Tillotson, retreating. 'It's just that the police are here again. They want to see everyone. They say that Mrs Greave is dead.'

He left and Bonnie poked Dalziel hard with her forefinger.

'You knew about this?'

'Aye,' he said, sitting up and yawning.

She watched him in silence as he got out of bed and began to dress.

'Listen, love,' he said as he peered in the mirror and dragged her silver-backed brush through his greying and retreating stubble. 'It's no good lying there looking suspicious. My shoulders are no good as public leaning posts. I either carry you or I drop you. Partnership means doing things my way.'

She laughed at this, realized he hadn't intended a joke, frowned, then flung back the sheets and jumped out of bed.

The brush paused in mid-stroke as Dalziel regarded her in the mirror.

'All right,' she said. 'You're the boss. Lead on, Sydney. Even if we are travelling by tumbril.'

16

Dead Ducks

After a brief preliminary consultation Dalziel kept very much in the background as Balderstone and Cross worked their way steadily through everyone in the household, taking statements about the events of the previous day with particular reference to conversations with and last sightings of Annie Greave.

Papworth excited particular interest, of course, but even old Hereward was fed with black coffee and interviewed in his own bed. Dalziel meanwhile wandered outside to see how Gibb and his men were getting on. The progress they had made was not perceptible to the inexpert eye, but the little builder assured him that all was proceeding to schedule.

Dalziel continued his perambulation, returning eventually to the front of the house where he stood looking out over the lake. It really wasn't much of a lake, he realized, now that the sinking of the flood waters was making its normal limits much more clear. Not your Windermere or your Loch Lomond. But it might be a useful adjunct to the restaurant if you knew how to exploit it. A floating bar perhaps. Or gondolas.

He laughed to himself. It would be easy to start thinking in the nutty fashion of the Lake Housers.

Suddenly a dull explosion shattered his thoughts. Birds screamed and rose from the trees and the lake. But a couple did not rise and lay instead staining the water with dye as bright as their bills.

From behind the small island which Dalziel had examined for signs of Nigel only two days ago emerged the duck punt. The gun in the bows was still smoking and Tillotson waved triumphantly when he saw he had a spectator.

'Great,' said a voice behind Dalziel. 'Roast duck stuffed with lead for supper.'

'The buggers'll sink before he reaches them,' said Dalziel.

'You were looking for me earlier,' said Uniff.

'Not really,' said Dalziel. 'I was just poking round your room.'

'Hey, man,' said Uniff, grinning through his tangled beard. 'You're too honest to be honest. What'd you find?'

'Tell you what I didn't find. I didn't find a serial number on your camera and I didn't find those dirty pictures you showed me.'

'Dirty? Those weren't dirty! Man, I could show you pictures that would blow your mind!'

'I doubt it. Your sister said she posed for 'em. She's a liar.'

Suddenly Uniff drew himself upright, placed his left hand on his hip and thrust the other forward as if holding a sword.

'Call my sister a liar, sir? Zounds, you besmirch our family honour. On guard!'

The change of accent was very good, rather better on the whole than his American.

'I got Sergeant Cross to check with Epping,' said Dalziel. 'Annie Greave had that tattoo on her inner thigh.'

'Ain't you the clever one,' said Uniff, reverting. 'So what?'

'So why did Mavis lie?' said Dalziel. 'You know the question I'm really asking myself, Mr Uniff? Why did you get so worried after you'd shown me those pictures?'

'Like I said, you're the law.'

'Never forget it. No. Two answers are possible. One: you were worried in case Annie blabbed when we picked her up. If you and Bertie were forced into a position of your word against hers, it wouldn't help matters if it could be shown that you knew her well enough to use as a model. So get rid of all the photos. Two: if you knew Annie was lying like one of the babes in the wood all cold under a pile of leaves, then you'd be even less keen to let me find a connection.'

'What're you trying to say, friend?' asked Uniff uneasily.

'I'm not your friend, friend,' said Dalziel. 'And you don't need an interpreter. Now, I don't know what time you went missing from the little party last night, but I do know what time you got back. Empty roads, fast car. You could get to Epping and back in five hours easy.'

'I told you, I was drinking after hours,' said Uniff.

'That's what they all say round here,' mocked Dalziel. 'I'll tell you something else for nothing, seeing as this is one of my helpful days. You can file, file away at a number stamped in metal; we've got machines in our labs that'll bring it up like a chicken pox.'

'Man, I'm shaking,' said Uniff. 'What's it to be – the rubber truncheon or the water torture?'

He sounded quite recovered from his momentary uneasiness.

'Tell you what,' said Dalziel thoughtfully. 'I think I understand you. You really do think that money's just a game.'

'No. An evil,' said Uniff.

'Oh aye. But you need it.'

'Yeah. *That's* a game. Getting it, spending it. But I don't like the game so I won't play to the rules.'

'You'll commit crimes?'

'Not against people. Just the money system,' said Uniff. 'Look, man, money's immoral, right? Then all activities aimed at getting hold of money are immoral, right? Your pay-cheque at the end of the month is just as immoral as . . . as . . .'

'As defrauding an insurance company,' suggested Dalziel.

'Nice example, Andy,' grinned Uniff. 'That's about the strength of it.'

'So when I suggest you're crooked with money, all I get from you is a laugh. But when I suggest you might have something to do with Annie Greave's death, you begin to shake.'

'Hurting people's something else,' said Uniff seriously. 'You gotta see that. Humanity makes me shake.'

'Is that it? Or guilt?'

Suddenly their conversation was interrupted by two sodden, bleeding birds thrust between them by Charley Tillotson.

'You two look very serious,' he said cheerfully.

'Not as serious as those things,' said Uniff. 'I thought Bonnie said no shooting.'

'Yes. I believe she did. But she didn't seem to mind when I gave her a couple earlier for dinner. There's plenty to spare just at the moment with the flooding. Think of what it must have been like in the old days.'

'You need a licence for that thing,' warned Dalziel.

'Do I really?' asked Tillotson. 'Well, Bonnie might have one. It's her gun, after all. I'll go and ask her.'

'Have you made your statement?' asked Dalziel.

'Oh yes. First in,' said Tillotson proudly.

He went into the house dripping blood and water.

Dalziel turned to follow him, but Uniff placed a restraining hand on his arm.

'Would you answer me a question for a change, Andy?'

'Mebbe.'

'Well, man; like, you keep on dropping hints and making threatening noises, but I just had a little talk with the prodigal son and what he said made you sound more like a mother hen than an avenging angel. This fire business, which is all fantasy, you dig, I mean I admit nothing, but if that's what you believe, then shouldn't we all be down at headquarters having our fingernails pulled out? What's the name of the game, man? Or can I guess?'

Dalziel didn't answer, but turned away and went back into the house.

Behind him Uniff laughed provocatively but Dalziel ignored him. Very soon, he was beginning to realize, he would have to make a decision. In fact he supposed that already that afternoon he'd taken very definite steps towards making it. At the moment he could examine his professional conscience and find it pretty clear if you ignored those small shifting misty areas which always swirled around on the periphery. What he knew to be relevant he had passed on to Balderstone and Cross. And what he merely suspected to be relevant he had not yet consciously decided to withhold.

Ideally Balderstone and Cross should sort things out for themselves without reference to his own special knowledge gained as a guest in this house. Yet they felt, as he would do in their shoes, entitled to share this knowledge. The only way to remove himself from this pernicious position was indeed to remove himself and that might be as painful as remaining.

The interviewing had taken place as nearly all semi-formal activities seemed to in this house in Herrie's sitting-room. At least with the old man sleeping the sleep of the stoned upstairs, there should have been no indignant outbursts.

He met Nigel coming out of the door.

'All right?' said Dalziel genially.

The boy said nothing but looked at him with an expression which might have been accusation or fear. As he moved on, Dalziel watched him with a troubled mind.

Inside Cross and Balderstone sat drinking tea. Bonnie must have made it, thought Dalziel with absurd possessive pride. She was the only one in the house who would even have considered making the policemen comfortable.

'Finished?' asked Dalziel, looking at the pile of statement forms which lay on the table by the teapot.

'Yes, sir,' said Balderstone.

'Except for one,' said Dalziel.

'What?'

'Mine.' He produced from his inside pocket a

foolscap sheet folded in quarters and placed it with the others.

'I was here too, don't forget.'

'We hadn't forgotten, sir,' said Balderstone.

'Tell me then. What's new?'

'Well, nothing much, sir,' said Cross. 'As far as we can make out, Annie Greave was last seen about the place at two-thirty yesterday afternoon. It was Mrs Fielding that saw her. That was just before the presentation ceremony. So any time after that she could have packed up and gone. We've checked with taxi services, bus and train ticket offices, but no joy yet. She could have been picked up by a passing motorist, of course.'

'Passing where?' asked Balderstone. 'The road past the gate runs between Low Fold and High Fold and it's still under a foot of water most of the way.'

'Yes, sir,' said Cross. 'So either she walked to Low Fold and got a bus there, which no one recalls. Or she was given a lift by someone in the house though no one admits it. Now this could have been just before the ceremony . . .'

'No,' interrupted Dalziel. 'I was walking back from the village between two-fifteen and two-forty-five and no cars passed me coming from the house. And everyone was gathered in this room when I got back.'

'Except Papworth,' said Cross reprovingly. 'But the rest were here till the drinking started. No one's so sure who was where doing what from about four o'clock on.'

Dalziel felt they were both regarding him significantly. His shoulders rose in a small non-typical Gallic shrug.

'The thing is,' said Balderstone, 'no one would surely be much bothered by admitting they'd given her a lift and just dropped her in Orburn, say, or even farther afield. So I think we've got to accept that nobody did this. Which raises the much more important question. Could anyone have taken her all the way to Epping, either dead or alive, and got back here within the known period of their absence? The answer is, only two. Papworth and Uniff. Now they're both vague enough to be suspicious. Uniff won't give us the name of the pub he claims he was drinking in after hours and Papworth won't give us the name of the woman he claims he was rogering. They both have highly developed senses of honour, it seems. Well, I've tried to avoid waving the big stick . . .'

'Why?' interrupted Dalziel. 'They shouldn't give us big sticks if they don't want us to wave 'em. Any road, that's up to you. I tell you this, though, on my patch we wouldn't need to ask. We'd know the pub and we'd know the woman.'

Cross and Balderstone exchanged glances in the face of this large and unmannerly claim. Dalziel glowered at them, recognizing in himself a desire to fall out with them and then let ill-temper cut the ties of co-operation.

'Of course, we're approaching it from that side

too, sir,' said Balderstone calmly. 'Now, the other possibility, and this looms very large in view of the statements we have received, is that Mrs Greave left with one of the visitors.'

'Visitors?'

'The people here for the presentation. You can't recall when any of them left, sir?'

'No,' said Dalziel, shaking his huge head slowly. 'They'd all gone, except Arkwright, when I came back downstairs.'

'After your ... discussion with Mrs Fielding,' said Balderstone, glancing at Dalziel's statement. 'It's a pity, but they all seem to have got away fairly quietly. Lots of cheeriohs inside the house, but no one seems to have escorted them to the door.'

'Do you know *where* they went?' asked Dalziel.

'Your own surmise, London, seems very likely. But we've passed on the information to Epping and no doubt they will be checking down there. Well, I think we've done all we can here and it's getting on.'

He began to gather up the sheets of paper from the table. Dalziel glanced at his watch. It was after six.

'By the way, sir,' said Balderstone, 'Mr Albert Fielding while we were talking to him made enquiries about the procedure for bringing a complaint against a police officer.'

'What did you do to him? Forget to kiss his arse?' asked Dalziel.

'No, sir. The complaint, I gathered, was aimed at you.'

'*What!*'

'He seemed to think that certain insinuations you made in the presence of his young brother, Nigel, were slanderous. I indicated that as you were not here in an official capacity, he would be best advised to seek redress through a civil action, when the police, I assured him, would investigate the alleged offences thoroughly. This seemed to quieten him down.'

'The puffed-up nowt!' said Dalziel. 'He needs to be locked up for a few months.'

'Perhaps. But it seems unlikely now. Conspiracy is very difficult to prove, especially when the conspirators are forewarned.' His voice was studiedly neutral.

'It would never have stuck,' said Dalziel.

'You're probably right,' agreed Balderstone. 'This boy Nigel puzzled me a bit, though. The one you talked to.'

'Yes?'

'Well, we just had him in as a matter of form. So we could say we'd seen everyone in the house. His mother had told us he just came back this morning. That struck me as odd. He's how old? Fifteen? Sixteen? And she hadn't been much bothered when he ran away. Strange, even in this day and age.'

'He'd done it before,' said Dalziel. 'And he did ring.'

As though on a cue the telephone rang and Dalziel grabbed it. It was the uniformed sergeant at Orburn Police Station wanting to talk to Cross. Balderstone and Dalziel moved across into the window bay to avoid disturbing him.

'The lad seemed very disturbed by it all,' continued the inspector.

'He's very young,' offered Dalziel. 'I suppose from his point of view, Annie Greave was almost one of the family. And he still hasn't got over his dad's death.'

'You're probably right,' said Balderstone. 'It can't have helped for him to hear you saying what you thought his father had been up to either.'

'No,' said Dalziel. 'An error of judgement, that. I'm sorry.'

'There's been a sight too much death about this house,' said Balderstone. 'Mr Fielding, Mrs Greave. And Spinx, of course. We found his car by the way. When he came through the gates he turned right and ran it down through the trees to the lake edge. A good spot to hide. You haven't picked up any hint of what he was after, have you?'

'No. Everyone seemed baffled. Probably he was just trying a last desperate snoop before reporting failure.'

'It was his last, sure enough,' said Balderstone. 'Tell me, sir, you said you'd leave it to us to break the news of Annie Greave's murder so you could have a chat with the people here before they knew about it. Did anything come out of this?'

'Not really,' admitted Dalziel, thinking guiltily of how he had spent a great deal of his time since getting back to the house. 'I had a good go at Papworth, but got nowhere. He says he picked Annie up one night in the Pool, struck up a regular liaison with her and brought her out here when the chance presented itself.'

'It's possible, I suppose,' said Balderstone. 'When they're getting on a bit, some of these girls fancy a steady relationship even if it means a cut back in pay. But not out here, I shouldn't have thought. You indicated to Sergeant Cross that you were pretty certain Papworth was knocking her off, though.'

'Yes, I did,' agreed Dalziel. Another prevarication.

'So there might be something in it. What about connecting the others with her?'

'I think there's a chance Uniff might have been using her as a model for some candid camera shots. Hard to prove, though. Liverpool CID might be able to establish a connection, but what would it prove?'

'I don't really know, sir,' said Balderstone blankly. 'So no one said anything which suggested a foreknowledge of Mrs Greave's death.'

Dalziel shook his head. He could do this quite honestly.

Cross put the telephone down and joined them in the bay, shooting a quick glance at Balderstone. It seemed to Dalziel that the inspector nodded almost imperceptibly as though indicating to the sergeant that it was all right to go ahead. If true, this both piqued and alarmed him.

'They've been on from Essex again,' he said. 'Trying to baffle us with speed, I reckon. But fair dues, they've done well, or the Met has. They found the Yanks at Claridge's and seem pretty convinced they're in the clear. Penitent, the BBC man, they got hold of also. He started talking about his civic rights a bit quick, but in the end they were sure he hadn't seen Annie Greave.'

'Pity,' said Dalziel, feeling much more disappointed than the single word showed. He was surprised to find how much he wanted Annie to have been seen alive and well and a long way from Lake House.

'You fancied him?' asked Balderstone.

'He was alone.'

'No, he wasn't,' interrupted Cross. 'I think that's what bothered him. It turns out that he gave a Miss Nicola Sugden a lift back . . .'

'Who?' asked Balderstone.

'The lass in the green tunic!' said Dalziel. 'The photographer.'

'That's her,' said Cross. 'And she seems to have spent the night in Penitent's flat. His wife and two kids arrived home from a visit half-way through the interview.'

'No wonder he abandoned poor Arkwright!' said Dalziel. 'That means Butt was by himself.'

'Yes, sir,' said Cross, looking at his notebook.

'They contacted the paper he was doing the feature for and got his address. It's in Chigwell, Essex, only five or six miles from Epping.'

Dalziel began to scratch his ankle, bending forward to conceal the relief on his face.

'Butt,' he said. 'Nasty bastard. I'd have said touching up typists on the Underground was his limit but you can never tell.'

'We mustn't jump to conclusions, sir,' said Balderstone in a tone of admonition too mild to be insubordinate. 'What did Mr Butt have to say for himself, Sergeant?'

'Nothing, sir,' said Cross. 'They couldn't get hold of him. It seems he flew out to Brazil first thing this morning. On an assignment. They checked, of course, and it's genuine.'

'Damn!' said Dalziel. 'Yes, he was going on about it yesterday. You'd have thought it was a royal visit. Here, what about his car?'

'Yes, they thought of that as well, sir,' said Cross. 'It was parked at the airport. They opened it up, had a good look. In the boot they found an old travelling rug. On it were traces of make-up, some hairs and a small patch of blood. They're doing tests on them, of course. Also in the boot was a small spade, the kind of thing motorists sometimes have in case of heavy snow. This one had traces of fresh earth on the blade. They're cross-checking that too.'

'It sounds promising,' said Balderstone. 'When's he come back?'

'He has a return flight booked for a week on Saturday,' said Cross. 'But they won't wait that long, will they?'

Dalziel shrugged.

'I don't know. They won't want to alarm him. There's no extradition treaty with Brazil, remember. And after that balls-up with Biggs, everyone will be treading very carefully.'

'In any case,' added Balderstone, 'they haven't finished their tests yet. Mind you, it would all fit very nicely. Very nicely indeed. Now we must be off, Sergeant. Mr Dalziel will be wanting his dinner. Goodbye, sir. We'll keep in touch.'

Dalziel walked with them to the front door and watched them drive away with much unprofessional relief. When he turned to re-enter the house, Bertie was standing there.

'All right, Dalziel,' he said. 'You've got your car back now, so there's nothing to stop you following your friends.'

Dalziel pushed by him with enough force to make the stout youth stagger. He made for the kitchen, followed closely by Bertie who talked incessantly.

'This isn't a fascist state, Dalziel. You can't go around bullying people and slandering them without being made to pay for it. Just shove off, get out of our lives, go and decompose somewhere else.'

They were all in the kitchen except Hereward. There was a smell of roast duck in the air and Louisa was setting the table.

'Have they gone?' asked Bonnie.

'Yes, just,' said Dalziel. 'They asked me to say cheerioh and thank you for the tea.'

'How frightfully polite,' mocked Uniff.

'Wasn't it?' agreed Dalziel. 'More than I can say for laughing boy here.'

He sat down and smiled at Louisa.

'Don't forget to lay a place for me.'

Bonnie looked coldly at Bertie.

'What have you been saying?'

'I told him he'd outstayed his welcome. His car's back on the road and there's nothing to keep him here. There's enough to bother us without having to lock our doors because we've let a nasty creeping spy into the house.'

'He's right, you know, Andy baby,' said Uniff. 'Nothing personal, but, hell, we'd be crazy to keep you.'

'Wait a minute!' interjected Louisa. 'Who's giving orders? Let me remind you whose house you're in. If anyone decides who goes, who stays, it's Bonnie and me.'

'And what do *you* say, love?' asked Dalziel.

'I'm not sure.'

'Well, while you're deciding, shall we eat?' asked Dalziel.

He almost fell out of his chair as Bertie seized it from behind and pulled.

'To hell with this!' cried the stout youth. 'Just get packed, Dalziel, and get out.'

'Quieten down, lad,' said Dalziel soothingly. 'It's

271

ill-mannered to talk like that to a guest. It's down-right stupid to talk that way to a business associate.'

Something in his voice quenched Bertie's wrath. 'What do you mean?' he asked uneasily.

'What I say,' Dalziel said. 'Earlier this afternoon I accepted your chairman's invitation to invest a couple of thousand of my hard-earned savings in your business. Ask your mam. So you're no longer just my friends, you're my colleagues. And I'll tell you what, Bertie. I'll be worth my weight in fire insurance.'

No one spoke for a moment, then Uniff began to laugh.

'Bonnie!' cried Bertie. 'It's not true?'

Slowly his mother nodded.

'Right,' said Dalziel, seizing a knife and fork and holding them in clenched hands. 'Madam Chairman, if the meeting has been called to order I think I'm ready for item number one.'

17

Opening Night

It is a truth universally acknowledged by all married men that their wives are rational, understanding, submissive and amiable only in proportion as they are distanced from their mothers.

'For God's sake, Ellie,' protested Peter Pascoe. 'We've only called in to pick up the presents. It's Saturday. I start work on Monday. I need all of tomorrow to get myself organized!'

'We can still be home by mid-morning,' said Ellie firmly. 'If you keep off the booze, that is. Which might not be a bad thing.'

'What's that mean?'

'Well,' said Ellie maliciously, 'that was a nasty case of brewer's droop you caught last Tuesday. I understood CID men were immune. You'll be back in uniform if you're not careful.'

'It was that southern beer,' protested Pascoe, grinning. 'That's why I want to get home really. Surely they'd understand?'

'No,' said Ellie. 'Mum and Dad have gone to

a lot of bother. Just look at the way they've done up this bedroom. As for tonight, the table's booked and it's not been cheap, I can tell you. They're not all that well off and I'm not going to let their efforts be wasted. So resign yourself to it. And let's go downstairs before they start worrying. In my family decent folk don't screw in the afternoon.'

'All right,' sighed Pascoe. 'They said it would be like this but I never believed them. You know, I wouldn't mind so much if we were being treated to the best French cuisine in Lincolnshire. But a medieval banquet! Jesus wept!'

It was even more hideous than he anticipated. For a start the car parking was chaotic. A tall blond youth in a see-through tunic and knee-breeches was directing operations with a fine disregard for the laws of space, time and dynamics. Leaving the car was almost as dangerous as remaining in it, but they finally reached the bar where even Ellie's isn't-this-nice expression fractured momentarily when she found they were attached to a gaggle of Townswomen's Guild members, many of whom insisted on dredging up anecdotal treasures from her distant childhood. Fortunately their simultaneity made them mostly incomprehensible.

Pascoe caught Ellie's expression and smiled; and smiled yet again when he saw his father-in-law demand confirmation of the exorbitant prices the striking middle-aged barmaid had charged him for their apéritifs. He suddenly felt that the evening might prove ghastly enough for an objective student of the social sciences to be able to enjoy himself.

Inside the alleged medieval Banqueting Hall, which was more like a parody than an imitation, goodies continued to spill out of the cornucopia. The room was illuminated by electric candles whose dim religious light showed rows of benches and tables set with wooden platters, plastic-handled daggers and goblets made of some alloy so light that, once filled to the brim with unctuous mead, they became dangerously unstable. Which, decided Pascoe after a careful sip, was more than he was likely to do. The diners were packed close on the benches. Pascoe had Ellie's mother on one side and on the other a statuesque townswoman from whose close-pressed thighs he might have derived much harmless pleasure had it not felt strangely corrugated.

From a gallery at the far end of the hall came music vaguely Elizabethan in style, and a girl so slightly built that in the best Elizabethan tradition she might have been a boy was singing about the pleasures of her hey-nonny-nonny-no. The assembled diners, who seemed not to have been much deterred by the price of pre-dinner drinks, joined in the chorus with prurient enthusiasm.

Pascoe leaned over to Ellie who sat opposite.

'I was wrong,' he bellowed. 'I think I shall enjoy this.'

Behind him someone was beating a tin plate and a strangely familiar voice was shouting, 'My lords and ladies, pray be silent for the entry of the first course.'

No one took much notice except Ellie who ignored Pascoe's words and stared over his shoulder with an expression of pantomimic incredulity.

'Peter,' she said. 'You'll never believe this.'

Slowly Pascoe turned. What he saw came as such a shock he had to use the townswoman's thigh as a support.

'My God!' he said.

Standing at the far end of the hall clad in a green velvet gown and wearing a floppy blue cap embellished with a peacock's feather was Detective Superintendent Andrew Dalziel.

Pascoe laughed so much he couldn't drink his Baronial Brose and was still having difficulty by the time he reached the Cavalier's Capon. The townswoman fortunately put this down to her own rib-tickling conversation. Only Ellie understood his amusement, though after an initial outburst she no longer seemed to share it.

'What's he *doing*, Peter?' she asked under cover of an outbreak of screams as some wit, immediately imitated, demonstrated the Tudor method of chicken-bone disposal.

'God knows,' said Pascoe. 'But he hasn't spotted me yet. Here!'

He beckoned to a bearded youth in a jester's out-fit who was going round taking flash photographs at fifty pence a time.

'Right, man. Grab hold of the little lady and smile.'

'No, no. Not me,' said Pascoe. 'I'd like a picture of him. The portly gent in the green nightie.'

'No, Peter!' protested Ellie. But the photographer, after a quizzical raising of the eyebrows, had moved away.

'Andy, baby, you've got fans,' said Uniff.

'What?'

'Guy over there wants a pic. So make with the medieval merriment. Say cheese.'

'Shit,' said Dalziel as he followed the direction indicated by the jerk of Uniff's head.

'What the hell are you doing here?' he growled into Pascoe's ear a couple of minutes later.

'Just having a lot of fun,' grinned Pascoe, on whom the mead was having a greater effect than anticipated.

'It's about time you had a piss,' said Dalziel. He nodded sternly at Ellie and moved away.

'Everything going OK, Andy?' asked Bonnie whom he met outside the door.

'Fine,' he said. 'What are you doing?'

'I just stepped out of the kitchen for a quick drag. It's red hot in there.'

Dalziel could believe it. It was a close, humid night with wreaths of mist rising from the unmov-ing lake.

'Back to it, I suppose,' said Bonnie. She rested her hand on his arm for a moment and raised her face to his. As he kissed her the door to the hall opened and someone came out.

'See you later,' said Bonnie and moved away.

'Hello, hello, hello,' said Pascoe.

'You'd best sober up before you say summat you'll be sorry for,' said Dalziel grimly. 'Let's go outside.'

They stood together in the cobbled yard hardly able to see each other in the dim light which forced its way out of the Banqueting Hall through the stained plastic windows. Noise escaped more successfully and the overall effect was rather like overhearing an orgy in a church. Pascoe took a deep breath and tried to think of something inoffensive to say.

'Having a nice holiday, sir?' was the best he could manage.'

'Grand,' said Dalziel, and then repeated the word with a note of surprise in his voice.

It was in many ways true, he realized. Certainly in this past week he had been almost totally immersed in getting the restaurant into operation. After the initial reaction to his involvement, they had settled down quickly into a remarkably good team. There were various kinds of expertise present in Lake House but what Dalziel had had to offer was momentum. He got things moving and kept them moving, generally by brute force.

The hard work involved served a double function. It distracted his attention from both the past and the future. The Dalziel whose nights were filled with doubt and sorrow had retreated into some limbo with that other Dalziel whose constabulary soul would shortly have to go marching on.

Or perhaps not. He had always been a liver in the present, never one of those who tried to take the golden moment and beat it out thinly to cover more ground. But just as his mind in the past months had gradually started to plague him with visions of vacant futurity, so in these last few days, unbidden and almost undetected, an insidious optimism had begun to rise in his subconscious like curls of mist on the lake. He still woke early but now Bonnie was by his side. As one who had long opined in many a Yorkshire club and pub that there were nowt wrong with most discontented and unhappy women (e.g. all female politicians, jockeys, journalists, etc.) that couldn't be cured by application of a healthy well-endowed man, he should not have been surprised to find the therapy reversible. He was not a man given to self-analysis, however, but he knew that a future with Bonnie felt a much better prospect than a future without her.

Now here was Pascoe to remind him of the realities of his life starting next Monday morning.

'Something going on here, is there, sir?' enquired Pascoe.

Before Dalziel could reply the door into the

yard opened again and another figure emerged and joined them.

'Evening, sir,' he said.

'Hello, Cross,' said Dalziel. 'Bowls Club enjoying themselves?'

'Yes, thanks. Sorry if I'm interrupting. I thought you might be with Mr Balderstone, but he can't have arrived yet.'

He looked with open interest at Pascoe. Dalziel introduced them, then said, 'Look, I'd best get back inside. I'm supposed to be working and we're a bit short-handed. Cross, would you fill in Mr Pascoe here before he pees himself out of curiosity.'

He turned abruptly and left them.

'Smoke, sir?' asked Cross.

'No, thanks,' said Pascoe. 'Just tell me all.'

Briefly Cross outlined the course of events as he knew it which had resulted in Dalziel's involvement in Lake House.

Pascoe listened avidly and when Cross finished his relation he said, 'Yes. Good. That's the police evidence bit and very nicely done too. But what about the rest?'

'Sir?'

'Look, Sergeant. I know Mr Dalziel well. Fair enough, if he sniffs out some dirty business, whether he's on holiday or no, he'll worry away at it. But it'd take more than you've told me to get him to invest money with a gang of people he suspects to be crooks and to go around dressed up like Henry the Eighth's butler.'

Cross considered carefully before replying.

'Well, sir. I think he feels a bit protective towards Mrs Fielding. In a way by staying on he's looking after her interests.'

'Mrs Fielding? The big good-looking woman behind the bar? Ah yes, I saw them together just before.'

Pascoe grinned broadly for a moment, then loyalty wiped his amusement from his face.

'Now, this fellow Butt?' he enquired.

'Due back from Brazil today, sir. The police over there were asked to keep an eye on him, just in case he showed any signs of slipping away. But it was felt best to leave him alone till we had him back on British soil.'

'A bit dangerous, isn't it? If it's not down to him, then the trail will be damned cold,' said Pascoe.

'Not really, sir,' said Cross politely. 'If Butt didn't do it, then the trail leads right back here. They went over his car with a fine-tooth comb. Annie Greave was in his boot all right, there's no doubt about it. And Butt has probably spent the last hour explaining how she got there. Mr Balderstone, Chief Inspector Balderstone, was going to contact Mr Dalziel as soon as he heard anything. I thought he might be here by now.'

So, thought Pascoe. Dalziel is hanging on here in the hope that this guy Butt will cough everything and life at Lake House can go on undisturbed.

How deep is he in? he wondered uneasily. He had not liked the way Cross now and then seemed to be lining the fat man up with the Lake House gang rather than with the forces of law and order.

Yet it was Dalziel who had stirred things up, he reassured himself. He couldn't believe that he would ever have anything to do with suppression of evidence. Though, of course, technically there was nothing illegal in the suppression of theory. But the Dalziel who had been his mentor these many years would not indulge in such hairsplitting.

'We'd better go back inside,' said Pascoe. 'Our wives will be getting worried.'

'I've been married fifteen years,' said Cross. 'After the first ten, policemen's wives stop getting worried. They start getting angry instead. Come on.'

But inside the building they encountered Dalziel once more. He looked anxious and uncertain, expressions which Pascoe had observed on his face as rarely as smiles on an undertaker's.

'Balderstone just rang,' he said without preliminaries. 'The plane arrived, but no Butt.'

'What?' exclaimed Cross.

'He was taken ill at the airport, it seems. Ambulance took him to hospital in Rio.'

'Very convenient,' observed Cross. 'That seems to wrap it up, I'd say. It looks as if we'll have to do it the hard way from now on in. I don't suppose they'll be asking for volunteers to spend a couple of days in Rio chatting him up, will they, sir?'

Dalziel didn't answer but turned away and disappeared towards the kitchens. Cross shrugged at Pascoe and the two men re-entered the Banqueting Hall.

'Thought you'd got lost,' observed Ellie's father.

'There was a queue for the loo,' lied Pascoe as he attempted to squeeze back on to the bench beside the townswoman whose thighs seemed to have settled and spread like wedges of ripe Brie.

'You missed the Sir Toby's Syllabub,' observed Ellie.

'I don't think I did, really,' said Pascoe.

They had now reached the stage in the evening when the historical was at war with the nostalgic – a war it could not hope to win. The bearded photographer had reappeared armed with a guitar and though the mead-sodden audience were happy enough to listen to one verse of 'Drink to Me Only', further than that they would not go. The guitarist read their mood and gauged their taste perfectly, and soon the composition rafters were ringing with such fine medieval songs as 'Bless 'em All', 'She'll Be Coming Round the Mountain', and 'The Rose of Tralee'.

After some thirty minutes of this, during which time the tables were cleared completely (a pre-empting of the souvenir hunters in which Pascoe thought he detected Dalziel's hand), the guitarist announced that coffee was available and the bar would be open until ten-thirty. Clearly authenticity stopped at the licensing authorities.

Ellie and Pascoe sat fast while all around them their fellow diners scrambled for the exit.

'They'll be able to charge a quid a drink from now till closing time,' observed Pascoe. 'That should please Dalziel.'

'Why?'

'He's a shareholder.'

Quickly he passed on all he had learned that night. Ellie whistled speculatively when he finished.

'What's she like?' she asked.

'Who?'

'This woman, Bonnie Fielding, is it?'

'I don't know, do I? I've only seen her distantly. Your dad thinks she overcharges.'

'Let's hope she doesn't overcharge big Andy,' said Ellie. 'Come on, let's take a look.'

'He can look after himself, you know,' said Pascoe, rising to follow her.

'Huh!' she snorted.

'What's that mean?' he asked as they squeezed through the crowd towards the bar.

'It means that the way he was babbling on at our wedding reception, he was ripe for plucking. He no longer deems his soul immortal. I've seen the symptoms developing. You getting married was the last straw.'

'Bollocks!'

'Well, one of them,' amended Ellie in the face of this forceful argument. 'I don't mean he fancies you. And I don't think he objects to me like he used to. But he's unsettled. I mean, wasn't it a bit odd that he should take his first holiday in God knows how long at the same time as your honeymoon?'

'No wonder you can't flog your novel!' said Pascoe.

They had finally reached the bar at which all hands seemed to be manning the pumps, or rather taps, optics and bottle openers. Dalziel was among them. Pascoe watched his technique for a while with interest. He poured the drinks with swift efficiency then charged eighty pence for a round of two, one pound forty for three, one ninety for four and three pounds for anything over. It seemed to be generally acceptable. Pascoe studied the list of prices, took from his pocket the exact amount required for two scotches, ordered them from an old man in a black doublet and passed over the money.

'That's Hereward Fielding,' whispered Ellie.

'Who?'

'The poet. I knew he lived locally, but I didn't link him with this lot.'

Somewhere behind the bar, a phone rang. The big woman who Pascoe supposed was Bonnie Fielding retreated to answer it.

'It's for you, Andy,' she called a moment later.

Dalziel was a long time on the phone and, though the bar service went on as efficiently as ever, Pascoe sensed an awareness among the servers of what was going on in the background. Finally Dalziel reappeared and beckoned to Bonnie and the two disappeared from sight.

'Let's try to find somewhere less crowded,' suggested Ellie.

Again Pascoe followed her, but he protested when she opened a door marked 'Staff' and led him through.

'Friends of the proprietor,' she grinned.

'Can't you read?' demanded a most unfriendly voice. A stout youth had appeared at the other end of the corridor they were in and was glowering at them.

'We're friends of Mr Dalziel,' said Ellie firmly.

'Are you? Well, I'm sorry, but we don't let our staff socialize during business hours,' said the youth pompously.

'You're Bertie Fielding?' asked Pascoe.

'Yes. Why do you ask?'

'No reason. Someone described you to me, that's all.'

Fat and nasty had been Cross's words. To another auditor he might have used the same words of Dalziel, thought Pascoe.

'You might tell Mr Dalziel I'd like to see him,' continued Pascoe, resolved not to retreat before this creature. 'Inspector Pascoe.'

'Not another!' groaned Bertie. 'What do you do? Breed from mud?'

But he went all the same and a moment later Dalziel emerged from the bar. He shook Ellie's hand formally.

'Nice to see you,' he said.

'Hi,' she answered.

'Come on through,' said Dalziel. 'I'll be glad to take the weight off my feet.'

They followed him into the main house. He moved around, observed Pascoe, with the familiarity of the inmate.

'We'll go in here,' said Dalziel. 'It's the old boy's sitting-room, but every bugger uses it.'

'Cosy,' said Ellie. 'You seem to be enjoying your holiday.'

'Aye,' he grunted, looking at her ironically. 'He'll have told you everything, I suppose?'

'I wouldn't know that,' said Ellie. 'He may be holding something back.'

'He's daft if he doesn't,' said Dalziel. 'The practice'll come in useful later.'

'If I may interrupt this curiously oblique conversation,' said Pascoe. 'Look, sir, is this private business or a case? I mean, I don't want to stick my nose in . . .'

'Why not?'

'Because if it's private, it's private, and I've no right to interfere,' said Pascoe steadily. 'Unless requested, of course. But if it's a case . . .'

'Cross gave you a run-down, didn't he?' said Dalziel. 'How'd it look to you?'

'It looked like you were dancing on a tightrope, sir,' said Pascoe. 'With a high wind blowing up.'

'Did it? Well, I'll tell you what, Inspector, I'll just put you right in the picture, you and your missus both, and we'll see what the combined might of two university educations can make of it.'

Dalziel lit a cigarette. He looked, thought Pascoe, a bit like Cardinal Wolsey might have looked in a private moment, worn down by, rather than relaxed from, the cares of office.

'There's a possibility that this man Butt may have given Annie Greave a lift from Lake House, fallen out with her somewhere along the road home, killed her and dumped her body in Epping Forest. We mustn't discount this.'

'But you don't believe it?' said Pascoe.

'I wouldn't say that,' Dalziel answered. 'There's another possibility though. Only one other, really. Annie Greave was killed here and hidden in the boot of Butt's car. Butt didn't find her till he was nearly home. He stopped for a drink and a sandwich just before closing time at a pub just off the A1 at Baldock. They back-tracked him there. Perhaps he opened the boot for some reason when he came out of the pub. There was Annie's body. Now he'd be very bothered. I mean, Christ, who wouldn't? But he'd be particularly bothered. First he was half-cut. He'd got stoned here to start with. I bet he hadn't got much idea how he'd driven to Baldock! So he didn't fancy talking to the police in that state.

'And second, he was off to Brazil in the morning. A big job, lots of prestige. Now, you and me, we know a hundred reporters who'd just love to get so close to a murder enquiry. But not Butt. At best, if he rang the police it'd mean cancelling his Brazil trip. At worst, it could mean a lot more. For all we

288

know, he was so stoned that he couldn't positively remember that he *hadn't* given this woman a lift and perhaps even killed her! Remember, he hadn't seen Annie Greave up here, so he had no direct link in his mind with Lake House.

'So the stupid sod, half pissed still, does the obvious stupid thing. Drives to Epping, scrapes a bit of a hole, drops Annie in it, covers her up, and goes home. Next morning he flies off to Brazil.'

'Well, it's a theory,' said Pascoe dubiously. 'It is only a *theory*, isn't it, sir?'

Dalziel ignored him.

'There was another person died here last night,' he said. 'Spinx, an insurance claims investigator. It looks like an accident. It looks to me less like an accident if Annie died here at the same time.'

'The old police text,' observed Ellie. 'Wherever two or three die together, there shall Old Bill be also.'

'What's the connection, sir?' asked Pascoe with a warning glance at his wife.

'Spinx came to the house for some reason,' said Dalziel. 'Suppose Annie rang him? She'd decided to take off, not liking the look of me. But Annie's kind like to make a bit of money wherever they can. So she rings Spinx telling him she's got a bit of information to sell him. She fixes for him to come out to the house. That'll mean she'll get a lift as well, very useful. He turns up, parks his car at the agreed spot by the lake. But she doesn't come. He waits an hour, then goes looking. He's

289

been to the house before, of course, so he knows his way around. When he gets to her room, there's someone in the bed, so he gives them a shake.'

'How do you know this?' demanded Pascoe.

'I've talked to the guy in the bed,' said Dalziel. 'He can't identify Spinx, of course, but it fits. You see, everybody else in the house knew Annie had gone by then.'

'So why should anyone kill Spinx?'

Dalziel lit another cigarette. He's back up to forty a day, assessed Pascoe.

'He ran into the killer perhaps. Said he was looking for Annie. That made him dangerous. What had Annie said to him on the phone? Perhaps he hinted at more knowledge than he had. He was an absurd little git. Bang, he gets hit on the head with a lump of wood. And drowned.'

'Out there, on that landing-stage?' asked Pascoe incredulously. He had risen and was peering out of the bay window which overlooked the lake.

'It's pretty black tonight, but I think I'd still notice any funny goings-on,' he said. 'And this would be earlier than now, I take it?'

'Yes,' said Dalziel. 'I think it probably happened by his car. I think that someone then took the punt along the shore to those trees where the car was parked, loaded the body in it and brought it back to the landing-stage to fake the accident. I noticed that the water where I found the body was pretty oily. His suit was badly stained with oil. So was mine. I got it from sitting in the punt.'

'Why did you take a *quiet* look, sir?' asked Pascoe.

'Because,' said Dalziel slowly, 'because this is all guess work. Because I don't want to stir things up for the people in this house if I don't have to.'

'Mrs Fielding in particular?' asked Ellie.

'Have you seen owt else here I'm likely to fancy?' snapped Dalziel. 'Any road, that's my business.'

'You said,' interrupted Pascoe in a thoughtful voice, 'that Annie might have had some info to sell Spinx. Would that have been about the fire insurance? Or the theft?'

'What's it matter?'

'Well, the allegedly stolen stuff wasn't insured, Cross said. And there was no fire claim pending, was there? I mean, even the fraud scheme had gone into abeyance because (a) Fielding had died and (b) you had come to life.'

Dalziel looked at Pascoe with a faint smile.

'I taught that lad,' he said. 'Well, that's my business too.'

He's still not telling us everything, thought Pascoe, peering out of the window again. There was someone down there by the landing-stage, he observed, only a shadow moving darkly against the misty grey of the water's surface. One of the Townswomen's Guild keeping a lecherous rendezvous? More likely one of the Bowls Club honking his ring.

'Well, it'll be settled one way or another soon enough,' he said.

'How's that?'

'They won't leave Butt to his own devices now, will they? It looks damn suspicious already, having a nice convenient illness just before coming home. He'll have read about the discovery of the body in the English papers and probably thinks the longer that he takes to come back, the safer he'll be. No, it'll be the old bedside interrogation technique. A man on his back soon cracks. I wonder which he'll go for when the first British copper walks through his door – the sudden relapse or the miraculous recovery.'

He laughed as he spoke.

'He went for the relapse,' said Dalziel.

Pascoe stopped laughing.

'I'm sorry . . . ?'

'Butt's dead. That's what the second phone call was about. Heart attack. He never recovered consciousness.'

'Oh,' said Pascoe, rapidly considering the implications. 'You've got to give it to him. If it was an act, then he really died the part.'

'What've you been feeding him on?' Dalziel asked Ellie. 'It's a joke a minute.'

'I suppose we'll never know now,' continued Pascoe. 'One thing's certain, if anyone up here does know anything about Annie Greave's death, this must have been a happy bit of news. You'll have talked to Mrs Fielding?'

'Yes,' said Dalziel.

'Oh,' said Pascoe, keeping disapproval out of his

voice with difficulty. 'Then all you've got to do is arrest anyone with a big smile. Sir.'

He reverted to peering out of the window and musing on the mutability of things.

'I don't really see what difference it makes,' said Ellie, puzzled. 'Even if Butt had come back and was questioned, surely he was bound to deny killing the woman and you'd be no further forward?'

'That'd be right,' agreed Dalziel. 'If it wasn't for the diary.'

'The *what*?' asked Ellie.

'Butt was sober enough when he buried Annie to attempt to lay a bit of a false scent. He helped himself to the contents of her purse to make it look like robbery. But as well as her cash he got hold of a notebook she kept which gave details of her relationship with everyone in this house.'

'Oh,' said Ellie, nonplussed. 'I didn't know that. In fact, come to think of it, how do *you* know that?'

'She's got the makings of a jack,' said Dalziel to Pascoe who had been listening in puzzlement to the conversation. 'No, of course it's not true. But it's not too unlikely a story, is it?'

'It is if you know that Butt's lying dead on the other side of the world,' said Pascoe.

'Right,' said Dalziel. 'Fortunately that's not common knowledge in this house. No, I told Bonnie, Mrs Fielding, that Butt was alive and well and waving this notebook under the noses of our interested colleagues at Heathrow.'

It was at best a compromise, he admitted that. And like most compromises, it was a fusion of small betrayals. Lying to Bonnie was one; holding out on Balderstone another. As a trap it was too feeble; he saw this in Pascoe's face. But as a way of treating those who trusted him, it was too brutal; he saw this in Ellie's.

But it was the best he could do. Having decided that, no bugger was going to get in his way.

'What do you think's going to happen, sir?' asked Pascoe in the kindly voice he reserved for lady magistrates and Ellie's relations.

'Likely nothing,' said Dalziel. 'I told Bonnie that the Essex police were pretty satisfied that Butt had nowt to do with the murder and that Balderstone would be coming out here tonight. And I asked her to let everyone know that they should hang around after the bar closes and the customers go home.'

Pascoe glanced at his watch. It was twenty past ten. The bar closed in ten minutes.

'Ellie,' he said. 'Your mum and dad will be wondering where we've got to. It would be kind to reassure them.'

'When policemen start being kind to their in-laws, let wives beware,' said Ellie. 'What are *you* going to do?'

'I'll hang on here for a while. Look, if they want to head for home, tell them not to worry. I'll cadge a lift into Orburn later.'

Ellie glanced from her husband to the fat man in the floppy hat.

'OK,' she said.

After she had gone the two men kept their silence for a while. Dalziel lit yet another cigarette and Pascoe prowled lightly round the room peering at the old man's books and examining the furniture.

'None of your antiques here,' said Dalziel finally. 'But if yon cupboard's open, you'll mebbe find a drink in it.'

The cupboard was indeed open and Pascoe straightened up with a bottle of Rémy Martin in one hand and Glen Grant in the other. Hereward had not put all his money into the business. The scotch had been purchased in recognition of Dalziel's personal taste and the fat man had acknowledged this kindness by spending at least an hour each night sitting here with the old poet drinking and exchanging tales of the criminal and the literary underworlds.

Pascoe poured Dalziel a scotch and helped himself to a generous measure of cognac.

'This man, Balderstone,' said Pascoe. 'What's he like?'

'Not bad.'

'Is he relying much on you? For inside information, I mean?'

'He'd be bloody daft if he was,' said Dalziel acidly.

Pascoe sipped his drink thoughtfully. At least there was no self-deception here.

'So what happens tomorrow when nothing happens tonight?' he asked.

'You're a detective,' said Dalziel. 'They've questioned everyone twice, taken statements. What'd you do?'

'Well, normally I'd go and solve some easier crime, and thank God this one was down to Essex, not me!'

'Now suppose you're the killer. What then?'

Pascoe considered.

'Unless I was very stupid, I'd laugh myself to sleep at this all-revealing diary story. Then when I discovered that Butt was actually dead, I'd laugh myself awake. If I wanted to be *really* clever, I might just start recollecting that I caught a glimpse of Butt driving away that night with someone beside him in the car. But that'd be gilding the lily a bit.'

'There you are then,' said Dalziel. 'There's nowt to be done.'

'Not quite,' said Pascoe. 'You haven't asked me what I'd do if I were *you*.'

Dalziel reached up one voluminous sleeve and began to scratch under his armpit.

'No, I bloody haven't,' he said uninvitingly.

'I'd be worried sick,' said Pascoe, 'in case by not telling the investigating officer what I suspected I was impeding the course of justice.'

'What's suspicion?' asked Dalziel. 'Bugger all. It's what you know that counts.'

'And what makes you think that Balderstone's told you everything *he* knows?' demanded Pascoe. 'Have you given him cause to take you into his confidence? Put what you suspect and what he knows together and bang! you may have a solution.'

Dalziel glared at him angrily and Pascoe realized he had gone further than he intended. He sank the rest of his drink quickly in an effort to anaesthetize himself, but before the storm could break, the door burst open and another high-pressure centre flowed in on a wave of distant noise like the honking of a flight of geese.

'Andy,' cried Bonnie. 'Have you seen that half-wit Charley anywhere? God Almighty, it's like Brand's Hatch out there! Where the hell has he got to?'

The noise he could hear wasn't geese, Pascoe realized, but the gabbling of human voices raised in anger commingled with a variety of car horns.

'What's up?' asked Dalziel.

'It's the car park. He got in such a muddle that he told the last people to arrive just to leave their cars on the drive with the keys in and he'd sort them out. Well, they're still there, blocking the way, but the keys have gone. Some twit tried to go round them across the garden, but it's so wet with all this rain that he's got stuck. God, what a mess!'

'And Charley's gone?' asked Dalziel, very alert.

'I've been telling you, yes! You must have directed traffic sometime, can't *you* do anything?'

They all make cracks about a cop's job in the end, thought Pascoe. But she was a fine-looking woman. A bit long in the tooth perhaps, but what she'd lost in youthful athleticism she could probably more than make up in expertise. Which was a male chauvinist pig thought he'd do well to keep hidden from Ellie.

'Come on,' said Dalziel, rising and making for the door. Pascoe realized that he was being addressed, not Bonnie, and rudely pushed past her in the fat detective's wake.

'This Charley,' he said. 'Could he be the one?'

Dalziel didn't answer but began to climb the stairs.

If so, he's probably long gone, thought Pascoe. All those cars to choose from. Unless . . .

He caught Dalziel's green velveteen sleeve.

'Those keys,' he said. 'You've got 'em!'

'Right,' said Dalziel. 'No bugger drives out of here till I'm done.'

He flung open the door of a room which was in darkness. Neither of them needed the light to know it was empty.

'It doesn't look as if he's taken anything,' said Dalziel, puzzled. 'He won't go far in his fancy dress surely.'

'Where'd he go anyway?' asked Pascoe. 'I mean he'd hardly set off walking to Orburn if he thinks Balderstone's coming driving along that road any moment. Hang on, though. Downstairs when I was looking out of the window, there was someone by the lake.'

'Oh no!' groaned Dalziel.

They turned, met Bonnie looking bewildered

half-way up the stairs, pushed by her once more and ran out of the front door.

The night was warm and almost windless. The mist on the lake surface had crept a little further up the garden in the last fifteen minutes and the rail of the landing-stage was barely visible, an indistinct line of faded runes scratched on a limestone wall. Though the noise of the car park chaos was more clearly audible here, its effect was to increase the feeling of isolation, like traffic heard beyond a prison wall.

'Andy!' called Bonnie from the doorway. But Dalziel did not pause.

'Careful!' he said to Pascoe as he ventured out on the landing-stage. 'This stuff's rotten.'

With sixteen stone going before me, what have I got to worry about, thought Pascoe.

Dalziel stopped short of the broken and still-unmended section beneath which he had discovered Spinx. The duck punt had gone.

Pascoe began to speak but Dalziel gestured impatiently and peered out across the lake, his head cocked to one side. Like a St Bernard on an Alpine rescue mission, imaged Pascoe.

'Do you hear anything?' asked Dalziel.

'Only the waters wappe and the waves wanne.'

'Come on.'

Grasping Pascoe's arm for support, the fat man clambered down into the rowing-boat which rocked dangerously under his weight.

'You want me to come in that?' asked Pascoe incredulously.

'Someone's got to row,' said Dalziel.

'But what's the point?' protested Pascoe as he stepped down. 'If you think he's out there, just get the locals to start a search. I mean, what's at the far side?'

'America,' said Dalziel. 'Just row.'

Grumbling, Pascoe unshipped the oars and began to pull away from the shore while Dalziel sat in the stern with the tiller in his hand. It took only a few strokes to put the house and garden out of view and the sense of being alone on a limitless expanse of water grew rapidly.

'I'm sorry, sir, but what *are* we doing?' demanded Pascoe for the sake of hearing his own voice rather than in hope of an answer. But to his surprise, Dalziel laughed, a short bark reminding him once more of his St Bernard image.

'We're on the track of a very dangerous man.'

'Dangerous?' said Pascoe in some alarm. 'The car park man?'

'You'd be surprised. Look there!'

Dalziel put the tiller hard over so the boat came round as sharply as a shallow-bottomed leaky rowing-boat could. Pascoe glanced round in alarm as he felt his left oar strike something. He would not have been too surprised to see an arm reaching out of the water and brandishing a sword. Instead he saw a punt pole, its top pointing drunkenly at the sky and its other end presumably buried in the sludge at the bottom of the lake.

'I told you he was dangerous,' said Dalziel. 'Listen.'

They listened. After a while, out of the other small water noises, Pascoe picked an intermittent slapping noise, as though some aquatic creature were beating the lake with its flippers.

Dalziel nodded imperiously and Pascoe began once more to strain at the oars. This form of exercise was not one he was accustomed to and his arms and shoulders were already beginning to ache.

'Who's there?' a voice suddenly called out of the darkness. 'Is there anyone there?'

'Aye, is there,' answered Dalziel.

'Is that you, Mr Dalziel? Could you give us a tow? I'm afraid I've lost the pole.'

Pascoe glanced over his shoulder and saw the silhouette of a punt. In the stern a lanky figure was pushing himself upright, his hands dripping. The halfwit must have been paddling with them since he lost his pole, thought Pascoe. His feeling of superiority was almost immediately dissipated as he caught a double crab and fell backwards over his bench. From this undignified position, he heard another voice.

'No closer please, Andy. Just pass over your oars and we'll be on our way.'

Pascoe struggled upright. The punt had now swung round or perhaps the boat had moved as a result of his mishap. In any event, they were now broadside on to the bow of the punt and in it, sitting behind a formidable-looking gun, was a second man.

'Evening, Herrie,' said Dalziel.

'Just the oars, Andy.'

The old man's voice was steady but not quite right, thought Pascoe. Strain showed through it. It was like Gielgud playing Little Caesar.

'Come on, Herrie,' said Dalziel jovially. 'What's all this about?'

'I couldn't get the car down the drive,' said the old man. 'Charley said he'd shift some of the visitors' but the keys had gone. That'd be you, I suppose, Andy. So I rang up a taxi, arranged to be picked up on the road at the far side of the lake. I'd have been there by now if my Charon had not proved more than usually incompetent.'

The two craft had moved almost to the point of touching and Pascoe, upright once more, was able to view the strange tableau in all its absurd detail. The fact that he was the only one present in normal twentieth-century garb accentuated his sense of being an audience. The old man was the centre of the tableau. His finely sculpted patrician head was perhaps more suited to a toga than a black doublet, but he made a good Duke Vincentio or even a Hamlet played by some English actor who had left it too late. Dalziel, standing now looking down at the punt, was an imposing figure in his long green gown, but his was not a head for philosophy and suffering; beneath the absurd cap flopping down over his brow, his eyes were calculating and shrewd: Ulysses assessing a tricky situation, or even an overweight Prospero, feeling a bit regretful that he'd drowned his book.

As for the third figure whom Pascoe had already seen at work in the car park, he too was one from the magic island. Ariel and Caliban combined, grace and awkwardness. Look at him now as he began to advance down the punt; his first couple of steps movements of ease and elegance, he looked as if he had been wearing thin silks and pink hose all his life. He spoke.

'I say, I don't know what's going on . . .'

Hereward Fielding turned his head, Dalziel saw his chance and stepped from the rowing-boat into the punt, Ariel took another step and became Caliban, stumbling over a loose cushion and falling heavily to the deck. The punt rocked violently; Dalziel, standing precariously on the gunwale, swayed like a clipper's mast in a gale, Hereward rose from his gun and reached out a saving hand but it was too late. Like the undermined statue of some deposed dictator, the massive bulk of the man toppled slowly sideways and entered the water with a mighty splash. Tillotson and Fielding knelt anxiously at the side of the punt, eager with apologies and assistance. And Pascoe, feeling it was time the twentieth century asserted itself, stepped calmly into the bows and took possession of the gun.

It struck Pascoe as odd that a man who had recently been threatening to blow a hole in his boss should now be so solicitous about his health, but Tillotson's words as he helped drag the water-logged Dalziel aboard seemed to explain this.

'I'm so sorry, but really all I was going to say was there's no need for any fuss. I mean the gun's not loaded, you don't think I'd leave the thing loaded do you? I told Herrie, he knew it wasn't loaded; please, what's going on? Oh gosh, you are wet, aren't you?'

Pascoe, squatting by the duck gun, began to chuckle quietly. The unloaded gun doubled the comic dimensions of the thing by removing altogether the heroic element. Of course, if there had been a risk . . . idly he pressed the trigger.

The resulting blast tore the mist apart for about five yards in all directions. More devastatingly, the rowing-boat, which was in the direct line of fire at very close range, had a hole nine inches across punched in its side close enough to water-level for each rocking motion to ship some water. Very quickly the craft began to settle and the lake poured in.

'Not loaded,' said Dalziel to a dumbfounded Tillotson. 'Jesus Christ. Pascoe, grab those oars!'

Pascoe obeyed just in time. As he began awkwardly to paddle the punt back towards the shore, the rowing-boat sank with a quiet burp, leaving only a few bubbles and Dalziel's floppy hat to show where it had foundered.

Back at the house they found the car chaos was

under control. Cross had taken over and the only cars now remaining were those stranded by Dalziel's removal of the keys, which fortunately had survived his immersion. But the confusion in the car park seemed now to have been internalized by the members of the household who hung around in their fancy dress like actors uncertain of their cue. Pascoe was particularly sorry for Bonnie Fielding whose anxiety about her father-in-law and distress at Dalziel's half-drowned state were doubled by the discovery that her son Nigel had decided to run away again. Another note had been found saying that one night of working in the restaurant had convinced him this was no life for a sensitive spirit, or words to that effect.

Pascoe tried to keep Hereward apart from the rest of the household but his effort was in vain without resorting to the strong arm of the law and, as Dalziel had retired to dry himself without firm instruction, he contented himself with keeping the old poet in sight. He was not at all surprised to find Ellie waiting at the landing-stage. She had sent her parents home by themselves and returned just in time to hear the boom of the duck gun. The look of relief on her face as she saw them emerge from the mist had been a great boost for Pascoe's ego, even though her first words to him were, 'You've got oil all over your best suit!'

Now they were all gathered in the old man's sitting-room. Hereward had poured himself a large brandy and Pascoe was interested to notice that he filled up a glass with Glen Grant also. Cross came into the room accompanied by a new figure whom he introduced to Pascoe as Chief Inspector Balderstone. Briefly Pascoe outlined what had taken place. Obscurely he felt the need to somehow cover up for Dalziel, but he had no idea how to do this. The fat man would have to look after himself.

Balderstone listened carefully but ventured no comment and a couple of minutes later Dalziel reappeared.

He had changed quickly into sports jacket and slacks. On his feet incongruously he wore a pair of multi-coloured carpet slippers. But casual though his garb was, Pascoe realized it separated him from the medieval/Tudor costume of the Lake House people as clearly as if he had come down in full police uniform.

He greeted Balderstone and spoke quietly to the two local policemen for a few moments, after which Cross slipped out of the room.

'Andy,' called Hereward Fielding. 'There's a drink waiting your attention here. And for your friends too.'

The atmosphere had subtly changed, realized Pascoe. From confusion and doubt a kind of optimism had emerged. He felt he could guess its source and the next minute confirmed this.

'Thanks,' said Dalziel, taking the drink. 'I need that.'

'I'm sorry about your soaking,' said Hereward. 'And about that gun! When I think what could have happened, my blood curdles.'

He shivered and took a long pull at his drink.

'My fault really,' added Tillotson. 'I'm so sorry.'

'But even with the gun empty, it was a silly joke,' resumed Hereward.

'Joke?'

'Holding you up like that! It's true what they say about second childhood. I never thought I'd start playing pirates!'

He laughed and all around him the others laughed too.

Dalziel didn't laugh.

'Where were you going, Herrie?' he asked.

'I told you. I couldn't get out of the gate because of those damned cars, so I organized a taxi.'

'At the other side of the lake.'

'That's so. You see I wanted to get into High Fold and, as you'll recall from our first encounter, that's over that side.'

'And why did you want to get into High Fold?' asked Dalziel. He was speaking very calmly and with hardly any inflection, as if, thought Pascoe, he merely wants to get this out of the way so he can get on with the real business. Pascoe had no doubt that this was Dalziel's intention, but where he could go from here he could not see. It was clear that the truth about Butt had been unearthed, probably from Sergeant Cross who would have no reason to withhold it. This is what came of acting alone, as Dalziel had often warned him. Almost certainly this stupid pretence about the diary had been exploded also. So Hereward had now learned the truth. There was no need to run. The evidence such as it was pointed to Butt and no one else.

Pascoe wondered uneasily if Dalziel *had* assumed he would keep the old man incommunicado, but he himself had made no effort in this direction when they first re-entered the house.

'I wanted to get to the pub there and buy a couple of bottles of cherry brandy. Revolting drink, I know, but very popular with the lower orders. We had run short. Bonnie asked me to see what I could do.'

He glanced at Bonnie who met Dalziel's disbelieving gaze full on and nodded.

'Why go to High Fold. Why not Low Fold? It's a mile closer.'

'It's the licensing hours,' said Hereward. 'Different authorities. They have an extra half-hour at weekends in High Fold.'

It all fitted together rather nicely, thought Pascoe in whose mind a little doubt had begun to stir. Could it be *true*? No! He had been there, had heard the exchange between Dalziel and this man. But what had he heard? A joke. Why not?

Dalziel had remained silent since Fielding's last answer and the old man decided to press home his advantage.

'What's all the fuss, Andy? Is it the gun? I'm

sorry about that, but you have to make allowances for the mentally handicapped. Hank has promised to dismantle it tomorrow. He's good with his hands.'

Uniff waved them before him like a Negro minstrel.

'Yeah, man,' he said.

Balderstone coughed gently.

'Excuse me, sir,' he said to Dalziel. 'Have you any instructions?'

'It's your case, Chief Inspector,' said Dalziel. 'I'm a guest here. Though there's one suggestion I could make.'

'What's that, sir?'

'Arrest the bloody lot of them,' snarled Dalziel. 'Charge 'em with obstructing the police and with being accessories before, after, and during the fact.'

'What fact is that, sir?'

'The fact that Open Annie Greave was done to death in this house ten days ago.'

He glared malevolently at the group before him. Their reactions all looked to Pascoe like bad acting, but perhaps it was their theatrical costume which gave this impression. Only Hereward remained firmly in character.

He laughed disbelievingly.

'Can that be it, Andrew? You think that absurd story you told Bonnie made me start like a guilty thing surprised and set off across the lake like Lord Ullin's daughter? For God's sake, you know me well enough by now. Even if I were guilty, if at my age I had found sufficient strength first to roger then to strangle this unfortunate woman, can you imagine that I would take flight in such a futile and undignified fashion? Dressed like this?'

His hands touched his doublet, his face lengthened in amused surprise, till finally he began to laugh at the self-evident absurdity of the idea. It was an infectious laugh and gradually, one by one, the others joined in. Even Pascoe felt tempted. Dalziel's face didn't change.

'Come on, Andy,' said Bonnie. 'Let's have a drink and count the takings. Your friends can help. At least it'll be an honest count with the law so well represented.'

She advanced smiling. She was an extraordinarily attractive woman, thought Pascoe. Something of this must have shown on his face as a sudden sharp kick on the ankle reminded him that Ellie was standing close by.

'I'm sorry,' said Dalziel.

'Sorry? Never apologize,' laughed Bonnie.

But Dalziel stood aside and pushed open the door. The smile faded and with it ten years from Bonnie's face.

'Oh, Andy,' she said. 'Whatever happened to Sydney Carton? This is a far, far shittier thing than you have ever done.'

Dalziel considered this while Pascoe's eyes flitted from the stricken woman to the even more devastated visage of her father-in-law. Then he looked through the door.

Standing in the hallway with Sergeant Cross's protective or retentive arm around his shoulders was Nigel Fielding.

'No, it isn't,' said Dalziel to Bonnie.

18

The Last Days of Pompeii

'Was she your first?' asked Dalziel.

'Yes.'

'And Hank fixed you up?'

'Yes.'

'Well,' said the fat detective with an effort at jocularity, 'we've all got to start some time and it's best to start with an expert.'

The room had been cleared except for Nigel and his mother. They sat on the sofa while opposite them Dalziel and Balderstone lounged in armchairs. Cross had gone upstairs with Hereward who had folded up like an evening daisy when the boy appeared. Pascoe stood quietly in the window bay.

'So you had been intimate with Mrs Greave since she came to this house?' asked Balderstone delicately.

'Come on, Inspector,' said Bonnie scornfully. 'I didn't bring up my children to be mealy-mouthed!'

'Did you know of this relationship, ma'am?' enquired Balderstone.

'Not till too late,' said Bonnie.

'And when you found out, what did you do?'

'What should I do?' she asked. 'I saw no harm in it. I thought she was Pappy's daughter, remember. A nice respectable widow who happened to have hot pants. Like the Superintendent says, we've all got to start somewhere and it was better than getting some local kid into trouble.'

Dalziel took up the questioning again. His voice had a strange quality which puzzled Pascoe, who had attended the fat man's interrogations more times than he could remember. But this intonation was new to him.

'After your father's funeral you decided to run away?'

'Yes,' said Nigel. He had spoken only the minimum necessary to answer questions. He looked pale but composed. Only occasional quick flickers of his eyes from one extreme of vision to the other hinted at agitation.

'But you didn't get far. It was too wet. You came back to shelter.'

'Yes.'

'And you hid in Mrs Greave's room?'

'Yes.'

Dalziel nodded and scratched his nose.

'I thought it was Papworth,' he explained to Balderstone. 'Only, when I searched his room, I couldn't find any suede shoes. Any road, I doubt if he eats doughnuts for breakfast! We nearly bumped into each other once or twice, eh, lad?'

The boy nodded.

'So you were here all the time. And when I found you in the billiards-room with your rucksack, you hadn't just come back. No, you were just on your way out then. I wondered how you knew my name! You were waiting till Herrie got me safely out of the way to Orburn, then off you would go and as far as I was concerned the one person who could know nothing about Annie's death was you. Right? But you did know something about it, didn't you, Nigel?'

The boy nodded. His mother put her arm protectively over his shoulder. They were large shoulders, Pascoe realized. The large frame of the elder brother was all here, though unhung as yet with Bertie's superfluous flesh. He was a powerful young man, powerful enough to . . .

'I killed her,' he said blankly.

'Tell us about it,' said Dalziel gently.

Why doesn't his mother intervene? wondered Pascoe. There's no need to let him answer these questions now. She could get her solicitor here for a start.

'She just packed up and said she was going. I found her getting ready and when I tried to persuade her to stay, she just laughed at first. I tried to stop her and we had a fight. We ended up on the bed and, well, I thought it was going to be all right then. But after we'd finished, she just went back to her packing.'

He fell silent and glanced at his mother.

Dalziel coughed phlegmily.

'You were fond of her?' he said.

'Yes,' said Nigel lowly. 'I told her I loved her. I thought she felt the same. But she laughed again, told me to grow up. She'd never treated me like a child before. I started unpacking her case and she got angry. She pushed me away, I hit her, she said things about my father . . .'

'What things?' demanded Balderstone.

'About your father making love to her?' said Dalziel quickly.

'Yes. She said that. She said that I was being a bloody nuisance now like he'd been. I didn't believe her, but then she started saying things about my mother too. We had another fight, only this time . . .'

His agitation was quite clear now. His mother's arm tightened around him, but still she didn't speak.

'But you didn't mean to kill her,' urged Dalziel.

No wonder Bonnie doesn't bother with a solicitor, thought Pascoe. This was the unfamiliar intonation in Dalziel's voice. Defence counsel trying to lead his witness.

'No. I was just angry.'

'And afterwards you went out and found Herrie?' said Dalziel. He was recalling the photos he had looked at in Uniff's room. In one of them Herrie had been standing by the door, apparently talking to someone in the corridor. In the subsequent shots, the old man had disappeared. Everyone else was accounted for except for himself and Bonnie, upstairs on the bed (his mind quickly suppressed the image), Papworth allegedly drinking in the Green Man, and of course Annie Greave, already by this time, he now knew, lying dead in her room. His mind had been toying with the limited permutations for ten days now. Nigel had made an appearance at a subconscious level long before he would permit him to take the lead.

'Yes,' said the boy. 'I locked the door. Charley tried it, but I just kept quiet. Then I slipped out and nearly bumped into you and my mother.'

He turned to Bonnie and said, 'I was going to look for you but I couldn't say anything when I saw you with him, could I?'

Bonnie shook her head slowly.

'No. I'm afraid you couldn't, darling.'

Balderstone took up the questioning.

'Why did your grandfather and yourself put the body in Butt's car?'

'He wanted to use the Rover, but Mother had the keys and she was with Mr Dalziel. Mr Butt had left the keys in his car. Herrie thought that Mr Butt was so drunk he'd be hours. But just after we'd got the boot shut, he came out of the house. He didn't see me, but he saw Herrie by the car. They talked for a moment, then he drove away.'

No wonder the old man had believed he could offer himself as a decoy. If Butt's memory had been stimulated by interrogation, then the meeting with Hereward by his car would have been strong circumstantial evidence. Pascoe wondered how far he had intended to go. Would his actions have been merely diversionary or was he willing to go the whole hog and confess in order to protect his grandson?

And how far would Nigel have let him go? There was in this boy, Pascoe suspected, a broad vein of the tough self-interest which characterized both his brother and, by report, his father.

'What about Mr Spinx?' Balderstone now demanded. 'Hadn't Annie rung him and asked him to give her a lift?'

Pascoe wondered if Dalziel had outlined his theory to Balderstone or if the local man had arrived at the same conclusion independently.

'I don't know anything about Mr Spinx,' said the boy emphatically.

'All right, son,' said Balderstone unexpectedly. 'That'll do for now. Mrs Fielding, we'll have to take Nigel down to the station with us, you realize that. You may accompany him, of course, just as you or your representative may be present at any further interrogations. Perhaps you'd like to put some overnight things together for the lad.'

As Bonnie left the room, Cross entered.

'I've got a statement of sorts from the old man,' he said. 'He doesn't half ramble on! The doctor's here now and he's given him a sedative. I thought there'd be plenty of time for another go later, when he's more himself.'

'Yes,' said Balderstone. 'Plenty of time. Would you take Nigel out to my car, Sergeant?'

The boy turned at the door and said very formally, 'Good night.'

'Watch how you go, son,' said Dalziel. 'By the way, Sergeant Cross, I've been meaning to ask, you ever catch your chicken thief?'

'No, sir,' said Cross.

'We served chicken tonight. I've a notion Papworth supplied them. We never did find where he was the night Mrs Greave disappeared. And his room stinks. A word to the wise.'

'Thanks,' said Cross, ushering the boy out.

'Well, sir, that seems to wrap it up,' said the Chief Inspector. 'I was surprised that the mother was so co-operative, but it looks as if we'll have a nice detailed confession all signed and sealed before we get to bed.'

'It's good for the soul,' answered Dalziel. 'What's your guess – manslaughter?'

'Not for me to say,' answered Balderstone. 'You'll call to see me tomorrow, sir, and we'll get what you've got to say down on paper too? Then it's back to your own patch.'

'That's it,' said Dalziel. 'Eight sharp on Monday morning.'

'Right then. I'm sorry how it's worked out, all this,' said Balderstone, making a vague gesture with his hands. 'Tell Mrs Fielding we're waiting in the car.'

He left and Pascoe came out of the bay.

'You still here,' grunted Dalziel.

'You forget, my in-laws have gone off home in my transport. Perhaps I should ask Balderstone for a lift.'

'No. He'll be crowded. You come along with me. I'll just put my gear together.'

'You're leaving?' asked Pascoe in surprise. Such diplomatic gestures were not usual in his superior.

'I can hardly stay on, can I?' said Dalziel. 'Not after . . . well, anyway, it's back to the Lady Hamilton for me. Fitting, really. That's where it all started. Which reminds me.'

He stuck his head out of the door and shouted, 'Charley!'

After a few moments, Tillotson appeared. With him was Louisa. On the whole, Dalziel decided, studying the effect of their almost identical silk tunics, Tillotson was the curvier of the two.

'Is it true?' asked Charley. 'That you've arrested Nigel, I mean?'

'Yes, it is,' said Dalziel. 'I'm sorry.'

'Poor sprout,' said Louisa. 'I told you no good would come of it.'

'But you couldn't foresee this!' protested Tillotson.

'Not precisely. But I could foresee *something*, which is more than you could do. It takes you all the time to foresee past your stupid pointed nose!' snapped Louisa.

'Don't be ridiculous, Lou,' said Tillotson. 'All Hank did was fix Nigel up with a bit of sex. My God, I sometimes wish he'd fix *me* up.'

The fist came snaking out in the same fierce, uninhibited punch as before. Tillotson, in whom familiarity seemed to have bred faster reflexes, managed to duck and take the blow on his temple. Even so he staggered a pace backwards and the girl had gone by the time he recovered. Dalziel wisely avoided involvement this time.

'Why did she punch you in the Lady Hamilton?' he asked. It was a question that somehow he had never got round to asking.

'Much the same thing,' answered Tillotson, gingerly touching his head in search of a wound. 'She said it was disgusting, especially as Conrad, her step-father, had been having it off with Mrs Greave too. I told her I didn't blame him, I wouldn't mind myself, and bang! I was knocked flat.'

'You mean you knew? You all knew? About Nigel and Conrad and Annie? Then you must have suspected what had happened when Annie's body was found?'

'Certainly,' said Tillotson. 'You didn't have to be a detective to work that out. Nigel will be all right, won't he? He's only a boy. I say, we made a hell of a lot of cash tonight. We've just been counting it up in the kitchen. Shall I show you the figures?'

'Go away!' said Dalziel. 'Just go away.'

He went upstairs to pack. In the hall he passed Ellie who glowered at him inimically from the shadowy corner she was sitting in. They did not speak.

Before going to his own room he went along the landing and tapped at Hereward's door. There was no answer and he peered inside. The old man's head lay on the pillow, still majestic in repose. He breathed deeply and regularly. It was good to see him looking so peaceful, thought Dalziel, approaching the bed.

'I'm sorry about all this, Herrie,' he said. Apologies were easy to the sleeping and the dead. He turned to leave but, as he did so, the old man's eyelids flickered and his thin tenor piped almost inaudibly.

'Oh the life of the spirit's a very fine thing
 But you can't be a monk without flogging
   your ring.'

Then the regular ebb and flow of his breathing resumed.

Downstairs with his case, Dalziel found Pascoe and Ellie waiting for him. Bonnie had left with Balderstone, Pascoe told him.

'Did she say anything?' asked Dalziel pointlessly.

'No.'

In the car on their way to Orburn the trio sat in silence for the first five miles. It was Ellie who broke it.

'I suppose we should congratulate you,' she said suddenly.

'What for?' asked Dalziel.

'Coming through with flying colours. All these

temptations to act like a human being and you still managed to be true to yourself. The patron saint of policemen must be proud of you. You've told the truth and shamed the devil!'

'Aye,' grunted Dalziel. 'I'm glad to see marriage has mellowed you.'

He pressed viciously on the accelerator and the car leapt forward. Pascoe, sitting in the back, rammed his knees into the back of Ellie's seat, partly as a safety precaution and partly as a warning. His married life was going to require many such warnings, he told himself. He didn't rate his chances of being a Chief Constable by forty very highly.

'There are still some things I don't understand,' he said in what Ellie called his let's-change-the-subject tone of voice.

'Me too,' said Ellie.

Pascoe ignored her and ploughed on.

'This business of Nigel running away and then coming back and hiding round the house. I mean, why do it? You're not telling me his mother didn't know.'

'No,' said Dalziel. 'Old Herrie didn't at first, though. We almost got ourselves drowned looking for the lad, so Bonnie faked a phone call from him saying he was safe and sound. Quick thinking, that. Someone rang, Spinx I think, and she must have pressed down the rest and pretended she was talking to Nigel.'

He spoke admiringly.

'Yes. But why?' pressed Pascoe. 'And why did Annie Greave ring Spinx? What was she going to tell him? And what really happened to Spinx? You said you thought he might have been lugged around in the punt? What does Balderstone think?'

'You know me,' said Dalziel. 'I wouldn't presume to tell anyone else how to run their case.'

Jesus wept! thought Pascoe. He'd tell God how to run heaven if he got the chance.

'And I still don't understand why Hereward really decided to invest in the business,' he went on.

'Pressure,' said Dalziel. 'You heard Charley Tillotson. I bet they all knew what was going on. I wouldn't be surprised if Big Brother Bertie hadn't threatened to shop Nigel if Herrie didn't shell out.'

'Happy families,' said Pascoe.

'God, you two are so smug and superior!' exploded Ellie. 'They're *people*, some nice, some nasty.'

'I know it,' said Dalziel.

'But you don't let the distinction bother you?' she demanded.

He didn't reply and they completed the journey in silence.

'See you on Monday morning, sir,' said Pascoe as they parted outside his father-in-law's house.

'Good night,' said Dalziel and drove away.

'Ellie,' said Pascoe. 'Why don't you practise what you preach some time?'

'Meaning?'

'Meaning that you might try to understand rather than just judge.'

She slammed the front gate so hard that a light went on in her parents' bedroom. Pascoe smiled. It was a small sign of remorse. Slowly, thinking about Dalziel, he followed her up the garden path.

Dalziel had been in bed an hour when the phone rang. He answered it instantly.

'I've just got back from the police station,' said Bonnie. 'The night porter at the Lady Hamilton didn't sound pleased at being woken.'

'Sod him,' said Dalziel.

'Andy,' she said finally. 'Will they find out?'

'About Conrad? I don't know.'

'Anchor are going to pay up, did I tell you?'

'Are they?'

'Yes. Andy, why didn't you say anything?'

'Because I don't know anything. Not for certain.'

It was true. He did not know for certain that the Propananol tablets in the bathroom cabinet had been prescribed to Conrad Fielding for his heart condition, though he did know for certain that no mention of the condition had been made to Anchor Insurance. All Conrad had to do to get the life cover required by the finance house for a short-term loan was to sign a declaration that he was in perfect health and give the address of his local doctor. The tablets had been obtained in London, where no doubt the diagnosis had been obtained also.

Nor did Dalziel know for certain that Conrad had had an attack while up the ladder in the Banqueting Hall. Nor that Nigel had found him and fetched his mother. Nor that Bonnie, realizing that death from a long-established heart condition would invalidate the insurance policy, had taken the still running drill and held it to her husband's chest. Perhaps it *had* caught him as he fell, perhaps that was what gave her the idea. In any case, Dalziel knew none of these things for certain. But, if true, they explained much. They explained why, once she discovered he was a policeman, she wanted to keep Nigel out of his way. They explained why Mrs Greave, who could have seen Conrad taking his pills on one of the occasions he slept with her, had felt her knowledge might be worth money to Spinx.

This was all reasonable supposition.

But some things Dalziel did know for certain. He had seen the pathologist's report on Conrad Fielding's post mortem examination. The doctor had had no inducement to examine the tattered remains of the man's heart for any damage other than that caused by the drill. Told of a suspected heart condition, he might indeed have been able to find traces. But it wouldn't have mattered.

For beyond any doubt, Conrad Fielding had died from the cause stated. When the drill plunged into his heart, he was still alive.

Bonnie could not have known that, Dalziel assured himself. She had believed that the physical effect of mutilating a dead man was the same as a live one. Her crime (if there were a crime) had been an attempt to obtain insurance money fraudulently.

But he could never be certain of this without becoming certain of all the other things he did not care to know.

'When will we see you again, Andy?' she asked.

'I don't know,' he said. 'I'm a busy man.'

'Lots of crime in Yorkshire,' she said with an effort at lightness.

'Aye.'

'But you've got business interests here.'

'Happen Bertie would be pleased to buy me out.'

'If that's what you want,' she said.

'That's it.'

'Well then. We'll be in touch.'

He put the receiver down without saying good night and let his great grey head relax on the pillow. Thoughts flitted madly through his mind. He lay there waiting for their mad whirling dance to exhaust itself. In the end, as always, the last to fade was a policeman's thought. What had been the circumstances in which Bonnie's first husband had drowned in the lake – and how much insurance did he have?

He didn't want to know that either. He felt exhausted but reluctant to sleep. With a sigh he turned over on his side, reached out to the bedside table, picked up *The Last Days of Pompeii* and opened it at his place.

A CLUBBABLE WOMAN

For Pat

Chapter 1

'He's all right. You'll live for ever, won't you, Connie?' said Marcus Felstead.

His head was being pumped up and down by an unknown hand. As he surfaced, his gaze took in an extensive area of mud stretching away to the incredibly distant posts. Then his forehead was brought down almost to his knees. Up again. Fred Slater he saw was resting his sixteen stones, something he did at every opportunity. Down. His knees. The mud. One stocking was down. His tie-up hung loose round his ankle. It was always difficult preserving a balance between support and strangulation of the veins. But it was worth it. Once the mud hardened among the long black hairs, it was the devil's own job to get it off. Up again. He resisted the next downward stroke.

'Why do you do that, anyway?' asked Marcus interestedly.

'I don't know,' said a Welsh voice. 'It's what they always do, isn't it? It seems to bloody well work.'

'You all right then, Connie?'

Connon slowly got up with assistance from the Welshman whom he now recognized as Arthur Evans, his captain.

'I think so,' he said. 'What happened?'

'It was that big bald bastard in their second row,' said Arthur. 'Never you mind. I'll fix him.'

There was a deprecating little cough from the referee who was lurking behind Connon.

'I think we must restart.'

Connon shook his head. There was a dull ache above his left ear. Marcus was rather blurred.

'I think I'd better have a few minutes off, Arthur.'

'You do that, boyo. Here, Marcus, you give him a hand while I sort this lot out. Not that it matters much when you only get twelve of the sods turning up in the first place.'

Marcus slipped Connon's arm over his shoulder.

'Come along, my boy. We'll deposit you in the bath before the rest of this filthy lot get in.'

They slowly made their way to the wooden hut which served as a pavilion.

'Get yourself in that bath and mind you don't drown,' said Marcus. 'I'll get back and avenge you. It must be nearly time anyway.'

Left to himself, Connon began to unlace his boots. The ache suddenly began to turn like a cogwheel meshing with his flesh. He bowed his head between his knees again and it faded away. He stood up, fumbled in his jacket pocket and took out a packet of cigarettes. The smoke seemed to help and he took off his other boot. But he couldn't face the bath, he decided. He wasn't very dirty and he hadn't moved fast enough to work up a sweat. He washed the mud off his hands and bathed his face. Then, after towelling himself down, he got dressed.

The others trooped in as he was fastening his tie.

'You all right, Connie?' asked Marcus again.

'Yes, thank you.'

'Good-oh!' said Marcus. 'Let's get into that water before Fred gets in.'

He began to tear his rugby kit off. Within seconds the bath was full of naked men and the water was sloshing over the side. There was a general outcry as Fred Slater settled in. Connon looked at the scene with slight distaste.

'Goodbye, Marcus,' he said, but his voice was drowned in a burst of singing. He made his way to the door and out into the fresh air.

He picked his way slowly over the muddy grass towards the distant club-house. The hut the fourth team used had originally been all the accommodation the club possessed, but the present of an adjoining field and a large loan from the Rugby Union had enabled them at the same time to develop another two pitches and build the pavilion. But even here the showers could not really cope with more than two teams, so the Fourth soldiered on in the old hut.

Connon thought ruefully that he had rather missed out on the development. The season the club-house was opened had been the season he retired. All those years in the first team had been centered on the old hut. Now when he was stupid enough to let himself be talked into playing, it was back to the old hut again.

He pushed open the glass-panelled door and stepped into the social room. Tea and sandwiches were being served.

'Hello, Connie,' called Hurst, the club captain. 'Been over at the Fourths? How did they get on?'

Connon realized he did not know. He could not even recollect the score when he had left the field.

'I don't know how it ended,' he said. 'I got a knock and came off early.'

Hurst looked at him in surprise.

'You haven't been playing, have you? Good lord. You'd better have a seat.'

Connon helped himself to a cup of tea.

'I'm only thirty-nine,' he said. 'You're nearly thirty yourself, Peter.'

Hurst smiled. He knew, and he knew that Connon knew, this was his last season as captain.

'They won't get me out there, Connie. When I finish, I finish.'

'Sandwich, Connie?' asked one of the girl helpers. Connon recognized her as the girl-friend of the second team full-back. He shook his head, remembering when Mary had used to come down on Saturday afternoon. The catering like everything else had been more primitive then. Once they became wives they stopped coming. Then they

4

tried to stop you coming. Then they even stopped that.

'I won't do it again in a hurry,' he said to Hurst. 'How did you get on?'

But Hurst had turned away to talk to some members of the visiting team.

The ache was turning again in Connon's head and he put his cup down and went across the room to the door which led into the bar. This was empty except for the club treasurer behind the bar sorting out some bottles.

'Hello, Connie,' he said. 'You're early. You know we don't serve till tea's done and the girls have got cleared up.'

'That's all right, Sid. I just feel like a quiet sit down. It's rather noisy in there.'

He sank into a chair and massaged the side of his head. The treasurer carried on with his work a few moments, then said, 'Are you feeling all right, Connie?'

'Fine.'

He lit another cigarette.

'Make an exception and pass me a scotch, will you, Sid?'

'Well, all right. Medicinal purposes only. Don't let those drunkards smell it.'

He poured a scotch and handed it over.

'Two shillings and sixpence.'

'Isn't my credit good?'

'Your credit's bloody marvellous. It's my accounts which are bloody awful. Two and six.'

5

Connon dug into his pocket and produced the money. He sat down again and sipped his whisky. It didn't help.

The door opened and Marcus stuck his head in.

'There you are, then. I saw your car outside so I knew you must be hiding somewhere. How are you feeling?'

'Not so bad.'

'Good-oh. I see you've got a drink. Hey, Sid!'

'No.'

'Right, I'll have to share yours, Connie.'

He sat down beside Connon. Connon pushed the drink towards him.

'Have it.'

'Here. Watch it or I'll take offence.'

Connon smiled.

Marcus Felstead was short, bald, and fat. His face was not really the face of a fat man, Connie thought, but of a tired saint. He could not recall the name of the tired saint he had in mind but he remembered very clearly the picture in his illustrated Bible which was the source of the idea. The saint, his sanctity advertised by a dome of light which sat round his head like a space helmet, had been leaning on a staff and looking despondently into the distance which seemed to offer nothing but desert. Perhaps the thing about Marcus's face was that the fleshiness of it formed a framework round rather than belonged to the thin nose and lips and narrow intelligent eyes which peered at him now curiously.

'Are you sure you're OK, Connie? You're not usually knocking the booze back so early.'

'Well, I did feel a bit groggy. But it's gone now. How did we get on by the way?'

'What do you think? Two men short with one of their reserves playing at full-back. Can you imagine? A reserve for a fourth team. Jesus, he made me feel young. They scored another couple after you'd gone. Thirty-two – three it was at the end.'

Connon was surprised. He could not recall any scoring at all, certainly not the kind of regular scores needed to build up a total like that.

'Who scored for us?'

Marcus looked at him strangely.

'What are you after? Flattery? You did, you silly bugger. A moment of glory, like the old times.'

Connon drank his whisky absently. He had distinct memories of the game, but they bore no relation to Marcus's account.

The door burst open and a group of youngsters came in, their faces glowing with exercise and hard towelling.

'Come along, barman, this isn't good enough, this bar should be open now!' one cried.

'It'll be open at the proper time,' said the treasurer, 'and then I'm not sure you're old enough to be served.'

'Me? The best fly-half the Club's ever had. I'd be playing for England now if I hadn't got an Irish mother, and for Ireland if I hadn't got an English father.'

'And for Wales, if you didn't fancy Arthur Evans's old woman.'

Marcus frowned disapprovingly and spoke sharply into their laughter, affecting a Welsh lilt.

'Somebody talking about me, is there?'

There was an edge of silence for a moment, but only a moment.

'It's only Marcus!'

'It might not have been,' said Marcus sharply.

Unconcerned, a couple of boys strolled over and sat down at the table. They were only eighteen or nineteen. Still at the stage where they were fit rather than kept fit, thought Connon.

'Did you play today, Marcus?'

'Yes.'

'Great! How did you get on?'

'Lost.'

'Pity. We won and the Firsts won.'

'Not playing for the Firsts yet, a young and fit man like you?'

The youth smiled at this attack on his own con-descension. 'Not yet. But I'm ready. I'm just waiting for the selection committee to spot me.' He grinned, a little (but not very) shyly, at Connon. 'Didn't you like my line-out work today, Connie?'

The boy had never called him Connie before. In fact, he couldn't recollect the boy's ever having called him anything. This was the way with these youngsters – noncommittal or familiar, there was no earlier formal stage. Not that I mind, he admonished himself. This is a rugby club, not an office party.

'I didn't see it, I'm afraid,' he replied.

Hurst stuck his head through the hatch which led into the social room.

'Right, Sid,' he said. 'All clear.'

'Your order, gentlemen. Marcus, you're on tonight as well, aren't you?'

'Christ, so I am. I could have been legitimately behind the bar all this time. Are you staying, Connie?'

Connon shook his head.

'I'm late already. Mary's expecting me for tea.'

'She doesn't know you were playing, then?'

'How could she? I didn't know myself till Arthur grabbed me when I got here and wept Welsh tears all over me.'

'Best of luck, then. See you tomorrow.'

'Perhaps.'

'Come on, Marcus!' came a cry from the bar. The room was now full and the social room hatch was also crowded with faces. Marcus barged his way through the crowd and was soon serving drinks from the other side of the counter.

Connon held the last of his whisky in his mouth. He felt reluctant to move though he knew he was already late. In fact he tried to catch Arthur Evans's eye but the little Welshman either missed him or ignored him. Connon smiled at himself, recognizing his own desire to be pressed to stay. A group of young men with their girls crowded round his table and he stood up.

'Thank you, Mr Connon,' said one of the girls as

she slipped into his chair. Connon nodded vaguely at her, suspecting he recognized one of his daughter's school-friends under the mysterious net of hair which swayed over her face. She brushed it back and smiled up at him. He was right. Seventeen years old, glowing with unself-conscious beauty. She had a piece of tomato skin stuck in the crack between her two front teeth.

'You're a friend of Jenny's, aren't you?' he asked.

'That's right,' she said. 'How's she enjoying college?'

'Fine,' he answered, 'I think she's very happy there. She'll soon be home for the holidays. Perhaps we'll see you at the house. It's Sheila, isn't it?'

'That's right. It depends where I fit into Jenny's new scale of friends, I suppose. I'd quite like to see her.'

Connon reluctantly digested another piece of the revolting honesty of the young and turned to go. He heard a burst of laughter as he moved to the door. Arthur noticed him this time.

'Hey, Connie, how are you there, boyo? How's the head?'

'It's all right now.'

'Good. I settled that fellow's nonsense anyhow. Time for a drink?'

'No thanks, Arthur. Gwen coming down tonight?'

'Why yes, she is. Always does, doesn't she? Why do you ask?'

'No reason. I haven't seen her for a while, that's all.'

'That's because you're always bloody well rushing off home, isn't it? Why doesn't Mary come down nowadays?'

Connon shrugged. For a second he contemplated offering Arthur a long analysis of the complex of reasons governing his wife's absence.

'Too busy, I expect,' he said. 'I'd better be off. Cheers, Arthur.'

'Cheer-oh.'

The car park was quite full now and his car was almost boxed in. He had once proposed at a committee meeting that the club-house facilities be restricted to those who at least watched the game but this voluntary restriction of revenue had not won much support. Finally he got clear without trouble and drove away into the early darkness of a winter evening.

He glanced at his watch and realized just how late he was. He increased his speed slightly. Ahead a traffic light glowed green. It turned to amber when he was about twenty yards away. He pressed hard down on the accelerator and crossed as the amber flicked over to red.

There was no danger. There was only one car waiting to cross and it was coming from the right.

But it was a police-car.

Connon swore to himself as the car pulled ahead of him and flashed 'Stop'. He drew carefully in to the side and switched off his engine. Its throbbing continued in his head somehow and he rubbed his temple, in an effort to dispel the pain. Out of the car ahead climbed two uniformed figures who made their way towards him slowly, weightily. He lowered his window and sucked in the fresh air.

'Good evening, sir. May I see your licence?'

Silently he drew it out and handed it over with his insurance cover-note and test certificate.

'Thank you, sir.'

The gears in his head were now grinding viciously together and he could not stop himself from rubbing his brow again.

'Are you all right, sir?'

'Yes, thank you.'

'Have you been drinking?'

'No. Well, no. I had one whisky but that's all.'

'I see. Would you mind taking a breathalyser test, sir?'

Connon shrugged. The policeman accepted the negative result impassively and returned his documents.

'Thank you, sir. You will hear from us if any further action is proposed concerning your failure to halt at the traffic lights. Good evening.'

'Good evening,' said Connon. The whole business had taken something over fifteen minutes, making him still later. But he drove the remaining five miles home with exaggerated care, partly because of the police, partly because of his headache. As he turned into his own street, his mind cleared and the pain vanished in a matter of seconds.

He drove carefully down the avenue of glowing lampposts. It was a mixed kind of street, its origins contained in its name, Boundary Drive. The solid detached houses on the left had been built for comfort in the 'thirties when they had faced over open countryside stretching away to the Dales. Now they faced a post-war council estate whose name, Woodfield Estate, was the sole reminder of what once had been. This itself merged into a new development so that the boundary was a good four miles removed from the Drive. Mary and her cronies among the neighbours often bemoaned the proximity of the estate, complaining of noise, litter, overcrowded schools, and the comparative lowness of their own house values.

This last was certainly true, but Connon suspected that most of his neighbours were like himself in that only the price-depressing nearness of the estate had enabled him to buy such a house. Even then, it had really been beyond his means. But Mary had wanted a handsome detached house with a decent garden and Boundary Drive had offered an acceptable compromise between the demands of social prestige and economy.

His gates were closed. He halted on the opposite side of the road and went across to open them. While he was at it, he walked up the drive and opened the garage doors. It was quite dark now. The only light in the house was the cold pallor from the television set which glinted through the steamed-up lounge windows.

When he went back to his car a man was standing by it with the driver's door open. Connon recognized him as the occupier of the house directly opposite his own, a man named Dave Fernie whom he also knew as a chronic grumbler at work.

'Evening, Mr Connon. You left your engine running. I was just switching it off.'

'Thank you,' said Connon. He never knew how to address this man. He worked in the factory of the firm for which Connon was assistant personnel manager. But he was also a neighbour. And in addition, possibly with malice aforethought, Mary had made of Mrs Fernie the only friend she had from the council houses.

'I was just opening my gates,' he added, climbing into the car.

'That's all right,' said Fernie graciously. 'I've just been down the match. Were you there?'

'Yes,' said Connon. 'I mean, no. I was at the rugger match.'

'Oh, that. I meant the football. We won, 3–1. How did your lot come on?'

'Oh, we did all right.'

'Good. Rugby, eh? Here, you used to do a bit of that, didn't you? My wife saw the pictures.'

'Yes, I did once.'

He turned the key in the ignition and felt the turn in his skull so that the pain in his head shook with the roar of the engine, then settled down as quickly.

'You OK?' asked Fernie.

'Yes, thank you.'

'Well, good night then.'

'Good night.'

He swung the car over the road and into the drive, slamming his foot hard on the brake as the branches of an overgrown laburnum slapped against his wing. He was used to this noise, but tonight it took him completely by surprise. He had stalled the engine and this time it took two or three turns of the starter to get it going again.

At last he rolled gently into the garage. He shut the main doors from the inside and went through the side door which led into the kitchen.

In the sink, dirty, were a cup and saucer, plate and cutlery. From the lounge came music and voices. He listened carefully and satisfied himself that the television was the source of everything. Then he took off his coat and hung it in the cloakroom. He looked at himself in the mirror above the hand basin for a moment and automatically adjusted his tie and ran his comb through the thinning hair. Then, recognizing a desire to delay, he grinned at his reflection and shrugged his shoulders, grimaced self-consciously at the theatricality of the gesture and moved back into the entrance hall.

The lounge door was ajar. The only light within was the flickering brightness of the television picture. A man was singing, while in the background a lot of short-skirted dancers sprang about in carefully choreographed abandon. His wife was sprawled out in the high-backed wing chair he thought of as his own. All he could see of her were her legs and an

15

arm trailed casually down to the floor where an ashtray stood with a half-smoked cigarette burning on its edge. The metal dish was piled full of butt ends, he noticed. The burning cigarette had started another couple of stumps smoking, and Connon wrinkled his nose at the smell.

'Hello,' he said. 'Sorry I'm late,' still hesitating at the door.

The music and dancing seemed to be approaching a climax. The trailing hand moved slightly; a gesture of acknowledgment; a request for silence, a dismissal.

Connon let his attention be held for a moment by a close-up of a contorted face, male, mixing to a close-up of a shuddering bosom, female. The cigarette smell seemed to catch his throat.

'I'll just get a cup of tea, then,' he said and turned, closing the door behind him.

Back in the kitchen he found a slice of cooked ham, evidently his share of the meal whose débris he had noticed in the sink. He slapped it on a plate and lit the gas under the kettle. Even as he did so, he felt his head begin to turn again and this time his stomach turned with it. He pressed his handkerchief to his mouth and moved shakily upstairs. Distantly the thought passed through his mind that he was well conditioned. Being sick in the downstairs toilet might disturb Mary. Now he was on the landing and his knees buckled and he gagged almost drily. Wiping his mouth, he pulled himself up, one hand on the handle of his bedroom door.

16

The next time he fell, he fell on to the bed and the wheels in his head went spinning on into darkness.

'Do we have to have that tripe on?' asked Dave Fernie.

'Please yourself,' said his wife. 'You usually like it. All those girls. You must be getting old.'

'Too old for that.'

Alice Fernie glanced across at her husband with a smile, half ironical, half something else.

'Old enough for what, then?'

'Aren't you going to switch it off?'

'I didn't switch it on.'

'No. I did. So you could see your precious football results after you rushed back from your precious match. And when you didn't come, I even marked them down for you. Don't you want to see?'

Fernie reached across and took the paper from the arm of his wife's chair.

'Thanks,' he said.

The singer was off again, alone this time; a ballad; his voice vibrant with sincerity.

'For God's sake, switch that bloody thing off, will you!'

Angrily she rose and pulled the plug out of its socket.

'I don't know what's wrong with you these days. I'm getting pretty near the end of my tether with you. Other women wouldn't put up with what I do.'

Fernie ignored her and peered down at the news-paper, but she sensed he wasn't really seeing it. She stood in the middle of the room and glowered down at him. He was in his early thirties, the same age as herself, but there was a puffiness about his face and a sagging at the belly which made him look older. Normally the contrast to her own advantage pleased her. Now she screwed up her face in distaste. Then, quickly as it came, her anger drained from her and she sat down again.

'Are you ready for your tea yet?'

'No, love. I told you I wasn't hungry.'

'Is there anything bothering you, Dave? Are you feeling all right?'

She steeled herself for the irritability her con-cern for his health always seemed to cause, but unnecessarily.

'No, I'm fine.'

'You were late tonight.'

'Yes, I'm sorry. I got held up. It was a good gate. I met his lordship on my way up the road.'

He jerked his head towards the window which faced the street. Alice affected not to understand.

'Who's that you mean?'

'You know who. Connon. Bloody twat.'

'Why? What's he ever done to you?'

'Nothing,' he grunted. 'I just don't take to him, that's all. Too bloody stand-offish for me.'

'That's what he was. A stand-off.'

'A what?'

'Stand-off. His position at rugby. Mary told me.'

Fernie laughed. 'Stand-off, eh? That's bloody good. Wait till I tell them on the bench. That fits him.'

'Anyway I think you're wrong. When I met him he was very nice. Charming. A bit quiet perhaps but he's just a bit shy, I think.'

'If he's shy he shouldn't be a bloody personnel manager, should he? Anyway he's more than that. He's a snob.'

Alice laughed with a slight edge of malice. 'I'd have thought you could say that about Mary Connon. But not him.'

Fernie shook his head dismissively. 'Her. That's different. She'd like to be better, but knows she isn't. He believes he is. Bloody rugby club.'

'Oh, Dave, don't be daft. It's not like that these days. Anybody plays rugby. Maisie Curtis's boy next door, Stanley, he's in the Club.'

'So what? Things don't change all that quick. What a game. Organized thuggery, then they all sing dirty songs like little lads. Yet they all tut-tut like mad if one of our lads runs on the field and someone shouts "shit" from the terraces.'

'There's no need to get excited, Dave.'

'No? No, I suppose not. Here, I think I'm ready for my tea now.'

Alice rose and went into the kitchen.

'I'll tell you something about your precious stand-offish Mr Connon, though.' His voice came drifting after her.

'What's that, then?'

'He'd had a couple tonight. He was swaying around a bit. And I thought he was going to drive across his lawn and in through the front door.'

Alice came back to the sitting-room door.

'That doesn't sound like him.'

'Doesn't it? Don't tell me that you've only heard good of him from Madam Mary?'

'She doesn't talk much about him at all.'

'I don't know why you bother with her. You've only got your age in common.'

Alice took an indignant step forward.

'What do you mean? I can give her ten years, and more.'

Fernie caught her hand and pulled her down beside him on the settee.

'As much as that? Mind you, she's well preserved. And game too, I should think.'

'I don't know what you mean,' said Alice, struggling to get up.

'She must have caught him young then, very young. He's only thirty-nine, you know.'

'How do you know?'

He didn't answer but went on, 'And they've got that girl of theirs . . .'

'Jenny.'

'Yes, Jenny, at college. He must have been caught young. Very young. She's a pretty little thing, now.'

'Don't you want any tea, Dave?'

Fernie's brawny arm held his wife in a clamp-like grip round the waist. He looked thoughtfully into her face, then pressed gently with his free hand where it rested on her leg just above the knee.

'No,' he said, 'I think I've changed my mind again.'

Jenny Connon hadn't quite made up her mind what to do about the hand on her knee. Adaptability was an important quality in a teacher, her education tutor had told the class that morning. How to cope with the unexpected.

Though, as she herself had arranged that her roommate should go out and she herself had turned the key in the door to prevent interruption, the situation was not all that unexpected.

'Do you really want to be a teacher?' she asked brightly.

Antony (he insisted on the full name) pushed the hair back from his brow with a gesture almost girlish (but he used the hand not on her knee) and smiled.

'If you mean, have I got a sense of vocation, no. If you mean, are my natural inclinations to be something else being repressed, the answer is equally no. Being at college is less distasteful than most of the alternatives, and it pleased my parents. Anyway, think of the holidays. I have a sense of *vac*ation very strongly developed.'

Antony Wilkes was without doubt the smoothest man in the South Warwickshire College of Education at the moment. As he was in his third year and Jenny was in her first, the opportunities for the relationship to develop were limited. As it was, Jenny had decided to feel flattered that she was the second girl he had chosen from the year's new supply. Her college 'mother' in the second year had assured her (rather sadly) that Antony was most discriminating in his selection. Her room-mate had been even more positive. She had been the first of the year. This gave Jenny the advantage of being well briefed in the Wilkesian technique, but being forewarned she was discovering did not prevent her from being disarmed. Antony was one of the few people she had met who really did talk in long well-organized speeches like people in plays. Most of her acquaintance, she realized, hardly ever strung together more than a couple of dozen words at a time except when telling an anecdote, and in fact the few who did talk at length were down in the catalogue as bores and therefore to be avoided.

But Antony talked eloquently, interestingly, without strain; with none of those changes of direction, grammatical substitutions, syntactical complexities, whose existence her linguistic lecturer assured her was the real framework of the spoken language.

His speech, Jenny decided, was the smooth, reassuring surface of his amatory technique. Even the slight sense of staginess it conveyed worked for him, creating a faintly non-real, therefore non-dangerous, context. But beneath the surface . . .

The obvious survival tactic was to stay afloat. She seized at a bit of driftwood in his last speech.

'Is it important to please your parents?'

'But of course. It's important to please everyone who deserves it, even a little beyond desert if possible. Financially it's not important. My father has a strict scale of values. He gave me the precise amount necessary to bring my grant up to the level he has worked out to be sufficient for my well-being. Less would be neglect; more would be luxury. So I never get more or less for any reason. And to use money as punishment or reward is quite out of the question.'

'He sounds like a Puritan banker.'

'Not at all. If you wish to combine his religion with his profession, you'd have to call him an Aston Villa butcher. Mind you, my mother slips me the odd note now and then. But, as I say, this has nothing to do with the question. The only real answer is that, despite the fact that in many ways they find me utterly incomprehensible, they have always felt inclined by nature to please me; similarly I them.'

'You mean you love them?' asked Jenny, half-consciously trying to embarrass him.

'Yes, of course. Had I not made that clear? I'm sorry. And you, do you love your parents?'

'Yes, I think so. My father, I like him a lot and we mean a lot to each other. It's a matter of talking and understanding, but my mother's different. Irritating in so many things. I want to scream at her sometimes.'

'But you never do?'

Jenny grinned. She had tried to stop grinning. She thought it made her face fall apart in the middle, and

23

she still had to count her teeth to assure herself she had not got twice as many as other people. But she kept on forgetting.

Antony Wilkes was glad she forgot.

'Oh, sometimes. I give a quick forty-second-psycho-analysis. Rather nasty stuff it can be. She's a bit of a snob; uses me to get at Dad, whom she resents in some odd way. She's a few years older than he is, though I only use that as a last resort. I don't know why, I suppose I just know that for her age is the ultimate insult, stuck a long way after vanity and dishonesty! But sometimes I feel I'm a lot more like her than Dad, than I'm like Dad I mean, though I like him more.'

Ruefully she compared her own performance as a speech-maker with Antony's. Still, it wasn't all that bad. And her hesitancies arose from uncertainties of emotion. Perhaps it would have flowed more smoothly if she hadn't been so aware of the tensions, the fight for survival at home.

Antony's hand patted her knee sympathetically. She realized that her attempt to stop on the surface had somehow gone wrong. She had entered into a conversational intimacy with him without even noticing it. She would have to keep very much on the alert now. His other hand was pressing her shoulders round. She turned to him and he kissed her. She'd have to do something about his other hand. But not yet. Mini-skirts and tights, she thought dreamily. Action and reaction. The invitation to attack might be more compelling than ever before, but the defences were stronger. She grinned again, which produced a very invigorating kind of kiss.

She could postpone her decision for a while yet.

'Christ, Marcus, where the hell have you been? You just said half an hour. It's been more like an hour and a half.'

Marcus Felstead manoeuvred his bulk under the flap into the bar.

'Sorry, Ted, old son. Got held up a bit. Look, have a pint on me and push off now. I'll spell you when you've got a Saturday.'

'OK. And I'll have that pint. I've been so bloody busy that not a drop's passed my lips since you left.'

'It'll do you good. Give you an edge when they start fighting for the spare.'

'Some hope. There won't be much of that around now. See you, Marcus, Sid.'

Sid Hope, the club treasurer, looked askance at Marcus.

'Nice of you to come back and give us a hand.'

'Come off it, Sid. I did get Ted to stand in.'

'Ted! Have you seen him at the till? He's got some peculiar decimal system of his own. Where have you been to anyway? On the prowl?'

'Nowhere important. Just out.'

A peal of uninhibited female laughter cut through the noise and fume of the bar. Marcus turned. Sitting in the furthermost corner surrounded by half a dozen men was the woman he expected to see after hearing that laugh. Dressed in a low-cut cocktail dress whose demure whiteness set off the gleaming black of her hair and the shining silver of her tights, she was looking up and smiling at the young man who bent over her, obviously telling a story.

The treasurer followed Marcus's gaze and shook his head.

'Trouble,' he said laconically.

'What do you mean?'

'You know what Arthur is. He's been hopping around like a cat on hot bricks all evening waiting for his precious wife to turn up. Finally off he goes about half an hour ago to fetch her. Decides she must have forgotten. Forgotten! Well, he's hardly out of the place before she comes sailing in like the figurehead on the good ship Venus. And of course within two minutes of coming into the most crowded room in the county with a queue six deep at the bar, she's sitting in the corner surrounded by drinks. Just wait till Arthur gets back.'

Sid drew a couple of pints for a complaining customer, then looked over at Gwen Evans again.

'Mind you,' he said, 'what a pair of bristols, Jesus! There hasn't been anything like that in here since Nancy Jennings went off with that traveller. And Mary James – Connon, I mean – was the only thing I've ever known who could have beaten it.'

'Connie's wife?'

'Yes. She doesn't get in here much now, does

26

she? Nor does Connie for that matter. But I can remember the days. Jesus! Connie was married when you came to live here, wasn't he, Marcus?'

'Yes. Just.'

'It must have been a full-time business with that one. No wonder he lost his edge after that. God, he once looked a cert for a cap. First we'd have ever had. Never been a sniff since. All for love.'

Marcus poured himself a scotch.

'He did crack his ankle.'

'Of course he did. I'm not really suggesting, mind you, that kid of theirs came out pretty smartly. Like Connie's pass, they said. And the responsibility can't have helped. But they seemed to make out all right. Didn't see all that much of Mary after that. But it was before. Like her over there. And Nancy Jennings. Trouble.'

Marcus, his eyes still fixed on the noisy corner, ran his glass along his lower lip.

'Are you putting forward as a general proposition, Sid, that women with big breasts cause trouble?'

'Not absolutely. Though there's a bit of truth in it, isn't there?'

'Mary Connon never caused any trouble down here that I saw.'

'Like I said, after they married, she didn't get in here so much. Tailed off. That's an apt phrase if you like. She was six years older than him, you know.'

'Still is, isn't she?'

'You know what I mean. She'd had her fling down here. Not here exactly. That was in the days before this bloody roadhouse came into being. Remember? We had the tea-hut. None of your polished floors. You could get splinters through your shoes if you weren't careful. Then over to the Bird-in-Hand. No, Mary did the right thing – for her, anyway. Married someone half a dozen years younger. And stopped coming so much. Nancy Jennings, she buggered off. It's when they marry someone ten years older than themselves *and* keep their wares in the shop window that the trouble starts. Here, my lad, if you're going to have another whisky, pay for the last one first.'

'Sorry, Sid. There it goes; and for this one too. Witnessed?'

But Sid wasn't paying attention.

'Here we go,' he said in a low voice. 'Here we go.'

Marcus had never seen anyone whose face was really black with rage, but Arthur Evans was pretty close to it as he pushed through the door. A path opened up before him. It led to the corner where his wife sat. She looked up, flashed him a quick smile, then returned her attention to the youngster who had been talking to her. But he had seen Arthur too and seemed disinclined to talk further.

With a tremendous effort, obvious to all who watched, which was about three-quarters of those in the room, Arthur turned to the bar. Marcus could almost feel the man's will forcing his broad shoulders to turn. Then his trunk followed. And finally his legs.

Quickly Marcus thrust a glass up against the whisky optic. And again.

'Arthur, old son, I'm in the chair. Wrap yourself round this and tell us about your childhood in the green valleys of old Wales.'

Evans took the drink in one.

'Thanks,' he said.

Over his shoulder, Marcus saw Gwen casually disengaging herself from the group in the corner. Exchanging a word here and there as she came, she passed easily across the room till she arrived at her husband's shoulder.

'Hello, dear. Going to buy me a drink? I've got no money and I can't sponge off your friends all night.'

'Where've you been, Gwen?'

She smiled ironically.

God, you're a beauty, thought Marcus. Sid, in an excess of desire to share his admiration of the sight before them, kicked him painfully on the ankle.

'Oh, I got tired of waiting, so I came on by myself.'

'But you were supposed to be coming with Dick and Joy.'

'Was I? Oh, I forgot.'

'They called for you.'

'Then I must have left.'

'To come here? You took your time, didn't you, girl?'

'Do you want to quarrel, Arthur?'

29

She raised her voice just sufficiently to cut into the attention of those immediately adjacent to them.

Marcus looked at Arthur. Surprisingly, he seemed to be considering the question on its merits.

Finally, calmly, 'No,' he said.

'Then let's have that drink. Marcus, love, see if you can add a bit of gin to that slice of dried-up lemon which seems to be all that's left of a once proud fruit.'

'A pleasure, ma'am,' said Marcus. 'A real pleasure.' He meant it.

Two hours or so later, just after eleven, he put the lights out in the bar. Outside he could hear the din of departure. Car doors. Impatient horns. Voices. Song.

As he passed the Gents, the door opened and a large figure fell out.

'Marcus,' it said.

'Ted. Christ, you certainly caught up, didn't you? Come on, old son. We'd better get you home.'

Arm in arm they walked out into the car park.

Jenny Connon opened the door to let her roommate in.

'Hello,' said the newcomer brightly. 'Not too early, am I? It's after eleven.'

'What you really mean is, not too late, you hope. How are you, Helen?' said Antony. 'Well, must be off. See you both. Bye.'

Jenny watched him go down the corridor.

'Had a nice time?' asked Helen.

'Oh yes,' said Jenny noncommittally as she closed the door. She hoped she had done the right thing.

'The time is ten minutes past eleven,' said the announcer with evident relief. 'You are watching . . .'

Alice Fernie switched him off in mid-sentence and yawned.

'Well, I'm off to bed. Coming?'

Behind her, her husband stood in the small bay of the window looking out into the front garden.

'No, dear. You go on. I'll be up in a minute.'

'What are you looking at?'

'Nothing. I thought I saw that bloody black and white cat from next door digging up my lawn. Off you go.'

'All right, then. Good night.'

'Good night.'

And over the road, Sam Connon stood pale-faced and trembling in the darkened hall of his house, the telephone in his hand.

Behind him in the lounge, stretched out in the high-backed chair he would never want to call his own again, was his wife.

She was quite, quite dead.

Chapter 2

Superintendent Andrew Dalziel was a big man. When he took his jacket off and dropped it over the back of a chair it was like a Bedouin pitching camp. He had a big head, greying now; big eyes, short-sighted, but losing nothing of their penetrating force behind a pair of solid-framed spectacles; and he blew his big nose into a khaki handkerchief a foot-and-a-half square. He had been a vicious lock forward in his time, which had been a time before speed and dexterity were placed higher in the list of a pack's qualities than sheer indestructibility. The same order of priorities had brought him to his present office.

He was a man not difficult to mock. But it was dangerous sport. And perhaps therefore all the more tempting to a detective sergeant who was twenty years younger, had a degree in social sciences and read works of criminology.

Dalziel sank over his chair and scratched himself vigorously between the legs. Not absent-mindedly

– nothing he did was mannerism – but with con-scious sensuousness. Like scratching a dog to keep it happy, a constable had once said within range of Dalziel's very sharp hearing. He had liked the simile and therefore ignored it.

'You should have seen him, Pascoe. He went round their cover like a downhill skier round a line of snowmen. And he was a big lad, mark you. Still is, of course. But even then. Not one of your bloody Welsh dwarfs, but a good solid-built English fly-half. How we roared! He'd have captained the Lions if we'd been selectors.'

'Yes, sir,' said Sergeant Pascoe with the resigned condescension of one certain of the intellectual superiority of Association Football.

'Graceful, too. Ran upright. Always looking for the quickest way to the line. God, he found it that day. He was picked for the final trial, of course. Nearest thing to a certainty since Lily Jones left Crown Street. Then bang! his ankle went. The week before. No one's fault. He was overtaken by a loose scrum. Never afraid to mix it, was Connie. Solid defender, sharp attacker. But he never came again after that. Played for another eight years. No diffi-culty in holding his place in the club. Stood up for the County a dozen times. But never sniffed at a cap again. But he was a great runner with the ball, a great player.'

He nodded two or three times and smiled faintly as though at some pleasant memory.

'A great player.'

'Then he could hardly commit a murder, could he?' said Pascoe, hoping by this irony to recall his superior to the realities of their work.

'No. Probably not. Or not one like this. He'd use his head, that one. Which,' added Dalziel, standing up and walking to the window, 'is what you should do, Pascoe, before wrapping up another of your little ironies for me.'

Pascoe refused to be squashed.

'Perhaps he is using his head, sir. Perhaps he is, in the sporting idiom, selling us a dummy.'

Dalziel flung up the window with a ripping sound from the parts where the paint had fused, and let in a solid cube of icy air which immediately expanded to fit the room.

'No one ever sold me a dummy. Point yourself at the man and bugger the ball, you can't go wrong.'

'But which man?' said Pascoe.

'No,' said Dalziel, slapping his thigh with a crack which made Pascoe wince, 'at this stage the question is, which bloody ball? Is that enigmatic enough for your scholarship, eh?'

Pascoe had grown used to jokes about his degree when a constable, but Dalziel was the only one who hung his wit on it now.

The trouble is, he thought, looking at the broad slope of the back whose bulk stopped the light but not the draught, the trouble is, deep down he believes that everyone loves him. He thinks he's bloody irresistible.

'What did you make of him last night anyway?'

'Not much. That doctor of his had pumped him full of dope and was hovering around like a guardian angel when I got there.'

Dalziel snorted.

'At least you saw him. He was tucked up in bed by the time I arrived. I'd have liked a go at him while the iron was hot.'

'Yes, sir. The early bird . . .'

'Only if it knows what it's all about, Pascoe.'

Pascoe did not let even the ghost of a smile appear on his lips. He went on speaking.

'In any case, the iron wasn't all that hot at eleven. She'd been dead at least three hours, possibly five. The room temperature seems to be a rather uncertain factor. Signs of a big fire, but the place was like an ice-box by the time we got there. That was a sharp frost that set in last night.'

'Bloody science. All it does is give us reasons for being imprecise. I can manage that without logarithms.'

'The cause of death's a bit more exact, isn't it, sir?'

'Oh, yes.'

Dalziel rippled through the papers scattered on the desk before him. Pascoe tried to show none of the offence this lack of organization caused him.

'Here we are. Skull fracture . . . bone splinters into frontal lobes . . . blow from a metal implement, probably cylindrical . . . administered with great force to the centre of forehead . . . perhaps long enough to permit a two-handed grip. That's a great help. Found anything yet, have they?'

'No, sir.'

'I should bloody well think not, eh? Not if you knew and I didn't. Where is this man, anyway?'

Pascoe pushed back his stiffly laundered white cuffs to glance at his watch.

'The car went for him half an hour ago.'

'Waiting for him to finish breakfast, I expect. Hearty, I hope. He'll need his strength.'

Pascoe raised his eyebrows.

'I thought you said . . .'

'I didn't think he'd done it? But I might be wrong. It's been known. Twice. But whether he did it or not, if it wasn't done casually by an intruder, he'll probably know why it was done. He might not know he knows. But know he will.'

'Have we dismissed the possibility of an intruder, sir?'

'We? We? You're not my bloody doctor. No, I haven't. But if you look at your bloody scientifically based reports, you'll see that she seems to have been sitting very much at her ease.'

'Could it have been from behind? With, say, a narrow-headed hammer. That way you'd get the force . . .'

'Pish and cobbles, Pascoe! Didn't you see the height of that chair-back? And she was sprawling in it at her ease. You'd need arms like an orang-outang. No, I think it was someone she knew pretty well.'

'And how narrow does that make the field?'

Dalziel grinned lecherously.

'Not as narrow as you'd think. Twenty years ago

there were a hell of a lot of people down at the Rugby Club who knew Mary James pretty well. I've had a bit of a nuzzle there myself. And that kind of acquaintance doesn't get forgotten all that quickly.'

'You make her sound like a professional.'

'Don't get me wrong, son. She wasn't that. Not even an enthusiastic amateur. She just liked the gay life. There's one in every club. Where the booze is strongest, the dancing wildest. The girl who doesn't flinch when the songs get dirty. Who can even join in. It's the gay crowd she likes, not the slap and tickle in the dark corners. But her image demands she has a large following. And she's bound to be overtaken from time to time.'

'Was Connon an overtaker?'

'Oh no. He was taken over. Your old stager begins to smell danger when the gaiety girl passes the quarter-century with no strong ties. Your young lad's easy meat, though. Easily frightened too.'

'Frightened?'

'They got married at a dead run. Their girl appeared eight months later. Premature, they called it.'

Pascoe listened with distaste to the rasp of laughter which followed.

'But you'll find out all about that, my lad. Have a walk down there this lunchtime. They always get a good crowd in. Have a chat with one or two of them. See if anything's known. They'll all be eager to natter. Here, I've scribbled out a list of who's who down there. It's not definitive by any means, but it'll tell you whether you're talking to a mate of his – or hers – or not.'

He passed over a scruffy sheet of foolscap, one corner of which looked as if it had been used for lighting a cigarette.

'You're best at this stage. If we haven't sorted this lot out in a couple of days, I'll drop in for a social drink myself. The tension'll have gone by then and they'll all imagine they're pumping me for information.'

Whereas you pump stuff into barrels, not out of them, thought Pascoe.

Dalziel turned to the window again and took a couple of deep breaths. His fingers drummed impatiently on the sill.

'Anything in from house-to-house yet?'

'Not yet, sir.'

'They'll all be in bed. Christ. Bloody Sundays!'

There was a long pause. Then . . .

'Here he comes,' said Dalziel, slamming the window shut with even more violence than he had used to open it. 'Anything you want here, laddie?'

'Well, no; I mean yes,' said Pascoe in puzzlement.

'Grab it and go, then. What's the matter? Did you hope to see the master at work?'

'No. But I thought that as you know him – I mean, you are a vice-president of the Rugby Club and something of a friend . . .'

'A friend?' said the superintendent, twisting his fingers in one pouchy cheek so that his big mouth was dragged sinisterly out of shape. 'You've jumped to conclusions, Sergeant. Perhaps I better had let you watch the master some time. He's a great player, but I never said I liked him. Nor he me. Oh no, I never said I liked him. Push off now. We'll save you for later if need be.'

Quickly Pascoe gathered a couple of files and some papers together and made for the door. There was a knock and it opened just as he reached it.

'Mr Connon, sir,' said the uniformed sergeant standing there.

'How are you, Mr Connon?' said Pascoe looking at the pale-faced man who stood a pace or two behind the sergeant.

Solid. Yes, he looked solid all right. Still firm. No flabbiness in the face. Just the paleness of fatigue. But what is it that has drained your blood, Mr Connon? Grief? Or . . .

'Please come in, Mr Connon.' The loud voice broke his thoughts. He glanced round. Dalziel, his face a mask of sympathy so obviously spurious that Pascoe shuddered, was advancing with his hand outstretched. He stood aside to let Connon enter, then stepped out into the corridor leaving them together.

'He's like Henry Irving,' he said to the sergeant, shaking his head.

'Which one?'

'Which one? I don't know. Perhaps both. I'll be in here if I'm wanted.'

And for all his resentment at his dismissal, he found he wished that he had been wanted.

'It might be nice to see the master at work.'

The sergeant turned round, but Pascoe had closed the door of his temporary office behind him with a bang.

The sergeant went back to his desk whistling, 'Dear Lord and Father of mankind'.

It was, after all, Sunday.

'Sorry to get you out of bed, Mrs Fernie,' said Detective-Constable Edwards.

'Don't apologize,' interjected Fernie. 'I told her this might happen last night.'

'Last night? Why was that, Mr Fernie?'

'Well, I happened to notice your cars pull up outside Connon's house . . .'

'Happened to notice!' sneered Alice Fernie, pulling her nylon housecoat closer round her. 'You must have been stood at that window for half an hour or more.'

Fernie started to reply but the constable interrupted them.

'The important point to ask both of you is, did you notice anything earlier on?'

'Anything? What kind of thing? How much earlier?' asked Alice.

'Anything at all concerned with the Connons or their house. Any time yesterday.'

'Well, no. I was over there in the afternoon . . .'

'Over there?' The constable leaned forward.

40

'Did you know the Connons well, then?'

'Mary Connon, I know – knew her very well. We were friends,' said Alice; then, 'We were friends,' she repeated softly to herself, as though the import of the comment was just beginning to sink in.

'And how did Mrs Connon seem to you then?'

'Oh fine, fine. Just the same as ever. Nothing out of the ordinary.'

'Did she say anything that struck you as unusual?'

'No.'

'Were there any phone calls? Any callers?'

'No, nothing.'

'What time did you leave?'

'Shortly after four. I don't know exactly. I came back to get Dave's tea ready.'

'What were Mrs Connon's last words?'

'Last words?'

'I'm sorry. I didn't mean it to sound . . . what did Mrs Connon say as you left?'

'Well, nothing really. Cheerio. And something about getting Mr Connon's tea ready, if he got home in time for it.'

'What did she mean by that?'

'Well,' said Alice, 'I'm not sure . . .'

'Come off it, Alice,' said Fernie. 'She meant that if he didn't get home on time he'd get his own tea. She was a stickler for that, you've often told me. And he didn't get home on time either.'

'How do you know that?'

'I saw him. About half past six. And I'll tell you something else.'

41

'Dave!' said Alice with real annoyance in her voice.

'What's that?'

'He was drunk. Could hardly stand.'

The constable scribbled assiduously in his note-book.

'You're certain of that?'

'Dave!' said his wife again.

'Oh yes,' said Fernie, looking at his wife. She ignored his glance.

'If you're finished with me, I think I'll go back to bed,' said Alice, standing up so that her housecoat fell open revealing her thin nightdress.

'Thank you very much, Mrs Fernie,' said Edwards. 'You've been most helpful. We might want to see you again.'

'I'll be ready.'

She went out, leaving the constable smiling and her husband scowling.

'Now, Mr Fernie. What exactly happened when you met Mr Connon last night?'

'So that's all you can tell me, Mr Connon?'

'That's right, Superintendent.'

'You got home about half past six. How positive is that time?'

'I don't know. Pretty approximate.'

'That's a help. You say the television was on when you stuck your head into the lounge?'

'That's right. I see what you mean. There was some variety show. Dancers, girls, not much on. Dancing

42

behind a singer. Big youth, rather Italianate, singing something about flowers.'

Dalziel smiled sardonically.

'So you were out for four hours?'

'That's right.'

'Nasty that. What'd your doctor say?'

'I don't know what his diagnosis was. He just seemed concerned with getting me to bed.'

'You'll be seeing him again?'

'Of course.'

'I wonder if you'd mind if our man cast his eye over you while you're down here? It might save your McManus a crisis of conscience.'

Connon smiled wanly.

'Again I see what you mean. I have no objection.'

'Good. Good. But first, there's one thing that puzzles me. You felt sick in the kitchen. You end up by passing out on your bed. Why not be sick downstairs? The kitchen-sink. Or if your notions of hygiene are so strong, why not use the downstairs toilet? I noticed you had one.'

Connon spoke the words of his reply very slowly and distinctly as if learned by rote from a linguaphone record.

'I did not wish to disturb my wife.'

Dalziel crossed his legs cumbersomely and started prying into his nostrils with thumb and forefinger.

'Tell me, Mr Connon, Connie, I always think of you as Connie, do you mind?'

'I always think of you as Bruiser, Superintendent.'

43

Dalziel was amused and gave a few snorts of laughter.

'If the name fits, wear it, eh? Give a dog, eh? But yours doesn't tell us much. Doesn't fit, does it? Connie. A bit girlish. Which reminds me. You did not wish to disturb your wife. Now me, I'm a blunt Scottish lad by birth, a blunter Northcountryman by domicile. So perhaps the finer points of marital diplomacy have passed me by. (I wish my lad Pascoe could hear me!) But I don't quite follow the workings of your mind here. You come home, you're a bit under the weather, your wife ignores you, you've got to make your own tea. And you don't want to disturb her. There are some men would've disturbed her. Men you've played rugby with who'd have put their boots through the telly screen.'

'Men who have no respect for their wives do not deserve to keep them, Superintendent.'

That was a mistake, thought Connon. He's taking it personally.

Dalziel's wife, now divorced, had gone off with a milkman fifteen years before. At least, she had gone off. The milkman might have been malicious invention.

'Yes, Mr Connon. You're right. We should respect those who are weaker than us. Or older. Of course we should. Like forgiving our enemies.'

The phone rang.

'Excuse me,' said Dalziel. He listened for a moment.

'The doctor's ready for you now, if that's OK.'

Connon stood up.

'He won't keep you long, I expect. Like the Army. Just a cough and a piddle.'

'Will you want to see me again, Superintendent?' Dalziel opened the door for him.

'Just for a moment perhaps. Sergeant!'

The uniformed sergeant who had brought Connon to the room appeared. The expression of unctuous sympathy with which Connon had been greeted reappeared on Dalziel's face for the first time since the interview began.

'This is very good of you. It's a trying time. Sergeant, show Mr Connon to the doctor. And get him a cup of tea, or coffee if you prefer it.'

'No, thank you,' said Connon and set off after the sergeant.

'No,' said Dalziel to himself as he watched them go. 'I expect you'll manage a piddle without it. Or I'm losing my touch. Sergeant Pascoe!'

'You're not intending to go down to the Club in that rig, are you, girl?'

Gwen Evans turned before the mirror and peered back over her shoulder.

'What's the matter? My bum's not too big, is it?'

She was wearing a tight-fitting dress of flowered silk, whose style was distantly Chinese in origin.

'No, but if that slit went any further up the side, you'd be able to see your belly-button.'

'Don't be vulgar, Arthur. What's the matter? Don't you want me to go to the Club?'

'No, it's not that at all . . .'

'No? I think you'd much rather have me here slaving over roast beef and two veg, waiting for you to come back full of love and beer.'

'Be fair, Gwen. Most of the time you complain that I'm too keen to get you down there.'

'Oh ay. Where you can keep an eye on me at night. But it doesn't seem to worry you at lunchtime. Do you think I've got a time switch on it, then, and can't get it to work in hours of daylight? You should know better.'

Evans crossed to her in three swift strides. Instinctively she cowered back, holding her hands before her face, but he made no move to strike her. Instead he reached down, seized the hem of her dress and tugged violently upwards.

There was a tearing noise as stitching came apart and the oriental split up the side extended to the waist.

'There,' he said. 'Now you can really see your belly.'

She relaxed, leaned against the wall and began to laugh. At first there was a very faint note of hysteria in it, but this rapidly faded and the laugh deepened to genuine amusement.

'Give us a fag, will you, Arthur?' she said finally, regarding her husband with something like real affection. 'You're not such a bad old faggot when you're roused.'

Evans sat on the bed and lit two cigarettes, one of which he passed over to his wife.

46

'Thanks,' she said, drew on it deeply and placed it carefully on the edge of the dressing-table while she began to remove her ruined dress.

Evans watched her impassively.

She went to the wardrobe in her slip and opened its door.

'Well,' she said, 'what's it to be? Club-wear, or kitchen-wear?'

'Where were you last night, Gwen?'

'At the Club with you, dear. Remember?'

She smiled sweetly.

'Gwen,' he said, 'you're right. It's a daft question, isn't it, girl? I know where you were. Or at least who you were with.'

She stiffened and reached down a dress from the hanging rail.

'Oh, do you?'

'Yes, of course I do, Gwen. And I suppose if I know, every other sod in the Club has known for months. But I don't understand you, Gwen. I can see why you encourage all those young lads who come sniffing around you. That'd be flattering to any woman. But a man of my own age. And a friend. What made you pick him, Gwen? What made you pick Connie?'

'A-1, I hope,' said Dalziel when Connon reappeared.

'I hope not, Superintendent. That would mean I couldn't get better. And I don't think I've recovered from that knock yet. I hope we won't be much longer.'

'This is a murder enquiry, Mr Connon. We need your help. Your wife is dead.'

I think that I am at least as aware of that as you, Superintendent. My daughter will be arriving home some time this morning. I'd like to be there to meet her.'

Dalziel looked sympathetic.

'Of course. A father's feelings. But have no worries on that score. My sergeant was just telling me. Your daughter's got here safe and sound. We were able to assist a little there.'

Connon stood up.

'Jenny? Here? You mean, *here*?'

'Oh no. Never worry yourself. I mean at home, of course. We wouldn't bring her here.'

'At home. Then I must go.'

Dalziel let him reach the door.

'Just one question, Mr Connon.'

'If you must.'

'You left the Club at twenty to six, and got home about six-thirty. Rather a long time isn't it? It's only seven or eight miles at the most. And there's not much traffic about at that time.'

'There was enough.'

Dalziel, expert at detecting ironies, thought he heard one here.

'You didn't stop for any reason? A drink perhaps? Or had you had enough at the Club?'

'Why do you ask?' said Connon quietly.

'Well, it's just that we've had a statement. Not guaranteed reliable, mark you. But admissible, and voluntary, and therefore carrying some weight. This man . . .'

'Which man?'

'A man called Fernie, says he met you last night. Is that true?'

'Yes.'

'About six-thirty?'

'Yes.'

'Outside your house?'

'Yes again.'

'He says that you were acting oddly. In various ways. He says, in fact he was willing to swear, but we introduced a degree of moderation, as is our wont. He says he got the distinct impression that you were drunk. Very drunk.'

'Thank you for telling me, Superintendent. Now I must go. Goodbye.'

'Wait!' bellowed Dalziel.

Connon turned once more, half out of the door.

'If you want a fairly precise statement of the amount of alcohol I had taken up to about ten past six, I suggest you contact the constables who administered a breathalyser test to me at that time in Longtrees Road. I thought that this was what you were going on about, not malicious gossip. Good day. I must get to my daughter.'

Dalziel sat for a minute looking at the open door. Then he stood up and walked slowly over to it, scratching the back of his neck with an intensity that made his skin glow redly through the grey stubble.

'Sergeant,' he called, pitching his voice low, but with an intensity which easily carried it along the corridor to the desk. 'Would you step along here for a moment, if you'd be so kind? To discuss an organizational point.'

At the desk, the sergeant stopped whistling.

'Sorry, we don't start selling till twelve.'

'I'm a police officer,' said Pascoe. 'I don't start buying till I'm off duty.'

Sid Hope slowly rose from his crouching position behind the bar.

'Oh yes? I'm Hope, the club treasurer. What can I do for you? Is there some trouble? About the licence, I mean?'

'Should there be?' said Pascoe. 'You don't allow non-members to buy drinks, do you? Normally?'

'Of course not. When we know, that is. But I didn't know who you were. On my knees, trying to set up a new keg. It's like a bloody heart-transplant operation getting one of these things operational.'

Pascoe merely looked thoughtful at this attempt to bring in a lighter note.

'Anyway, I don't know them all. You could be a member. There's one or two from the police who are. Superintendent Dalziel for one.'

'Is that so? How do you run the bar, Mr Hope? A duty roster?'

Sid looked happy to get on to more general ground. 'That's right. We have a committee, me in charge, plus half a dozen others. We take it in turn to look after things for a week.'

'Just one of you? By himself?'

Sid laughed.

'Not bloody likely. No, we get some of the boys to help us when it's very busy, like weekends. Or even take over for a couple of nights. Some of us are married, you know. But, like I say, weekends the committee man in charge has really got to be here all the time. It's not just the serving, but the stock, and the till.'

'Sounds like hard work.'

'It is. Like now. Getting things set up for the great rush.'

'Popular, is it?'

'Christ, yes. It's our main source of income. Apart from the odd dance or raffle. We've just about paid back our loan now and . . .'

Pascoe turned on his heel. The man was beginning to be at his ease. He stopped talking at the sight of Pascoe's back.

'How many do you get in here on a Saturday night?'

'I don't know. Sixty, seventy, and there's the other . . .'

'You'd be on last night?'

'That's right.'

'Busy?'

'Very.'

'Was Mr Connon in at all, Mr Sam Connon?'

'Connie? No. Well, yes. I mean he was in at the

beginning of the evening right after the match. Look, what's all this about? Have you got any proof you really are a policeman?'

'I thought you'd never ask.'

Pascoe produced his warrant card. Sid examined it closely.

'What time did Connon leave?'

'I'm not sure. About five-thirty. Quarter to six, I think. I can't say for certain. He stopped to have a word with Arthur on his way out, but he might just have gone through into the other room.'

'Arthur?'

'Evans. Captain of the Fourths. That's right. Connie had been playing. Got a knock. Wanted a medicinal scotch. Hello, Marcus.'

Pascoe looked to the doorway. Standing there was a short fleshy man dressed in slacks and a polo-neck sweater. Pascoe felt that he had been standing there for some time.

Now he came into the room.

'Hello, Sid. Sorry I'm late again.'

'That's all right. I've been managing. As long as you didn't send Ted.'

Marcus didn't look at Pascoe but went behind the bar as though he wasn't there and began to busy himself with bottles.

'Marcus,' said Sid, 'this is – who is it?'

'Sergeant Pascoe.'

'Sergeant Pascoe. He's asking about Connie.'

Marcus looked at Pascoe now.

'What about Connie?'

'You know his wife?'

'Mary? Yes. What about her?'

'Was she a friend?'

Sid and Marcus looked at each other.

'Not exactly. But I know her pretty well. Connie's a close friend,' said Marcus.

'Why do you say "was"?' asked Sid.

'She's dead I'm afraid.'

You learn nothing from their faces, thought Pascoe. A split second of surprise, incredulity, shock; perhaps not even that. Then they're all busy arranging their features to the right expression.

'She was killed last night. I'd like to ask a few more questions, please.'

Marcus sank down on a bar stool. His left foot hooked repeatedly at a non-existing cross-rail.

'Where is Connie?' he said.

'I don't know. Home by now, I expect. His daughter's arriving.'

'Jenny. That's good. That's good.'

But the look on his face didn't seem to go with the words somehow.

'Daddy?'

'Yes.'

'Is that you?'

'Yes.'

She was sitting on the edge of a dining-room chair like a nervous candidate for interview.

For a moment they looked at each other as though this indeed was why she was there.

53

Then she ran to his arms and sobbed once into the wool of his overcoat, then rested there quietly for a long minute.

'Come and sit down, Jenny,' he said.

'Yes.'

They sat side by side at the table.

'Why don't you take your coat off?' he said.

'Why don't you?'

'Yes. I will.'

He stood up and undid the buttons. Jenny glanced down at the white and brown mock-fur coat she wore.

'It's all I had. I had to wear something, it was so cold coming. There was nothing else. And I was so worried about people seeing me in this. It's a bit gay, isn't it? That's all I thought as I walked up the path. But I don't have anything darker. Jesus! I never thought I'd give a damn about the neighbours.'

'You never used to. Some of the things you'd lie around the garden in when it was hot.'

'Oh yes. Do you remember old Mr Hawkins? He'd go in to get behind the curtain. But Mr Hall would come rushing out with his lawn-mower. All to look at my bumps.'

She laughed, then stopped in mid-note.

'We're talking about them as if they're all dead.'

He laid his coat on the table and put his arm round her shoulders.

'No, my dear. Not them. Just those days.'

She stood up away from his arm and took off her

coat. He looked at her, long-legged, short-skirted, well-rounded.

'They were wise to look,' he said with a smile.

She trailed her coat along the floor as she walked to the window and ran her finger along the sill.

'Tell me about it, Daddy.'

'Are you sure?'

'Yes. Please.'

'There's not much to tell.'

'Not much. My mother's dead! And that's not much?'

'No, I mean . . .'

She sat down on the sill.

'I'm sorry. I know what you mean.'

'I came home. I was late. I'd let myself be talked into playing and I got a bit of a knock. Your mother had had her tea and was sitting watching the television. I just stuck my head into the room and said hello. She didn't say anything. I could feel the atmosphere. You know how she hated anything to spoil her timetable, no matter how unimportant. So I went into the kitchen to get myself some tea.'

He stopped and after a moment Jenny turned from the window which she had been staring out of since he started talking. Connon was resting his head in his hands, his elbows on the table.

'Are you all right?'

'Yes, yes. It's just this pain again. That's what happened on Saturday. It came on then, in the kitchen. I couldn't eat. I felt sick, so I went upstairs. And I passed out on the bed.'

'What is this pain? Have you seen about it?'

'Not really. McManus has had a look. And a police doctor, but he didn't give me a diagnosis. I told you I got a knock during the game. Anyway, when I awoke it was nearly eleven. I still felt a bit groggy, but I remember thinking it was rather odd your mother hadn't been up to look for me. I came downstairs. The telly was still going in the lounge. I went in.'

He stopped and made a gesture which might have been a shudder, or a shrug, or an incipient reaching out to his daughter. Jenny didn't move and Connon became still again.

'Go on.'

'She was sitting in the big chair. Sprawled out. She was dead.'

He was silent again, studying his daughter from between half-closed lashes. As if making a decision, he stood up and walked over to her so that he was standing close to her, not touching, not offering to touch, but there if required.

'Her eyes were open. Her forehead was smashed in just above her nose. She was obviously dead. I stood there for a minute. It was odd. I was quite calm. I thought, I mustn't touch anything. And I walked out into the hall and picked up the telephone. Then this thing in my head started again. I could hardly dial. But I managed.'

'Who did you ring?'

'Old Dr McManus first. Then the police. McManus was more interested in me than your mother. Just took one look at her. But gave me a shot of something

56

and put me to bed. There were police all over the place, but they didn't get far with asking me questions. I was out like a light.'

'And this morning?'

'They were round first thing. That's where I've been. They told you that?'

'Yes.'

'It's that fellow Dalziel. I know him vaguely from down at the Club. He's a brute of a fellow. I don't know what they expected him to find out.'

'Have they any ideas?'

'Yes, I think so. A couple.'

'What are they?'

'Firstly, that I am lying about this pain in my head and passing out. I came in last night, smashed your mother's head in and waited a few hours before calling the police.'

'Secondly?'

'That I'm telling the truth about passing out. But, unknown to me or forgotten by me, I nevertheless killed your mother.'

Now there was the longest silence of all. Finally Jenny opened her mouth to speak but her father gently laid his index finger across her lips.

'You needn't ask, Jenny. The answer is no, I did not consciously kill her.'

'And unconsciously?'

'I don't think so. What else can I say?'

Now she took his hand and pressed it to her cheek. Connon looked fondly down at her flowing golden-brown hair.

He ran his fingers through its softness; it was a happy mixture of her mother's once vivid red and his own light brown.

'Don't worry, darling. It'll soon pass over, all this. Perhaps we can go away. It's almost your Christmas holidays. Would you like that, to go away, I mean?'

She looked up at him.

'Is that what you want? To go away, I mean?'

He rolled the question round in his mind for a moment, trying to read her thoughts. But nothing of them appeared in her face.

Finally he settled for the truth.

'No, I don't think so. No. It isn't.'

She nodded her head in serious accord.

'No. Neither do I. We'll stay. There'll be lots to do here. We'll stay and do whatever we have to. Together.'

She kept on nodding her head till her hair fell in a golden curtain over her white face.

Chapter 3

It was a glorious day. The sun laid a deep shadow obliquely across the polished oak of the coffin as it was lowered into the grave. The sky was cloudless, its blue more thinly painted than the blue of summer but the sun was too bright to stare in the eye. The air was just cold enough to make activity pleasant and the mourners shifted gently, almost imperceptibly, under their coats from time to time.

Only Connon and Jenny stood in absolute stillness.

Dalziel was scratching his left breast, his hand inside his coat moving rhythmically.

'Ironical,' he whispered loudly. 'Suit you, my boy. Subtle.'

'What?' said Pascoe.

'This,' he said. 'Nature.'

'Human nature? Or red in tooth and claw?'

'Don't get bloody metaphysical with me. The day, I mean. Fine day for a funeral. Sun. No wind blowing dead leaves or any of that. Fine day for golf.'

'What are you doing here then, sir?'

Dalziel sniffed loudly. A few heads turned and turned away. He obviously wasn't about to break down.

'Me? Friend of the family. Last respects must be paid. Heartfelt sympathy.'

He fluttered his hand inside his coat so that the cloth pulsated ludicrously.

'What's more to the point, what are you doing here? I come within smelling distance of having a reason. You're a non-starter. Bloody policeman, that's all. You'll get the force a bad name. Intrusion of grief, it could be grounds for complaint.'

'In his master's steps he trod,' murmured Pascoe softly.

'Which of us does that make the very sod? And what *are* you looking for, Pascoe? You're not nursing any nice little theories, are you? And not telling me?'

'No,' said Pascoe, 'of course not.'

Not bloody much, thought Dalziel. You keep working at it, lad. Nothing like the competitive spirit for sharpening the wits.

'Not a bad gate,' whispered Arthur Evans to Marcus.

'Arthur!'

Evans looked sideways at his wife. She had put hardly any make-up on in deference to the occasion and wore a plain black coat, loose-fitting. But the bite in the air had brought the red blood to her lips and cheeks and the looseness of the coat just made it more obvious where it did touch.

Dressed like that, thought Evans with bitter admiration, she wouldn't stay a widow long.

Marcus, on his other side, looked pale beyond the remedy of frost. He swayed slightly.

'You all right, boyo?'

Jesus, on and off the field, I spend half my life nursing them.

'Yes, I'm fine. Just a bit cold. Poor Connie.'

Poor Connie. Poor bastard. Evans remembered the shock last Sunday when they had finally got to the Club, arguments buried for an hour. That detective had been there, he was somewhere around now, bloody ghouls, one of Dalziel's lackeys, there's a right thug for you, like all these Scotsmen, no finesse, first up first down, feet feet feet. Sid had got in first. Snipped his indirect line, gave the news right out, loud and clear. Mary Connon's dead. And all I could do was look at Gwen, watch Gwen, see her age beneath the words, then gradually come back to life with awareness of her own life.

Poor Connie. He deserves sympathy. He deserves . . . perhaps he will get what he deserves. There he stands with that little girl of his. Not so little. She's a pretty little thing.

She's a pretty little thing.

The service was over. Out of the corner of his eye Pascoe had noticed two men with spades move tentatively forward from the cover of a clump of trees, then retreat. Their movement startled half-a-dozen crows whose caws had been a harsh burden to the words of the prayer-book and they went winging from the tree tops in ragged grace, as the black-coated mourners moved in twos and threes away from the grave-side, silent at first, but speaking more and more freely as the distance grew between themselves and the motionless couple who remained.

At the car park they formed little groups before dispersing. Dalziel convened with three or four elder statesmen of the Club, his face and manner serious. He produced a cigarette-case and passed it round.

Black Russian perhaps, thought Pascoe. That would amuse Dalziel if I could tell him. Do I want to amuse Dalziel? And if I do, is it to keep him sweet so I can manipulate him, like I pretend? Or is it because he puts the fear of God into me? Just how good is he anyway? Or is he just a ruthless sucker of other men's blood? 'Don't get bloody metaphysical with me!' But said quite nicely really. Like a jocular uncle. Uncle Andrew. You had to laugh. But not here. It's colder now. Christ, I'm holding conversations with myself about the weather, the mental Englishman, that's me. Now there's something to warm us all up, that woman getting into the back seat, back seat's the place for you, dear, are you sitting comfortably, now get them off. Don't be shocked, love, that's what all the detectives are thinking this year, you'll be giving yourself a scratch in a minute Andrew, you randy old devil. Randy Andy. Now if she'd been killed, her, Gwen, wasn't it? Evans, that would have been easy. Jealous husband, spurned lover, or one of those tumescent young men who'd been hanging around her from the moment she set foot in the bar, yes, one of those provoked just that bit too far, just over the edge where playing starts to be for real. But not Mary Connon, not that parcel of middle-aged lumber they'd just stored away. Though why not? She'd been built on the same lines, streamlines, take a hundred lines, so they said. Forty-five. Inches. Years. Was forty-five too old? No kind of age at all these days.

And she wasn't looking her best when I saw her, was she? There's something about a hole in the head . . .

So who knows? But I don't quite see the young men . . . more like one of these old fogies Randy Andy's chatting up, best prop-forward the Old Sodomites ever had, don't you know; or perhaps the best fly-half who never played for England, himself perhaps, selling us all a dummy as he stands there remembering how he smashed her head in so he could look for it inside, for the years lost, the place out in the glow of the crowd at Twickenham, could a man love a game that much? And smashed her with what, for God's sake? Where was it? I'd like a look round that house. Whatever it is could be lying at the bottom of his wardrobe. He'd get used to it after a while, like an egg-stain on a waistcoat, you get used to anything after a while. Lying there for someone to find, a friend, Felstead, Marcus, what's he got to look so sick about? And what'd he be doing in Connon's wardrobe anyway? Homosexual jealousy, that's the answer, I'll try it on Dalziel for a giggle. More likely his daughter, she'll find anything there is. Christ, what a thing to find out about your father, she'd do all right in the back seat too, I wouldn't mind carrying her away at a student riot. Here they come. And there goes fat Marcus, I come to bury Mary not to, he's taken his time about extending heartfelt sympathy though there's always the phone. Still, for a nearest and dearest friend . . .

'Hello, Connie, Jenny.'

'Marcus.'

'Hello, Uncle Marcus.'

Marcus had invited her to stop calling him 'Uncle' about three years earlier when she had flourished into young womanhood. 'It makes me feel old and you sound young.' So he had become plain Marcus.

Till now.

I have reverted to my old role, thought Marcus.

'I would have called round,' he said apologetically, addressing himself to Jenny rather than Connon. 'But you know how things . . . how are you both?'

'Well,' said Connon. He did not look as if he was really listening, but glanced back to the grave.

'What will you do now, Jenny? Is your term over?'

'No, there's another couple of weeks yet, but I've got leave of absence. I needn't go back till after Christmas.'

'How is it? Are you liking the life?'

'It's not bad. A bit crowded. There's more students than space. I can sympathize a bit more with these people who write indignantly to the *Express* about "smelly students".'

Thank God for the resilience of youth, thought Marcus. No damage there, or not that's going to show. But you, Connie, out of the cage at last, you look as if another sniff of free air will shrivel your lungs. No bloody wonder, the shock, the strain of investigation. There's a new life waiting, if only you'll believe that, I must make him believe it before it's too late . . .

Jenny made a move down the path towards the car park. Marcus touched her arm.

'I'll stay here and chat to your father a bit till the others have thinned out. We'll catch you up. You'd better go and sit in the car out of the cold.'

Jenny was surprised to find herself resenting Marcus slightly as she moved away.

She was my mother after all, and he's my father. Why should he be treated like the sensitive plant and me chucked down to face this lot?

Because you can think like this at a moment like this, she admonished herself humorously and the shadow of a smile must have run over her face for she caught 'Bruiser' Dalziel eyeing her sharply as she stepped on to the car park.

Standing a little behind Dalziel she saw a tall young man, elegantly dressed, with a thin intelligent face – the kind of actor-type who played ambitious young Foreign Office men on the telly.

She thought momentarily of Antony. She hadn't had time to see him before she left, everything had happened in such a hurry. But no doubt Helen would have passed on the news to him. Perhaps even made a come-back in her original starring role.

Definitely her last appearance, thought Jenny, but didn't find it particularly funny. She intended to make straight for the car and shut the door firmly on all condolences, sympathetic noises, keen-edged questionings probing for vicarious pain. But her arm was taken firmly and she was brought to a halt.

'I just wanted to say that I shall miss your mother, Jenny,' said Alice Fernie.

The annoyance that had tightened her lips for a moment eased away. She could not remember anyone else saying this. They were all 'dreadfully sorry', it had come as a terrible shock to them, but no one had really suggested that Mary Connon would be missed.

'Yes, I shall too,' she replied, then feeling this was a bit too cold she squeezed the gloved hand which still rested on her arm and went on, 'I know how much she relied on you.'

This was nothing more than the simple truth, she realized, as the words came out. Mary Connon had rarely mentioned Alice Fernie to her except in faintly disparaging or patronizing terms. Her lack of taste; the unfairly large wage her husband earned on the factory floor; the excessive subsidization by the ratepayers of council-house rents. She was capable of blaming the Fernies ('and all those like them,' she would say inclusively) for the very existence of the Woodfield estate. It had only been a very few years previously that Jenny had realized that the council estate had been there already when her parents bought the house. She had come to accept a picture of rolling countryside being savaged before her mother's eyes as the bulldozers rolled in, prompted by the Fernies and 'all those like them'. But Alice Fernie had been, perhaps by the mere accident of proximity, the nearest thing to a real friend she had. And now Jenny felt real gratitude that this large handsome woman who could only be in her early thirties had thought enough of her mother to accept the condescension of manner and get closer to her.

Closer than me perhaps, she thought.

'How did you get here, Mrs Fernie?' she asked. 'Can we give you a lift back?'

There were no funeral cars other than the hearse. 'I will judge what is fitting,' she had heard her father say to the oblique remonstrances of the man from the undertakers.

'No, thank you, dear. You'll want to be with your dad. And I'm not going straight back anyway. 'Bye now.'

'Goodbye. Please call round, won't you? I shan't be going back to college till next month.'

I'll have to watch myself there, she thought as she watched Alice move away with long confident strides, I could become as patronizing as Mum.

As she got into the car, she glanced back and

caught the eye of the young man who could have been from the Foreign Office. He took a step forward. She thought he was going to come across and talk to her. But a rumbling, phlegmy cough from Fat Dalziel caught both their attentions and the young man turned away.

Policemen, she thought, angry at her disappointment, and slammed the car door.

Connon watched Marcus walk away from him down the path through the rank and file of headstones.

The car park was nearly empty now. The Evanses' car was just pulling away. He looked after it thoughtfully. Gwendoline. He formed the syllables deliberately in his mind and smiled. All those youngsters competing to provoke the loudest laugh, craning forward to get the deepest view of bosom, pressing close to feel the warmth of calf or thigh, and imagining a returned pressure. Tales to be blown up into triumphs over a couple of pints. But the real triumphs were never boasted of, but remembered in secret; first with reminiscent delight, but soon with fear and cold panic.

Dalziel was gone, he observed, and his puppy-dog, Pascoe. Mentally he corrected himself. He had no reason for thinking Pascoe was merely that, though he was sure Dalziel would make him that if he got the chance.

And me, what would he make of me if he got the chance? he thought.

A parcel for the lawyers. Strongly wrapped, neatly labelled.

Samuel Connon. Wife-killer. There must be some long Latin word for a man who killed his wife. Dalziel might know it, though he probably wouldn't admit to it if he did. Pascoe would know. He seemed a highly educated kind of cop. The new image. Get your degree, join the force, the Yard's the limit. Or . . . leave school at sixteen, start as office boy. You can be assistant personnel manager by the time you're forty. If you're lucky. And if the general manager is a big rugby fan.

I'd better be getting down to Jenny. Poor Jenny. I wish I knew how hard this has hit her. Perhaps I was wrong. Perhaps we should get away for a bit. Where? What on? There's not all that much spare in the account. All this costs a bit. Even if you haggled over headstones. Now if I'd gone first, Mary'd have been sitting pretty. But what kind of man insures against his wife's death?

At least they can't say I killed her for profit. But it'd be nice to get away. Soon. When things had quietened down. It'd be nice to get far, far away. To somewhere as unlike this as possible.

Back to the desert.

Over twenty years earlier, Connon had been sent to join his unit in Egypt at the start of his National Service. He had only been out there a couple of months when the regiment returned home, and at the time the few weeks he spent there seemed to consist of nothing but endless liquid motions of the bowels. He had been as delighted as the rest to return to England and it was this period that saw the blossoming of his rugby career. He had played only a couple of times since leaving school but now he became quickly aware of the advantages traditionally enjoyed by the athlete in His Majesty's forces. His natural talent exploded into consummate artistry in these conditions and only the simultaneous service, as officer, of the current Welsh stand-off kept him out of the Army XV.

But something of his brief acquaintance with the desert did not easily die. It remained with him as dreams of luxury hotels in the remote Bermudas haunt some men. He read anything he could get hold of on the desert. Any desert. He collected colour brochures and handouts from the travel agents. Fifteen days in Morocco. Three weeks in Tunisia. Amazing value. But always too much for him.

In any case the desert Connon really wanted to visit was not in any of the brochures, not even the most expensive. He recognized it by its absence, that is, he knew what he wanted was something out of the reach of a camera; something untranslatable into colour photography and glossy paper. He wanted rock that had absorbed terrible, endless heat for a million years, that had writhed in infinitely slow violence till its raw bowels lay on the surface, yet without a single movement noticed by man. He wanted sand which rose and fell like the sea, but so slowly that it was only when it drowned his own civilization that a man recognized its tides.

It was a vision he confided to no one. Least of all Mary, who had found his collection of travel brochures nuisance enough.

Perhaps Jenny . . .

Hs saw that she had got out of the car again and was standing against the bonnet looking up towards him. Otherwise the car park was now completely empty.

He began to walk towards her.

'I wasn't going to ask her anything,' repeated Pascoe. 'Not then. Not there. I felt sorry for her. Just standing there. She looked, I don't know, helpless somehow.'

This, he thought, is a turn up for the book. Bruiser Dalziel lecturing me on tact and diplomacy. It was like Henry the Eighth preaching about marital constancy.

'Well, watch it. We don't harry people at funerals. At least not unless we think they did it. And we don't think young Jenny Connon did it, do we?'

'No, sir.'

'You checked, of course?'

'Of course. She was nearly a hundred miles away. We know that.'

'It's about all we bloody well do know. The only thing we make any progress with is the list of things we don't know. Item: who had a strong motive to kill her? No one we know, not even the great Connie as far as we know.'

'Strength of motive is in the mind of the murderer, sir.'

'Confucius, he bloody well say. To continue. Item: what did he kill her with? A metal object or at least an object with a metal end, cylindrical in shape, long enough to be grasped probably with both hands and smashed right between the eyes of a victim who sits there smiling and doesn't even try to duck.'

'The pathologist's report did say that Mrs Connon had unusually fragile bones, sir. Perhaps we're over-estimating the strength needed.'

'So what? Thanks for nothing. And Mary Connon fragile? I don't believe it. It couldn't be true. With tits like those she'd have broken her collar-bone every time she stood up. To continue again. Item: who saw anything suspicious or even anyone any-where near the house that night? Not a soul. Not even the eyes and ears of the Woodfield Estate, your friend Fernie. All he can swear is that Connon was rolling drunk. Which Connon can disprove with con-bloody-siderable ease.'

'It does fit with Connon's account, though. About his giddiness, I mean. Makes his story that bit stronger, don't you think? And our doctor did find signs of a slight concussion. He's still seeing his own man, too. I checked.'

Dalziel slammed his fist so hard on the desk that Pascoe broke his rule of stony non-reaction to his superior and started in his chair.

'I'm not interested in the bloody man's health. If

72

he's innocent, he can drop dead tomorrow for all I care.'

'A sentiment that does you credit, sir. But there is one thing about this injury to Connon that's a little bit odd.'

'What's that, and why isn't it in your report?' asked Dalziel suspiciously.

'Apparently irrelevant. But I felt you might like it, sir.'

Dalziel licked his lips and looked as if the task of strangling Pascoe personally and instantly might not be unattractive.

'It's just that when I was down at the Club, I talked among others to a chap called Slater.'

'Fat Fred. I know him.'

'Slater remembered Connon being laid out. But, he added casually and as far as I could see without malice, that he reckoned the boot that did the damage belonged to Evans, his own captain. He seemed to think it was just a case of mistaken identity.'

'Fred would. He's thick as pigshit, that one. But Arthur Evans isn't made that way. He plays hard, but he'd never put the boot in.'

'So?'

'So Fred Slater should start wearing his glasses on the field. Or better still, give up. It's indecent a man that size exposing himself in public. I don't know how his wife manages him.'

He chuckled to himself at the thought and murmured, 'Levers, I should think.'

'Pardon?'

'Sergeant,' he said quietly, 'is there anything we've left undone which we ought to have done?'

'I don't think so, sir.'

'Right. Then somewhere, in some area we are covering, or have covered, lies the clue.'

'The clue?'

'There's always a clue, boy. Don't you read the Sunday papers? All this started somewhere and it wasn't Boundary Drive. Or if it was, we're not going to get much help there. Now where's our best bet?'

Pascoe spoke like a bored actor who was thinking of things other than his lines.

'At the Club.'

'That's right. I think I'll just drop in there tonight. No, tomorrow. That's a training night. They'll all be there. Socially, I mean, for a pot of ale. If there's anything known, they'll tell me by chucking-out time. They'll tell me.'

He spoke with some satisfaction.

Like a . . . but the phone interrupted Pascoe's search for the right simile.

Dalziel nodded at it.

'Well, get it, then.'

Pascoe lifted up the receiver.

'Sergeant Pascoe here. Yes?'

He listened for a few moments then replaced the receiver and stood silent.

'Not a private call, I hope, Sergeant,' said Dalziel. 'Or are you just playing hard to get.'

'I'm sorry, sir,' said Pascoe. 'No. It's the Connons. They got home and there was a letter. For the girl, it seems. Something unpleasant. Connon wants us to go out there straight away.'

Alice Fernie had gone straight home from the funeral, not doing some shopping first as she had told Jenny. She possessed a great deal of natural tact as well as independence of spirit, a quality which had made possible her friendship with Mary Connon. But the journey had involved two buses and a great deal of waiting. So she had plenty of time to think.

Buses and trains both set you thinking, she thought. But not in the same way. Trains gave you a rhythm, sent you into dreams, cut you off from reality. Buses were always stopping and starting; traffic, road-junctions, lights; and of course, bus-stops. The world you passed through was observable. And real.

So was the world inside your head.

Buses were good places to worry on.

Alice Fernie was worried. She was wondering what the law might do to her husband if it caught up with him.

'Hello there, Alice. What a grand drying day it is, eh?'

Maisie Curtis from next door had got on the bus and was easing herself into the seat beside her. They were both broad-hipped women and the woeful inadequacy of the Corporation's transport service was very apparent. Alice didn't mind. The Corporation didn't provide much heating either and the warmth generated by the collision of two such large areas was very welcome.

'Hello, Maisie.'

'You're looking smart. You've been to her funeral, then?'

'That's right.'

There was a short pause while Maisie paid her fare.

'Many there?'

'A few.'

'Oh.'

She'll want names, thought Alice resignedly. She'll want a guest-list. And she'll get it.

'There's no funeral meats, then?'

'No. Everyone's just going home. Quietly. Like me.'

'Was there anyone from the police there?'

Alice sighed.

'As a guest, I mean, a mourner. They wouldn't be there official, would they? Not unless . . .'

'What?'

'Unless they wanted to watch him, keep an eye on him.'

'Who?'

'Mr Connon, of course.'

Alice shifted herself in the seat so that Maisie had to give a couple of inches. The conductor looked in awe at the overhang.

'Why should they want to watch him?'

'I don't know. In case he decided to skip, that's why. Well, he might, mightn't he? If he felt like it.'

'Like what?'

'Like getting away.'

'In his shoes, who wouldn't feel like getting away?'

Maisie was used to deliberate obtuseness on the part of her neighbour and was neither distracted nor offended by it.

'I mean escaping. If he did it.'

'If he did it? What makes you say that? You should watch what you say, Maisie. That kind of talk could get you into trouble.'

Alice found herself speaking with greater vehemence than she'd intended, but once more Maisie greeted the affront with a smile.

'Well, if I'm in trouble, I won't be the only one. There'll be lots of company,' she said smugly.

Alice's heart sank.

'Who do you mean?'

'Why, your Dave for one.'

Oh God, she thought. Was he still at it? In spite of the row last night? He'd say it to someone who mattered sooner or later. And then, then the law would have its course with David Fernie. Alice knew nothing of the law of slander. But she knew how much compensation she herself would demand for being falsely accused of murder.

She tried to speak casually.

'Dave? What's he been saying to you?'

To you. Maisie Curtis. Queen gossip of the Woodfield Estate. Which meant of the town.

'To me? Nothing. Your Dave doesn't pass the

time of day with me. No, it was our Stanley he was talking to.'

This was worse. Maisie Curtis's Stanley was a direct channel to the Rugby Club. The only one Dave had, probably. And, equally probably, he'd know it. There'd be gossip enough at the Club. Bound to be. Suppose Stanley, young, bumptious, keen to impress . . . lived nearly opposite the murder-house . . . next to a key witness.

Witness! To what?

Like that time in Bolton. That was a few years ago, but her memory was longer than her husband's. The law had been brought in then, but only to ask why anyone should have wanted to break Fernie's jaw and kick three of his ribs in.

But Mr Connon was a different kettle of fish. It wouldn't be the law of the jungle this time. Gossip was one thing. Innuendo, knowing winks, impudent questionings. But someone saying he *knew* was quite different; someone saying he was certain.

Dave Fernie, big Dave Fernie. He knew. He always bloody well knew. Not even God Almighty was as certain about things as Dave Fernie.

'What's Dave been saying, then?' she asked as calmly as she could, shredding her ticket with meticulous care.

'Well, according to my Stanley, your Dave says he knows how he, Mr Connon that is, killed his wife. And he knows why.'

Maisie nodded as affirmatively at this point as if she had been Fernie himself.

Soul-mates, thought Alice. They're soul-mates. Born under the same star.

'Was that all?'

'All? Wasn't it enough? It quite upset our Stanley, it did. That's how I got to hear of it. I could see something was bothering him. And he's not been in the best of health lately, had a few days off work with one of his tummy upsets. So I asked him and he told. He's always looked up to Mr Connon, you see. Well, I mean, they all do, down at that Club. He's on the selection committee as well, you see.'

Alice didn't see, because she'd stopped listening. To think they said that it was women who had the vicious tongues. There'd been one or two near things since Bolton. One or two unpleasant moments. One or two lost friends.

But this could mean the law.

'Alice! Are you not getting off, then?'

The pressure had gone from her flank. Maisie was standing in the aisle, looking down at her.

'Yes, of course.'

They set off down the main road together, Maisie chattering away about other matters now. She was unoffendable herself and never considered for one moment that anyone could be hurt or angered by anything she might say.

After fifty yards they turned left into Boundary Drive.

It was quieter here, away from the main course of traffic. The private side of the road was lined with trees which, even though stripped for winter, added something to the peacefulness of the scene. The trees which should have been on the other side of the road had been swept away at one fell swoop, without warning, when the Corporation bulldozers had moved in at the end of the war. An act of civic vandalism, the residents had called it, complaining even more when they realized they would have to pay road charges now the council was making up the road-surface. But the trees had gone beyond recall, and their absence accentuated as much as the architecture the differences between the old and the new.

Still, the trees and the pleasant outlook over to the more solid and architecturally varied private houses had made Alice glad that they had been offered a house here rather than in the middle of the estate.

Up till now.

Maisie's voice suddenly rose so sharply that it penetrated the confused web of her own thoughts.

'That's them, isn't it, Alice? In that car. I thought I recognized them.'

Her eyes focused ahead. A black saloon had just driven by them. She remembered seeing it in the cemetery car park. She watched with trepidation as it slowed down further along the street. For a moment of heart-sinking shock, she thought it had pulled over to stop in front of her own house. But the driver was merely giving himself enough room to swing round to the left, over the pavement and into the Connons' drive.

'I wonder what they're after?' asked Maisie, increasing her pace.

Alice didn't wonder. She didn't care. As long as they weren't after Dave. She'd have to talk to him again. She'd have to make it quite clear that he was worrying her silly with his slanderous gossip. She'd have to get him to realize that he could get himself into very serious trouble with these terrible accusations against Mr Connon. Very serious trouble.

Unless . . .

It was curious that the thought had never entered her mind before.

Unless they were true.

She began to lengthen her stride to keep up with Maisie Curtis.

'"Dear Miss Connon,

'It must be terrible for you to find that your mother is dead and to realize your father is a murderer. Nothing can bring your mother back. But it may be some comfort to you to know that the man you think is your father is not. Your mother married him only so that her baby (you) would have a name. What a name! It is a murderer's name. Think yourself lucky he is nothing to do with you."'

'No signature.'

'Let me see,' said Dalziel.

Pascoe handed over the letter. The superintendent took it carefully by the same corner that Pascoe had used and glanced down at the writing.

'At least it's clean,' he said.

'That's little consolation,' said Connon, who was standing with his arm protectively over Jenny's shoulders. To Pascoe the girl did not look particularly in need of protection. In fact she had the same rather dangerously angry look he'd seen wrinkle her brow after the funeral.

'Let's get this clear . . .' Dalziel began.

Connon interrupted him.

'I presume that means you want me to repeat myself.'

Clever sod, thought Dalziel. Clever-clever. I'm beginning to hope you did it, clever Connie.

'No, I'll repeat you,' he said. 'You just confirm. It's a question of making sure we're talking the same language. Now, you came straight back after the funeral arriving . . . when?'

Connon looked at his daughter.

'Quarter to twelve,' she said. 'I put the radio on. There was a time-check.'

Then she added, almost apologetically, 'I wanted a noise in the house. Something lively.'

Pascoe looked at her sympathetically. She didn't avoid his gaze but stared back till he looked away.

'You picked up the letter as you came in, but didn't open it immediately?'

'No,' said Jenny. 'I thought it'd be just another condolence note or card.'

'Anyway, you made a pot of tea, brought it through to your father who was sitting in here, then you opened your letter?'

'That's right.'

'And?'

'And what? I showed it to Daddy.'

'And I,' cut in Connon, 'decided we ought to get in touch with you instantly.'

'Quite right too, sir.'

'Well, Superintendent, what next?'

Dalziel looked around with the kind of heavily underlined hesitance that could be clearly marked in the back row of the gods. Pascoe watched in awe.

He invites them to join in his games, he thought. That's the secret of his success. He reduces it all to the level of a pantomime.

'I wonder,' said Dalziel, 'I wonder if I could perhaps have a word with you alone, sir?

Connon looked doubtful.

If he's not careful, he'll be playing. If he's not playing already.

'My sergeant can be taking a statement from Miss Connon while we're talking,' added Dalziel.

That'll be nice, thought Pascoe, trying to keep any trace of the thought off his face.

Jenny Connon did not seem to think it would be particularly nice at all and made little effort to keep her thoughts off her face. But she turned readily enough and went to the door.

'We'll go into the lounge, then,' she said. Connon nodded. Dalziel wondered if he detected a hint of relief.

The chair had been moved, Pascoe noticed. He didn't suppose anyone else had sat in it since Mary

Connon had relaxed to watch television on Saturday night. Then he laughed inwardly and changed his mind. The chair probably hadn't come back from County Forensic where Dalziel, despite the scorn he poured on Science and all its works, had sent it. The boys down there, their work once finished, would have no compunction at all about sitting in it.

'Well,' said Jenny, 'are you just going to stand there, all hawk-eyed, or are we going to get on with this statement? What would you like me to state?'

'Yes, the statement.' Pascoe fumbled in his pocket for his notebook. 'Won't you sit down?'

'In my own home, I prefer to issue the invitations. Please sit down, Sergeant.'

Only the remembrance that her mother had died in this room not a week earlier stopped Pascoe from grinning.

He sat down.

'The words in that letter were printed, of course, but even printing is sometimes recognizable. Did the writing remind you of anyone's you had seen before?'

Jenny shook her head.

'No.'

'Sure?'

'Yes, I'm sure.'

'Can you think of anyone who would send such a letter to you?'

'Yes.'

Startled, he ceased his pretence of making notes.

'Who?'

'The man who killed my mother.'

He shook his head slowly.

'Now why should he do that?'

'To divert suspicion from himself.'

'How can he hope to do that when we don't know who wrote the letter?'

'But you do know who you're suspicious of.'

Of whom you are suspicious, Antony might have said. But it sounded a little clumsy for Antony. He never let his passion for correctness trap him into clumsiness. In any field.

She noticed that this time Pascoe had let his grin show through. She felt like grinning back, whether at Pascoe or at the thought of Antony she wasn't sure. But she didn't, for at the same time she felt guilty, as she did whenever she found herself acting normally, as if her mother hadn't been done to death, here, in this very room, last week, on an ordinary Saturday evening with the television set babbling uncaringly on in the background.

The thought had stopped the grin even if her willpower had failed. But even now she recognized how diluted the emotional shock of remembering had already become.

I could go out tonight, she thought. Have a drink and a laugh, no bother. I know I could. I feel I shouldn't be able to, but I could. They've got to catch him soon, they've got to, I'll make sure they do, he deserves it, he must be caught. Must.

That'll be an end of it then, some more distant part of her mind whispered.

Dear God! the most conscious level replied, aghast. Is that it, then? Is that what the pursuit of vengeance is – not the instinctive reaction of deep and lasting grief, but an attempt to compensate for shallowly felt grief, to give it body, to make testimony to it?

Confused, she became angry. Angry at herself for thinking like this. Angry at the police for making no progress. Angry at Pascoe for talking to her here while the real interview was taking place in the next room.

'Let's stop this farce, shall we?' she said.

'Farce?'

'Yes. You don't want a statement from me. What the hell can I state that's any help or even needs recording? All you want is me here so that disgusting Dalziel can chat Daddy up by himself.'

Pascoe's face relaxed again at her choice of adjective and this time an answering smile almost broke through.

'Now why should we want that?' he asked politely.

She turned away from him.

'So that he can ask Daddy if what the letter says is true, I suppose. About me not being his child, I mean.'

Pascoe seemed to be trapped like a disembodied spirit somewhere in the room where he could see and hear an unemotional policeman, disguised as himself, ask in an absolutely even voice,

'And is it?'

*　　*　　*

'The question's purely biological, I presume, Super-intendent?'

'Pardon?'

'You're interested in the narrow question of whether I am physically the girl's father, rather than in my attitudes towards her?'

Christ! another talking like a Sunday supplement article. Pascoe's bad enough and at least the bugger's on my side. But this . . . cold fish, Connon. He'd work out which side your balls were hanging before he made his sidestep.

'That's right, Mr Connon. I think. I mean, was young Jenny born as a result of you having inter-course with your wife?'

Connon shrugged. He looked very tired.

'I think so.'

'Think!?'

Dalziel took a rapid command of himself so that though the word began as a roar it ended as an almost gentle interrogative.

'I have never had any positive evidence to the contrary. At the same time, I can't point to any proof positive on the other side. There have seemed to me and others to be physical resemblances, but parents and relations in general are notoriously blind in these matters.'

'So you admit that it's possible the terms of the letter could be accurate?'

'Not all of them, Superintendent.'

Hair-splitting now. Don't answer. Let the sod go on in his own sweet time.

'It's a question of faith, I suppose. I suppose it always is.'

'And you didn't have that faith?'

'Once. But it went. Too late to matter as far as Jenny was concerned, I'm glad to say.'

'Why did it go? Was there anything in particular, talk, anything like that? Gossip?'

'No. Probably. I never heard, but then I wouldn't. More in your line.'

The truth of this simple statement half surprised Dalziel. He ran his mind back over the narrow little track signposted 'Mary Connon', but came across no landmarks of interest.

'Well, then . . .' he said.

'She told me.'

'She what?'

'Told me. Several times. She wanted me to give up playing almost from the start. Said it was too much to expect her to cope all week with a baby and then to be left to herself on Saturdays as well. I daresay there was something in it.'

'But you didn't.'

'You know I didn't. I went on. Every Saturday from September to April. It was important.'

'To you?' said Dalziel very softly. He didn't want to disturb his man. He thought he recognized the beginnings of that half-dreamy inward-looking state in which a thought-monologue could easily lead to a confession.

But his soft interjection seemed to blast into Connon's mind like a hand-grenade.

'To me?' he said, laughing. 'Of course. But that sounds selfish, doesn't it? The outskirts of a motive. No, important to us all, the three of us, my wife and child, as well as me.'

'But you said she told you. What?'

'She told me that I might as well keep on going to the Club. At least that way I might run into Jenny's father.'

'She said that!'

I'd have broken her neck, thought Dalziel. Motive? What better? I'd have broken her bloody neck!

But the thought went on against his will: perhaps that's why she told you by telegram, perhaps that's why you ended up standing stupefied in the lobby of your little semi-detached, reading and re-reading the jumble of words on the buff form. He'd often thought since of his wife in some post office writing those words down, then passing the form to some clerk to count them up. Had he said anything? Had there been an expression on his face as he counted? Was there a query perhaps?

It must have cost her a packet.

But, he thought now, with a self-irony which had only developed of later years, but, he thought as he looked down at his tightly clenched fist, it had been money wisely spent.

'When was this?'

'Too long ago for a motive. Fourteen, fifteen years.'

'What did you do?'

'I forget.'

Dalziel let this pass for the moment.

'Did she ever say more?'

'She repeated the claim, twice I think, both times at moments of great anger.'

'Did you believe her?'

Connon shrugged.

'I've told you, it's a matter of faith. I knew she'd been with other men before we married. But I believed she loved me. So I had faith.'

'And?'

Connon looked at Dalziel with the self-possession the detective found so irritating.

'No "and", Superintendent. I think I've said as much as I want to say.'

Dalziel infused a threatening rasp into his voice, more from habit than expectation of producing any result.

'You've either said too much or too little, Mr Connon. I need to know more.'

'Or less.'

'I can't unknow what you've told me.'

'No. But you can reduce it to its proper proportions surely. Many years ago my wife implied to me that I was not the father of her daughter. She later withdrew the implication. It's doubtless the kind of nasty thing husbands and wives shout at each other fairly frequently when they're rowing. It didn't worry me, at least not too much. And less as time went on. I never thought of it. Jenny was mine, my daughter, my responsibility, even if you could have proved Genghis Khan was her father. So why

90

should I be bothered? Now my wife's dead and my daughter's had a vicious letter. Now I'm bothered. I'm telling you all this in the hope it might be some help to you to catch the writer of that letter.'

'And your wife's murderer?'

Connon nodded wearily.

'If you like. Though I don't see how. And his bit of harm's done, isn't it? This boy's got his still to finish.'

Dalziel rose ponderously and belched without effort at concealment. Connon remained seated, looking up at him.

'Good day to you, Mr Connon. Please contact us instantly should any further attempt be made to contact your daughter, by letter or any other means.'

'Other?'

'This kind of thing can become a habit. I should try to get to the telephone first in future, for instance.'

As if at command, the phone rang.

Connon looked startled, the first unguarded emotion he had shown, then moved rapidly across the room and out into the entrance hall.

Pascoe was standing there with the phone in his hand.

'Hello,' he said. 'Hello.'

Jenny was in the doorway of the lounge. So he can think too, thought Dalziel.

Pascoe put the receiver down.

'No answer. It must have been a wrong number.'

'Surely,' said Dalziel. 'Well, we'll bid you good day, Mr Connon. Jenny.'

He moved to the front door. Behind him he heard Pascoe say in a low voice, obviously not intended for Jenny's ears, 'Just one thing further, Mr Connon. Could you let us have a list of the TV programmes you think your wife would have been likely to want to see on that Saturday night? It might help.'

'Might it?' said Connon. 'But not two lists, surely? I passed that information to your office at Mr Dalziel's request yesterday.'

'And,' said Dalziel, smiling smugly as they walked to the car together, 'I'd have let the girl get to the phone first if I could have managed it. It was probably the only chance we'll ever get of listening in.'

'If it was our man.'

'Oh yes. I'm sure of that.'

Across the road, the curtain fell back into place in a bedroom window.

'He asked me if it was true.'

'Me too.'

'What did you tell him?'

'What I told you when you asked.'

Outside they heard the car start up. There was the familiar slap as it brushed against the laburnum tree, then it was on its way. Jenny put the chain on the door and the simple action filled Connon's heart with the grief he had not yet felt.

He had been telling nothing less than the simple

truth when he said that his love for Jenny was in no way dependent on his being her father. But he saw that his own indifference was not shared and he regretted now that he hadn't been absolutely affirmative with her.

What has she done that she must share my doubts? he thought. What have I done that I can expect her to understand my certainties?

The urge to tell her it made no difference was strong in him once more, but he knew it would be a mistake. She must find for herself how little difference it did make. Now all that was necessary was to remind her she wasn't facing a stranger.

'Jenny, love, what about a pot of tea?'

'If you like.'

She was pale. Her face had the shape which could take paleness and make it beautiful, but she was too pale.

Connon hated the writer of that letter which had taken his daughter's colour away.

'Will they find him?'

The question slotted so neatly into his thoughts that he was slow in formulating a spoken reply.

'I don't know. He's out there somewhere. Out there.'

'At the Club?'

'Perhaps. I don't know.'

'Have you any idea?'

He moved back along the hallway to the dining-room door. He spoke suddenly with a new resolution in his voice.

'There's a committee meeting tomorrow night. I think I'll go. Will you mind?'

She smiled and his heart split with love and anger.

'If you don't mind, I'll come with you. It's a long time since I showed my face there.'

'Right then.'

'Right.'

Connon turned from the dining-room and moved across to the door opposite.

'We'll have tea in the lounge, shall we?' he said casually.

'All right.'

'Then a quiet night. Save our strength for tomorrow.'

'Right.'

Again he hesitated, looking for words.

'Jenny, I miss your mother. More now somehow. More than I thought.'

Then he stepped into the lounge for the first time since Saturday night.

In the kitchen Jenny whistled softly as she made the tea.

Chapter 4

They were dancing in the social room. A record-player shuffled a few simple chords violently together, then dealt them out with heavy emphasis. The upper reaches of the room were vague with cigarette smoke, the lower reaches voluptuous with long legs and round little bottoms.

Dalziel watched with awful lust as the girls twisted and jerked in total self-absorption. A hand squeezed his knee.

'Watch it, Andy, or you'll be spoiling your suit.'

Dalziel laughed but didn't turn his eyes to the speaker.

'It's as if they were being rammed by an invisible man,' he said.

The music stopped and now he gave the new-comer his full attention.

'They weren't like this in our day, Willie,' he said.

Willie Noolan, small, dapper, grey, bank manager and President of the Club, smiled his agreement.

'They were not. We had to earn our wages in those days.'

'The wages of sin, eh? Not that it was always difficult, if you knew where to look. Do you recall a little animal called Sheila Cripps? Eh?'

Noolan smiled reminiscently. These two had known each other for well over thirty years, meeting first at school and then finding their paths crossing again and again as they shifted with their respective jobs, till finally they had both come back permanently to the town they started from.

'She's a dried-up old stick now, Andy. Sings in the Methodist choir. I can't believe my memory when I look at her.'

'Ay. They don't weather like us, Willie. Even when the shape goes,' he said, slapping his belly, 'the spirit remains constant. It's a question of dedication. But I'm sorry that little Sheila's been a backslider.'

'Oh, she's been that in her time too.'

They laughed again, each enjoying the joke, but each with the watchfulness of his profession.

The third man at the table did not join in.

'Careful, Jacko, or you'll have hysterics,' said Dalziel.

The long thin mouth was pulled down at the corners like a tragic mask, the eyes were hooded, the shoulders hunched, head bent forward so that the man's gaze seemed fixed on the surface of the table.

God, thought Dalziel as he had frequently thought

for the past twenty years, you're the most miserable-looking bugger I ever saw.

'You're like a couple of little lads. Act your age,' Jacko said, half snarling.

'John Roberts, Builder' was a familiar sign in the area. He had built the club-house they were sitting in.

He was reputed to have arrived in town at the age of sixteen with a barrow-load of junk and two and ninepence in his pocket. The war was on. He was an evacuee, said some; others that he had absconded from a Borstal. No one took much notice of him then. No one who mattered. It was only when he plunged, wallet-first, into the great post-war building wave that people began to take notice. He lived chancily, moved into many crises, both business and legal, but always emerged from the other side safely – and usually richer, more powerful.

Those who remembered him with his barrow recalled a cheerful, toothy smile, an infectious, confidence-inspiring laugh. Armed with this information, they wouldn't have picked him out on an identity parade.

Dalziel wouldn't need an identity parade if he wanted to worry Jacko. He knew enough about him, had done enough research on his origins and his company, to worry him a great deal. But his knowledge wasn't official. Yet.

He was saving it up for a rainy day.

'How's business, Andy?' asked Noolan. 'Putting many away?'

'Not enough. Not near enough.'

There was a pause. A new record had started. Slower, softer. Some of the dancers actually came in contact now. Sid Hope was doing the rounds, having a friendly word with those who were late in paying their subscriptions. They were due at the start of the season. Sid gave plenty of leeway, right up to Christmas. But, Christmas past, he was adamant – non-payers were ejected, quietly if possible. But noisily if necessary.

'These two coughed up, have they, Sid?' asked Noolan with a laugh.

'Oh, ay,' replied the treasurer as he passed. 'See you at the meeting.'

'Meeting?' asked Dalziel.

'Yes. The committee. At eight. Just time for another, eh? Jacko?'

'You'll be one short tonight,' said Dalziel casually.

'One? We usually are. Oh, you mean Connie? Yes, I expect so. Can't expect anything else in the circumstances. Sad. Very sad.'

'Man gets shot of his wife, that's not sad.'

'Jacko, my lad, you're lovely.'

'Didn't some bastard offer to get them in?'

'That's very kind of you, Jacko,' said Dalziel. 'Another pint. Please.'

Without a word, Roberts rose and headed for the service hatch.

'You've got a way with Jacko, Andy. I've often noticed.'

'Observation's anyone's game. Detection's my business, though. Don't start looking too deep.'

Make them feel almost a part of it, thought Dalziel. Just a hint's enough.

He's after something, thought Noolan.

'You were saying about Connie.'

'Was I? What?'

'About it being sad.'

'Well, it was. Very. Not that we'd seen much of Mary lately. In fact I can't remember the last time. It was probably at the bank, anyway, not here.'

'Bank with you, do they?'

'Yes.'

'Interesting account?'

'Not particularly. Just the usual monthlies, and weekly withdrawals for the housekeeping.'

'Nothing out of the ordinary, then. Recently? In or out?'

'No. Not a thing.'

Dalziel pulled up his trouser-leg and began scratching his ankle.

'Much left at the end of the month?'

'Enough. Not much. But enough to give them a week in Devon.'

Dalziel scratched on.

'You're not trying to extract confidential information from me, are you, Andy?'

They both laughed.

'And what the hell's wrong with your ankle?'

'I've got an itch. Nasty inflammation.'

'Been putting your foot in it, have you?'

They both laughed again.

'Still at it?' grunted Jacko, slamming a tray laden with three tankards on to the table. 'Like a couple of bloody tarts.'

'Is that the time?' said Noolan. I'd better go and convene this damn meeting. You'll be here for a while?'

'What do you think?'

'See you later, then. Cheers, Jacko. See you later.'

They watched him shoulder his way jovially through the dancers towards the door of the committee room at the far end of the social room.

'A real card,' said Jacko, dead-pan.

'He's been a good help to you, Jacko. Saw you through when many wouldn't have.'

'Surely,' said Jacko. 'Beneath these pinstripes hang three balls of brass. Did he tell you owt?'

Dalziel shrugged.

'Nothing helpful.'

It was no use playing games with Jacko Roberts, he thought.

But then it was even less use trying to play games with Andy Dalziel – unless he'd invented the rules.

'Was she insured?'

'No. No cover at all as far as we know.'

'No cover? That'd be a sight for sore eyes with that one. By God!'

Dalziel put down his tankard in mock amazement.

'Do I detect a note of enthusiasm, Jacko?'

'There's plenty as was. Once.'

'Just once? Nothing lately?'

Jacko scowled.

'How the hell would I know?'

Dalziel nodded thoughtfully.

'I'd have heard, too. What about Connie? Has he been having anything on the side?'

'Nothing said. But he moves without you noticing, that one.'

On and off the field, thought Dalziel. Yes, it's true. Not inconspicuous, nothing grey about Connie, no blurred edges there. But self-contained. An area of calm.

Like the eye of a storm.

'Jacko,' he said.

'Yes.'

'If you hear anything . . .' but as he spoke he became aware of someone standing behind him and Jacko's gaze was now aligned over his head.

'I didn't know you were bringing the wife,' said Jacko.

Dalziel was startled for a moment and twisted round in his chair.

'Hello,' said Pascoe.

'I'm going for a run-off,' said Jacko.

He stood up, his lean hunched figure making his clothes look a size too large for him. He leaned forward and said softly to Dalziel: 'I'll tell you something. Someone's fishing in Arthur Evans's pond. Welsh git.'

Pascoe watched him go with interest.

'Tell me, sir. Does he always take his tankard to the loo with him?'

'What the hell are you doing here? I told you, you'd had your go. Now get out.'

Pascoe sat down.

'Nothing like that, sir. I'm here socially.'

He felt in his top pocket and produced a blue card.

'Here you are. I'm a paid-up member. The place interested me. I decided to join. I don't think that your Mr Hope was all that happy, but what could he do?'

'I'm not happy either. And I can do something, Sergeant.'

But Pascoe's attention was elsewhere.

'Before you do it, sir, just have a look at who's come through that door.'

Dalziel knew who it was before he turned.

Connon, rather pale but perfectly composed, wearing a dark suit and a black tie, stood in the open doorway. His eyes moved swiftly over the scene before him, registering but not acknowledging Pascoe and Dalziel. Then he pulled the door to behind him and moved quickly and efficiently across the floor between the dancers and disappeared into the committee room.

'I bet hardly a soul noticed him,' said Pascoe.

'Why should they? Our interest's a bit specialized. And half these buggers wouldn't recognize him if he came in with a label on. Rugby supporters, pah! They know nothing.'

'And we know?'

'At least we know where he is.'

Pascoe scratched his nose ruminatively then stopped in horror as he realized who he was imitating.

'Yes, where *he* is. But I wonder where his daughter is? He should have more sense than to leave her alone. These letter boys are sometimes persistent.'

Oh do you now? thought Dalziel. Then you should have looked through the door before he closed it behind him. But you worry on a bit longer, lad. Just a bit longer. It's good for the soul.

Jenny got half way to the bar before anyone noticed her.

'Well, hell-oh,' said a large man as she tried to slip by him with an 'excuse me'. He was clutching a pewter tankard with a glass bottom. Now he drained it and squinted at her through the glass. He was still a good two hours from being drunk and even then he would probably manage to drive home without attracting unwanted attention.

There were faint flickers of real recognition at the back of his eyes, but he preferred the mock-lecherous approach.

'What's a nice girl like you doing in a joint like this?'

'I've come about the woodworm. How are you?'

Jenny could only judge the effectiveness of her cool self-possessed act from its results. Inside, it felt so phoney that the merest glimmer of amusement would have sent an embarrassed blush swirling up from her neck to her forehead. The stout man, however, was obviously nonplussed. His own opening gambit made it impossible to take offence.

'Hello, Jenny,' said a voice from a side-table.

'Excuse me,' said Jenny to the man, who now obviously recognized her and was recomposing his face to a rubbery concern. But he couldn't quite get the mouth right and traces of the leer still showed through. By the time he felt able to add sound effects, Jenny was sitting down at a table with two girls and three youths.

'Hello, Sheila,' she said, 'Mavis. How's the world wagging?'

'Fine,' said Sheila. The other girl in contrast to both Jenny and Sheila was so heavily made up that it was like looking at someone behind a mask. She nodded carefully as though afraid of disturbing it.

The three boys rearranged themselves rather self-consciously.

'You know these creeps, do you? Joe, Colin. And the gooseberry's Stanley.'

Jenny smiled.

'Hi. I've seen them around. How's your dad, Stanley?'

'Fine,' mumbled the boy.

Jenny smiled again, feeling a kind of desperate brightness sweeping over her, a need to avoid silences.

'Stanley lives in our road. It used to be his main

ambition to see my knickers. Stanley the Watcher I used to call him.'

She laughed, the others smiled politely. Stanley went very red, then very pale.

'That's a lie. That's a stupid thing to say. I don't know why you . . .'

He trembled to a stop as the others looked at him in mild surprise.

'You mean you didn't want to see her knickers?' said Sheila. 'That's not very complimentary. Why don't you make yourself useful, get Jenny a drink or something? You can't expect her to get them in on a student's grant.'

Miaow, thought Jenny as young Curtis stood up awkwardly and set off for the bar, turning after a couple of steps to ask, 'What do you want?'

'Bitter, please. Pint.'

'Female emancipation,' said Sheila. 'I can remember doing that for "O" level history.'

'So?'

'Well, so old Wilson used to tell us that lots of men opposed it because they felt it would lead to women in trousers sitting in pubs drinking pints of bitter. It was one of his jokes. He'd laugh if he could see you.'

'Perhaps he can,' said one of the two remaining boys. 'He's dead, so he might be watching.'

Something violent happened under the table, and the boy looked startled, then apologetic.

'Look, Jenny,' said Sheila, 'we were all dead sorry to hear about your mother. That was rotten.'

They all nodded agreement, Mavis carefully as ever.

'Yes, it was. Thanks,' said Jenny. 'But life goes on.'

'That's one way of looking at it,' said Sheila.

'No, that's two ways of looking at it,' answered Jenny. 'One way, my life goes on despite my mother's death; the other way, someone else's life goes on because of it.'

'My, college has made you even sharper,' said Sheila with a thin smile.

Jenny sensed she was losing a friend, or rather, cutting the last few strands which held their friendship together. She and Sheila had been very close at school up to the Fifth Form. They had both planned to stop on in the Sixth, then at the last moment, half way through the summer holidays in fact, Sheila had announced she was getting a job.

That had all been more than two years before. They'd seen each other fairly regularly since, but more and more competitively as time went on.

Now it didn't matter who won or lost.

'Thanks, Stanley,' she said, taking the pint which had been deposited rather ungraciously before her. 'Cheers.'

She took a mouthful, coughed and grimaced wryly at Sheila, who smiled back with something of their old affection.

In fact Jenny was really very fond of beer, but she recognized that while an attempt to show off could be tolerated, careless expertize would only antagonize further.

'What're you all up to, then?' she asked.

'We, that is Mavis and me (or I, should I say?) are being entertained by these young gentlemen. Lavishly, as you can see.'

'What about you, Stan?'

'He's waiting,' interjected one of the boys quickly.

'For what?'

They all laughed. Stanley shrugged and tried to look unconcerned. He made quite a decent job of it too.

'Cheer up. She might be along later,' said Sheila.

'He fancies Gwen Evans.' It was Mavis who spoke. Jenny remembered that the joke had always stopped at Mavis.

'All the men fancy Gwen,' said Sheila.

But not all the women, eh? thought Jenny. She knew Gwen Evans only slightly; she had seen her at the funeral, and previous to that a couple of times, but the memory stuck.

'I'd have thought she was a bit old for you, Stanley,' she said.

Sheila wrinkled her nose scornfully.

'It's all in the mind anyway. This lot read about all these teenage orgies and think they're missing out somehow.'

Joe and Colin grinned unconcernedly.

Now you don't look as if you're missing out, my lads, thought Jenny.

'Anyway,' Sheila went on, 'it's all happening at the universities and colleges, isn't it, Jenny? The intellectual-sexual bit.'

Here we go again.

'Yeah,' said Colin with some enthusiasm, 'all those wild birds. It's all wiggle-waggle and jiggle-joggle at those places.'

'We have our moments,' said Jenny. She looked around the room. She wasn't quite sure why she had come here at all, but it certainly wasn't so she could sit and chat with this lot. They were too young for a start. Whoever it was that was menacing her with letters (a letter, she corrected herself, but feeling certain there would be more), whoever it was that had anything to do with her mother's death, that person, or those persons, would belong to her father's age group.

What do I want anyway, she thought. To find out who wrote that letter? To find out if there was any truth in it? He could have denied it, he could have been positive, but all he did was tell me he loved me, that it didn't matter. Not matter? Something matters. If it doesn't matter, *that* matters. Miss Freud, that's me. Shortly to be Miss Sherlock Holmes. But how to start? What do people like Fat Dalziel and Popsy Pascoe *do* to get things moving? On the telly they just talk to people and find things out. But how do you know who to talk to in the first place?

'There she blows, Stanley,' said Joe.

Jenny turned her head. Her first impression was of an exotically beautiful woman lightly covered in a very revealing dress. But this was only for a second. Gwen Evans wore neither less nor more make-up than most other women in the room, her skirt was by no means the shortest there, her dress zipped up the front right up to the collar and she had a cardigan draped casually over her shoulders.

It was the way she moved, the animation of her face, the way she held herself that made her presence so electric, not any ultra-daring revelation of flesh.

Her husband was in close attendance at the moment but Jenny knew he was due at the meeting. The man behind the bar said something to him, probably a reminder, for he nodded, spoke to his wife, then with a quick look round the room, he left.

Gwen too was looking round the room, more slowly, deliberately. Her gaze met Jenny's and paused. Then she smiled an acknowledgment and dropped an eyelid in half a wink. Jenny was surprised to feel herself flattered by this hint of intimacy between them.

'What're you waiting for, Stan?'

Stanley stood up awkwardly.

'Excuse me,' he said. 'I've got some work to do at home.'

He moved across the room and out of the door without a glance at Gwen.

'My!' said Sheila. 'Perhaps he's got delusions of grandeur and is playing hard to get.'

Jenny suddenly didn't care for her in the least. She downed the remaining beer in her glass in one easy draught.

'I think I'll circulate a bit,' she said. 'It's been nice having a chat.'

'Suit yourself,' said Sheila.

'Cheerio.'

Near the bar she caught a glimpse of Marcus's round head and began to make her way towards him. When she got a little closer she saw he was talking to the man she'd had the brush with when she first came in, and she hesitated in her progress. Marcus turned at that moment and saw her. His face showed surprise, then pleasure.

'Jenny,' he said. 'Come and have a drink, love.'

She smiled back and squeezed through the intervening people to his side.

'Are you by yourself?' he asked, his eyes probing the further corners of the room.

'Daddy's in the committee meeting.'

'Of course. I'm glad he decided to come. It'll do him good to get out and about. You too. Here, what'll you have?'

'I'll have a scotch if you insist.'

'Oh, but I do. One scotch. You ready for another, Ted?'

He took the large man's glass without waiting for a reply.

'You know Ted, do you? Ted Morgan. This is Jenny Connon, Connie's daughter. This is Ted. He's the biggest gossip in the Club so be careful what you tell him about me. Won't be a sec.'

Marcus turned to the bar and ruthlessly elbowed his way through to the pole position.

Jenny looked at Morgan with interest.

'Look,' he said. 'I'm sorry if I was rude before. But

110

I didn't recognize you at first. I've only ever seen you a couple of times, with your dad at matches.'

His face was set into the perfect sympathetic mould now. But his eyes were still assessing what lay beneath her Marks and Spencer jumper.

Perhaps I should introduce them to him. Now this one on the left is Marks, and this other is Sparks. Say hello nicely.

She grinned at the thought and the solemn angles of Ted's mouth relaxed also.

'I'm sorry if I was rude to you, too, Mr Morgan.'

'Call me Ted.'

'Is it true what Marcus said? That you're the biggest gossip in the Club?'

'Certainly,' said Ted. 'Bigger than that, even. There's not much happens here that I don't know.'

He nodded with mock-solemnity. Jenny found herself quite liking him.

'And how long have you been a member?'

'Since I was a nipper. My dad didn't like to beat me, so he made me join him.'

Jenny laughed with more enthusiasm than the witticism merited.

'Ted hasn't told you one of his jokes, has he? Be careful, Ted, will you? Jenny's not one of your ancient barmaids.'

Marcus handed her a goblet of scotch and Ted another pint.

'I'm being entertained very well, thank you, Marcus.'

'Good-oh. Well, here's how.'

They all drank. A loud outburst of laughter came from the bar. Jenny glanced over. The source was the group round Gwen Evans. Beyond them, just coming in through the door, she saw Pascoe. He edged his way through the standing drinkers and for a moment she thought he was going to join her, but he merely nodded and drifted down the room, taking up a position by the wall where he seemed to become engrossed in watching the efforts of a group of youngsters on the one-armed bandit.

I shouldn't be at all surprised if he didn't fancy me, thought Jenny. Perhaps not though, I seem to fancy every man I meet fancies me at the moment. Either I'm at the height of my powers or I'm suffering from delusions of grandeur. Like poor Stanley. Gwen Evans wouldn't bother with a kid like that, not when she could have the pick of the men in this room. Or any of the other rooms either.

And her heart gave just a little kick of worry as she turned to Ted Morgan again.

Clickity, clickity, clickity, click. A lemon, a bell and a cherry. Clickity, clickity, clickity, click. Two bells and an orange. Clickity, clickity, clickity. If you had stood as I have done for five hours in a draughty ante-room of a courthouse sticking six-pences into one of those things to see how frequently it paid out, you wouldn't be so keen to chuck your money away, son. Couldn't understand it, could he? Two or three jackpots a night in the Club. Anyone'd tell you. My client wonders if the police have been as thorough in their research as they seem to imply. Perhaps the constable who carried out the test was merely having a run of bad luck. It is in the very nature of the entertainment offered by these machines that the result should be irregular, unforecastable. Odds must be measured over weeks, months, not hours. And me with my second-class honours degree, standing there with corns on my hands saying yes sir, no sir, till I made my smart answer, my quick repartee. Then everyone tut-tuts. And they all jump on me from great heights till corns on my hand seem like the fringe benefits of delirious joy. But no joy for Pascoe, nowhere. Little Jenny there, glad she's there, not elsewhere, listening to phone calls, opening letters; but no joy there for you Pascoe. Not yet. Not ever? She's very friendly with those two, though; Felstead, Marcus, and Morgan, Edward. Lucky them, but not her style, not big Ted. He looks as if the pools have come up for him. And over there, beyond the blue horizon of desire, Gwen, backseat driver. Gwen, change any gears and we're airborne. That brass ring at her neck, attached to the zip all the way down that dress, like the ring you hold on to when you leap from a plane, plunging in free fall till you dare no more, then you pull the ring down, down and float in airy freedom, master of all you survey.

For a CID man you've no head for beer. Another

pint and you'd be like those young lads all falling over themselves to make an impression. Or like fat Dalziel. Worse. Please God, don't let me become like fat Dalziel. But he at least is probing, sniffing around, trying to get things moving, not losing himself vainly in mazes of mental erotica. Listen. Look. Look and listen. That's why you're here. And don't just look over there.

'Everything?' said the highly made-up girl on the table behind him, her eyes rounding with interest into O's of mascara.

'Yeah,' said one of the two boys at the table, 'that's what he told me. He said he reckoned she wanted him to see. You know. Sort of egging him on.'

'More wishful thinking,' said the other girl scornfully.

'Mebbe. Mebbe not. Anyway, you know what he did?'

'No. And I don't want to. Let's go next door and dance a bit. Coming?'

'Oh, all right then. Off we go.'

Even when I eavesdrop I hear nothing but sex, thought Pascoe watching the four of them disappear out of the bar. Now there was that fellow Roberts. Jacko Roberts. He seemed an interesting kind of man. Perhaps worth a word or two.

Dalziel might not like it, of course.

'Dalziel,' he murmured audibly enough for the fruit-machine victims to glance his way, 'is not bloody well going to get it.'

He began to move towards the end of the bar where Jacko Roberts was drinking alone.

'Any other business,' asked Willie Noolan.

'There's this competitive rugby survey thing that's come round from *The Times*,' said Reg Certes, the club secretary.

'Propose that a general meeting of members be convened to discuss the whole question,' said Connon.

'Seconded,' said Sid Hope.

'Any opposition? Right, carried. What about timing?'

'Week Friday'd be all right,' said Certes.

'Agreed? Right. Anything else?'

'Just one thing if I may, Willie.'

Noolan glanced at his watch. If it had been anyone other than Connie . . . but he could hardly choke him off.

'Yes, Connie.'

Connon looked round the table for a moment as though choosing his words carefully. But they had been chosen for some little time already.

'Mr President,' he said, and the formality of his voice made the others pay him even closer attention. 'Yesterday, the day of my late wife's funeral, my daughter received an anonymous letter. I believe it came from someone connected with this Club.'

Evans let out a long whistle. The others merely looked stunned. Then Noolan and Sid Hope both spoke at once.

'What grounds have you . . . ?'

'What did it say . . . ?'

They both tailed off.

'Your ball, I think, Willie,' said Hope.

'I'll answer you both. Or rather, I won't,' interjected Connon. 'I won't reveal my grounds. Nor will I tell you what the letter said. The writer already knows. It concerns no one else.'

'Well, Connie,' said Noolan expansively, 'I'm sure we're all very sensible of the strain of your situation and the shock this kind of thing, whatever it said, must have caused both you and Jenny. But I don't think that a committee meeting is the proper or best place to discuss this, do you? Let's close the meeting, then we can talk informally. This isn't the kind of thing we'd want to see in the minutes, is it?'

'Yes,' said Connon. 'It is. I'd like to propose that the writer of this letter when known should be barred for life from the Club.'

'You're being a bit bloody silly there, aren't you, Connie?' snorted Arthur Evans. 'I mean, how can you bar him from the Club if you don't know who it is, then?'

He looked round, acknowledging the triumph of logic by a small rocking movement of the head. The others were looking at Connon, however, each doubtful what to say. Certes, the first team secretary and the youngest there, the man most likely to succeed Hurst as captain, had a rather different problem. He was the least well acquainted with Connon and had no intention of saying anything at the moment. His problem was knowing what to write. His pen rested, unmoving, on his note-book.

'Connie,' said Noolan finally, 'I don't think this is an admissible proposition. Firstly, Arthur's right. We can't bar someone we don't know.'

'I didn't say I didn't know him,' said Connon. Now jump, you buggers. Now stare in wild surmise. This is that thing called change. Things will never be the same again. Till I let them.

Noolan was the only one who did not react.

'Then it is your plain duty to inform the police of your knowledge.'

'Haven't I just done that, Willie?'

Now there's one in the breadbasket for you, you old goat, thought Evans. That's got you nonplussed. Spend all your life hanging around on the edge of the scrum and it comes as a bit of a shock to get a pair of fingers up your nostrils.

'Our discussions at these meetings are minuted, Connie, and as such are published to our members.'

'I know. I haven't noticed Reg writing much for the past few minutes, though. Have you made a note of my proposition, Reg?'

Still without speaking, Certes began to scribble.

'Very well, Connie,' said Noolan resignedly. 'We have a motion proposed by Mr Connon. Is there a seconder?'

The blare of music from the social room came in very loud. Connon felt a drum start beating in his head. The edge of pain began to intrude between the muffled notes. He put up his hand and began to massage his temple.

'Are you all right, Connie?' asked Hurst.

'Yes, fine. Just a headache.'

The wheels were turning now. He hadn't felt anything for three days now. But it was back. McManus would have to do something. Old fool. Long past it. What can he know about . . .

'I'll second it.'

Well, that's scuppered you, Willie.

It was Arthur Evans's distinctive lilt.

'In that case, unless there's any further discussion we'll take a vote.'

'Just one point,' said Hurst. 'What does it mean if we pass this motion?'

'Nothing until they catch this fellow, whoever he is. Then if he's in the Club, he gets thrown out. If he's not in, he can't get in.'

'We're still very much in the dark though, Connie. Can you assure us that the contents of this letter were such as make such action reasonable?'

'You know my daughter? They caused her very real distress. Actionable assertions were made.'

'Right-oh. Go on, Willie.'

'Let's have a vote then. Those in favour?'

Firmly, Arthur's hand went up. Hurst's. Certe's. More slowly Hope's.

'And you, of course, Connie.'

'Of course. And you, Willie?'

'It's not part of my function to vote here, unless

118

the meeting is deadlocked. Carried unanimously. Anything else? No? Then I declare the meeting closed.'

They sat still for a second, then Evans stood up and pushed his chair back and the others followed.

'Let's get a drink,' said Evans.

'Just hang on a moment,' said Certes. 'I've got the tickets we ordered for the Welsh match at Twickenham next month. They're a bit scattered around – we must have been near the bottom of the pile, I'm afraid.'

'Bloody inefficiency,' said Evans. 'It wasn't like this when I was secretary. Eh, Sid?'

'Too true. The nearest we ever got to Twickenham was Cardiff.'

Certes grinned amiably.

'Anyway, I've sorted them out so we can all sit next to our nearest and dearest.'

'With the best seats for committee members, of course?'

'But of course. Here you are Sid. Three it was, eh? One for you, Peter. Two for you, Willie.'

He hesitated and a note of uncertainty came into his voice.

'And you too, Connie. There's two here for you.'

'Two?' said Connon.

'Let's go and have that drink,' said Noolan over-loudly. 'All this talking!'

'That's right,' said Connon, reaching over and taking the tickets. 'It was my turn to get Marcus's this year. I hope we can see this time. I was behind a post last year and the Irish scored three tries right on the other side of it.'

'Trust the bloody Irish. Second only to the Welsh in low cunning,' said Hurst.

'Are you sure you're OK, Connie?' he whispered to Connon as the others went ahead through the door.

'Yes. Just a bit of a head, that's all. I don't think I'll go through just yet, Pete. I'll catch you up in a minute or two.'

'OK, Connie. See you do. It's good to see you around again. We missed you at the selection meeting earlier. There's copies of the teams on the board there. I'd be interested to hear what you think.'

'I'll have a look.'

'Right. Don't linger too long, though. There's not much drinking time left.'

From the far end of the social room, Superintendent Dalziel noted with interest the order of emergence from the committee meeting.

'Sit down, Willie,' he said to Noolan who was so deep in thought he'd almost walked past the table. 'What kept you so long?'

Pascoe found Jacko Roberts fascinating and Roberts himself seemed to be almost obsessively interested in the (to him) paradoxical situation of a well-educated man joining the police force.

'You went to college, did you?' he asked again.

'Yes. University.'

'Like them posh-talking bastards over there in the corner?'

'Yes. That's right. Beneath this rough exterior lies the education of a posh-talking bastard.'

'But they'd make you a sergeant straightaway? No uniform or anything?'

'No. I had to spend the usual time on the beat, in uniform.'

'Directing traffic?'

'Yes. That too.'

'That's what your boss should be. Directing traffic. I can understand him, but *you*!'

'What's a nice guy like me doing in a dirty job like this? Well, I'm trying to get information out of you for a start.'

For a while as Jacko's interest grew, Pascoe had seen the outline of a softer, happier, younger face beneath the deeply etched misanthropy of his usual expression. But now the mask returned – or the illusion faded.

'It's your round.'

Pascoe brought Roberts two pints.

'It'll save time.'

'What do you want to know?'

'Simple questions, really. Who'd want to harm Mary Connon?'

'Next question?'

'Who'd want to harm Connon?'

'Next?'

'Who's knocking off Gwen Evans?'

He jerked his head slightly towards the other end

121

of the bar where someone was describing to the lady in question some event which seemed to involve a great deal of grappling with her unresisting frame. It could have been anything from a dance routine to a loose maul.

'Anything else?'

'That'll do for starters.'

Another half-pint gulp.

'I'm no bloody oracle. And I don't see why I should help you. But I'm big-hearted. That's why I'm so poor. Last first. That thing along the bar there, there's so many trying it's hard to say who's succeeding. But I'll tell you who Evans has elected front runner.'

'Yes?'

'Connon. That's right. The boy wonder. And that answers two of your questions, doesn't it?'

Perhaps, thought Pascoe. Perhaps it answers three. More likely it doesn't answer any. Not a word of this before, not a hint; surely there'd have been a hint, a nod, a wink? Surely Dalziel would have known?

Perhaps Dalziel did know.

Or perhaps there was nothing to know. Perhaps Gwen Evans was as pure as the driven snow. Perhaps.

But it didn't matter. No woman could look like that without *someone* starting a rumour about her and *someone*. But there had been no mention of Connon exercising his talents there.

Of course, there wouldn't be. You didn't mention that kind of thing to a detective investigating the death of a fellow club-member's wife. Especially when he was the best fly-half the club had ever had. No, it just wasn't done. Not unless you were a jumped-up bastard like Jacko Roberts.

Or a woman. He hadn't talked to any women down here. But the place seemed full of them. Camp-followers. Regulars as regular in their attendance as any man. He'd have to pick one out. They had a different scale of loyalties.

'Do you believe it?' he asked.

'Me? I'd believe anything bad about anybody, if I didn't know they were all a load of bloody liars.'

'Evans, now. I thought he was an old mate of Connon's?'

'The first people you suspect are always your friends. Usually you're right.'

'Is Evans right?'

Jacko looked him in the eyes for the first time since they'd met. His head, ill-constructed out of sharp edges and loosely-hung skin, rested against the wall, out of place between two framed photographs of past successful teams, young men, glowing with health.

'Welshmen weren't born to be right. They were born to be bloody tragic.'

He finished the second pint with a definitive swallow and the backward movement of his head shifted one of the pictures.

Pascoe reached forward to straighten it. The fifteen young men smiled brightly at him. One face, happier than the others, caught his attention. He looked at the names underneath.

'Aye, that's him. In his Golden Boy days.'

'Connon?'

He looked closer. Yes, unmistakable now. Connon's face looked back at him.

'He looks as if he'd been made King of the Harem.'

Now Jacko peered closely, this time at the date.

'He had,' he said. 'Twenty years old. Happy in the day time, happier in the night-time. Just picked for the first trial. Six weeks later he's bust his ankle and put this girl in the club. He wakes up one morning and though he doesn't know it, he must suspect it – the party's over. And no one's ever going to ask him to another.'

'Never?'

'Never. From now on he's a gatecrasher.'

Jacko nodded sagaciously and rattled his glasses together. Pascoe smiled and shook his head.

'No thanks, Mr Roberts. I'll be getting on, I think. Thank you for the chat. Cheerio!'

Let me find some nice little girl, with someone else's drink swilling inside her nice flat little belly, who'll talk and talk and talk, and be nice to look at. Or even just one who's nice to look at. I wonder where Jenny is?

But when he turned to look, she was gone and Marcus was talking to someone else.

Ted Morgan had gone too.

*   *   *

124

The price of information was too high, decided Jenny. So far she had got no information and she had come dangerously near to paying the price.

Ted Morgan's car was parked high above the town about five yards down a narrow cart-track which led off the road between two steeply sloping fields. Jenny was heartily relieved that the recent bad weather had made the track so muddy that even the passionate and rather drunk Ted had not dared go any further.

They were not really out of the town. The hill, or knoll, they were on was almost completely surrounded below by two horns of suburb. The gossip was that the farmer who owned the land was merely hanging on till the price came up to his requirements, then some builder would carve out of the hillside a super executive-type estate, with views for fifteen miles and mortgages for fifty years.

The only bit of information Jenny had got out of Morgan was that he 'knew' the builder was Jacko Roberts.

It was obviously a popular site, if not for builders, then certainly for lovers. Four or five sets of headlights had blazed rudely into the neck of the lane, then turned in disappointment away.

The sudden illumination did not seem to inhibit Ted, but Jenny found it comforting. She'd also refused to transfer from the front seat and the gear-lever, handbrake and steering-wheel were welcome allies.

At the moment there was a truce. She lit her

second cigarette. She didn't really smoke, but it was time-consuming and also provided a potential weapon.

Ted puffed energetically at his, uncertain yet whether to congratulate himself on being parked up here with this very attractive young girl, or to commiserate with himself for his failure to make more than token progress.

'Ted,' said Jenny brightly, 'how long have you known my father?'

Morgan shifted uneasily. He didn't like any of the implications of the question.

'Oh, a good few years.'

'Are you one of his special friends?'

'I wouldn't say that. Not really. Not like Marcus. Or Arthur.'

'Gwen's very pretty, isn't she?'

'So-so,' said Ted casually.

Jenny laughed and started coughing.

'Don't be so offhand,' she spluttered. 'You wouldn't say no, would you?'

He grinned.

'No, I don't suppose I would. Chance'd be a fine thing.'

'I suppose there's a lot of competition for a pretty woman?'

How the hell do you get a man to gossip about your dead mother? she thought. I bet Pascoe could.

Ted grew enthusiastic.

'You bet there is. It can be fun.'

'Fun?'

'Depends whether you join it, or watch it. Me, I weighed up my chances and decided to watch it. Then it's fun.'

He's still talking about Gwen, she thought disappointedly. But what can I expect? If he knew what I wanted he'd be out of the car and away in a flash of shock. But I can't sit here all night. It'll be time for round two soon. Come on, my girl, you're supposed to be a budding teacher. Skilful questioning of the child can make him tap sources of knowledge he didn't know he had. But it'd be easier to give him a work-card.

'Tell me, Ted,' she began, but he wasn't finished yet. Like the good gossip he was, he had merely been marshalling the various elements of his anecdote to their best advantage.

'You should have been there last Saturday night. Arthur starts looking at his watch about seven. She should have been there by then. He doesn't go home after the game, you see, not worth it, has his tea here and starts straight in on the beer. Well, I was there, behind the bar, standing in for Marcus, for a few minutes he said, more like two hours, so I saw it all develop. He'd look at his watch, then at the clock on the wall, then at his watch. Finally about quarter to eight he shoots through to the other room and finds Dick and Joy Hardy there, they were supposed to be picking Gwen up and bringing her round. But it turns out she wasn't in. So he comes back through trying to look unconcerned. But he's shooting some pretty piercing glances around, I tell you. I let him see me there bright and clear!'

He paused to chuckle.

'Why?' asked Jenny in puzzlement.

Ted sighed at the stupidity of women.

'Because those who were there couldn't be where his old woman was, could they?'

'And who wasn't there?'

Suddenly the impetus of Ted's narrative seemed to fail.

'Oh, lots,' he said without enthusiasm. 'I mean, I couldn't see, could I?'

'But you were behind the bar? That means Uncle Marcus wasn't there.'

Ted cheered up.

'That's right. He wasn't. Though I can't imagine Marcus . . . anyway it doesn't matter.'

He reached over and put his arm round her shoulders, more paternalistically than passionately.

'Is that the end of the story, then? It's a bit pathetic.'

'Pathetic? Yes, I suppose it is. You've got to feel sorry for him, haven't you? I'm sure there's nothing to any of it, really. Anyway, let's talk about something interesting, like you and me.'

Poor Ted, she thought. He's just remembered what happened last Saturday night. But it's more than that, isn't it? He's remembered that Daddy wasn't there either; he's remembered who he's talking to and he's just sober enough to mind his p's and q's. Does he really know something about

128

Daddy and Gwen? I wonder. Or is it all in that cotton-wool mind?

She half turned to look at the figure beside her and this proved a near fatal mistake.

Ted mistook the move completely and his other arm came round with an enthusiasm which had nothing paternal in it. Jenny found herself dragged uncomfortably over the gear-stick and hand-brake, her left cheek was pressed in against her teeth by the pressure of an ardent but misdirected kiss and she felt a button on her cardigan give with a violence which boded ill for Marks and Sparks cowering beneath.

Round two, she thought, and I didn't even hear the bell. Now this long metal rod with the knob on the end which is doing God knows what damage to my pelvis is the gear-lever. From the freedom of play it seems to have in relation to my belly it must be in neutral. This other more rigid lever which is gouging a hole in the knee of my tights must be the hand-brake. Therefore if I move my hand down there, poor Ted, he's shifting out of the way, God knows what he imagines I'm going to do, there we are, rather stiff, but there she goes, I think.

It took Ted several seconds to realize the car was moving. Jenny clung to him tightly, partly to delay his attempts to remedy the situation, partly to buffer herself against any possible impact.

By the time he got his foot to the brake pedal they were down among the mud and the car slid on for several yards before coming to a halt.

Below them the lights of the town twinkled unconcernedly on. Jenny had a very poor topographical imagination and needed to apply herself with great concentration to the task of relating the main lines of street lights to her own knowledge of the town. It was a task she devoted herself to while Ted with a most ungentlemanly violence of language put the car into reverse and tried to back up the lane.

The wheels spun in the mud-lined cart-tracks. Jenny let them spin on for a while; but she was above all things a sensible girl and had no desire to find herself irretrievably stuck. That would be jumping out of the frying-pan into a raging inferno.

'Why don't you,' she said in the ultra-kind voice she reserved for very recalcitrant children, 'get out, put some branches or stones or something under the wheels, then start pushing? I will drive. I do have a licence and I'm really quite good.'

Without a word, Ted climbed out of the car and began pulling at the hedgerow. Jenny felt quite sorry for him.

She wound down the window.

'I think we'll need some more branches,' she said.

Dave and Alice Fernie were walking like a couple of children down the private side of Boundary Drive. They were hand in hand, about a yard apart, swinging their joined hands high and indulging in a tug-of-war every time they encountered a lamp-post or a tree.

Alice screamed with laughter as Fernie gave her a jerk which pulled her forward so hard that her left shoe stayed behind, its heel bedded deep in the grass verge.

'Oh-Dave-you-silly!' she half-panted, half-laughed, hopping towards him as he retreated, holding her at arm's length, but didn't finish for he let her catch up, caught all her weight to his body and kissed her passionately.

It had just been an ordinary night, starting like a hundred others. They had walked to the local pub, about half a mile into the estate, to have a couple of drinks with a handful of old acquaintances. But things had gone absolutely right from the start, contrary to usage. Perhaps the Christmas decorations in the pub had helped. Dave had had just the right amount of drink, he hadn't been tempted to display his superior knowledge in argument; he hadn't produced any slanderous gossip, he hadn't felt it necessary to demonstrate his virility by being over-attentive to someone else's wife. He had irritated no one, offended no one; he had been moderate in speech, witty in comment, generous in purchase and was now obviously amorous in intent.

There was a sharp edge of frost in the air. Above, clouds ragged as crows' wings beat across the sky, turning the moon into a pale flower drifting beneath the sea. When for a moment it floated into a clear patch of the sky, it turned to silver the branches and few tenacious leaves of the tree against which they now leaned. There had been nights like this years ago, when they were younger, before there was a house and a television set, before they were married. Memories real as the rough bark pressing against the back of her hands came crowding into her mind. But she did not speak them. Dave did not like the past and she was not going to risk losing any part of the present.

The wind rose suddenly and her foot began to feel the cold. Gently she pulled away.

'I'll get my shoe, Dave, and we'll get on home,' she said.

'Right, love.'

His arm was round her waist now as they walked on, quietly, anticipatingly.

It was darker on this side of the road. The trees, the older less efficient lamp-posts, all contributed. Ahead they could see the telephone box which stood almost outside their gate. 'They didn't need one till the *hoi polloi* came,' Fernie had once commented. When he was in the mood, everything appeared as evidence of the difference between 'us' and 'them'.

Now it looks like a beacon, welcoming us home, thought Alice, though not without a wry glance at her own romanticism.

They were nearly there and she turned to cross the road. But he pulled her back and leaned her against another tree.

'Dave!' she said.

He kissed her again.

'Afraid of the neighbours?'

'Of course not. I'm afraid of me. There's some things you can't do out on the street.'

'Why not?' he whispered. 'It'd be fun.'

'Oh, you fool,' she murmured.

They kissed once more.

'Let's go in now,' he said, eagerly.

As they stepped out from behind the tree, a figure, walking rapidly and glancing back over his shoulder, stepped off the pavement a few yards up and came at them on a collision course. There was an urgency about the way he moved which caught Alice's attention, but it was her husband who spoke first.

'Hey, Stanley! What's up, then?'

The figure stopped dead and saw them, obviously for the first time.

'Mr Fernie. It's you.'

Then no more.

It was Stanley Curtis, his face rather pale, breathing deeply, quickly.

'Is something wrong, Stan?' asked Alice.

'No. Well, yes. It's just that, well, I was passing Mr Connon's house and I just looked over the hedge and I saw someone. Someone there.'

He stopped again.

'Where, boy?' asked Fernie, sharply. 'What doing?'

'In the garden. Just prowling around. Then he disappeared up the side of the house. I thought it might be . . .'

'Yes, Stanley?'

'. . . the man who killed Mrs Connon.'

133

Fernie nodded vigorously, not so much, it seemed to Alice, at what Stan had said, but rather at some thought going through his own head.

'Right. Come on, lad. Alice, you stay here.'

'Dave! What are you going to do?'

'To have a look. What else? There's two of us. Come on, Stan.'

But Stanley made no movement. Poor kid, thought Alice, he's scared stiff.

She moved to him and put her arm over his shoulders. He was shivering violently.

'Don't be a fool, Dave,' she said sharply. 'Stan's not coming with you. And you're not going either. There's the phone box. Get on to the police straight-away.'

Fernie stood irresolutely for a moment. Alice glanced round. The Curtis house was in darkness. Maisie and her husband were obviously out.

'I'm taking Stan inside,' she said. 'You come on in when you've talked to the police. You can watch in comfort then.'

So much for the perfect end to a perfect night, she thought resignedly as she walked up path. All that build-up gone to waste. It'd have been better if I'd told him to go ahead up against the tree. We might have missed Stanley. And he was too scared to notice us. But he'd have called the police anyway and they might really have caught us at it. Against a tree!

The thought made her smile. Alice Fernie was a woman of indomitable spirit.

Behind her, her husband stepped into the telephone box and began to dial.

'Connie,' said Hurst, 'I've brought you a drink. You're not going to hide in here all night, are you?'

Connie recognized the half-jocular, half-sympathetic note in Hurst's voice. It was a tone he was growing familiar with. Condolences first. Then afterwards talk as if nothing had happened, but inject enough sympathy into your voice to show you're still aware that something has.

He hadn't meant to sit so long by himself. He had come down to the Club that night with a real purpose, a purpose only half of which had been carried out at the meeting. The sight of Dalziel and Pascoe had disconcerted him more than he had cared to show. He felt illogically that somehow he was responsible for introducing a dissonant element into the Club. It was a rugby club. He had long been disturbed by the growing diversification of the Club's interests. And therefore of the Club's membership.

But he put these thoughts to the back of his mind now, with a silent promise that they would be uttered one day soon.

'I've been glancing through the teams, Peter,' he said. 'What's happened to Jim Davies?'

'He knocked his knee on Saturday. Seemed all right at first, but came up like a balloon over the weekend.'

'So you brought in Gerald on the open side. He'll

135

never hold the place, will he? Did you think of any of the youngsters? Jo Walsh? Or Stan Curtis?'

Hurst laughed.

'You might almost have been eavesdropping, Connie. Yes, both of them. But Joe's best-manning at a wedding on Saturday so he's not available. Though he'd come along, white carnation, wedding-ring and all, I reckon, if he was asked to play for the Firsts. But we couldn't do that. And young Curtis has been a bit under the weather, missed training this week, so he's out. Anything else?'

'Yes. I see Marcus's name's missing from the Fourths.'

'Time marches on, Connie! He's asked not to be considered, for a while at least. Feeling his age, he says.'

'Considered!' smiled Connon. 'You don't get considered for the Fourths. You get press-ganged. He'll have to join the great gang of us who move around in disguise on Saturdays till half an hour after kick-off time. You'll be one of us soon, Peter.'

Hurst nodded and started to pin the team-sheets back up on the board.

Then he seemed to make his mind up about something.

'Connie, that letter. I was desperately sorry to hear about it.'

'Yes?'

It was a calm, simple interrogative, inviting but not pleading for a continuation.

'I'd like to see it if I might,' said Hurst.

'Why?'

'I might be able to help. Might, perhaps; there's just something; that's why I asked at the meeting, but I'd have to see the letter first, partly to see what's in it, partly just to see it.'

'Well now, Mr Hurst. I think that might be arranged. We'll get in touch with you tomorrow shall we?'

In the doorway stood the solid bulk of Dalziel. Hurst flushed an angry red. But Connon remained as cool and unmoved as he had been while listening to Hurst.

'He'd have to know, Peter,' he said calmly. 'The police have the letter. Did you want to speak to me, Superintendent?'

'That's right. I didn't come just to eavesdrop. We've had a report on an intruder on your premises. The station have just phoned me here. I've told them to observe, but keep off till I get there. I'd like you to come too, if you would.'

'Of course. Who reported this?'

'Your friend Fernie. He seems to spend most of his spare time keeping an eye on your house.'

Connon smiled thoughtfully.

'Yes, he does, doesn't he? Good night, Peter. Perhaps we can talk again tomorrow.'

They moved out into the social room. As they passed through the dancers, Connon noticed Pascoe moving slowly around with an attractive young girl. Sheila, he thought. I saw you last Saturday. It seems like a thousand years.

Dalziel noticed him also and made a motion of the head. Pascoe didn't seem to notice and carried on dancing. But as they walked towards the car park, buttoning up their coats against the frost, footsteps came up quickly behind and Pascoe joined them.

'Jenny,' said Connon suddenly.

'She left,' said Pascoe laconically. A cold fear gripped Connon's stomach.

'Where?' he asked. There was no reason why they should know the answer, but he felt sure they would.

'It's all right,' said Pascoe. 'Not home, I shouldn't think. She left with Ted Morgan.'

Connon tried not to let his relief show. Ted Morgan was manageable. Ted was forecastable. As far as anyone was forecastable, that was. And perhaps that was not very far at all.

He reached into his pocket for his car keys. The frost on his windscreen was merely dampness still and after four or five sweeps of the wiper-blades he began to see more clearly. Dalziel's car was waiting for him by the exit. Carefully he began to follow it out on to the main road.

It was a silent drive back down into the town. Ted lived with his mother, an arrangement which, while it lacked many of the usual tragi-comedy trappings of such situations, did present certain problems. Ted was not altogether happy at the prospect of explaining to her how he came to be covered with mud down the front of his suit.

Jenny had put Ted quite out of her mind and was threshing over problems and questions she would not have believed could have existed a week ago.

She felt very lonely. There was only her father. She loved him deeply, but their relationship had generally been tacit; there had never been a need for definition, explanations, analyses. Love didn't need these things. But now she needed someone to talk to, with; at, if you liked. She needed someone to take her thoughts and rethink them. Look at them in a new way.

She had thoughts she did not wish her father to look at.

And she was certain that whatever was going on in his mind, only the sheltered, leeward aspect would be revealed to her.

I don't want to be protected, she thought angrily. I want to be consulted, listened to, argued with. I'll make him talk to me, I'll force him. I know I can. I know!

But even in her anger she also knew she could not add anything more to the heavy burden of worry and doubt she had seen her father was already carrying.

'Is it right here?' asked Ted in the voice of one speaking only through dire necessity.

'That's right.'

Poor Ted. He'd had a bit of a raw deal. And to slip in the mud must have been the last straw. If Daddy was home, she'd invite him in for a coffee and a clean-up. But only if Daddy was at home.

'This side of the road, just before that phone box,' she said.

There seemed to be a lot of cars parked in the street tonight. Without lights. Like taxis. Or . . .

She rubbed the side-window and peered out. She had been right. That was her father's car.

'Stop here,' she cried.

They were almost at the house and Ted was already braking. But her sudden command made him stand violently on the pedal and they were both jerked forward against their seat-belts.

Jenny smacked the release button sharply, opened the door and stepped out.

Connon came trotting up the pavement towards her.

'Daddy,' she said, her voice full of relief. 'What's hapening? What's the matter?'

'No need to worry, my dear,' said Dalziel, coming up behind her.

She ignored him and looked expectantly at her father.

'Someone's been seen prowling round the house. Or at least Mr Fernie believes he saw someone.'

'You have too little faith in Fernie,' said Dalziel. 'A man who feels his civic responsibilities more than some. Still, we'll soon see. My ferrets are in. We'll see what they nip out.'

Connon put his arm over his daughter's shoulder as she shivered at Dalziel's imagery. There was some kind of sound made remote and distant by the night.

'Ah, action, I think,' said Dalziel. 'Let's have a look, shall we?'

He strode out energetically towards the gate. Connon and Jenny followed. Jenny was curiously reluctant to come face to face with this intruder whoever it was.

A small group of men were coming down the path. Some were uniformed policemen. One silhouette she thought she recognized as Pascoe's. And another outline looked strangely familiar.

'My dear officers,' said a rather breathless but still well-modulated voice, 'of what am I accused that you should treat me like the nucleus of a civil rights demonstration? Is this the effect television-watching is having upon the constabulary? Have a care – my father sells meat to the wife of a prospective Liberal candidate.'

'Antony,' she said with delight. 'Daddy, it's Antony.'

The group stopped before them.

'Ah, there you are, Jenny. I cannot say how touched I am at the warmth of the reception you have arranged for me.'

Even dishevelled as after a slight struggle and with his arms firmly gripped by two impassive policemen, he looked elegantly in control of the situation.

'Do you know this man, miss?' asked Dalziel.

'Of course I do. Please let him go at once. How bloody stupid can you get?'

Dalziel nodded at the policemen, who released Antony's arms.

'I think we had better go inside for some explanations,' he said with a sigh. 'If you don't mind, Mr Connon.'

Connon nodded and set off up the drive. Jenny put her arm protectively round Antony's waist and led him after her father, the uniformed police still in close attendance.

Dalziel looked around. At Ted Morgan who stood against his car, hardly able to take in what was happening. At Dave Fernie who was coming over the road. At Alice Fernie and Stanley Curtis who stood at the Fernies' gate.

'You look after matters out here, will you, Sergeant? Make a thorough job of it, eh?'

He too went up the driveway into the house.

Pascoe looked after the vanishing figure. Then turned back to those remaining, letting his eyes run coldly over them, finally coming to rest on Morgan's mudstained suit.

Yes, he thought, I'll make a thorough job of it, never fear. Sir.

Chapter 5

Connon came up out of blackness into a dream. It was as if he had fainted in his sleep and the recovery from the faint made the level of sleep seem reality by comparison. There stretched before him a great expanse of mud-trodden grass, gleaming brokenly like water viewed from a height in the summer sun. Immeasurably distant on the horizon stood a pair of rugby posts, so high that they were clearly visible despite the miles that seemed to separate them from him. He set off running towards them, smoothly at first, balanced, feeling all the old confidence in his muscles, the ability to shift his weight at will in any direction, to stop dead, accelerate, turn, sidestep. He knew when he felt like this that, given a yard to move in, no man on earth could stop him.

But here there was no one to try to stop him.

Nevertheless he made a few feints out of sheer exuberance, suggested a turn with his hips, moved at right-angles to his forward path with no loss of speed, changed step three times in successive strides, kicking hard on the last change and accelerating away in the joy of being able to run for ever.

The posts did not get nearer.

Suddenly he felt a change. His stride shortened; his legs felt leaden; his breathing, till now perceptible only in a slight flaring of the nostrils, became harsh and ragged, his mouth wide open, his teeth biting desperately at the intangible air.

The sun exploded into whiteness and the muddy grass turned to sand so fine that he sank in it ankle-deep as he ran.

I am in the desert, he thought. At last I am in the desert. And I shall die if I do not reach that rock.

The rock towered on the horizon where the posts had been. The sun sat on top of it like the flame on a black candle.

Desperately, failingly, he ran towards the sun.

Out of the rock's foot grew a shadow so dark that it contained all colours. Its edges, at first three-dimensionally sharp and rigid, after a while began to wave and shimmer on the red heat of the sand. Soon the undulation spread to the whole shadow and the blackness curved smoothly away from the rock. Then at the crest of each polished wave, the blackness broke for a moment into the dark green of very deep water, and the sun shimmered in it like light varnished over.

The shadow stretched towards him like a great

shining path. There was a beating in his ears like the roar of a mighty crowd.

He sat up in bed and heard the singing of a solitary bird in the tree outside his window.

Then that noise stopped too and he was not sure if he had heard even that.

It was still dark. The sun came late in December if it came at all. He sat on the edge of the bed and felt for his slippers.

Soon it will be Christmas, he thought. Not more than a week. Season of promises. Vows that this year it will be different. This year those brief moments of feeling, of affection while sharing the task of putting up the decorations, of humility while listening to carol-singers, of joy when waking on Christmas morning, this year these brief moments will spread and grow and shape themselves to fit the whole year, the whole of our life. But there was scarcely enough to colour the greyness of Christmas Day itself. And this year there was no use even in making promises.

Mary is dead, he told himself, and we are to each other for ever what was bearable only in my intuition of its impermanence. Death doesn't change things, then. It merely petrifies things for those who go on living.

He stood up and went out on to the landing. As he passed Jenny's door he paused momentarily, but shook his head at himself and went on down the stairs.

If he is in there, then he is in there, and they might

145

as well bring each other what comfort they can. To know would not help me. To know I know would probably distress Jenny. So I must be careful not to find out. As long as he is capable of tenderness, and I think he is.

He laughed softly to himself.

At least there'll be no shortage of pillow talk with that one. If kids learn by example, he'll turn out whole classfuls of pedants.

At the bottom of the stairs he was surprised to find himself putting on his overcoat. He started to take it off again, then sighed and pulled it back over his shoulders.

My body knows more than my mind, he thought. I might as well get it over with.

Shivering a little he went through into the kitchen and opened the back door. The cold morning air struck damply into his face. A familiar but still timid stray cat peered at him from beneath a blackcurrant bush and howled piteously.

'In a minute,' he said.

He stepped across the strip of lawn which separated the side of the house from a small garden shed. Inside the shed it was dark. There was a smell of fertilizer and insecticide. Against the wall opposite the door and clearly visible in the shaft of relative light falling through the doorway was a chair. High-backed, comfortable-looking. His mind a careful blank, he reached to the shelf over it and took down a small plastic bag. Then he turned and went out in the garden again, closing the door behind him.

When he got back into the kitchen the cat, finally courageous in its search for food, was sitting in the corner. It made a dart for the door as he came in, but he was too quick for it. Realizing it could not get out, it sat down and started washing itself.

'That's right,' he said. 'Breakfast in a minute.'

Then he tipped the contents of the plastic bag on to the kitchen table and began to sort through them.

'Good morning, Mr Connon,' said a man's voice, pitched deliberately softly in order not to startle. Connon was a hard man to startle in any case, as those who knew him well could vouch. Now he hardly glanced up at the dressing-gowned figure standing at the door.

'Good morning, Antony,' he said. 'Sleep well?'

'Like a log,' said the boy. 'Jenny and I sat up until the early hours chatting.'

'You're up early.'

A statement not a question. Connon continued to sort through the objects before him.

'I'm very good at toast and coffee. May I be permitted . . . ?'

'Go ahead.'

Connon now brought his full attention to bear on the objects before him.

There were four groupings on the table top. The first group contained seven pennies and three half-pennies. Some of the coins were almost green with age.

The second group contained pieces of paper. Old

147

bus tickets, theatre-tickets, a golf score-card, a shopping list, the items almost unreadable.

He picked this up, and looked at the writing for a moment, then put it gently down.

The third group contained a variety of items. Hairgrips, a pencil, a bobbin, a teaspoon with an apostolic head.

The fourth group wasn't really a group at all. There was just one item. A very small piece of lead, like a tiny cupola with a lightly-milled edge.

Connon poked at it with his forefinger. It rolled round a semi-circle and came to rest.

'Coffee,' said Antony. 'Toast follows in a trice.'

He put a large mug of steaming black coffee in front of Connon and looked enquiringly at the stuff which littered the table.

Connon picked up the plastic bag, opened it, put it at the edge of the table and swept the items into it with one efficient movement of his hand. Then he tossed the bag lightly on top of a wall-cabinet behind him.

He sniffed.

'Do your habits include burning toast?' he asked.

Antony turned the grill off and looked at the dark brown slices of bread.

'It is only by going too far sometimes,' he said, 'that we know we have gone far enough.'

They drank their coffee and ate their toast (rejuvenated with a sharp knife) in silence at first.

'Is there any more coffee?' asked Connon.

'In a second,' said Antony.

'Mr Connon,' he said as he busied himself with the kettle and the jar of instant coffee, 'I didn't really have a chance last night to explain myself to you very fully. I was too occupied in explaining myself legally to that rather brutal man, Dalziel, then in explaining myself emotionally to Jenny, to have much chance of explaining myself rationally to you. Here's your coffee.'

He sat down again.

'Explain away,' said Connon.

'I was distressed, as were all her friends, to hear the sad news of Jenny's bereavement. That it was unexpected I knew. I had just been talking with Jenny about her family, yourself and Mrs Connon, that same Saturday night.'

'Had you now?' murmured Connon.

'When I read in the newspapers the details of the matter, I was even more distressed. I determined to contact Jenny, but letters and telephone conversations seemed quite inadequate means of discovering what I wanted to know, that is whether I could be of any use to her. So I vacillated, most uncharacteristically I might add, for several days. Finally I went to the Principal of the college, a sympathetic dame whose ear I have for any amount of services rendered, and told her I had decided that term must end slightly earlier for me than the others. So off I set. My intention was to arrive here during hours of daylight, but the charity of our road-users is not what it used to be. The rest you know. I arrived to find the house empty. I settled down to wait in the passageway between the garage and the house where I was a little protected from the inclemency of the weather and whence I was eventually plucked by the constabulary. More toast?'

'Thank you, no,' said Connon, looking reflectively at the youth. 'How well do you know Jenny?'

'In terms of time, not well. But in terms of attraction, very well indeed. I am her current beau.'

'If the archaism is meant to help me understand you, I don't like the implication,' said Connon with a smile. Antony looked apologetic but Connon did not let him speak. 'And now you've seen Jenny, have you learned anything that letter or telephone conversation would not have told you?'

'Possibly not. But what I have learned is absolutely clear, which it might not otherwise have been.'

'And that is?'

'That I can be of help, that she is delighted to have me here and that my presence can be of great comfort to her during these very trying times. I would like to have your permission to extend my stay, Mr Connon.'

'Do I have a choice?' asked Connon. 'If I do, which I doubt where Jenny's concerned, then I unhesitatingly offer you my hospitality for as long as you care to accept it. I also noticed Jenny's reaction to your arrival. But make sure your presence remains a comfort to her and doesn't become a complication.'

'Is this a private party or can anyone join?' said Jenny's voice from the door.

She was wearing an old dressing-gown, her hair was uncombed, her nose shiny. And her eyes too shone as she looked at the two men sitting there.

Antony rose to his feet and stood gazing intensely at her.

Connon sighed.

'If you're going to stay with us, Antony, you'll have to learn that in this household we don't pay all that much attention to the courtesies. You'll have to break yourself of the habit of bobbing up and down every time my daughter appears, especially when she looks like this.'

'It is not a matter of habit this time,' replied Antony. 'It is a small tribute I offer to beauty.'

'Jesus wept!' said Connon, laughing loud.

Jenny sat down, laughing even louder and eventually Antony, a pleasant glow of satisfaction in his mind, sat down laughing also.

In the hall the phone rang.

Jenny, nearest the door, turned in her chair, but Connon was up and out in one smooth movement.

As soon as he went through the door, Antony leaned over and kissed Jenny lightly on the lips. She smiled happily at him and took his hand. They sat looking at each other without speaking. Connon's voice came drifting in from the hall.

'Hello? Connon speaking.'

A long pause. The youngsters kissed again.

'Is that all you know? But why?'

Jenny shook her head in mock severity as Antony leaned nearer.

'Yes, of course we must. What? I don't know, do I? You'll have to think that out yourself.'

A very short pause.

'All right. Later. Goodbye.'

The phone clicked back on to its rest.

Jenny and Antony moved a few inches further apart, then giggled at each other because of the involuntary movement.

Connon came back into the room. One look at his face and Jenny stopped giggling.

'Daddy,' she said. 'What's the matter? What's happened?'

'I'm not sure,' said Connon slowly. 'It may be nothing, but the police have picked up Arthur Evans. They've got him down at the station for questioning. About . . . about last Saturday night.'

'Listen, Arthur,' said Dalziel in his heartiest voice. 'We've known each other a long time. All I want's a bit of cooperation. Anything you tell me will be in strict confidence if it's got nothing to do with our enquiries. As I'm sure it hasn't. I give you my word as a public official, and a friend. I can't say fairer.'

'Confidence?' said Evans. 'You talk of confidence, do you, with laughing boy sitting here with his pencil and paper at the ready? What's he doing, then? Sketching the bloody view, is it?'

Dalziel sighed and looked over at Pascoe who was sitting quietly in the furthermost corner of the room. The sergeant raised his eyebrows interrogatively. Dalziel shook his head fractionally.

'I'm sorry, Arthur. Sergeant Pascoe has to stay. I have to have someone here, you see. It's the regulations. It's in your interest, you see. It's for your protection.'

You bloody old hypocrite, thought Pascoe. You'd lie to your own grandmother. Suddenly it's regimental Dalziel, the slave of the rule book. Poor old Bruiser! If he didn't want me here, I'd be out like a rocket. Though why he does want me here's a bit of a mystery. Why not try the old pals' act, just the two of us together, it'll be off the record? Why not? I'll tell you why not, you half-wit. Because he knows it wouldn't work, that's why not. These two are about as near to being old pals as Judas Iscariot and the Pope. Just look at them. Perhaps Bruiser joined the queue knocking at Gwen Evans's back door at some time. He's not promising poor old Arthur silence if he co-operates. He's threatening him with lots of noise if he doesn't!

'If it wasn't Sergeant Pascoe here, Arthur,' Dalziel continued, 'it would have to be someone else. In fact technically I ought to have someone else here as well, but I thought that as the sergeant knew the facts of the enquiry (in fact he was instrumental in getting the information we'd like to question you about), it would keep it in the family so to speak if he acted as my amanuensis, that's the word, isn't it, Sergeant Pascoe?'

Pascoe smiled bleakly at the appeal to his erudition. Dalziel nodded enthusiastically as if he had received encouragement.

'Of course, you're entitled to have your own legal representative present, if you wish to be really formal about things. Would you like that? It's Stubby Barnet, isn't it? It'd be nice to see Stubby again, haven't seen him since last year's Club dinner.'

Stubby Barnet! thought Pascoe. Nice to see Stubby again; Good God, the power structure in a town this size was more formidable than politics in New York City. Come on, Arthur, you can't complain, boyo! You're being offered all the protection of the law. We'll keep the crowds back as you wash your dirty linen in public.

'Listen, Dalziel,' said Evans, 'I don't know what you're getting at, see? This is Saturday morning and I've got things to do. The only reason I came in here was that I was on my way into town when your boys called and they said it would be quicker if I came in to see you. So let's make it quick, shall we?'

'With pleasure, Arthur. Then I'll just ask again the only question you've allowed me to put so far. Would you tell me where you went when you left the Rugby Club about eight-fifteen last Saturday evening?'

'This is to do with Mary Connon, is it?'

'Just answer the question, please, Arthur.'

'I went home, then, that's where I bloody well went. Can I go now?'

'Why did you go home?'

'It's where I live, see? That's what home means, don't you remember, Superintendent Dalziel? Ask your bloody amanuensis.'

Dalziel was unperturbed by the outburst.

'But why did you leave the Club? You came back later, didn't you? Oh come on, Arthur! You're among friends. We have information. It's no use being coy, there's others who aren't.'

'I bet there bloody well is. Old gossiping women dressed up like men. I know them.'

'Sergeant. What is our information again, please?'

'Sir!' said Pascoe, sitting to attention. 'Our information is that Mr Evans left the Club in order to go and see what was delaying the arrival of his wife whom he had been expecting for some time.'

'I see. Is that true, Mr Evans?'

'Yes. Anything wrong with that?'

'Not in the least. Did you try the telephone?'

'Yes.'

'But without success.'

Evans grunted.

I can't put that down in words, can I? said Pascoe to himself. If I did it would probably read, if someone's rogering your wife on the hearth rug, you can't expect her to answer the phone.

Dalziel was looking happier now.

'You see, it's really all straightforward, isn't it? What happened then?'

'When?'

'When you got home.'

'Nothing. I mean, she wasn't there.'

Dalziel pushed his right index finger through the small hairs which fringed the cavity of his ear, and wriggled it sensuously about.

'But you knew she wasn't there.'

'What?'

'You knew she wasn't there. Your friends Dick and Joy Hardy had already called as arranged and had got no reply. They told you when you asked them at the Club. And you had telephoned yourself without success. So you knew she wasn't there.'

He knew she wasn't answering, thought Pascoe. That's what you knew, wasn't it, Arthur?

'I had to be sure.'

'In case she'd had an accident or something?' suggested Dalziel sympathetically.

'Yes,' replied Evans, hardly bothering to sound convincing.

'Relieved?'

Evans looked up suspiciously, his body tensing, his trunk leaning forward as if he were going to rise.

'Relieved she wasn't there. She hadn't had an accident.'

'Yes.'

'What did you do then?'

'Well, I came back to the Club, didn't I? You know that bloody well. You just said so.'

'Straight back.'

'Yes.'

'So you left the Club about ten past eight, went home, found all was well, and went straight back?'

156

'That's right. Yes. Though,' he added slowly as if thinking something out, 'I didn't leave there for, oh, about twenty, perhaps thirty minutes, I shouldn't wonder. Yes. That's right.'

Dalziel clapped his hands together as though a tricky point had been made simple.

'Good!' he said. 'That's why you didn't get back till after nine-fifteen. It's only five minutes' drive, isn't it?'

Now Evans did stand up.

'Yes,' he said. 'Is that all then? I don't see the point, but if it helps you, you're welcome. And I'll be on my way.'

Dalziel shook his head with a sad smile.

'Don't be silly, Arthur. You're not daft. You know that's not all. I'm just giving you a chance to tell us, that's all. If you don't want your chance, then just sit down again, and we'll tell you.'

Slowly Arthur Evans resumed his seat.

'Sergeant, just refresh us with your information again.'

'Certainly, sir.' Pascoe rippled through the pages of his notebook, stopped, coughed and began to speak in an impersonal monotone as before.

'Information given to us states that Mr Evans's motorcar was seen parked in Glenfair Road just before its junction with Boundary Drive at about eight-forty p.m. on the evening of Saturday last.'

He raised his eyes from the page. He might have done this a good deal earlier if he had wanted for it was completely blank.

His interviews the previous night had been done with all his customary thoroughness, but the most productive one had been not the Fernies or young Curtis, those most directly concerned with the incidents which had taken him to Boundary Drive, but with Ted Morgan whom there was really no reason to interview at all.

Except that he had had mud down his suit. Anyone who came back covered with mud after an evening with Jenny Connon had some answering to do, Pascoe had decided, surprised at his own concern.

Or jealousy.

Me jealous? he thought. Nonsense. I'm questioning this man because he might be able to help us. Not jealous. Just zealous.

But whatever his motives, he soon realized that he had tapped a very useful vein of information in Ted Morgan.

Ted had been a little belligerent at first but a couple of hints that Pascoe had seen him drinking in the Club earlier and an oblique reference to the breathalyser test had calmed him down and made him most co-operative.

Once he got started, like all the best gossips, there was no stopping him. Ten minutes with Morgan was more informative than all the rest of his questioning put together.

What he said about Evans's movements and behaviour on Saturday evening plus his confirmation of Jacko Roberts's placing of Connon high on the Evans suspect list had set Pascoe's mind racing. He knew that the constable on patrol in Boundary Drive had noticed no strange cars parked in the road that night as he passed along. Now he checked with the policeman whose beat took him down Glenfair Road, the main thoroughfare into which Boundary Drive ran. The list of car numbers he had noted that evening for one reason or another was unproductive. Evans's was not among them. But after much thought the constable did vaguely recall noticing a car parked very near to the corner of Boundary Drive, not near enough to constitute a danger, but near enough for him to notice it.

'I didn't make a note,' he had said defensively. 'Why should I? There was no offence being committed. Nothing suspicious.'

But his vague memory was of a white or cream Hillman. Evans drove a white Hillman Minx.

It had all been so flimsy that Pascoe had hesitated about presenting it to Dalziel. But in the end, he knew he had to. The superintendent's reaction had been unexpected. He had been as near to complimentary as Pascoe could recall.

'I've been wanting a chat with Arthur,' he had said gleefully. 'I'm worried about that wife of his. A woman like that's a . . . one of those things that helps other things to get started?'

'A catalyst,' said Pascoe.

'Right. A catalyst to violence.'

'You can't question a man because his wife's well built!' protested Pascoe.

'I once questioned a vicar because his choir was too big. Other churches were complaining, he was poaching their kids. It turned out he was paying well over the odds. But it didn't stop at singing. Let's have him in first thing.'

'All right,' he said. 'So I was there. What of it?'

'Where is "there", Mr Evans?' asked Dalziel.

'There. At Connon's. You know. I'm damned if I know why I didn't tell you in the first place, back when all this started happening. Must look a bit odd, I suppose.'

'Perhaps. Perhaps not. Lies, evasions, we get 'em all the time, Arthur. I sometimes use them myself,' he said, chuckling.

'I've noticed,' said Evans drily.

'Tell us about it then, Arthur,' invited Dalziel.

Evans grunted again, then started talking. Having made up his mind to talk, he spoke rapidly and fluently and Pascoe's pen flew over the paper as he took shorthand notes. He was so occupied with the accuracy of his record that he scarcely had time to pay attention to the narrative as a whole and it wasn't until Evans fell silent that the statement jelled in his mind.

The Welshman had set off home in a cold fury. He was convinced that his wife was with another man. He was almost as convinced that this man was Connon. He went right through the house when he arrived home but there was no sign of Gwen; nor of anyone else. Connon had left the Club early, he remembered, saying he was going home. Now Evans got back into his car and drove round to Connon's house. He had not parked in front of the house because he had no desire to draw attention to himself. All he wanted to do was to see if Connon's car was in the garage. The only sign of life he could see in the house was the white light from a television screen shining through a chink in the living-room curtains. He went as silently as he could up the drive and peered into the garage. The car was there. Still unconvinced, he considered ringing the bell and inventing some pretext for coming to see Connon if Mary Connon answered the door. Instead, not wanting to risk a scene without more evidence of his suspicions, he went back to his car and drove back to the Club, stopping briefly at a couple of pubs on the way to see if Gwen was in either. But when he reached the Club she was there already.

It's a reasonable story, thought Pascoe. And if he had rung the bell at Connon's what reason would he have had to kill Mary?

'And *did* you find out where Gwen had been, Arthur?' asked Dalziel softly.

'She said she thought Dick and Joy had forgotten they were to pick her up, so she set off to catch the bus.'

'It must have been a slow bus.'

It was a flat, totally unaccented statement.

'She just missed one, so she dropped in at our local for some fags, and stayed to have a drink.'

'And did she?'

Evans was having difficulty in controlling his voice.

'I do not go around public houses asking if my wife is telling me the truth. That's more in your line.'

'Oh it is. Quite right,' said Dalziel with equanimity. 'We'll ask, never fear. But we won't bother you with our findings if you feel that way.'

A touch of the knife, thought Pascoe. Just a hint, a reminder.

Dalziel wasn't finished.

'Why do you suspect Connon of . . . whatever you suspect him of?'

'Don't be mealy-mouthed, Bruiser.'

'All right. Of having it away with your wife. Why Connon?'

Evans spoke softly now so that Pascoe had to strain to catch his words.

'Nothing positive. Things she let slip. We had a row. She said I should pay her more attention, I was always round at the Club with my drinking mates. I said at least I knew where I was with them. I could trust the men I drank with. So she laughed at that, see. Said, "oh yes?" I asked what she meant. She said that not all of them were overgrown boys like me. One at least, she said, was a man. Still waters run deep, she said.'

He fell silent.

'That's little enough to go on.'

'Oh, there's other things. I've seen 'em talking. Seeing her looking at him. And when she goes

162

missing like she did last Saturday he's usually not around either. But I wasn't certain, see? That's why I didn't ring the bell.'

'You were certain enough last Saturday afternoon when you put the boot in,' said Pascoe casually from his corner.

Evans flushed and looked far more embarrassed than he had done at any stage so far.

'What? Oh, that. How do you know? Oh, I don't know what made me do that, rotten thing to do, that was. I was really sorry afterwards. I'd got him to play, see? We were short anyway, always are, and I thought, right Connie, I'll know where you are this afternoon at any rate. Then he went down in this loose scrum, shouldn't have been there, but he was always a bit of a hero, and I put my foot in looking for the ball and there he was. I couldn't have missed him, but I could have slowed down a bit. But I didn't. Silly really, I've never done anything like it before. Never. Hard, you know, but never malicious. I was really sorry. Might have killed him. I thought I had for a moment.'

I wish he wouldn't get so blasted Welsh when he's excited, thought Pascoe. My shorthand doesn't have the right symbols somehow. I'll never be able to read it back.

'But I didn't, did I?' Evans went on. 'And I didn't kill his missis either, if that's what all this is about, which is all I can think.'

'No one has suggested such a thing, I hope?' said Dalziel, shocked. 'Your value to us, Arthur, is that you were there. In the road. Up at the house. At a significant time. We want to know what you saw. Tell us again what you saw.'

Halfway through the third telling, Pascoe was called out to the phone. He returned a minute later looking thoughtful.

'Now look,' said Evans. 'I've got to be going. Gwen will be thinking I've been put in a dungeon. And I've got to catch the team bus at twelve-forty-five. We're away today. So unless you've got ways of keeping me here you haven't revealed yet, I'm off.'

'Arthur,' said Dalziel reproachfully. 'You've been free to go any time. We've no way of holding you.'

'No,' agreed Evans, rising.

'Except perhaps for obstructing the police by not revealing all this a lot earlier.'

Ouch! thought Pascoe.

'Early or late, I've revealed it now. And it'll go no further, I hope.'

'Not unless needed, Arthur. We're always a little doubtful about statements that have to be forced out of witnesses by revealing the extent of our prior information.'

Evans laughed, the first merry sound he'd made since his arrival.

'Information nothing. It's piss-all information you had. I volunteered my statement because I wanted to volunteer, not because of your pathetic bluff. When you sort out your notes, Sergeant, you might include in them the additional information that my car was parked at the other end of Boundary Drive, the end furthest away from Glenfair Road, see? So it's purely voluntary isn't it? And now I'm going to volunteer to go home. Good day to you both.'

Dalziel and Pascoe looked at each other for a long moment after the door had slammed behind Evans. Then they both began to grin, and finally laughed out loud.

It was their first moment of spontaneous shared amusement that Pascoe could remember.

'Well now, boyo,' said Dalziel in a dreadful parody of a Welsh accent, 'you'd better watch your bloody self, see? Telling such lies to an honest citizen.'

'It might have been his car,' said Pascoe. 'White Hillman. I mean, why not? It didn't seem absolutely out of the question. By the way, we had a phone call.'

'From?'

'Connon. He was worried about Arthur. Wanted us to go easy on the thumbscrews, I think.'

'Did he now? And he asked for you?'

'Why yes. I expect so.'

'I see. Thinks I haven't got any better feelings to appeal to, does he? Well, go on.'

'There's nothing to go on with. I assured him we were only asking Mr Evans one or two questions that might or might not be connected with the case. And I suggested he should contact Evans himself for full details.'

'That was naughty. You didn't ask then?'

'Ask what? Sir?'

Dalziel looked pleadingly up to heaven. Pascoe sighed inwardly.

The party's over then, he thought. Like Christmas, a brief moment of good will and fellowship, then back to normal. You've spent your allowance, Bruiser. What're you going to do at the end of the week?

'You didn't ask who he got his information from. About Evans's being here.'

He's right. I should have asked. That's another of his blasted troubles. He keeps on being right.

'No, sir. I didn't. Sorry. I'll get back on to him, shall I?'

'Don't bother,' said Dalziel. 'If he doesn't want to tell us (and the minute you ask, he won't) there's no way of finding out. From him. But the possible sources aren't many, are they?'

'No, sir.'

'Our bobbies. A couple of nosey neighbours. Or the fair Gwen herself. Who's got your money, Sergeant?'

Pascoe's mind was racing.

'That'd mean, or might mean, that Evans is not altogether wrong. And if he's not altogether wrong, then Connon suddenly gets a great big motive.'

'Motive? What motive?'

'Why, she, Mary Connon that is, finds out.'

'How?'

'Accidentally by finding something,' said Pascoe impatiently. 'Or is deliberately told. Anonymous friend, a telephone call, that kind of thing. We've got one around that doesn't like Connie much, we know that.'

'So. She knows. What then?'

'She tells him, that night. Gets nasty. Says some more unpleasant things about his daughter. Connon sees red. He's had that crack on the head remember. He grabs . . .' Pascoe paused.

'What does he grab, Sergeant?'

'How do I know? Something odd enough in shape not to be a normal part of living-room furniture. Something, *anything*, he can use as a club. And swings it at her.'

'At his own wife? Sitting in his own lounge? Connon?'

Pascoe sighed.

'I didn't know the lady as well as you, sir, but she seems in all particulars to have been a pretty clubbable woman.'

'No, I didn't mean her. I mean Connon. It's out of character. You've met him. Sudden violence doesn't fit.'

The fat sod's fair, thought Pascoe. You've got to admit he's fair. I'm sure he'd like it to be Connon, but he doesn't try to bend matters.

'Perhaps the whole thing's a fake then, sir. Perhaps there was no concussion, no quarrel, no heat of the moment. Perhaps Connon decided he would like to marry Gwen Evans or just unmarry Mary Connon. So he goes quietly home, sits and watches the telly with her a while; then, in the commercial break perhaps, he leans forward, taps her on the head with whatever he has selected for the job, waits a couple of hours, then rings us.'

Dalziel was scratching with both hands, one on his inner right thigh, the other under his chin. One movement was clockwise, Pascoe noted, the other anti. Difficult.

'That sounds better. But not by much.'

Well, let's have your ideas, for God's sake. You're the great detective!

Pascoe kept back his exasperation with difficulty and put his thoughts as mildly as he could manage.

'What do you think then, sir? An intruder?'

Dalziel laughed without much merriment.

'You and your damned intruder. No, be sure of one thing, there wasn't any intruder, my lad. The answer's nearer home. Your intruders'll all turn out to be like that laddo last night. Bit of a disappointment that, eh? Christ, he could talk! Made even you sound like a board-school lad at the pit-face. But he seemed nice enough. He'll be good company for that kid of Connon's. He's not exactly the laughing cavalier, is he?'

Pascoe stood up.

He's going to try to get the knife in, he thought. Just a little wriggle this time.

'Will that be all then? I'd better try to tidy my desk up a bit.'

'Mind you,' continued Dalziel, ignoring him, 'it wasn't all waste, was it? I mean, Ted Morgan turned out to be a real find, didn't he? The eyes and ears of the world. You must have leaned upon him pretty hard.'

'Not really,' said Pascoe.

Dalziel leered at him across the desk.

'It's not a crime to take Jenny Connon out, you know. Eh? Now don't be offended. Just take care that fancying her doesn't make you go too soft on the rest of the family, or too hard on anyone else. I glanced at the stuff from young Curtis and the Fernies. Nothing much there, eh?'

Pascoe shook his head.

'Though the Fernies do seem to be around a lot, don't you think? And I met Mrs Curtis – she came in to see what it was all about. She'd just got in, and her husband. Do you know them?'

'No,' said Dalziel without interest. But Pascoe ploughed on.

'He's nothing, a little silent man, not much there, I think. She's a talker, gab, gab, gab. The Fernies got rid of her when I left and she walked me to the front gate. Made Ted Morgan seem like an amateur. But one thing she did say was that our friend Fernie is going around telling everyone Connon killed his wife. And claiming he knows how.'

Dalziel was now immersed in some papers and didn't even glance up.

'There's always plenty of them, isn't there?'

'I wouldn't know, sir. Is it worth a word with him?'

'I shouldn't think so. There hasn't been a complaint? See him if you want, though, but it'll be a waste of time.'

He glanced at his watch, opened the top drawer of his desk and swept the papers in.

'Come on,' he said. 'We'll be able to get a drink in a moment. You'll be wanting an early lunch, won't you?'

'Will I?' asked Pascoe, trying to conceal from himself the effort he had to make to keep up with Dalziel down the corridor. 'Why?'

'The rugby, Sergeant. Remember?'

'We're going to watch?' asked Pascoe, puzzled.

Dalziel sighed.

'I might watch. But the game you're concerned with is Arthur Evans. You heard what he said, his coach goes at twelve-forty-five. So you get round to his house at one. Have a chat. Stop a while. Who knows? Friend Connon might even turn up to keep you company. That'd be nice. You in your small corner, Gwen curled up on the mat and Connon taking his ease in Arthur's rocking chair.'

The thought obviously amused him. They were out in the street now. Dalziel was well known, hailing and being hailed by nearly every second person they passed, it seemed to Pascoe. Though he noticed there were some who spoke to the superintendent and were completely ignored, while others looked as if they would have preferred to creep past unknown.

Again there came to him a sense of how small

a town of some eighty-five thousand people really was.

'Talking of chairs,' said Dalziel, 'there was a report from forensic, wasn't there, on that chair of Connon's? Nothing useful, I suppose?'

Pascoe was never quite certain just how genuine his superior's casual contempt for science was. Had he really not even looked at the report? He felt tempted to find out by inventing a number of startling discoveries made through lab tests on the chair. But instead, as always, he thought, I'll play the game.

'No. Nothing. No indication that anyone had been killed in it or done anything else in it but sit in it. It went back to Connon's yesterday. He made them put it in the garden shed.'

'Did he now? Bit of degree work for you there, Pascoe! The psychology of the criminal.'

They came to a halt at a busy road crossing. The town was full of Saturday morning shoppers, more than usual even; there was only one more Saturday before Christmas.

'Sir, what about Hurst and the letter? You mentioned last night . . .'

'Did I? No, I didn't, Sergeant. I'm not senile. Who did?'

Pascoe looked a little shamefaced.

'Well, Connon actually, on the phone. He asked if anything had been done.'

Dalziel slapped his inside pocket.

'It's here. I'll be seeing him before the match. Any

171

other little reminders to me, Sergeant? Anything else I might have forgotten? No? Then what are we standing here for? Let's move on before some young copper picks us up for soliciting. Now, where did you say you were going to take me for that drink?'

Jenny and Antony looked at each other, brown eyes unblinkingly fixed on blue, over the rims of their upraised pint pots.

'Umh,' said Antony appreciatively, putting his glass down and nodding his head, 'not bad at all. Unpretentious, with a pleasant touch of wit, should travel quite well. There is perhaps a slight tendency towards making one drunk.'

They were sitting near a huge open fire in the lounge of a pub of that kind of indeterminate oldness which is the sign of constant use and development over many years. The fireplace was obviously very old indeed. It was large, and had once been larger. The table they sat at was wrought iron, with a bright brass guard-rail running round the top of it, more of a danger to glasses than anything else. In the ceiling there was visible what might have been an original oak cross-beam, but it had been unceremoniously distempered with the rest.

'I like it here,' said Antony. 'They have attempted neither to freeze the past, nor anticipate the future. Nor indeed to impress the present upon us with framed photographs of actors and actresses, cricketers and jockeys, the semi-famous sub-world, with duplicated scrawls of spurious well-wishings stamped across their corners.'

'I just like the beer,' said Jenny.

'It was nice of your father to chase us off together as he did,' said Antony.

'He's a nice man.'

'Yes, I'm sure he is. Well, Jenny, now we have got over the initial emotionalism of our reunion, perhaps one or two points might be clarified for me. Your father has extended to me the hospitality of his house for as long as I care to take it, or until he grows sick of the sight of me. It did not escape my notice, however, that you were accompanied last night by a rather large, rather muddy man who, I gathered from hints dropped from various quarters, had been your escort that evening. Competition I do not mind. I thrive on it. But we Wilkeses were never dogs in mangers. A word will be enough.'

'Which word is that?' asked Jenny.

'If you don't know it, then I shall not teach you it. Good. I'm glad that's out of the way.'

'I didn't know it was.'

'Well, isn't it?'

'Of course, you fool. Didn't you get a good look at him? I was after information, that's all.'

'Information?'

Quickly Jenny explained about Ted Morgan. At least it started off as a quick explanation, but almost without noticing, she was soon telling Antony everything she had felt or feared in the past week.

He listened gravely without interrupting her.

When she finished, he went to the bar and refilled their glasses.

'There are evidently some very nasty people in this little town of yours,' he said reflectively.

'And some very nice ones,' said Jenny with instinctive indignation.

He grinned at her and took her hand.

'But what goes on on the terraces seems to be very simple and almost harmless compared with that Rugby Club of yours.'

The look of strain which had been missing from Jenny's face most of the morning returned.

'You think it's all something to do with the Club too, do you? Daddy does, I'm sure. And I think fat Dalziel does too. Oh, I wish it was something simple, some burglar, a tramp or something, who broke in and did it. It would still be as horrid, but it'd end there at least. Instead of which it seems to be going on and on and I'm finding myself going round playing at stupid amateur detectives. And what it's doing to Daddy, I just don't know.'

'Hey, cool it, baby.'

The shock of hearing such an expression in the accents of Hollywood gangsterese come from Antony's lips pulled her up sharply. He was smiling at her, but there was concern in his eyes.

'Thanks,' she said. 'I was going on a bit.'

'Nonsense,' he said. 'Of course you're concerned about everything. But there's nothing wrong with playing games to ease your concern, whether it's playing detective or playing rugby. That's what

174

games are, recreational. They give us a space in the business of life to re-create ourselves. Don't you think I would teach R.E. extremely well? And talking of detectives, aren't those two gentlemen, who have just come in like Laurel and Hardy, of that ilk?'

They were Dalziel and Pascoe. They looked around the room.

'See that? All good detectives look around the room,' murmured Antony. Jenny giggled and kicked his ankle.

Dalziel saw them and waved. Pascoe glanced over and nodded almost imperceptibly.

'You know,' said Antony, 'I think that Laurel there fancies you.'

'Don't be silly,' replied Jenny, feeling the fringe of a blush caressing her cheek.

'Silly? Am I then so esoteric in my taste as to be the only man in the world who fancies you?'

Jenny finished her second pint with a swallow that reminded Pascoe, who was watching her surreptitiously through the bar mirror, of Jacko Roberts.

'Come on,' she said. 'I've got to get home and make the dinner.'

'Right,' he said. 'And this afternoon?'

'Well,' she said, 'I wondered if you'd mind going out with Daddy. Get him off to the rugby match or something.'

'Of course. But what are you going to do?'

'I want to clear out their, his, bedroom. Of Mummy's things, I mean. I've been meaning to do it, he

175

doesn't seem to have the will, and it's more my job, I think. All her clothes and everything. I must do it now. He's been sleeping in the spare room, you see, but when you turned up last night, he moved back in. I think that's why he was up so early this morning.'

'I'm sorry,' said Antony. 'I didn't realize.'

'Why should you? Anyway, I'd like to do it. I know he's been through her papers and that, not that there was much. But the police asked, in case there was anything there to help. So if I can get rid of the rest . . .'

'Of course. Well, let's be on our way. I haven't really tasted your cooking yet, have I? I mean, I did in fact make my own breakfast. Not at all what I am used to.'

Jenny grinned, that wide, slightly toothy grin which she tried so hard to avoid, and which filled her whole face with an animation and glow that turned Antony's heart upside down.

He laughed back at her and they left the pub hand in hand.

Dalziel looked meaningfully at Pascoe, but said nothing. Pascoe felt the cold beer fill his mouth and listened to the landlord's radio distantly above playing 'White Christmas'.

It was twelve o'clock.

'Time for another,' he said.

Gwen Evans wasn't being very helpful. At least, not in any sense that had any bearing on the case.

But Pascoe found her a great deal of help in restoring his rather worn manly pride. She was not a coquette, he had decided. She did not deliberately set out to make herself interesting to men. There was nothing self-conscious about the way she moved, stood, sat down, or talked to a man. There was nothing suggestive about her, she gave no hints of interest or invitation. She was dressed in a sloppy brown sweater and an old pair of slacks.

Whoever else she might be expecting, he had thought on arrival, it surely can't be her lover.

But the overall effect of two minutes in her presence had been to fill him with an all powerful sense of her sex.

The beer helped, he assured himself. Three pints heightened most men's receptivity.

But what the hell! he added. I don't just want her. I like her! She's a nice woman. A nice, pleasant, unfairly sexy woman.

But she wasn't any help at all as far as Evans was concerned.

Yes, she knew he was jealous of Connon.

No, there was nothing in his suspicion.

No, there hadn't been anything odd about the previous Saturday, either about her husband or about her own behaviour.

She repeated what he had heard already from the lips of Evans. She had decided that her friends had forgotten to pick her up. Had set off to catch the bus. Missed it. Dropped into the local, the Blue Bell, to get some cigarettes. Stayed to have a drink.

No, she hadn't talked to anyone in there. It had been quite crowded, but she had sat quietly in the corner with a drink.

No, she could not remember who had served her.

'And what the hell business of yours is all this anyway, Sergeant?'

She spoke without animosity and Pascoe smiled at her apologetically.

'None, of course, in all probability. We never know what's our business, and what isn't, till we get the answers.'

He could afford not to press, he thought. All he had to do to check on her story was to ask at the pub. If she'd been there, no matter how quietly, someone would remember. You couldn't go around looking like Gwen Evans and hope to remain anonymous.

'Would you like a drink, Sergeant? Or a coffee?'

The beer was just beginning to turn a little sour in his stomach, and his bladder felt very full. Coffee would help one, but not the other.

'Coffee would be very nice,' he said. 'May I use your bathroom?'

She rose from the furry white armchair which he was sure was her choice. The thing he was sitting in felt hard and lumpy, almost certainly an Evans family hand-me-down.

'First left up the stairs,' she said in the hallway and went into the kitchen.

He had just shut the door, locking it from ingrained habit, when the front-door bell rang.

With a longing look at the gleaming white bowl, he hastily opened the door again and stepped on to the landing.

Through the railings overlooking the small entrance hall, he saw Gwen appear from the kitchen. She didn't even glance up the stairs.

Not much sign of guilt there, he thought. Perhaps it's just the baker.

He heard the door being opened. All he could see was Gwen's back from the waist down. It was a sight worth dwelling on, but not much use for present purposes. He wanted to see faces if this were Connon.

'Hello Gwen.'

A man's voice. Familiar. But not Connon's.

'Hello Marcus,' said Gwen evenly, with just a touch of surprise. 'I'm afraid you've missed Arthur. In fact I think you've probably missed the coach as well.'

There was a pause.

'The coach? Oh, damn. I'd forgotten. No, I'm not playing this week. I'd forgotten it was an away game.'

'Anything I can do?'

'No. I'll see him tonight. It was just that, well, I heard he'd been down at the police station this morning. I suppose I'm just being nosey, but I was worried. It's not nice this business. Anyway, I'd had a drink in the Club, that's where I heard. They were talking, you know how it is. So I thought I'd call in before Arthur got down there, just to see what was what. And to warn him the long knives were out. Some of them are like a lot of old women.'

'Thanks, Marcus. But don't worry. It was nothing at all really.'

It would be diplomatic, I suppose, thought Pascoe, to stay up here till she'd disposed of Marcus. If he sees me here, trouble will be confirmed. And if he is more nosey than friendly, then the rumours will fly. But, as Bruiser might say, if God had wanted me to be a diplomat, he'd have painted pinstripes down my backside. Which he didn't. So here goes.

He stepped back into the bathroom, pressed the little gleaming chrome lever, and moved hurriedly away from the sound of rushing water.

Gwen looked as if she were about to shut the door.

'Mr Felstead,' said Pascoe with a note of surprise more genuine, he felt, than anything Dalziel could produce. 'How pleasant to meet you again. Not playing today? You haven't been dropped, I hope?'

God, it sounded bad. Perhaps he wasn't much better than Dalziel.

'No, I'm not, Sergeant. But not dropped,' he added with a grin which made him look like the prototype jovial monk. 'You've got to die to be dropped from our Fourths, and then it's best to be cremated just to be on the safe side. No, I'm retired, temporarily at least. I'll leave it to the young men, like yourself. Do you play?'

'Not rugger. No, I used to kick a rounder ball in a less violent game, but now I'm kept far too busy.'

'Even on Saturday afternoons?' asked Marcus, raising his eyebrows quizzically in Gwen's direction.

'Even then,' agreed Pascoe. 'Though it is not without its compensations.'

Gwen yawned unconcernedly at the compliment. From the kitchen came a high whistle.

'Coffee,' she said. 'Marcus, would you care to step in and take a cup?'

'Of kindness yet, for the sake of auld lang syne,' ran absurdly through Pascoe's mind.

'No, I won't, thank you, Gwen. I'll get along. Cheerio. Cheerio, Sergeant.'

Pascoe followed Gwen into the kitchen.

'He didn't seem very interested in why I was here, Mrs Evans.'

She heaped a teaspoonful of instant coffee into a couple of beakers and poured a steaming jet of water on to it.

'No? Why should he be?'

'Because he seemed fairly interested in the police when he arrived.'

Silly twit, he thought as she turned to him, faintly amused.

'So you had a listen, did you? Well, well. It must be second nature.'

He smiled back and shook his head.

'I'm sorry. But it's not second nature. No.'

'No?'

'No. It required an act of will. In fact, now you've rumbled me, may I, would you mind if I postponed the coffee just a few moments more?'

181

He heard her laughing with real amusement as he went up the stairs once more.

Dalziel wasn't getting much co-operation either. He seemed to have been elected the most avoidable man in the club-house. Willie Noolan gave him a distant wave; Ted Morgan did an almost military about-turn when he spotted him and disappeared through the door; even Jacko Roberts seemed to consider his offer of a drink with more sardonic suspicion than usual.

'You've been found out,' he said.

'Found out?'

'That's right. The myth of rugby veteran, dirty story teller, hail-fellow-well-met Bruiser Dalziel's been knackered and they're seeing you as what you are.'

'What's that?'

'A nasty, nosey, nobody's-friend copper.'

Dalziel finished his drink and stood up. Peter Hurst had just come into the room, dressed in his track suit though there was some time yet till kick-off.

'Fat bugger,' said Jacko to the policeman's retreating back. Then he wondered if Dalziel had heard, and wished he didn't care.

Hurst doesn't look as if he's very delighted to see me, either, thought Dalziel.

He had always thought he had no illusions about the artificiality of people's reactions to him, but some must have taken root unaware. Tender young plants as yet, and all the more vulnerable to sudden blasts of cold.

'I've got that letter,' he said as jovially as he could manage.

'Oh yes.'

'Yes. Shall we go into the committee room?'

Hurst looked reluctant to go anywhere.

'Look, Superintendent,' he began.

'Andy,' interrupted Dalziel. 'We're in the Club, aren't we? This is unofficial.'

'That's it,' said Hurst. 'What I said to Connie last night was unofficial as well, between the two of us. I'd no idea you were listening.'

'Listen, Peter,' said Dalziel sympathetically. 'If you've got any information, you've got to give it to me. It's your duty.'

'Suddenly it's become official again, has it?'

Hurst's voice had risen a little, but he dropped it again as he realized that several pairs of eyes were watching them with interest.

Dalziel's mind gave the equivalent of a shrug.

These people never realize that I can stand a row better than any of them, he thought. They think a bit of sound and fury against me confirms something. It's like water off a duck's back.

'Mr Hurst,' he said formally, 'I have reason to believe you can help me with an enquiry. Now you can do that now. Or you can do it tonight. Or you can do it next week. But be sure of one thing. If you want to be out on that pitch when the referee blows his whistle, you'd better do it now.'

'Andy. Peter. For heaven's sake! Remember where you are!'

It was Noolan, attracted by the waves of interest emanating from all sides of the room.

'The committee room?' said Dalziel with a smile.

He put his arm over Hurst's shoulder as they went through the door, but removed it before the door was quite closed.

'Now, Mr Hurst,' he said. 'You wanted to look at the letter Jenny Connon received the day before yesterday. I have that letter here. Before I show it to you, however, I want to know your reason for wanting to see it.'

Hurst looked angrily at him, then questioningly at Noolan who had followed them in.

The bank manager nodded.

'Tell him, Peter.'

'So,' said Dalziel. 'Another in the plot? Don't say you've taken to concealing information as well, Willie?'

'No, Andy. Peter saw me last night after you'd left. Peter. Tell him.'

Hurst played with the zip on his track-suit top, moving it up and down.

Like a nervous tart on her first job, thought Dalziel. Will the man never start?

'It's nothing really,' said Hurst. 'It's just that a few days ago I heard one of our members say something about Connie. It was just after we'd heard about Mary. We'd been saying how awful it was, how sorry we were for Connie. And this chap said we might well be sorry for Connie, but not to overdo it. He said that there were things about Connie that he wouldn't like his daughter to know.'

'And?'

'Nothing really. We'd all had a few drinks. Someone said there were things about himself he wouldn't like his wife to know, we all laughed and went off happy. It kind of broke the gloomy atmosphere.'

'Exit on a joke. Is that *all*?'

'No. On Wednesday after the selection committee meeting, I realized I'd left my fountain pen in here. I came in to get it and found this same person using it. He finished off quickly as I came in, apologized when he realized it was my pen, and that was an end to it. But I got a distinct impression he didn't want me to see what he was writing. He folded it up and tucked it away very quickly.'

'Again, is that all? It's not much, is it? And why do you want to see the letter?'

Hurst obviously did not like what was happening. But he feels he ought to dislike it even more than he does, thought Dalziel. Jesus, it's all do-it-yourself public relations now. Everyone's sweating on their image.

'Whatever he was writing,' said Hurst slowly, 'he was writing in block capitals. I saw that much.'

'One block capital looks much like another, upside down, from a distance,' sneered Dalziel. 'Is that all?'

'No. It would be written with my pen, you see, if it was that letter. And that day my pen was filled with green ink. I'd run out and borrowed some from my boy. You know what kids are. Anything exotic. It happened to be green.'

Carefully Dalziel reached into his inside pocket and took from it a large envelope. Out of this he drew a Cellophane packet. Framed in it they could see a letter. He held it up to the light to give a clearer view.

The ink was black.

Hurst sighed deeply.

'I'm glad,' he said.

'Who was it you saw?' asked Dalziel.

'Why? Is that necessary,' he asked, turning to Noolan.

'You'd have named him if he seemed guilty. It seems odd not to do so when he is innocent. Eh, Willie?'

'It was Arthur Evans that Peter saw. We heard he was down at the station this morning. Peter wondered . . .'

'. . . if we in our own bumbling way had caught up with him? No. Well, thank you both very much indeed for your time.'

'Not at all,' said Noolan. 'I'm sorry yours has been wasted.'

Hurst left without a word.

'Andy,' said Noolan. 'Don't make such a big noise round the Club, eh? You put me in an embarrassing position.'

'I shall be so quiet you'll never notice me. In fact, with your permission, I'll start now and stop here for a while. All the best fictional detectives do it. Have long thinks, I mean.'

'Be our guest,' said Noolan and went back into the social room leaving the large figure, head wreathed in cigarette smoke, seated at the top of the big committee-sized table.

He was still there two hours later when the whistle went for no-side.

'A curious game,' said Antony as they drove away from the ground. 'Especially when seen through a glass, distantly.'

They hadn't cared to join the small crowd of spectators in the old stand, but had remained in the car parked about twenty-five yards behind one of the goals.

'A poor game,' replied Connon, 'seen from no matter what distance.'

'Why?' asked Antony, with a polite interest which ten minutes later had turned into the real thing.

Whatever else you know, Jenny's father, he thought, you certainly know your rugby. At least I think that if I knew my rugby, I would be in a good position to acknowledge that you know yours.

But he knew enough about the game to recognize the scope and justice of Connon's analysis.

'Now I feel I could watch the game again,' he said when Connon finished.

'Nothing is repeatable,' said the older man. 'Not even the moments that we relive a thousand times.'

Connon fell silent and Antony, great talker though

he was, knew when conversation was not being invited. The rest of the drive home passed in almost complete silence.

But I like him, thought Antony as they got out of the car. He might do for me very well. I could not bear a dull father-in-law. And Jenny, now Jenny, there's the find of the century.

He went towards the front door with pleasurable anticipation. But there was no reply to his enthusiastic bell-ringing and Connon, coming from closing the garage, had to get his key out to open the door.

The house was quiet and felt empty.

'Jenny! Jenny!' called Connon.

There was no reply.

'She can't have gone far,' said Connon. 'She'll be back in a minute I expect. Probably gone round the corner to the shops.'

Probably, thought Antony, but he didn't feel happy.

He went upstairs to change out of the heavy boots he had (unnecessarily) decided were good rugby-watching gear.

As he passed Jenny's bedroom door, he saw it was ajar. He pushed it gently open and looked in.

The room was quite empty. He looked at the furnishings, the pictures, the bed with its rich crimson bedspread. Seated on top of it was a fluffy white dog, its red tongue grotesquely hanging out, its head lolling to the side. It was a nightgown case and his eyes lit up as he saw it.

Quickly he moved into his own room, grabbed his

pyjama top and returned. His intention was simple, to substitute this for whatever garment he found in the dog.

But as he went across the room to the bed, something on the dressing-table caught his eye. It was a large sheet of paper with writing all over it.

Antony was a man with considerable respect for individual privacy. Looking at other people's letters was not something that attracted him. But something about the sheet of paper, lying with its contents reflected unreadably in the mirror, drew him towards it.

He picked it up.

'Dear Christ,' he said.

He read it again.

'Dear mother of God!' he said.

His pyjama-top dropped from his hand.

'Antony? Anything wrong?'

Connon stood in the door.

'I found this. On her dressing-table.'

He reached out the letter.

Connon read it with one sweep of the eyes. Then without a word he turned and ran downstairs. Antony walking out of the room to the landing heard him dialling the telephone.

Three numbers only.

'Give me the police,' he said. 'Quick.'

'As obscene letters go,' said Dalziel, 'I've seen worse.'

'Is that supposed to be some consolation?' asked Connon.

'It's pretty graphic I should have thought,' remarked Antony, trying to hide his tremendous concern under a calm exterior.

'Oh yes. It's graphic. It's that all right. Crudely so. But it's not perverted. This is all good straightforward stuff.'

'For God's sake, Dalziel!' exploded Connon. 'Can we cut the expert critical review and get on with the job of finding out where Jenny is!'

Dalziel made squelchy soothing noises in his throat.

'Take it easy,' he said. 'We have her description out. Every policeman in town's on the look out for her. I'm sure she'll have come to no harm.'

'Thanks,' said Connon. 'You realize there was no envelope with this thing. And there's only one post on Saturday and this had arrived well before I left?'

'Yes, sir. We realize that. So now you're imagining that he, whoever he is, popped this through the letterbox, waited till she had had time to read it, then rang the bell and invited her to take a stroll with him. Now is that likely?'

'Only if,' said Connon slowly, 'only if it was someone she knew well.'

The same thought had crossed Dalziel's mind much earlier, but he still found it hard to believe. In his experience those who wrote letters like this were unlikely to follow them up, at least so rapidly.

But there was something disturbing about the letter. Not just in its contents. He had been speaking nothing less than the truth when he put it well down the list of those he had seen.

No, there was something else.

The door of the lounge opened, and Pascoe came in. They all looked at him, Dalziel interrogatively, Antony hopefully, Connon fearfully.

A single shake of the head did for them all. He went across the room to Dalziel.

'Nothing yet, sir. We've got everything on it we can.'

He was plainly as concerned as anyone else there, really concerned, not just professionally.

Antony found himself quite liking Laurel after all.

He went up to the two detectives and coughed delicately.

'Forgive me for my effrontery,' he said. 'But my father always taught me never to be afraid of pointing out the obvious. I'm sure you have noticed the implication of the letter, that the writer has in fact observed Jenny undressing for bed? I just wondered if you also knew, as I'm sure you do, that her bedroom's at the rear of the house?'

'So?' said Dalziel.

'Well, as I know from personal experience it's almost impossible to get to the rear of this house from the front when the door at the end of the passageway between the garage and the house wall is locked. There is a very stout trellis on the other side of the house, with an equally well-barred door in it.'

'Through someone else's garden?' said Pascoe.

'From my brief observation of Mr Connon's hedges, he seems to have a peculiar fondness for a near lethal mixture of African thorn, briar rose, and bramble.'

'May we, Mr Connon?' said Dalziel, setting off without waiting for an answer.

They all stood in the rapidly darkening garden, most of them glad to have even the illusion of activity to take their minds off the unchanging situation.

It was a long garden, the kind of length which only generous pre-war builders gave to house-buyers.

There'd be a two-bedroomed bungalow tucked away there on a modern estate, thought Pascoe. Not that it bothers me. A bachelor gay.

The hedges were as Antony had described them. The door to the garage passage was bolted and locked, as was the door in the trellis work on the other side.

'You always keep these locked?' asked Dalziel.

'Always at night,' said Connon. 'It's habit. One of us, Mary and me I mean, always checked. Sometimes both. It was a bit of a joke.'

It was growing very cold in the garden. There was frost in the air. None of them was wearing an overcoat and Antony shivered violently.

'Over the tree?' suggested Pascoe.

A large sycamore tree growing in the front garden had branches which stretched along the side of the house over the trellis.

'I don't know,' said Dalziel. 'Possible, but I don't

see why. He could hardly know he was going to get a show for his efforts, could he?'

'No,' said Pascoe, glancing at Connon and Antony. 'I don't suppose he could. Shall we go back in? It's a bit chilly out here.'

Connon took a last look back at the gathering gloom before he stepped into the house.

I know what he's thinking, Pascoe told himself. If they don't find her before it's dark . . .

He didn't much like the thought himself.

Dalziel still wasn't happy about the letter. He let the others go on, sat down on a kitchen stool and took it out of his pocket. Pascoe stepped back into the kitchen.

'There you are,' he said.

'You checked the house?' asked Dalziel, not raising his eyes from the sheet of paper he held gingerly before him.

'Yes. She's not tucked away here.'

'Then she'll probably be all right. Sergeant, read this letter again.'

Silently Pascoe looked over his chief's shoulder and read. He felt again the anger which had gripped him when he first saw it.

'Any comment?'

'Well, sir, it's not really the same kind of vein as the last one, is it? I don't know if we can tell really much about such things, but I'd have said it wasn't from the same man.'

'I think you're right. But something else too. You're our expert here. Making allowances for the natural exaggeration of this kind of mind and the rather stereotyped language, does that sound to you like Jenny Connon?'

Pascoe was puzzled.

'Well, I don't know,' he began, but Dalziel wasn't finished.

'And look at this paper. Look at the way it's folded. You know what I think . . .'

But he didn't finish. Outside in the hall they heard the front door open, footsteps pattered along the polished parquet floor and a light high voice cried, 'Daddy? Antony? Are you there?'

Pascoe's stomach did a quick flip-over, he beat Dalziel to the door by a full two yards and almost fell into the lounge.

Jenny was being embraced by her father and Antony looked as if he was standing in the queue.

'Welcome home, Jenny,' said Dalziel. 'We were worried about you.'

She turned and saw them. Her face lost some of its animation.

'Hello,' she said. 'You're here.'

'Jenny, what happened?' said her father. 'Why did you go out when you got the letter? You should have phoned us at the Club.'

'Got the letter?' she said. 'Oh, the letter. You found it?'

Dalziel held it up gravely. Her face suddenly lit up with understanding.

'And you thought . . . oh, I see. Daddy, I'm so sorry.'

She put her arms around him again. Antony still stood patiently in the background. Connon looked puzzled.

'Sorry? What for, dear?' he asked.

Dalziel answered.

'Jenny is sorry she inadvertently misled us all, I think. You see, *she* didn't receive the letter. It wasn't meant for her. She found it. I think.'

'Among your mother's things!' said Antony with sudden understanding.

Connon's grip on his daughter relaxed.

'You mean, that letter was sent to Mary?' he said, incredulous. 'To Mary? No! She would have told me. You don't receive a letter like that and not . . .'

His voice tailed off and he sat down heavily on the arm of a chair.

'Where did you find it, Jenny?' asked Pascoe gently.

There were tears in the girl's eyes now.

'In the wallet pocket of one of Mummy's old handbags. I thought I'd better turn everything out, you see, and then this came up. I just glanced at it, I didn't want to pry, but I had to look to see if it was important. I felt ill when I read it. It wasn't what it said, I mean I've read books and heard jokes just as bad, it was just the thought of Mummy getting it. I went into my own bedroom and sat on the bed for a few minutes. But then, I don't know, I got a bit frightened. The telephone rang, but I didn't answer it. I just got my coat and went out. I didn't want to talk to anyone, you know, but I wanted to be near people. So I got a bus into town. I thought I'd walk down to the Club and see you and Antony there, Daddy, but there were so many people, I could hardly move. I'd almost forgotten it was so near Christmas. Anyway I realized I'd have missed you at the Club, so I turned round and set off back. It took me ages. I'm sorry. I should have phoned. I didn't want you to find the letter before I'd told you about it.'

She was crying hard now, tears coursing down her face over the pale curve of her cheeks.

'Sergeant,' said Dalziel, 'perhaps you'd take Miss Connon upstairs and ask her to show you where she found the letter.'

He waited till the door closed behind them.

'Now Mr Connon, I'll want to talk at length to you about this, you realize. But quickly now while Jenny's upstairs, do you have any knowledge, any suspicion even of the source of this letter?'

'None. Nor did I even suspect its existence,' said Connon. 'Superintendent, could this have anything to do with Mary's death?'

'I don't know. I really don't know.'

The door opened again and Pascoe came in alone. He motioned with his head to Antony, who nodded and went swiftly out of the room and up the stairs.

'Well, Sergeant?'

Pascoe held up a large envelope.

'I've put them in here. Three more in all, sir. In

the same place. Jenny must have just got hold of the first. And, sir.'

'Yes.'

'Mrs Connon's bedroom is at the front.'

Chapter 6

'It'll soon be Christmas,' said Pascoe inconsequently. Dalziel's gaze wandered suspiciously round the room as if seeking signs that someone had had the effrontery to deface the slightly peeling wall with festive decoration.

'What do you want, Sergeant? A present?' he asked sourly.

It's getting him down, thought Pascoe with a frisson of pleasure for which he was instantly and heartily ashamed.

It was, after all, his job too.

But the past few days *had* been depressing. Things had seemed to be opening up. For a while there had been a feeling that they were asking the right questions and that at any moment the individual answers would shuffle themselves into a significant total. But they remained ragged, unfinished, unproductive. The enquiry's initial impetus was being lost and now they were all groping. Other matters, important and routine, had arisen. New

198

demands on time and men were being made all the time.

'Yes, I suppose it will,' said Dalziel.

'Will what?'

'Soon be Christmas.'

'Thanks,' acknowledged Pascoe satirically, but for once Dalziel ignored him.

'Something'll happen soon. Something pretty big. We're stretched as it is. Something will happen that will almost snap us. It always does,' he ended with sour satisfaction. 'Just before Christmas.'

'What had you in mind?'

'Anything. Have you never noticed? Look, there's good reasons. People need more money at Christmas, even crooks. And there's more about. In the shops; in the wage-packets; moving to and from the banks. Right?'

'Right.'

'And it's darker. Gloomier. Half the bloody day. Makes it all seem easier. Darkness encourages other things too. Children have to come home in it. Women in lonely places are there more in the dark than at any other time of the year. Or if you want something else, the weather's rotten as well. Cars crash easier. Trains hit ice on the rails. Planes lose themselves in fog and drop out of the sky into city centres.

'But most often there doesn't seem to be any good reason. Things happen just because it's Christmas. Life showing its arse at the universal party.'

'It's the other way round, isn't it, sir? Things

are just more striking if they happen against the background of Christmas. Now I bet if you looked at it statistically . . .'

The very word, as Pascoe had half intended, was enough to jerk Dalziel out of his reverie back to his normal state of being.

'Statistically!' he sneered. 'If you're not superstitious yet, son, you bloody well get superstitious. And stuff your statistics!'

'Up life's arse at the universal party?' enquired Pascoe politely.

Dalziel laughed, almost sheepishly for him.

'I said that? It must be the high-class company I keep. But I mean what I say. Get superstitious. One of us had better get lucky soon.'

Pascoe looked ruefully at the piles of paper which had accumulated since the enquiry started.

'No, sir,' he said, 'I can't agree. It's not luck we want now. It's a computer. The answer, or at least, *an* answer, is in here somewhere.'

'We're just waiting for it to rise to the surface are we, Sergeant? Have you noticed in the detective books how there's always something bothering the private eye's subconscious? Some little oddity of behaviour or event which, when he recalls it, will prove the key to the whole problem. But it's not like that, is it, Sergeant? Nothing is odd because there's no norm. Or everything's odd. I mean, look at this lot we've got ourselves mixed up with. All of them, known and unknown, thrashing around in uncontrolled sexual activity like midnight at a Roman orgy.'

'It's like midnight all right. It's catching them at it that's difficult. If only we knew! Is there anything going on between Connon and Gwen Evans? That gives us some kind of motive if there is, but there's damn' little evidence. She might have phoned him up when we brought Evans in. It seems likely she did, but we don't know for sure. He might have gone to see her that Saturday night. Fernie saw him going into the house. Evans says the car was there when he went round. But the only person who could tell us whether Connon was in or not is Mary Connon, and she's dead.'

'Gwen Evans isn't.'

'No, but she says she was round at the local. The landlord knows her well, but couldn't remember seeing her that night. He said he'd ask the staff when they got in. He hasn't contacted me, so I assume no one saw her. But she could still have been there.'

Dalziel took a noisy sip from the cup in front of him and pulled a wry face.

'It's gone cold. Carry on Sergeant, do. I'm stuck for something else to do at this minute, so I might as well listen.'

Pascoe inclined his head in acknowledgment of the favour.

'Thank you for your enthusiastic reception. Then there's this letter writer, or rather, these letter writers. We're no further forward with either. You got no help on the first at the Club, and anyone from a dirty old man to a randy adolescent could have written the others.'

'They did suggest a combination of experience and athleticism,' smirked Dalziel. He must have caught a shade of disapproval in his sergeant's poker-face for he added, 'Don't be so strait-laced, Sergeant. They're just so much pornography and none of us turn up our noses at a bit of that now and then. They probably haven't anything at all to do with the case. And if it's that girl you're thinking of, forget it. They're tough nowadays. You heard her. It's a bloody permissive society.'

'Yes, sir,' said Pascoe. But he could not dismiss the thought of Jenny Connon so easily. He had never been short of girlfriends, not at university anyway. But he had discovered that joining the police had, for one reason or another, cut him off very largely from his old source of supply. The reaction of several members of his old student circle had surprised him. There had been nothing dramatic, no great debate, just a lot of jokes and heavy irony to start with, then a gradual, gentle separation.

Plus, of course, he admitted to himself wryly, the fact that the hours and the work don't make me the ideal boyfriend, let alone husband. Still, there's always that little bit of vitality Sheila whatsit, Lennox, that's it, down at the Club. Now she'd shown an interest. Young perhaps. But Jenny's age at least. *And* enthusiastic. If Dalziel found out he'd laugh for seven days.

'To get back to the letters, sir,' he said.

'We'd left them had we? Daydream on your day off, will you.'

'Sir. Well, I've read them pretty closely and though there's no date or any positive indication in them of the order in which they were written, there does seem to be a progression of a sort. I mean, two of them seem as if they are referring back to something which has happened since the first two.'

Dalziel was interested.

'You mean, they'd met. Or something like that?'

'No, nothing as positive as that. It's as though the show had become somehow more spectacular. All the time he's writing as if he'd seen her undressing, but there's something just a bit more theatrical about the last two.'

'You're being vague again, Sergeant. We'll get no further on with vagueness. We need something positive.'

There was a knock on the door and the station sergeant stuck his head round.

'Excuse me, sir. There's a Mr Wilkes here to see Sergeant Pascoe.'

'Is there now? Wheel him in here, then.'

'And there's a telephone call for you, sir. From a Mr Roberts.'

'Christ, I ask for something positive and they come shooting at us from all angles. Right, Sergeant, you take your boy elsewhere and I'll see what jolly Jacko, the life and soul of the party, wants.'

Pascoe got up and went out. He saw Antony standing talking animatedly to a rather bewildered looking police constable who looked relieved to get away.

'Hello there, Sergeant,' he said brightly. 'I was just enquiring of that officer whether in fact he was formally trained in deliberateness of manner. Perhaps you as a graduate in Social Sciences *and* a policeman could tell me?'

'I'm afraid I can't help you, sir,' said Pascoe woodenly.

'There you go!' said Antony. 'And the reason why I asked to see you rather than your superintendent was that you looked capable of rising above it.'

'What did you want to see me about, Mr Wilkes?'

'I'm sorry. Have I been offensive? It's just sheer nervousness, I assure you. It's like coming into a hospital.'

Pascoe looked closely at the smiling youth.' Suddenly he believed him. He was nervous. No one could appear as self-confident as this boy and not be nervous. Almost no one.

'Come in here,' he said. 'Sit down.'

'Here' was an empty interview room.

'What do you want to say to me?'

Antony perched himself comfortably on the edge of the table.

'It's about the letters. A piece of impudence on my part, really, but I have a strong sense of civic duty. Mr Connon when I arrived told me about the letter Jenny received and also about your warning to him that there might be phonecalls also. This made me think. I wondered if perhaps the letters Mrs

Connon had received could have been associated with phonecalls as well.'

Pascoe sighed at the arrogance of youth in general and this youth in particular.

'The thought had occurred to us, sir. There's little chance of checking up on it. We did ask Mr Connon if he recalled any unusual telephone calls – any that he answered, I mean, when the caller just rang off. He said no. And it would be curious if Mrs Connon took one while he was there and said nothing of it.'

'Or even when he was not there. But she hadn't mentioned the letters.'

'No, sir. Well, if that's all . . . ?'

He moved to the door.

'Oh please, Sergeant. I would not presume to try to do your job. No, I haven't come down here with suggestions – that would be presumptuous – but with information, or what might be. This chap had obviously been watching Mrs Connon in her bedroom, from the street almost certainly, or the garden. When I was waiting at the Connons the other night before you all so efficiently arrested me, I had occasion to use the phone box almost opposite the house. I rang my parents to say where I was. I also took the opportunity of giving them Mr Connon's phone number so they could contact me if they wished. To do this, I had to look in the directory.'

'And?'

'And it was heavily underlined.'

Pascoe's mind was racing so fast he had to make an effort of will to bring it under control. Two or three small elements on the edge of the puzzle seemed to be coming together. But whether they were related directly to the main body of the puzzle was not yet clear. But it was a possibility. But that's all it is, he told himself. A possibility has been suggested to you. Nothing more. A theory.

But he could hardly wait to get rid of Antony so that he could test it.

'It seemed odd at the time,' the youth went on, unconscious of his sudden undesirability. 'Why should anyone want the telephone number of a house only twenty yards away?'

'I can think of a dozen good reasons,' smiled Pascoe. 'But I'm very grateful to you, Mr Wilkes. Thank you for coming. If there's ever anything else you would like to tell me, please call in.'

'Do I detect a note of irony?' asked Antony cheerfully. 'Then I will be off. I am a sensitive plant. Like asparagus, I take a long time to grow and am easily killed off.'

'But you have a most delicate flavour all of your own,' said Pascoe as he ushered him out.

'Saucy,' said Antony. ''Bye!'

Dalziel was still on the phone. Pascoe began sorting rapidly through the papers on his desk.

Dalziel put the phone down with a ping that rippled violently across the room.

'Roberts,' he said.

'I know,' said Pascoe. 'Tell me, why do I have to

pay my informants a quid or more a time while you have snouts who could buy and sell both of us and who rush to buy you drinks whenever you appear?'

'Beauty,' said Dalziel. 'I have a beautiful soul. What're you doing?'

'Just reading a report.'

Quickly he told Dalziel what he had just learned from Antony and of the train of thought this had started in his mind.

When he finished Dalziel nodded appreciatively.

'I like that,' he said. Then, almost modestly he added, 'I've got a little something too. Perhaps there is a God.'

He rolled his eyes at the ceiling.

There isn't a God, thought Pascoe. No one capable of creating kangaroos could have resisted hitting him in the face with a divine custard pie.

'What did he give you?'

'Nothing much, really. Some odds and ends. But one interesting thing about a gentleman we may have overlooked. Mr Felstead.'

'Tubby little Marcus?' laughed Pascoe. 'Well, he is overlookable.'

'Don't underestimate him. He's a man of parts, used to be a very nippy little scrum-half, and he's still a very enthusiastic wing-forward.'

'Was,' amended Pascoe. 'He seems to have given up. That's what he said on Saturday. What about him anyway?'

'Well, his best service to the Club at the moment

is perhaps in the club-house. He's not married, he's keen, reliable, and he has a lot of time. So he helps a hell of a lot. With the bar, that kind of thing.'

'So.'

'He was on the bar the night Mary Connon was killed.'

'I know. It's in here somewhere.'

Pascoe struck his papers with the palm of his hand. A little dust drifted up.

'So was Sid Hope.'

'Yes.'

'So, from his own graphic account of the exit and reentry of Evans that night, was Ted Morgan. But you never asked him why.'

'Well, he did begin to go on about it being unusual for him to be that side of the bar, but I told him to get on with it.'

'Not bullying him, I hope, Sergeant,' he said reproachfully.

It was Pascoe's turn to roll his eyes at the heavens.

'Anyway,' said Dalziel, 'Morgan was on because Felstead was off.'

'Off?'

'For almost two hours. Off. No one knows where.'

He stood up and reached for his hat.

'What's worse, no one has *asked* where.'

Pascoe stood up too.

'Would you like me to . . . ?'

'No thank you, Sergeant. I'll have a chat. Tonight. You'll be out yourself, won't you? Drop in at the Club later and exchange notes.'

He put his hat on, flung his coat over his arm and went to the door.

'And Sergeant,' he said, as he closed it behind him.

'Marcus Felstead has a car. A cream-coloured Hillman. See you later.'

Dave Fernie was shouting at his wife. Alice Fernie was shouting at her husband.

The room was in a state of some disorder, but as yet, the little cool area at the back of Alice's mind told her, no permanent damage had been done.

The evening paper flung aside violently and scattering into its separate half-dozen sheets accounted for a good fifty per cent of the chaos. A coffee cup had been knocked off the arm of Fernie's chair, but there wasn't much left in it and the stain would be easily removable. The saucer had broken, however.

A single cushion had been hurled across the room and it lay on the edge of the fireplace. She would have to move it before it singed. It had struck the wall and disturbed a line of three china ducks. The middle one looked as if it had been shot and was going into its final dive. Even as she observed this, it did just that, slithered off the nail which supported it and plunged headfirst into the deep blue of the mantelpiece.

That was no great loss, either. She'd never liked them much; in fact she had only kept them up so long because Mary Connon long ago, almost on her first visit to the house, had been openly patronizing about them. It was a kind of V-sign, ever present, to keep them there.

But now that reason was gone, and the memory that remained of it seemed rather mean and cheap. It was time they were down.

All these thoughts and observations co-existed with the words she was hurling across at her husband.

'You'll end up in jail!' she yelled. 'Or you'll be paying damages for the rest of your life!'

'It's a free country!' he shouted. 'I'll say what I bloody well think. I'm as good as he is. There's one law for us all!'

'You were lucky last time!' she screamed. 'He didn't care for the law. He just worked you over a bit, put you in hospital, big man!'

'Let him try that! Bloody rugby players! Bloody creampuff. I'll take him apart.'

'Can't you *see*, Dave? Are you blind? You'll just get us all in trouble. We've had enough. Can't you leave it alone?'

The note of appeal in her voice was obviously analysed as a sign of weakness.

'Leave it alone? Why should I, for God's sake? I reckon the man's knocked off his wife and he's getting away with it! Someone's got to say something. The bloody law won't!'

There was a brief pause, Alice silent in despair, Fernie for want of breath.

Through the silence rang a bell as if signalling the end of a round in a boxing match.

'Who the hell's this?' snarled Fernie.

Alice didn't answer. She was moving round the room at great speed for so heavily built a woman. The newspaper resumed its normal shape, the broken duck and the pieces of saucer were dropped in the coal scuttle, Fernie got the cushion back hard in his chest.

The bell rang again.

Smoothing back her hair, Alice went to the front door and opened it.

Pascoe stood there.

'Hello, Mrs Fernie. I was beginning to think the bell was broken.'

'Who the hell is it?' asked Fernie again from the living-room.

Pascoe walked in with a smile.

'It's only the bloody law, Mr Fernie.'

Fernie glowered at him, corrugating his eyebrows to aggressive bristles.

'You've been listening at keyholes, have you? What a job!'

'Dave,' hissed Alice.

Pascoe was unconcerned.

'Not necessary, Mr Fernie. Anyone passing could hear you loud and clear.'

'We're not worried about what people hear, Sergeant,' said Alice fiercely.

'No? You sounded worried, Mrs Fernie. And I think you've got cause to worry.'

Alice's angry flush faded to pale anxiety.

'Is that why you're here?'

'Not primarily, but now it's come up we might as well talk about it. Mr Fernie, I gather you've been making certain allegations about your neighbour, Mr Connon.'

'Neighbour? He's no neighbour of mine. Neighbours are on this side of the road only in this street. And what if I have anyway? What's it to you?'

'Nothing officially, yet. If we think that what anyone says is likely to cause a breach of the peace, then we'll act. I gather you have said things in the past which caused a breach of the peace?'

'Mind your own bloody business!'

'Dave thought someone was running around with a neighbour's wife,' said Alice quietly. 'He said so. Often. Someone beat him up one night. They never got anyone.'

'But you think it was something to do with the slander?' asked Pascoe.

'Slander? What's this about slander?'

'Nothing yet, Mr Fernie. Slander normally involves a civil action. If you say a man has killed his wife, you are damaging his reputation and he is entitled to damages which could be considerable. Your only defence would be that you did not publish the slander, which in this case would be very difficult, I feel. Or you might plead that it was not slanderous because it was true. Even this is not always an acceptable defence, I should add. The truth can often be slanderous if it is put in certain ways. But still, it would be your best bet.'

'Best bet? But there isn't a case, is there? He wouldn't dare!'

'Why are you so certain of this, Mr Fernie? What proof have you got of your allegations?'

There was a long uncomfortable silence in which Pascoe noticed the missing duck, the broken china in the scuttle, and Alice noticed him noticing.

'You have no proof, do you, Mr Fernie?'

Fernie said nothing. Alice put her hand over his.

'You have nothing more than a dislike of Mr Connon and a very nasty twist in your mind which is going to get you into very serious trouble indeed. If I hear of one more occasion on which you make these allegations I shall feel it my duty to pass them on to Connon myself. Do I make myself clear?'

Fernie still said nothing.

'Very clear, Sergeant,' said Alice quietly.

Pascoe ignored her.

'I say you have no reason other than a dislike of Connon, Mr Fernie. I hope this *is* your only reason for wanting to accuse him?'

Fernie shifted uncomfortably. The anger seemed to have gone out of him.

'It stands to reason, doesn't it?' he argued. 'I mean, her, with her always flaunting herself.'

'What other reason, Sergeant?' asked Alice. 'What other reason could there be?'

'Mrs Fernie, I'd like to speak to your husband alone if I may.'

Alice looked from Pascoe to Dave, her face tense with worry.

'Why?' she asked.

'What's this then, Sergeant?' said Fernie.

'I won't go,' said Alice, with sudden determination. 'We've got nothing to hide from each other.'

Pascoe shrugged.

'All right. Mr Fernie, you said that Mary Connon was always "flaunting herself". Those were your words, I think?'

'That's right.'

'What did you mean?'

'Mean? Well, I meant she was, well, always showing herself off, you know, putting on the style. Mutton dressed as lamb.'

'Was that all?' asked Pascoe.

Fernie looked around the room, not quite focusing on anything. Alice felt a little knot of fear tying itself in her belly.

'Yeah, that's all. What else?'

Pascoe reached in his pocket and pulled out a notebook.

'Mr Fernie, Detective-Constable Edwards who interviewed you on the morning after Mrs Connon was killed, said in his very comprehensive report that you had noticed the police arrive the previous night. You knew something was up.'

'That's right. Make enough bloody noise, don't you?'

'To the best of my recollection, very little was made that night. In any case, according to Edwards, reference was made to you standing looking out of your front window for some time. Is that true?'

'No. Well, yes. I don't know. What's some time? I can look out of my own window, can't I?'

'Of course. What were you looking at? Or waiting for?'

Alice Fernie had taken enough of this. She leaned forward angrily.

'Come on, Sergeant. What are you getting at? Are you trying to suggest Dave *knew* something was going to happen?'

'Did you, Mr Fernie? Did you know? Or were you just hoping for something?'

Fernie was obviously in some distress. He looked at his wife, then at Pascoe, picked up the newspaper and began fiddling with it.

'Know? How could I know? Of course not. No, it was just that . . .'

Suggest an accusation of the larger to get an admission of the smaller, thought Pascoe smugly. But never forget, he admonished himself, that this is no proof that the larger isn't accountable also.

'Something to do with Mary Connon? Flaunting herself,' he prompted.

Fernie was now talking to his wife, rapidly, with just a hint of pleading.

'It was just that a couple of times I'd been looking out, or I'd just glance up as I passed, and, well, I'd seen her there. The light blazing, curtains not drawn. Well, Christ, of course I looked. What man wouldn't? I mean you could see everything. Everything. I'd have said something to you, love, but she was your friend.'

Alice just looked at him speculatively.

'Not very nice, really,' said Pascoe. 'Being a peeping Tom.'

Fernie grew indignant.

'Peeping Tom nothing! All I did was look. I wasn't hiding or anything. And make no mistake about it, she knew I was there. She knew she had an audience. That's what I meant by flaunting. She'd yawn, you know, like they do to show off, stretch her arms right back so that her . . .'

He glanced anxiously at his wife.

'Breasts?' she suggested amiably.

'. . . stuck right out. Right out,' he repeated.

'She had a big figure,' said Alice, as though some explanation was needed.

'Mr Fernie,' said Pascoe, 'do you ever use the phone box outside in the street?'

Fernie looked puzzled.

'Yes, I've used it. I phoned your lot from it the other night. Why?'

'Did you ever ring the Connons' house from it?'

'No,' said Fernie. 'Why should I?'

He looked even more puzzled but Pascoe could see from Alice's face that she was beginning to get the picture.

'Did you ever write a letter to Mrs Connon?'

'No. Never. What the hell's all this about?'

'Sergeant,' said Alice, 'had someone been phoning Mary? And writing to her?'

Pascoe nodded.

'Phoning her perhaps. Writing to her certainly. Did she ever say anything to you?'

Alice put her finger to her brow in the classic pose of thought. It did not look affected on her.

'No, nothing,' she said. 'But are you trying to say that Dave here might have been the man writing?'

Fernie's face lit up with amazement, followed by red indignation.

Could anyone really be that slow on the uptake? wondered Pascoe. Even complete innocence? Perhaps complete egotism could.

Fernie was on his feet now.

He's going to shout again, thought Pascoe.

'Now listen here, you, I don't know what you're up to, but I don't have to sit in my own house and . . .'

'Sit down and be quiet, Dave,' said Alice.

He obeyed instantly.

'Thank you, Mrs Fernie,' said Pascoe.

'Sergeant,' she said. 'These letters. Do you have them with you?'

'Not the originals,' he said. 'They've got to be carefully looked after and tested. Ink, paper, that kind of thing. Fingerprints. I'd like to take your husband's prints if I may. I've brought the stuff.'

He knew that only a few not very helpful smudges had been found after Mary Connon's prints, taken from the dead woman's fingers at the post-mortem, had been eliminated. But it was always worth putting a scare into people.

Fernie looked as if he was ready to explode again, but Alice nodded and he subsided.

'I've got a photostat copy of one of them, though,' he went on. 'Why?'

'May I see it?' she asked.

He looked dubiously at her.

'I'm a big girl now,' she said. 'I stopped reading fairy tales years ago.'

'Right,' he said. 'Here you are.'

He handed it over. She read through it quickly once. Then more slowly a second time.

To his surprise a smile began to tug at her cheeks and when she finished the second reading she laughed aloud as though in relief.

'Is there something funny?' he asked politely.

'Not to you, Sergeant. But to me. It's the thought of my Dave writing this.

'I'm no psychiatrist but I'll tell you one thing. That letter was written by some poor, unhappy, twisted, frustrated man with a rather scanty knowledge of women. My Dave may be a bit short on mouth control, he may talk too much, he may not know how to make friends and influence people . . .'

'Alice!' interjected her husband, outraged. But she went on as if he wasn't there.

'. . . but whatever else he is, he's not frustrated. If he sees a woman undressing in a window, he'll stop and have a look. Who wouldn't? You would!'

Oh yes, thought Pascoe, yes, I would.

'Especially if she's like Mary Connon. She was a big woman. But I'm no nymphet myself,' she

218

said proudly. 'Anything she had, I had too, and it was thirteen years younger, and readily available to my husband as, when, and how he liked to use it. Any man can be unfaithful, but it takes special circumstances to write a letter like that.'

She finished, slightly flushed, but looking him defiantly straight in the eye. Fernie was regarding her with some awe.

'You may be right, Mrs Fernie,' said Pascoe. 'Now, if I can just take your prints, Mr Fernie, I won't bother you any more.'

'Do you think whoever wrote those letters killed poor Mary?' she asked as she saw him out of the door.

'Perhaps,' said Pascoe.

'You can cut Dave right out,' she said with a smile. 'He couldn't hurt anyone. He goes queasy at those doctor programmes on the telly.'

Pascoe felt inclined to agree with her as he drove along Boundary Drive. Still, it was as well to keep an open mind. But all that had really happened that evening, he thought, was that he had developed something that was very nearly envy of Dave Fernie.

Dalziel's superiors would not have been happy to see him. He had already been seen once that day. A progress report had been requested. He had asked if what was wanted was a detailed account of the whole course of the investigation so far or a brief statement of what was known.

The Assistant Chief Constable had mentally spoken a prayer for self-control and asked for a brief statement.

'Enquiries are proceeding, sir.'

'Is that *all*?'

'I have sent in full and detailed reports of every aspect of the investigation, sir. Do you also require a digest of them?'

The Assistant Chief Constable had squirmed in his seat with irritation but, like the good golfer he was, he kept his head quite still.

'No thank you, Superintendent. I would like to suggest, however, that you might tread a little more carefully in certain places.'

'Like, sir?'

'Like the Rugby Club. If you go there as an investigating officer either do it more subtly or use the full paraphernalia of your office.'

'You mean dress up, sir?'

'I mean act either as a policeman, or a member. Don't try to be both at once.'

'But I am both at once, sir. All the time.'

The Assistant Chief Constable sighed.

'There have been one or two . . .'

'Complaints?'

'No. Words, gently dropped. But from a height. How important is this Club in your investigations?'

Dalziel thought a little, his hand working inside the waistline of his trousers.

If only he wouldn't *scratch*, thought his superior.

'Central,' said Dalziel finally. 'Will that be all?'

'For the moment. Keep me informed.'

'As always, sir.'

'And please. If you want to interview any more members of this Club, do it quietly, at the station preferably.'

'Sir!'

And here he was not many hours later sitting with Marcus Felstead in a relatively quiet corner of the club-house, twisting the guts out of him, though Marcus did not know it yet.

'Not bad beer here, is it?'

Marcus sipped his pint as if to make sure.

'No, not bad.'

'Many storage problems?'

'Not really,' said Marcus, a little surprised. 'It's all kegs nowadays, so as long as you keep it fairly cool, it comes up smiling.'

'How's the Club fixed for money now?'

Again surprise.

'I don't really know. Better ask Sid.'

'No, I don't mean figures. I just wondered if there was any thought of getting a permanent steward?'

'Not that I know of. It seems an unnecessary expense. There's plenty of us to do the work.'

Dalziel took a long pull at his pint and sighed happily.

'You do quite a lot, don't you, Marcus?'

'I do my share.'

'No; more, I'm certain. Just about every Saturday night.'

'Not every. But pretty frequently.'

'You were on the night Mary Connon died.'

That's a shot across your bows, my lad. Field that any way you like, thought Dalziel, observing his man closely.

Marcus's hand might have gripped the handle of his glass a little more tightly, but that was all.

'I think I was.'

Now a long pause. Let him wonder if it was just a casual remark. Let him try to organize his defences. Then let him relax.

'Hello, Willie!'

He waved his glass casually at Noolan, who smiled and waved back as he went to join a small group standing by the bar.

'Yes,' he said, returning his attention to Marcus. 'Yes. You were here all that night, weren't you?'

'I don't recall,' said Marcus, definitely a little ill at ease now.

'Oh, you were. We checked. All night. Except for the two hours when you went out and drove round to Boundary Drive.'

Marcus went white. He pushed the beer away from him with his rather small girlish hand.

'Don't be stupid,' he said. 'I never went anywhere near Boundary Drive.'

Dalziel laughed in a friendly fashion.

'Come off it, Marcus,' he said. 'Your car was seen. What's the matter? It's no crime, is it? That's what they usually say to me.'

'I never went near Boundary Drive,' repeated

Marcus, a little recovered now. 'You must be mistaken. It can't have been my car.'

'No? Well, there's a simple way to settle this, seeing as you're so worried.'

'What's that?'

Dalziel leaned across the table, pushing Marcus's glass back at him.

'Tell us where you really were, then.'

'Why the hell should I?'

Oh dear, thought Dalziel resignedly. He's going to start shouting. Time for us to go.

'Listen, Marcus, my lad,' he whispered confidentially. 'There's obviously some kind of misunderstanding here. We can't discuss it properly here in the Club. Why don't we take a drive down to the station to talk things out? Less embarrassing than shouting at each other in front of all these people.'

He waved his hand airily around, realizing as he did so that all these people now included Connon.

Connon didn't acknowledge the greeting but just continued to stare at them.

'Coming?' said Dalziel, smiling still for the benefit of the onlookers, but infusing a new grimness into his voice.

'For God's sake, Superintendent, sit down. Look, if it means that much to you where I was . . .'

'Oh, it does, it does,' said Dalziel.

Marcus stared into his beer broodingly for a long minute.

What's he hatching? wondered Dalziel. Have I hit

223

the jackpot? Jesus, that'd be a laugh, Connon's best mate bashing his wife's head in.

But there was still a large doubt sitting hugely at the back of his mind. What possible motive could this round, friendly, most amiable of men have for murder? It was no use going by appearances, but a man who reminded him so strongly of Winnie the Pooh . . .

Marcus seemed to have made up his mind.

'Come on,' said Dalziel. 'It's either the truth or a very complicated lie.'

'It's the truth,' said Marcus. 'But first, I must have your assurance that this is in the most absolute confidence.'

'As long as it has no bearing on the case.'

'It hasn't.'

'Then you have my word.'

The fingers he was scratching under his arm with were crossed. Dalziel preserved many of his old childhood superstitions.

'Well, look.' He was almost whispering and Dalziel had to lean even further forward to catch the words.

'Hello, Marcus, boy!'

Evans's heavy hand smacked down on the small man's shoulder. Marcus went white and jerked round sharply to look at the figure behind him. Even Dalziel, who was facing him, had not noticed his arrival, so intent had he been on catching Marcus's words.

'Give you a fright, did I? What're you two hatching anyway? You've got to be careful who you drink with these days, Marcus. Might lose your good name.'

'Evening, Arthur,' said Dalziel as unwelcoming as he could be in the limits of politeness. 'Gwen not with you?'

That should get rid of him, he thought with malice. He won't fancy a needling match on these terms.

But Evans merely grinned and helped himself to a stool from under a neighbouring table.

'She's in the loo making herself lovely for you, Bruiser. Marcus, boy, it's you I wanted to see. Listen, I'm having a hell of a job holding this team together. You know how important it is, a club's known by the quality of its fourth side. Now you drop out, one of the regulars. It's a big hole to fill. You should have seen us last Saturday. Walking bloody wounded! Couldn't you hang on till the end of the season?'

He's not listening to you, Arthur, thought Dalziel. He was going to tell me something, now he's having another little think. He's very worried. That's how I like them, worried. You'll have to go, Arthur. If you won't take a hint, I'll put it to you in terms even a thick-skinned Welshman can understand.

But before Dalziel could begin his dismissal operation, Marcus forestalled him.

'My round, I think,' he said. 'Arthur, will you have one? A pint? Right.'

He swept Dalziel's glass from under his nose and set off to the bar at quick march. Dalziel watched him go in amused exasperation. But it was merely a postponement.

'Here, Arthur,' he said. 'When Marcus comes back, piss off for a bit, will you? We're having a bit of a serious talk.'

'Are you now? It can't be more serious than the Fourths, can it? After all, this is a *rugby* club.'

Oh, they're all getting in on the act, are they? thought Dalziel. All dropping their little words in the direction of my bosses. But yours don't come from very on high, Arthur.

'In any case,' said Evans, 'what makes you think he's coming back? He seems to have bloody well disappeared altogether. And his round too!'

Dalziel looked sharply round at the bar. Noolan and his group were still there. Connon was standing a little apart from them, still looking across at the superintendent's table.

But of Marcus Felstead there was no sign.

Pascoe had pulled into the Club car park close behind the Evanses' car. He had not got out immediately, but sat and watched the broad Welshman and his wife pick their way carefully over the already frosted surface towards the club-house.

They looked just like any other couple, he reflected. Comfortable. Affectionate. Evans had taken Gwen's arm to help her circumnavigate a frozen puddle. She said something to him and he seemed to laugh. Then they disappeared through the door.

Perhaps it was all a mistake, thought Pascoe.

Perhaps it was just in Evans's mind, this other man. It would be impossible to live with a woman like Gwen and not know that other men envied you, would like to fish in your pond. And a temperament a lot less volatile than Arthur's could easily come to believe this was exactly what was happening.

What would it prove anyway if it turned out that there was a man and that man was Connon? A motive, he had said earlier to Dalziel. It would prove a motive. Or rather it would give a possible base for the possible erection of two or three possible motives. Lots of possibles. No probables. Probables versus possibles. And a young man, certain of his own strength and skill, running with balanced ease round all opposition as he made for the line.

I'm beginning to think in their imagery, he admonished himself, and lit a cigarette, somehow reluctant to leave his car and go in search of Dalziel. Or perhaps it was because Sheila Lennox might be there. He had had to stand her up on their second date. Nothing dramatically urgent to season an apology with; no startling new development, breathtaking chase, or a second murder. Just pressure of paper and organizational routine.

Her voice on the phone had been cold. His suggestion of another meeting ignored. Perhaps it was for the best. She was only a child. Nearly nineteen. That meant eighteen. And he was nearly twenty-nine. That meant thirty. But they grew up early these days. Or at least they seemed to. She had promised a wealth of experience on their exploratory first date.

But it had been mostly verbal. What lay behind it he would probably never know.

He opened the car door and dropped his cigarette end on to the concreted surface where it glowed with vulgar ruddiness on the silver sharpness of the frost till he ground it under his foot as he stepped out.

Then, half in, half out of the car, he suddenly became very still.

The club-house door had opened and a man came carefully out. He was unrecognizable at this distance, but the woman who followed him a moment later only had to take a couple of steps for Pascoe to know that this was Gwen Evans again. She had taken her coat off. He could see her bare arms gleam whitely for a moment as she too disappeared into the shadow down the side of the building.

Pascoe watched them out of sight. Then he slipped his hand into the glove compartment of his car till his finger rested on the heavy rubber casing of a torch. With this in hand and keeping low, he now stepped out of his car and closed the door quietly behind him, certain he was unobserved. He had long ago severed the connection between the door and the interior courtesy light. Three hours' extremely cold and tedious observation had been ruined by the sudden flash of this light several years earlier. Pascoe was a man who learned from his mistakes.

Silently he moved across to the club-house and made his way along the side wall. At first in the shadow of the wall it seemed pitch black, but his eyes rapidly adjusted to the light, or lack of it.

There was no one there.

He moved swiftly down the line of the wall, slowing as he neared its end. It was lighter here. A faint glow came through an opaque window which must belong to one of the cloakrooms.

He stopped beneath it. From round the corner came voices.

First Gwen's. Anxious. Tense. An edge of panic.

'Darling, darling. What're we to do? What's going to happen?'

Then a man's. Reassuring, but also anxious beneath. And familiar.

'It'll be all right, Gwen. I'll have to tell him. He'll want to talk to you. But we can still keep it quiet.'

'Quiet!' Almost a sob now. 'Quiet! I'm tired of it all. I'm tired of being quiet. I can't see where it's leading. I can't, I can't!'

The voices lowered to an indistinguishable mixture of near-sobbing and reassuring murmurs.

Pascoe took another step forward.

And trod on something.

A plastic coated cardboard cup, his trained ear told him. Or an empty ice-cream carton.

It cracked like a beechwood fire.

The talking stopped.

Oh dear, thought Pascoe. Well, here we go.

He switched on his torch and stepped round the corner. They were close in each other's arms and the beam of the torch was enough to catch them both.

'Good evening, Mrs Evans,' he said apologetically trying to keep the note of astonishment out of his voice. 'And good evening to you too, Mr Felstead. You'll catch your deaths out here if you're not careful.'

'I thought he'd made a bolt for it,' said Dalziel. 'He looked bloody scared.'

'I daresay he was,' grinned Pascoe. 'I mean, imagine you are about to confess you're knocking off Arthur Evans's wife and suddenly his great hand comes down on your shoulder. Anyone'd be scared. On the other hand he carried it off well. When he came back in, I mean. Did Evans notice anything?'

Dalziel nodded his great bull's head.

'Oh yes. He noticed something. I mean, I moved quite quickly when I saw Felstead had gone. But Connon stopped me, said Marcus had asked him to order while he went to the bog, and thrust a pint into my hand. You can't give pursuit under those conditions. Anyway, by the time he came back, Arthur was getting too impatient for his wife to put in an appearance to pay much attention to anyone else.'

'I told her to go into the other room and say she thought he was going to be in there. Not that I needed to coach her, she must have had plenty of practice. But what a turn up, eh?'

'You've never said a truer word, Sergeant. She confirmed everything?'

'Oh yes. They were at it in the house, then in

Felstead's car on the way to the Club, all the time he was away from the bar. The way they were hanging on to each other when I caught them, it's very easy to believe.'

Easy to believe? Dalziel asked himself, thinking of Marcus Felstead and trying to revise his mental picture of him. The physical reality couldn't be changed! Five feet four or five at the most, looking almost as round as he was high, with a balding pate that rose like a monk's tonsure through an unruly and still retreating fringe.

Then he thought of Gwen Evans. He had always felt he was a bit of an expert on Gwen Evans. He had spent many beery hours just assessing the value of all visible assets, and visualizing the invisible.

That she should spare a first glance, let alone a second, on this man was almost incredible.

But it all fitted. It had been Marcus who turned up at the Evans house on Saturday afternoon when Pascoe was there. He'd played it very cool, they both had. He could imagine the facial contortions, the mouthed warnings, at the front door.

It had also been Marcus who had phoned Connon with the news of Arthur's visit to the police station. And he, of course, had had it direct from Gwen the minute Arthur left the house.

'We were both very worried,' Marcus had said. 'We've got a very great respect for Arthur.'

Dalziel had laughed inwardly when he heard that. Tell that to him when the Celtic red mist's before his eyes and he's kicking your head in in a jealous rage, he thought.

But he hadn't spoken, just gone on listening.

Marcus told everything, reluctantly at first, but more freely after a few minutes. Then when Evans went in to a selection committee meeting, the reason for Connon's presence that night, Dalziel had had a long talk with Gwen.

They were obviously telling the truth about themselves. Too many details fitted. The affair had been going on for nearly two years.

'I bet he's been dying for an audience,' Dalziel said to Pascoe. 'It must be hell having a woman like Gwen and not to be able to strut around in public possession. Mark you, it might have worked both ways. Perhaps it was the secrecy that made Marcus acceptable to Gwen, eh? Christ, Arthur's no oil-painting, but he's like the Winged Victory compared with *him*!'

And where does that place you in the beauty stakes? thought Pascoe. But what's it matter? Hell, in one day I've been jealous of a sour-faced moron like Dave Fernie and of a little tub of lard like Marcus Felstead!

Dalziel shook his head finally in dismissive amazement at the inscrutability of woman.

'It can't be true,' he said. 'It's a bloody lie all of it. Only, Marcus wouldn't dare to tell a lie like that unless it was true.'

'Irish,' said Pascoe.

'You know what I mean,' said Dalziel.

'More important,' said Pascoe, 'is, where does it leave us? Does it put us any further forward?'

'It teaches us humility,' said Dalziel pompously. 'No other revelation in this case can possibly surprise us after this.'

'Not even if it turns out to be an intruder?' asked Pascoe.

'Not even if your intruder turns out to be Jack the Ripper. I'm off to my bed now. I might even go to church in the morning. Good night.'

He lumbered away shaking his head. Pascoe watched him go with a feeling he was disgusted to find almost resembled affection.

But as he climbed into his own bed in his little two-roomed flat half a mile from the police station his mind was occupied still with the case. He wished he had one of those 'feelings' which Dalziel had so efficiently mocked. But he hadn't.

All he had was the certainty that whatever steps had been taken that day had led them in one direction only.

Backwards.

He switched off the light and fell into an uneasy sleep troubled by dreams in which Gwen Evans, Sheila Lennox and Jenny Connon blended and merged into one.

Chapter 7

There were three days left till Christmas. The weather was dark, misty. The sky was low and constantly shifting as different layers of grey and black cloud were dragged around by gusty winds. Guiding stars were rarely seen. In any case, no one had much time to look.

The greatest money-spending competition on earth was coming to its climax. The streets were thronged all day with compulsive shoppers, inter-mittently spattered with hard-driven rain and tinted by the glow of festive lighting. And a constant background to everything was the music: carols, pop, sentimental, classical; now near, now far; on tape, on record, and occasionally even issuing from a real, live, human throat.

It was a strange unsettling atmosphere. No one could remain unaffected by it.

Some were hardened by it.

'I haven't given or received a Christmas present for more than a dozen years,' said Dalziel. 'Bloody idiots.'

Some were softened.

Should I have tried to go home this year? wondered Pascoe guiltily.

Home meant a suburban semi, two hundred miles away, grossly overcrowded for the holiday by his grandmother, his two elder sisters, their unsympathetic husbands and their four even more unsympathetic children, in addition to the normal complement of his parents.

He hadn't spent a Christmas there for three years. It was nearly time to try it again.

But not this year.

Some were worried by it.

'He's looking worse than he did when it all happened,' said Jenny. 'Perhaps it's Christmas. I think they always made a special effort at Christmas. For my sake as well, I suppose. He looks awful.'

'Is he seeing the doctor?' asked Antony.

'No. But I'm going to send for him. He had that knock on his head, I don't think he's recovered from that yet.'

'No,' said Antony staring out of the window into the front garden.

Some were made hopeful by it.

'Look, girl,' said Arthur Evans. 'I know we've had some bad times recently and a lot of it's been my fault. But let's make an effort, shall we? It's Christmas, eh? Let's see what we can make of ourselves, eh?'

'Yes,' said Gwen. But her eyes did not shift from the book she was looking at.

235

And the atmosphere of hectic unreality made some resolute. Marcus Felstead whistled a Christmas medley to himself as he carefully packed his suitcase.

But in a house in the heart of the Woodfield Estate there was no whistling as a man searched the streets for the fourth time for his child, then finally, belatedly, picked up a telephone and rang the police.

'It's happened,' said Dalziel.

'What?' said Pascoe, standing at the threshold of the room.

'Mickey Annan. Aged eight. One hundred and three, Scaur Terrace, Woodfield. Didn't get home from school last night. They broke up yesterday, had a bit of a party. It's the usual story. His parents thought he'd gone to a friend's house in the next street. He usually does on that night. But this time it was different, they were all going off for Christmas as soon as their kid arrived. So Mickey wasn't asked. So he wasn't missed till nearly ten.'

Pascoe raised his eyebrows. 'That's late.'

'They breed 'em hard in Woodfield. Anyway, they always kid themselves. Never admit that anything can be wrong until they've got to.'

'What's happening now?'

'The usual. One of his mates thinks he said he might go up to the Common. Someone had told him there might be some snow there. He was mad keen on snow.'

'Oh, Christ.'

The Common was the local term used to describe

an area of several acres on the western boundary of the Woodfield Estate. It was unfit even for grazing purposes and its main function in human terms was that its near edges provided a useful if unofficial dumping ground for anything and everything. The Common contained a disused quarry, two ponds and a steep-sided stream, all of which had been fenced off after years of complaint. But not even a full-time repair unit could keep up with the constant breaching of the fencing.

'We've got a full-scale search going on now. County are standing by with frogmen.'

'House-to-house?'

'No point yet. We're stretched as it is talking to every kid in the school now that they're on holiday.'

'He might have just taken a walk and got lost,' said Pascoe without conviction. 'Fell asleep behind a wall or in a shed.'

'He should have woken up by now.'

'What would you like me to do?'

'Look after the walking boys. It'll take them all morning to cover the kids from the school. By then if nothing's come out of the search, it'll be time to start asking everyone questions.'

'Anyone in particular? Streets, I mean?'

Dalziel looked surprised.

'Why, you'll start by asking everyone on the Woodfield Estate, and if we still haven't found him, we'll work our way through the rest of town. There's only eighty-five thousand of them.'

'Thanks,' said Pascoe.

'Think yourself lucky,' replied Dalziel, shaking a newspaper on his desk. 'At least they had the plane crash in North Africa this year.'

Funny man, thought Pascoe as he went swiftly and efficiently to work. Is it just a cover like we all put up? Or does he really not feel these things? What a man to spend Christmas with! I'd be better off at home with all those kids!

By midday the Common had been turned over with meticulous care, the pools dragged and the frogmen sent down. As far as Mickey Annan was concerned, the result was absolutely negative. But lots of other things were brought up. A list was always made on these occasions and Pascoe glanced quickly down it. A small part of his mind was still on the unidentified weapon in the Connon case. But there was nothing here which rang a bell. The usual household expendables, a suitcase containing some fairly valuable pieces of pewter (dumped by mistake? or stolen and dumped in fear?) and, an item which made Pascoe whistle slightly, two guns. But he had no time for idle speculation. A large-scale map of the Woodfield Estate lay before him. He still had to complete his detectives' schedules.

It was one-thirty before he had any lunch. He ate it alone in the police canteen.

Mickey Annan now went to the back of his mind. He had taken part in the search that morning for a while, talked to some of the children from the school, as well as helping to organize the house-to-house. But he knew it was a routine, automatic business, none the less essential for all that, and nine times out of ten effective. Mickey Annan would probably be found very soon. It was after the finding that the real work began, and Pascoe was not a man given to anticipating events. Except in the line of business.

His thoughts drifted back to the Connons. The missing boy wasn't really interfering with the progress of the Connon case, because the progress only existed in theory. Investigations were still proceeding, but unless Dalziel had some private little line well hidden from everyone else, the phrase was as empty as it sounded.

The only thing that was any clearer to him now than it had been when he started was his picture of the murdered woman. It wasn't a very complete one. She seemed to have been a reasonable kind of mother to Jenny; at least she hadn't stimulated any of the strong resentments which seemed to lie uneasily dormant in most daughters, especially those very fond of their fathers. And she seemed to have made Connon a bearable kind of wife. But she had told him his daughter had been fathered by another man and she had tried to separate him from his main interest in life, the Club. Add to this that she was a vain woman with a streak of snobbery, but one who had made a friend of Alice Fernie (who herself was unlikely to pick her friends haphazardly); that she was a man-hunting, high-life-loving girl who had shown no desire to keep up her connection with her old stamping-grounds; and finally, that she apparently received obscene letters with equanimity, merely folding them up and putting them away like love-letters sentimentally preserved; add all these things together and you had a woman who was as incomprehensible as women traditionally are.

Over his coffee, Pascoe toyed with permutations of possibilities in which Felstead or Evans had written the letter (*all* the letters?), in which Mary Connon had a lover (someone at the Club? Noolan? Jesus! Or what about Bruiser Dalziel? Joke); in which Connon swung a metal bar held like a spear into his wife's forehead (jealous rage? didn't fit. Careful plan? but was he so cold-blooded a man as *that*?).

He'd been along all these paths before. They led nowhere yet, except to fantasy in which Gwen Evans held a crow-bar to Mary's head and Alice Fernie struck it home with a sledge-hammer while Mary, unheeding, watched the television.

He sighed and returned mentally to the canteen. There was other work to be done. Connon would have to wait. Mary was dead. There was still the faintest of chances that Mickey Annan might still be among the living.

Connon was angry when the doctor arrived, but even in anger he didn't lose the moderation of speech or manner which Antony now recognized as his main characteristic.

'I didn't send for you, Doctor,' he said.

'Just a checking-up call,' replied McManus cheerily. 'Just because you don't send for me doesn't mean you don't need me any more.'

'I'm fine,' said Connon. 'You've had a wasted journey.'

'It's a good way to waste it, then. But I'll be the judge of how fine you are. You don't look so hot to me.'

Connon did not look well. He seemed to be visibly losing weight. His cheekbones were prominent and the paleness of the skin stretched over them was accentuated by the darkness which ran like a stain round his eyes.

'Come along, then, and let's take a look at you,' said McManus.

Connon had enough of himself left to give Jenny a sardonically accusing glance as he left the room with the doctor.

'He knows it was you,' said Antony.

'That doesn't matter. As long as Doctor Mac can do something for him.'

'I'm sure he can,' said Antony cheerfully. 'He'll come up with some witches' brew.'

But he could not feel so certain inside that Connon's malady would respond to physical treatment.

'Do you think the police have given up?' asked Jenny.

'I don't know. Do you want them to?'

'I'm not sure. I don't much care now whether

they catch someone or not. But I'd just like every-one to know for Daddy's sake that he had nothing to do with it. Do you think they took any notice of what you said about the telephone box?'

'They must have done. There's a new directory there now. I had a look. But I don't think my amorous rival Pascoe was too delighted to receive advice and assistance from me. As far as the police are concerned I suspect there's a very thin line between public support and amateur interference.'

'As if you would interfere in what wasn't your business!' said Jenny with mock indignation.

'I see you've come to know me well,' responded Antony. 'Come and sit on my knee.'

His hand stroked her leg as he kissed her.

I've been here before, thought Jenny. But she was very glad to be there again.

'Talking of interference,' said Antony a little while later, removing his lips from the side of her neck.

'Don't be disgusting,' she said.

'I think I shall interfere once more. There's something else which keeps on coming back to me which they might possibly be interested in.'

Jenny sat upright. 'What's that, Sherlock?'

But they heard a footstep on the stairs and Jenny rose swiftly, smoothing down her dress.

The door opened and McManus came in.

'How is he, Doctor?' asked Jenny anxiously.

The old man carefully closed the door behind him.

'He's just putting his shirt on. He'll be down in a minute.'

He looked enquiringly at Antony.

'It's OK, Doctor,' said Jenny. 'How is he?'

'Well, physically there's nothing I can put my finger on. He complains of being listless, loss of appetite, that kind of thing. But this we might expect. Also his head still pains him from time to time where he got that knock. But I think this is like his other symptoms. There's nothing wrong. It's purely nervous in origin.'

'But he seems to be getting worse, not better,' protested Jenny. Antony put his arm comfortingly round her waist.

'Yes. That's true. It's a delayed reaction, not uncommon. A kind of shock. He's been living on his reserves of nervous energy for the past couple of weeks. It can't go on for ever.'

He struggled into his overcoat which Antony brought him from the hall.

'But don't worry. I've been his doctor for many years, nearly all his life, I suppose. I've seen him like this before, before you were born, when he cracked his ankle the week before the final trial. He went as thin as a rake, and deathly pale then for a couple of weeks. You'd have thought the end had come. But it hadn't. He got back to normal in no time. No, no, it hadn't. It hadn't.'

He shook his head and laughed softly to himself at the memory.

Hadn't it? wondered Antony. And in what way could the end come twice?

'Well, I suppose you've told them three times as

much as you've told me,' said Connon from the door. 'I long ago noted that to a doctor keeping confidences meant telling your patient nothing and his relatives everything. You should all be struck off.'

McManus laughed as he picked up his bag.

'Goodbye, Jenny; and you, young man. I'll call in again, Connie, if you don't call to see me. Take your medicine now and stop worrying your friends.'

They watched him get into his car, then returned to the lounge.

'Well,' said Jenny, 'time for lunch, I think. Antony, make yourself useful for once, love. You'll find a table-cloth in the top drawer of the sideboard. Set the table, if it's not beneath your dignity.'

She went out into the kitchen. Antony grinned in resignation at Connon and began searching for the table-cloth.

'It's good of you to stay on with us, Antony,' said Connon. 'I hope your parents are not too disappointed.'

'It would be foolishly modest of me to say they will not be disappointed at all,' said Antony, 'but they are both very understanding. I hope to introduce Jenny to them very soon, when I think they'll be more understanding still.'

'Oh,' said Connon. 'Do I detect a note of serious intent creeping in?'

Antony pulled out a table-cloth and shook it open with a fine flourish like a bull-fighter showing his cape. Something fluttered to the floor.

'I think it highly probable,' he said seriously, 'that

I shall marry Jenny eventually, with, of course, her consent and your permission.'

He bent down to pick up the photograph which was what had fallen.

'In that case,' said Connon with equal seriousness, 'we must take an early opportunity of reviewing your prospects.'

Antony didn't reply. He was looking closely at the picture in his hand. For one brief moment he had thought it was Jenny, absurdly garbed and with a ridiculously short haircut. Then he realized that the only thing of Jenny's which was there was the familiar, wide, all-illuminating grin on the face of the young man in muddy rugby kit who was walking alone in the picture.

Connon took the photograph from him.

'That's the only picture of me playing rugby I ever kept,' he said.

'Why this one?' asked Antony.

Connon stared down at the young man in the picture as if he was looking at a stranger and trying to analyse what made him seem vaguely familiar.

'It was the first time I played for the County. I was nineteen. Still in the army, on a weekend pass. But nearly finished. There was a five-yard scrum. I was standing square over our own line ready for the pass back and the kick to touch. The pass came, I had plenty of time and shaped to kick to the near touch-line. Then I changed my mind. All their backs were coming up like the clappers. So I chipped it into a little space over the scrum, ran round, picked

245

it up and went up the middle of the field. I don't recall beating the full-back. They told me after I ran through him as if he wasn't there. All I could see was the posts and the exact spot centrally between them where I was going to touch down. Nothing else was real till I grounded the ball. Then I started walking back up the field. No one runs up and kisses you in a rugby match. In those days it was considered bad form even to slap you on the back. You just walked back to your position trying to look unconcerned and got your clap from the crowd. I could feel this smile on my face, feel it spreading out to a grin. The crowd all roared like mad. It was the biggest crowd I'd ever played in front of. I bent my head a bit, look, you can see on the picture, but I couldn't stop grinning. It was a grin of pure happiness. It felt as if it was fixed on my face for ever. I think I believed it was.'

He stopped talking. Antony for once was stuck for words. He's in the past, he thought, the poor devil's anchored there beyond hope of release. What a state to get into.

A wave of sympathy swept over him, some of which must have shown on his face, for Connon now smiled at him ironically.

'I think you may be misunderstanding me, Antony,' he said. 'I don't live down memory lane. What this photograph says to me is not that happiness is gone for ever, but that it's repeatable. I've often felt like this since, mostly on occasions connected with Jenny. The picture reminds me of what's possible again, that's all, not of what's gone for ever.'

'I'm sorry,' said Antony, rather shame-faced. 'I didn't mean to . . . you're very lucky. I'll go and set the table.'

He left the room with the cloth cast loosely over his shoulder like the end of a toga.

It suits him, thought Connon. Then he returned his attention to the photograph.

Repeatable? he asked himself. I wonder. Will it ever be possible again?

From the kitchen Jenny's portable radio began to play a selection of brass-band music. This faded almost at once, but then returned louder than before as though the set had been re-tuned.

Connie listened, then a smile moved slowly across his face.

I believe she's leaving it on for me.

It was five o'clock and dark and cold and wet. The shops were still crowded. Inside them it was bright and warm. Too warm. The crowds who had jostled close to each other all day, shoulder to ruthless shoulder, thigh to strange thigh, had left their unexpungeable smell. Sweat, scent, tobacco and damp clothing all mistily merged into an observable haze. The best shop-assistants were growing irritable, the worst had long been downright rude. But the artefacts of good cheer had not yet lost their power, the music was as merry as ever, the colours as gay, and nearly everyone was going home.

The festive spirit stalked abroad, reaching out to seize backsliders.

Mickey Annan had still not been found.

And Jacko Roberts was talking on the telephone to Dalziel.

'What the hell do you want, Jacko? I'm busy.'

'I wish I was. This weather's no good for my business.'

'It doesn't help mine much either. Come on now. Is this social? If it is, piss off. If not, get your finger out.'

One day, Jacko promised himself, one day I'll tap him on the head and wall him up in a brick kiln.

It was his perennial New Year resolution.

'A bit of both,' he said. 'I'm having a little party for a few select friends, tomorrow night. Christmas Eve. I'd like you to come.'

Dalziel hesitated. Jacko Roberts rarely entertained but when he did, it was usually lavish. He regarded it as an investment. Dalziel didn't mind being invested in as long as it was done the right way. A couple of years earlier, Jacko's investment had consisted of the introduction of a group of very willing young ladies to his previously well-liquored stag party of civic and other dignitaries.

Dalziel had been sober enough to leave early. He had noticed that the Roberts Building Company got a large share of municipal contracts the following year and had had words with Jacko.

Now he wondered if he had forgotten.

'Don't worry yourself,' snarled his prospective host. 'It's all respectable. They'll all be there, from Noolan to the Town Clerk. With their wives.'

'What time?'

'Any time after eight.'

'I can't promise. I'll try to make it.'

'Oh, and Bruiser. As you're short of a partner, why not bring that nice sergeant along? Whatsisname?'

'Watch it, Jacko,' said Dalziel softly. 'There's a notice on my overcoat which says, this is where Christmas stops.'

'All right. But I meant it. Ask him anyway. It pleases these old cows to have a virile young man about the place.'

Dalziel grunted and thought that Jacko must be doing well at the moment to be in, for him, so light-hearted a mood. He made a mental note to check on what the builder had been up to.

'Right,' he said. 'You said there was some business. Or is that what we've just been talking about?'

'That's an odd thing to say, super. No, but are you still interested in this Connon business or is it all neatly tied up?'

'Don't play clever buggers with me, Jacko. What have you got? Anything or nothing?'

'I don't know. It's just that Mary Connon and Arthur Evans were seen in close confabulation over a drink the Friday before she died.'

Dalziel digested the information for a moment.

'Where?' he asked.

'The Bull, on the coast road.'

'Anything else on a connection between them?'

'Not that I've heard.'

'It's probably nothing. That all?'

'Unless you're going to thank me.'

Dalziel put the phone down hard and sat looking at it. Then he picked up the internal phone and pressed a button.

'Sergeant Pascoe here.'

'Dalziel. Busy?'

'Well yes. I've just got in.'

'Had your tea?'

'Not yet. I was just going to . . .'

'Then you can't be all that busy. Step along here for a minute, will you. Bring your coat. I'll probably want you to go out.'

Pascoe sighed as he took his sodden riding mac off the radiator. A minute earlier he had been feeling sorry for the men who were still out on house-to-house questioning.

Now he began to wonder if his sympathy was misplaced.

Back in Dalziel's office the phone rang again. He picked it up crossly, but after listening for a few moments, his expression softened and he nodded twice.

'Yes, yes. That's good. I'm glad, very very glad.'

Pascoe was surprised to find him looking almost happy when he came through the door.

'Jesus H. Christ,' muttered Detective-Constable Edwards. It was his private theory that Woodfield

Council estate had been built as a series of experiments in wind-tunnelling. Behind him the door of the house whose occupant he had just been interviewing had been closed with considerable firmness. Some attempt had been made to turn the area immediately in front of the door into a rose-arbour by the erection of a bit of trellis work at right angles to the wall, and he crouched behind the little protection this afforded. The wind came howling down the street full of rain and incipient snow. A shoot of the rambler clinging precariously to the trellis whipped round and slashed against his face.

'Jesus,' he repeated and turned up his collar and went up the path. As he closed the gate he saw the curtain drop into position in the front window.

'All right. I'm off the premises,' he said aloud. What a thing it was to be loved. Not that we deserve it anyway. Bloody half-wits. God, to think how chuffed I was to get out of uniform. Detective! All I've done since seems to be walk around and knock on doors. First Connon. Now this. Poor little bugger. I wonder where he is?

He turned his mind away from the private conviction that little Mickey Annan was somewhere lying dead; deep beneath bracken on the moors; under an old sack in some outhouse; it didn't matter where. His job at the moment was to ask questions.

Someone must have seen the boy that night.

His heart sank when he saw where his questionings would take him next. It was a little cul-de-sac

251

of some two dozen semi-detached bungalows. Pensioners. Old Women. Mostly alone, often lonely. Welcoming, garrulous. He would be pressed to cups of tea, cocoa, Bovril, Horlicks. He tried to harden his heart in advance, but knew it was just a front.

I'm your friendly village bobby-type, he thought, not your hard-as-nails CID boy. This is going to take hours.

'Mrs Williams? Mrs Ivy Williams?' he said to the large heavily-made-up woman who answered his ring.

'No, that's my mam. What are you after, then?'

'I'm from the police. We're checking on the movements of people in this area last night, Mrs . . . ?'

'My name's Girton. Is it about that lad then what's missing? Well, mam can't help you. Never gets out at night, do you, mam?'

An elderly woman had appeared out of the kitchen which Edwards could see through the half-opened door at the end of the small hallway.

'What's that? What's up?'

'It's a policeman, mam. You weren't out last night, were you, mam?'

'No, I wasn't. Where'd I go?'

'That's right,' said Mrs Girton to Edwards. 'Where'd she go?'

'Well, thank you. You weren't here yourself last night, were you?'

'No, not me. Mondays and Thursday are my regular nights. Sorry.'

'Will you have a cup of tea, eh?' Mrs Williams

was already turning into the kitchen. Her daughter caught the look on Edwards's face and grinned sympathetically.

'Don't be daft, mam. He's got a lot of work to do, haven't you? Got to visit everyone in the road?'

'That's right. Thanks all the same. Good night.'

He turned to go.

'Everyone in the road, eh?' shrilled the old woman. 'Well, make sure you talk to Mrs Grogan next door, then. She knows something, eh? She'll be able to tell you something if you're from the police.'

She disappeared back into the kitchen.

Edwards raised his eyebrows quizzically at Mrs Girton, who shrugged.

'You never know. She's getting on now, but she takes good notice of whatever anyone says. I wouldn't pay too much heed myself, though.'

'Well, thanks anyway. Good night.'

'Good night.'

It was raining in earnest. He glanced at his sodden list under the street-lamp. Mrs Kathleen Grogan, No 2.

There was a sharp double blast from a horn. Turning, he saw at the end of the cul-de-sac a police-car. He went towards it.

'Hello, Brian,' said the uniformed constable cheerily. 'Enjoying yourself?'

'Great. What are you doing here?'

'They've found him. Mickey Annan.'

Edwards nodded and said, more as assertion than question, 'Dead?'

'No. Alive and well. We've come to tell you to jack it in. Hop in and we'll give you a lift back.'

Edwards was half into the back seat before he remembered Mrs Grogan.

He hesitated.

'Come on, then.'

'Look, John. Could you hang on just a couple of minutes? There's just one more call I'd like to make.'

'What're you on about? Playing detectives? I told you, the house-to-house is off . . .'

'Yes but . . .'

'Sorry, Brian. I've got to get on. There's at least two other poor sods trudging around in the wet when they could be clocking off and going home. Now hop in and let's go.'

Edwards got back out of the car.

'OK, John. You shove off. I'll make my own way back.'

'Have it your own way. But you're a silly bugger. Cheers.'

Yes, I'm a silly bugger. The silly bugger to end all silly buggers.

'Bugger!' he said aloud as he watched the car's tail-lights disappear into the driving rain. 'I must be mad.'

He made his way back along the pavement and turned up the narrow path.

Pascoe had sat in silence as his superior swiftly and efficiently did his part in calling off the search for

Mickey Annan. This was the first rule when an operation was over. Get your men back. There were too many working hours for too few police as it was without letting any be wasted unnecessarily.

Finally Dalziel was done.

'What happened?' Pascoe had asked.

'He was out looking for Jesus.'

'What?'

'It's these bloody schools. When I was a kid it was two-times table and the sharp edge of a ruler along your arse if you didn't know them. Now it's all stimulating the imagination. Christ! Show me a kid who ever needed his imagination stimulated! Anyway, little Mickey Annan was a wise man in the school Nativity play and got very interested in guiding stars in the East, and all. Especially when his teacher explained that Jesus was born again for everyone every Christmas and Bethlehem was never far away. How many bloody miles to Bethlehem! His favourite poem! Anyway, to Mickey the East was where his Uncle Dick and Aunt Mavis live at High Burnton out towards the coast.'

'How did he get there? He did get there, I take it?'

'Oh yes. Sat on a bus. Told the women he was sharing a seat with that he'd lost his money. He reckons wise men don't need to bother much with the truth as far as ordinary mortals are concerned. Anyway his uncle had gone off for Christmas with his family, the house was empty. He got in through a half-closed larder window. Very small evidently. Then he bedded down.'

'But what's he been doing today, then?'

Dalziel had looked pityingly at the sergeant.

'Wise men don't travel by day,' he said. 'You can't see any stars by day. You've got to wait till it's night.'

'Oh? I suppose you would, really.'

'Anyway the woman in the bus saw his picture in this evening's paper, told the local bobby and gave him the boy's uncle's address which the lad had passed on to her the previous evening. He was very chatty, evidently, not a care in the world when she was with him. She never associated him with the missing lad till she saw the picture. Off they went to Uncle Dick's just in time to meet Belshazzar taking off in search of a clear patch of sky. Kids! I hope his father whacks him till he's a confirmed atheist.'

Pascoe was still grinning at the story as he rang the doorbell of Arthur Evans's house. There were lights on all over the house but no one seemed in a hurry to answer the door. He hoped it would be Gwen Evans who came, though his business was with her husband. Analysing his emotions, he came to the conclusion that Gwen's affair with Marcus, far from making her more inaccessible, had merely confirmed her accessibility.

He rang the bell once more.

Almost instantly this time the door was flung open. Arthur Evans stood there. He looked distraught, his tie was pulled down and his collar open, his hair was ruffled, but even if he had been neatly dressed and groomed, the bright staring eyes and hectic cheeks would have warned Pascoe that something was amiss. And the smell of whisky.

'What the hell do you want?' demanded Evans, then with a sudden change of tone. 'Is anything wrong? Have you found them?'

'Found who?' enquired Pascoe politely.

'Oh, Christ,' said Evans, letting his shoulders sag as he turned and walked away from the open door. Pascoe hesitated a moment then followed him, closing the door quietly behind him.

Evans had gone through into the lounge and was standing leaning against the mantelpiece in the classic pose of grief.

But this was no mere pose, Pascoe decided.

'Mr Evans,' he said softly, 'what has happened?'

Evans looked at him wretchedly.

'What am I to do without her?' he groaned.

'Without Mrs Evans, you mean?' asked Pascoe. 'Why, where is she, Mr Evans. What's happened to her?'

He did not go any further into the room but stood in the door keeping a watchful eye on Evans. For all he knew, Gwen was lying upstairs dead and the man in front of him was building up to another outburst.

'She's left me,' said Evans with difficulty, mouthing the words in an exaggerated way as if examining them in disbelief as they came out.

'Left you? How do you know she's left you?' asked Pascoe, still suspicious that he might be listening to the self-deceiving euphemism of murder.

Evans reached into his pocket and pulled out a piece of paper, crumpled as though it had been thrust deeply and desperately out of sight.

Pascoe came carefully forward and took it.

'Dear Arthur,' he read, 'I am leaving you. Our marriage has been at an end for some time as far as I am concerned. I am sorry, but there's nothing else to be done. Please forgive me. Gwen.'

What the hell do I say? Pascoe asked himself. Oh, Bruiser, I wish you were here.

Evans sobbed drily, gulping in great mouthfuls of air, and rocked back and forward against the mantelpiece which was lined with Christmas cards. One rocked and fell. He looked up then and became aware of the others. Soundlessly, he swept his fore-arm down the whole length of the mantelpiece, scattering cards and ornaments alike.

Pascoe touched his arm.

'Come and sit down,' he said. For a moment it looked as if Evans might resist, then he let himself be led to the sofa where he sat down quietly with his head between his hands and began to cry.

Pascoe left him and ran lightly upstairs. It was his business to make sure that Gwen Evans was not still here. Arthur had obviously had the same idea. Every door was open, even wardrobes and cupboards, and all the lights were on.

He looked into the wardrobes and through the drawers in the dressing-table and tallboy.

She had packed well. Hardly a feminine article remained.

The same in the bathroom. Only, there on its side on top of the medicine chest was an unstoppered bottle. He picked it up. It was empty. He read the label, then turned and ran downstairs three at a time.

Arthur Evans was still on the sofa, only now he was sitting limp with his head resting against the arm. His eyes were closed and his breathing noisy.

Pascoe turned back to the hall, picked up the telephone and dialled.

'Ambulance,' he said. 'Quick.'

'How was I to know,' said Pascoe defensively, 'that there were only two tablets in the bottle? Anyway he must have had about half a bottle of whisky.'

'You do not pump out a man's stomach because he's drunk half a bottle of scotch,' said Dalziel. 'If you did, half the top men in this town would be swallowing rubber tubes every weekend. Christ, your common sense should have told you. Evans isn't your romantic suicide type, he's your find-'em-and-mash-'em type. He'll have you on his list now.'

'I hope they've gone a long way,' said Pascoe. 'They seem to have taken everything. Felstead's landlady says he told her that he definitely wouldn't be coming back. They're almost certainly in his car. Is it worth sending out a call?'

Dalziel shook his head emphatically.

'Nothing whatsoever to do with us, Sergeant. If a woman runs away from her husband that's their business. Our only concern is if and when Arthur catches up with them. I can't see him sitting down for a quiet civilized three-cornered discussion.'

Like you did? wondered Pascoe. Some hope! You and Evans are brothers under the thick skin.

'What did he say about meeting Mary Connon, that's the important thing,' went on Dalziel.

Pascoe tried to stop himself stiffening to a seated attention position and couldn't quite manage it.

'Nothing,' he said. 'That is, I didn't actually ask him. I mean, how could I? The occasion didn't arise.'

He wished his voice didn't sound quite so childishly defensive in his own ears, but Dalziel seemed happy enough with his explanation.

'It'll keep,' he said. 'Nothing's so important that it won't keep. Or if it is, and you keep it too long, it stops being important, and that's much the same thing. Look at the time! There's nothing more for us here. Come on!'

He stood up and took his coat from the chair over which it had been casually thrown.

'Well, help me on with it, lad,' he said to Pascoe. 'And hurry up. The most dangerous moment of a policeman's life is the time between getting his coat on and getting out of the station. You never know what's just coming in through the door.'

Just coming in through the door at that very minute was Detective-Constable Edwards. He was very wet.

'Where've you been, then?' asked the desk-sergeant aggressively.

'Out,' said Edwards with a nerve sharpened by cold and more than an hour in the company of Mrs Kathy Grogan. 'Is the super still in?'

Entry to the Grogan household had not been easy. Mrs Grogan had wisely taken note of the many warnings issued to householders, especially the elderly living on their own, to examine carefully the credentials of all callers before admitting them.

It took Edwards's warrant card, two library tickets, a pay-slip and a snapshot of himself and his fiancée on the beach at Scarborough to win him admittance. The snapshot was the clincher. The girl, Mrs Grogan told him, had the look of her late sister.

Once her doubts had been satisfied and the door unchained and unbolted, her attitude was one of reproachful expectancy.

'So you've come at last,' she said. 'You take your time don't you?'

'Pardon?' he said.

'Come along in, then. It's draughty out here. Gets right under my skirts if you'll excuse the expression. If I've written to the Council once about that front door, I've written fifty times. I told her next door you'd be coming, but I didn't think you'd be so long about it. If this is what you're like when you are anxious I wouldn't like to wait for you when you're not.'

The small living-room she took him into was made even smaller by the amount of stuff she had in there. Every ledge and shelf was crowded with ornaments of one kind or another, most of them bearing some civic inscription ranging geographically from 'A gift from Peebles' to 'A souvenir of Ilfracombe'.

Mrs Grogan, Edwards decided, was strongly attached to the past. He knew very well the dangers of any allusions to any of these articles, but the mere unavoidable act of looking at them was more than enough for his hostess.

He reckoned he had done well to get away with two cups of tea and forty minutes of reminiscence before an opening arose to thrust in a question.

'Mrs Grogan,' he said, 'you said before that you thought we were anxious to see you . . .'

'No,' she said. 'You said that.'

'Did I?' he asked, half ready to believe anything.

'Yes. Here. Look, I'll show you.'

She dived into a pile of newspapers which lay in an untidy stack beneath her chair and after a short search, triumphantly produced a neatly folded paper which she handed to Edwards.

He looked down at it and found himself reading an account of Mary Connon's death.

Mrs Grogan's gnarled and knuckle-swollen finger was interposed between his eyes and the paper. The meticulously clear and polished nail came to rest on a line near the end of the story.

'The police are anxious to interview anyone who may have walked or driven along Boundary Drive between seven and nine on the night in question.'

'But that means,' Edwards began to explain, then pulled himself up with a smile.

'I'm sorry we've taken so long to get round to you, Mrs Grogan, but we've been very busy. Now, I understand then that you did take a walk down Boundary Drive on that night?'

'Oh yes. Of course I did. I always do. I go to my nephew's for tea on Saturday afternoons and if the weather's not too bad I get off the bus in Glenfair Road and walk down the Drive. It saves me threepence on the fare that way. My nephew thinks I stay on the bus right into the estate, but I don't always. It would worry him if he knew. This won't have to come out in court, will it?'

'We'll try to keep it quiet,' Edwards assured her.

'Well, I'd just got opposite that poor woman's house, and I glanced up at it. I always look at the houses as I walk by them. It's really interesting. And then I saw the man.'

'The man.'

'Yes. I saw him quite clearly. A man.'

'Mr Connon?' suggested Edwards.

'Oh no. Not him. I saw his picture in the paper. It wasn't him. Someone quite different.'

'Evans,' interjected Dalziel when Edwards reached this part of his story.

'Probably,' agreed Pascoe gloomily.

'Evans?' asked Edwards.

'Yes. Arthur Evans. He was round there that night. I've talked to him about it.'

'Oh, I see,' said Edwards disappointedly. 'I didn't

know. I suppose you asked him, sir, what he was doing up the tree?'

'Up the tree? Up what tree?' said Pascoe, his interest revived.

'No. We didn't ask him that, Constable,' said Dalziel. 'Do go on.'

Edwards finished his story rapidly. Mrs Grogan had seen a man half way up the sycamore tree in the Connons' front garden. Despite the darkness and the distance, she claimed she saw him quite distinctly and, taking Edwards to her own window, she gave him a convincing demonstration of the excellence of her eyesight.

'What did you do then?' asked Edwards.

'What should I do? Nothing, of course. It's none of my business. I always look at the houses as I walk past, and I see a lot of things odder than that, but it's not my business, is it? No, it wasn't until I read about the murder in the paper that I thought any more about it. And when it said you were anxious to see me, I've been waiting ever since. I've even missed going out a couple of nights.'

'I'm sorry,' said Edwards gently. 'Next time why don't you come down to see us, to hurry us along a bit? Ask for Mr Dalziel if you do.'

But he didn't put that bit in his report.

'What price my intruder now, sir?' asked Pascoe, with some slight jubilation.'

'It depends who he is,' said Dalziel thoughtfully. 'And if he is. It's late now. And dark. Sergeant, first thing in the morning, you exercise your limbs round at Connon's and see what you're like at climbing trees. And I'll do a bit of sick-visiting, and go and talk to my old mate, Arthur, again. But watch yourself. Listen to that wind.'

And a few miles away Antony heard the boughs of the sycamore tree sawing together and watched the sinister patterns moved by the wind across the frosted glass of the bathroom window. He put his toothbrush down and rinsed his mouth out. Then moving quietly along the landing in his bare feet, he came to Jenny's bedroom door.

It made a small noise as he opened it and he paused.

'Jenny,' he whispered.

There was a little silence, then the sound of movement in the bed as she sat up. He could see her faintly, whitely.

'Come in,' she said.

They're looking very pleased with themselves this morning, thought Pascoe. Even from this angle.

'This angle' was almost ninety degrees. He had left the comparative safety of the platform of the step-ladder and was now clinging to what felt like a dangerously pliable branch of the tree.

Below him, hand in hand, staring up with lively interest, were Jenny and Antony.

Looking up, it had seemed no height at all. Looking down corrected the illusion, so instead he applied his mind to the business in hand.

If there had been a man up the tree on the night

of Mary Connon's death – and a conversation with Kathy Grogan earlier that morning had convinced him, though her interpretation of the written word might be naïvely literal, there was nothing wrong with her senses, then that man could have been there for only one of three purposes.

Unless he was a bird-watcher, he told himself. Joke. No, either he was up here to have a good look through one of the windows. In which case he'd be disappointed. Only if he really craned his neck sideways could he see anything of the front bedroom windows and then not enough to make the effort worthwhile. Or he wanted to get over the fence into the back garden. Which would be easy enough. Oops! Christ, nearly did it myself without trying. Or he was trying to get in through the one window in the house which was approachable from the tree side. The bathroom. Frosted glass. No good for your keen voyeur with an eye for detail, not even with the curtains open, blurred white shapes, very frustrating.

So, decided Pascoe, if it was the window he was after, he was trying to get in.

It was too much to hope that any sign of human presence in the tree would have survived two and a half wintry weeks. Not unless the climber had been wearing hobnailed boots. None the less Pascoe examined the likely branches conscientiously and as always in such cases, the satisfaction of expectation was a disappointment.

Then he selected what looked like the safest route

to the window and edged his way carefully out along the chosen branches. A sharp gust of wind set the whole tree in motion and he clung on desperately like a sailor in the rigging, remembering Dalziel's jocular injunction to 'watch himself'.

One thing's certain, he told himself, it wasn't fat Dalziel who climbed up this tree. Or anyone built like him. I reckon I'm about the limit. I reckon also I've reached the limit.

He was as near to the window as he felt he could get without falling. There was nothing to be seen. Again he had expected nothing. One of the first things that had been done when the police arrived at the house was to examine all windows and doors for signs of forcible entry. There had been nothing. There was still nothing.

The wind rose again, and again he tried to combine safety with dignity, thinking of the watchers below. And elsewhere. He had seen a few curtains moving in neighbouring houses.

It was time to descend, he decided, and began to move backwards, fixing his eyes on the wall of the house in his determination not to look down. Then he stopped moving and kept on staring. At first he thought it was merely the effect of looking too hard, and he blinked his eyes twice. But it was still there.

Just below the windowsill on the vertical brick there was something which looked like a footprint. Not much of a footprint, more of a toe-print. But it was there. As if someone scrabbling desperately for a hold had used even the little frictional grip pressure against the vertical could give.

Wind and height forgotten, Pascoe swung down from the tree like a gymnast.

Jenny's hair was blowing wildly all over her face, evading all the effort of her hand to restrain it. She was beautiful.

'Have you found anything, Sergeant?' she asked, pitching her voice high to get over the wind.

'Give us a hand with the steps,' he said to Antony. 'Over here.'

Together they moved the step-ladder right up against the wall. The earth was soft here and the feet of the ladder began to sink as he ascended.

'Hang on,' he grunted to Antony and clambered quickly to the top. The bathroom windowsill was not far above his head. He stood on his toes and peered up towards it.

'Look out!' cried Antony, and the steps lurched violently sideways.

But he was smiling as they helped him out of the herbaceous border.

It was definitely a print, most probably made by the toe of a rubber-soled sports-shoe; a tennis-shoe, perhaps, or basket-ball boot.

'Are you all right?' asked Jenny anxiously.

'He looks a bit dazed,' said Antony. 'It was the soil. One of the legs just went down as if it was on quicksand.'

'I'm all right,' said Pascoe, rather light-heartedly. 'Take me to my leader.'

Jenny and Antony looked at each other dubiously. 'Come inside and have a cup of tea,' suggested Jenny. 'Or a drop of Daddy's scotch.'

She took him by the arm and led him unresistingly into the house.

'Hello,' said Connon, looking at the sergeant's earth-stained suit. 'Had a fall?'

'Nothing to worry about, sir,' replied Pascoe. 'Winded me a bit that's all. May I use your phone?'

'Of course. Any luck with your tree?'

'Perhaps,' said Pascoe enigmatically, then seeing Jenny's look of enquiry, he relented and added, 'I think there may be a footprint.'

'On the windowsill?'

'On the wall.'

'That's absurd,' said Connon. 'No one could get in there. And the window was fastened in any case.'

Pascoe didn't answer but went out to the phone. Jenny looked worriedly at her father. Today he looked paler than ever.

'I wish they could have left this alone till Christmas was over,' she whispered to Antony. He squeezed her shoulder and went out into the hall after Pascoe who was just replacing the receiver.

'He's out,' said Pascoe, more to himself than Antony. 'He'll ring here when he gets back.'

'Sergeant,' said Antony. 'Forgive me if I seem to be playing the amateur sleuth once again, but something else occurred to me the other day, which might or might not be of interest to you.'

269

'Let's have it,' said Pascoe. 'Every little helps. Shall we go into the other room?'

'Well no,' said Antony. 'It would make my explanation easier if we stepped outside.'

Two minutes later Antony returned to the lounge.

'Has he gone?' asked Jenny, who was sitting on the arm of her father's chair.

'No. He's in the garden again. But he sent me in to ask you something. You know a girl called Sheila Lennox?'

'Yes.'

'He wants to know if you know where she works.'

Thirty minutes later the three of them were still sitting in the lounge.

'I hope he's going to pay for his telephone calls,' said Jenny.

'It's a little price to pay to see the great detective's great detective at work,' said Antony.

Connon sat with his hand pressed to the side of his brow.

'Have you got your headache again, Daddy?' asked Jenny.

'No. Not really. Just a little. It'll pass.'

'Oh, I wish . . .' but the front-door bell interrupted Jenny's wish.

Antony rose, but they heard the door being opened before he left the room.

'How do you do, Sergeant?' boomed a familiar voice.

'Oh God,' groaned Jenny, 'it's Fat Dalziel.'

'The gang's all here,' intoned Antony.

In the dining-room, Pascoe was speaking swiftly, persuasively to Dalziel who listened intently.

'All right,' he said when the sergeant had finished. 'I'll buy it. Let's ask him now, shall we? Where's he work?'

'He doesn't today. It's Christmas Eve, remember? He finished early for Christmas. That's why I left word for you to come here.'

'That makes it easier. Come on.'

Pascoe hung back, his memories of training thronging his mind.

'Shouldn't we call up a little support? Just in case.'

Dalziel laughed contemptuously.

'A strapping young lad like you? Not to mention me, the terror of seven counties. You must be joking. Anyway, it might still be a lot of hogwash. Let's ask.'

Jenny heard the front door close.

'That's bloody polite, I must say,' she said angrily. 'In and out without a by-your-leave, and they don't even say goodbye.'

'Perhaps they're not going far,' said Antony, peering through the curtains. 'In fact, they're not. They're just going across the road.'

'Where to?' demanded Jenny, jumping up and rushing to the window.

Connon stood up too and slowly followed her.

Over the road, Dalziel held his thumb down hard on the bell-push.

'Someone knows we're here,' he said laconically. 'Or there's a big draught behind the curtains.'

'Here we are,' said Pascoe.

The door opened.

'Good morning, madam,' said Dalziel with effusive politeness to the large woman who stood there, still rubbing her sleepy eyes. 'We're police officers. I wonder if I might have a word with your son.'

Maisie Curtis opened her mouth to say something. From somewhere at the rear of the house came the slam of a door.

'Sergeant,' said Dalziel. 'The back.'

But he was speaking to an already retreating Pascoe.

Stanley Curtis was young, fit, and had a good start. When Pascoe rounded the back of the house, he had already moved across the Fernies' garden and was clearing the next hedge like a trained hurdler. Pascoe made no attempt to follow him but rapidly assessed the situation. While the barriers between the Boundary Drive gardens were uniformly low, the hedges and fences which separated the bottoms of the gardens from those of the houses behind were generally much higher.

Pascoe took this in, turned and ran past Dalziel again without a word.

The Connons saw him leap into his car like a Le Mans driver and accelerate explosively up the street.

Two hundred yards on he brought the car to an equally violent halt.

Stanley Curtis, dragging in great mouthfuls of air through his hugely open mouth, was coming out of someone's gate.

He stopped when he saw the car and made as if to turn back.

Pascoe leaned over and opened the passenger door.

'Come on, Stan,' he said. 'It's no weather to be out without your jacket.'

His chest still rising and falling spasmodically, the youth came across the pavement and climbed into the car.

'Let's get Superintendent Dalziel,' said Pascoe, swinging the car in a turn which took him up on to the pavement. 'Then we'll go somewhere quiet and have a talk. I expect you're ready for a talk, aren't you?'

Chapter 8

'I didn't kill her,' said Stanley.

'No?' said Pascoe.

They were sitting, the three of them, in Dalziel's room at the station. Mrs Curtis had with some difficulty been persuaded to leave. She had become slightly hysterical and it had taken the intervention of the boy himself to get her out. He had spoken to her with a kindly firmness which seemed to surprise her and she had left without further protest.

Pascoe too had been surprised by the maturity the youth was showing. It was as if the desperate physical effort to get away had burnt off all the panicking, fearful element in him. For the moment anyway.

'Let's start with that,' said Stanley firmly. 'I didn't kill her.'

'I hope we finish with it too,' said Pascoe.

Dalziel sat back quietly, apparently happy to leave the talking to the sergeant at this stage.

'I'd been expecting you earlier,' Stanley went on.

'Everyone seems to have been expecting us earlier. But why should you?'

'Well, the Club mainly. I'd seen you talking to people round the Club, and I'd said one or two things to my mates. Just boasting, you know.'

'About watching Mrs Connon?'

'That's right. I thought someone would tell you. Sheila perhaps. You got pretty thick with her. Joe wasn't half mad.'

Pascoe nodded.

'Yes, she did. But only when I asked. And only today. I'd overheard something once, but it didn't mean anything then. Smoke?'

Curtis shook his head. 'Not when I'm in training.' He looked anxious suddenly. 'Am I still in training? I mean, what'll happen?'

'It depends on what you've done, lad,' said Dalziel sternly. 'Just speak up and tell us everything.'

Pascoe winked fractionally at Stanley, inviting him to join in a laugh at Dalziel's portentous manner.

'Tell us about the letters first, Stanley.'

'You found them, then? I hoped you wouldn't.'

'But we did. You went back to have another look for them, didn't you?'

'I was going to. I was dead worried. But that lad was there. I nearly died when he moved and I saw him. But he didn't see me, did he?'

'No, Stanley. But he realized that you must have

275

been in the garden to be able to see him where he was sitting. He just realized that today as well.'

'Christmas Eve,' said Stanley. His eyes suddenly filled with tears.

'Just start at the beginning, lad,' boomed Dalziel. 'And get a move on, eh? Or it'll soon be Boxing Day.'

'All right,' said Stanley. 'I'll have a fag after all, can I? Bugger training. Thanks.'

He took a long draw and then began talking.

'It began accidentally. I mean, I just looked out of my bedroom window one night and I saw her. Her curtains weren't right closed and she was getting undressed. She moved around a bit and sometimes I could see, sometimes not. Like a show. Well, after that I kept my eyes open. I had an old telescope, just a kid's thing that I'd had for years. But it brought things up pretty close. It happened quite often. I got to looking forward to it. I like big women,' he said almost apologetically, glancing at Dalziel.

'We all do, lad. But we don't go around making obscene phone calls to them. Get on with it, eh?'

Stanley stubbed his cigarette out.

'That's what I did first, made a call. I'd been watching her. I didn't dare say anything when she answered. I just put the phone down. Then I started writing letters. I didn't mean to send any. But she sort of got into my mind. You know how you sometimes start thinking about women and all, well, it was always her. Finally I sent her one. Nothing happened. So I sent another. And it was as if, well, after that, she seemed to be at the window more often, you know. As if she knew and she was putting on a real show. So I wrote again. And I telephoned her when I knew Mr Connon was out. It was stupid really but I got a kick out of it. I mean, I wouldn't have done it if it was frightening her, I wouldn't frighten her, believe me. But she seemed to join in. She laughed on the phone and told me to go on, to say more. I used to work out things to say to her, new things, you know.'

'You used to ring from the box in the street outside your house?'

'That's right. That was daft too, I suppose. But being able to see the house made it more exciting somehow. Anyway, I got into the box one night, but before I could pick up the phone, it rang. I nearly dropped dead. But it kept on ringing so I answered it. It was her. "Hello, Stanley," she said, laughing, you know. "What have you got for me tonight?" She'd found out somehow. Though, Christ, I suppose it was easy enough, really. I mean, I wasn't very clever. She might even have recognized my voice. I tried to disguise it a bit at first, but then it didn't seem to matter. But it was different now. It stopped being a game.'

He fell silent. Pascoe shifted his position in his chair and asked, 'How do you mean, Stanley?'

'Well, she started getting me to do things for her.

Like run messages. Go and get her cigarettes. Or just stupid things like walk three times round the telephone box. Or sit for an hour at my window in my overcoat and Dad's trilby.'

'How do you mean, she started *getting* you to do things, Stanley?' asked Pascoe.

'I mean, she had those letters, see? And she said she'd show them. To my parents, to Mr Connon, to the police. I don't know who she wasn't going to show them to.'

'So what happened?'

'Well, in the end I told her I wasn't going to play any more. I'd had enough.'

'Told her?' queried Dalziel.

'On the phone. She made me phone her regularly. We never actually met, except by accident outside and then she just smiled at me and said good morning or whatever. Anyway she said that was up to me. If she didn't hear from me in five days, she'd start showing the letters. I just put the phone down. I mean, it seemed daft. I didn't see how she could without making herself look silly. So I wasn't bothered much at first. But as the time got nearer, the Sunday, I mean, when the five days were up, I began to really worry. Then on the Saturday, I had a couple of pints after the game and I got this idea. It seemed dead simple really. I just had to get the letters back and I'd be all right. Then there was nothing she could do. Nothing at all. I knew she had them in her bedroom, she'd told me often enough. So I got this idea that I'd just get in the house somehow, pick up the letters and be away without anyone knowing a thing about it. It seemed really funny. I thought I might even ring her afterwards for a laugh. You know, ask her to make sure the letters were safe, and all. It seemed a real giggle.'

'Was it?' asked Pascoe gently. 'Was it a giggle, Stanley?'

'Was it hell!' the boy said. 'I nearly killed myself getting in for a start. I went up the tree and through the bathroom window. I made enough noise to raise the dead, I thought, but I knew they had the telly on downstairs. It was real loud. I couldn't wait till later, see, because it was the bedroom I wanted to get into. Can I have another cigarette, please?'

Pascoe handed one over again and lit it. The boy was frowning with the effort of recollection. He had a rather long, thin face, intelligent-looking, just beginning to fill out slightly, and firm into adulthood; but still with the fragility and the remains of the mild acne which is often the stigma of adolescence.

He's just on the turn, really, thought Pascoe. Eighteen years old, a foot in both camps. She got him just at the turn.

'Go on, Stanley,' he said.

'I stopped in the bathroom for ages. At least it seemed like that. Then I thought, "you stupid twit, if anyone does come up here for any reason, chances are this is the room they'll be heading for". So I got out then. The telly was still going strong below. It was easy to work out which must be the bedroom door, so I headed along the landing towards it. The door was open. I took a step in. Then I nearly died! Someone made a noise. A sort of groan. Then this figure moved on the bed. I hadn't noticed it before, it was so dark. Then he sort of pushed himself up.'

'Who was it, Stanley? Did you know him?' asked Pascoe.

'It was Mr Connon, I think. I'm pretty certain, but I didn't stop to look closer. I just ran. I was so terrified I didn't head back for the bathroom, I went the other way to the stairs. There was still a hell of a noise down below . . .'

'What kind of noise?' snapped Dalziel.

'Voices. And laughing. And music. It might all have been the telly, I don't know. I didn't have time to find out, did I? I just set off down the stairs. I was half way down when the lounge door burst open and Mrs Connon came out. She saw me and screamed.'

'Did she recognize you, Stanley? Surely she'd recognize you?'

Stanley looked rather shamefaced.

'Well, no. She wouldn't. I mean, I'd put this thing, a stocking, over my head, like they do, you know!'

'Oh Christ!' groaned Dalziel.

'What happened then?' said Pascoe.

'She just stood there. She only screamed once. Then this man . . .'

'Which man?'

'The man in the lounge with her.'

'Did you see him? Do you know him?'

'No. I mean I didn't see him. Not really. I heard him say something like, "What's the matter?" or something like that. And I sort of half saw him coming up behind her. But I wasn't going to wait, was I? I just threw my . . . this . . . something at her, you know, not to hurt, just in panic, and she stepped back and must have bumped into him, and I shot past and out of the front door. I don't even remember opening it.'

'What did you do then, Stanley?'

'There wasn't anyone in the road, luckily. I dragged the stocking off as I got out of the gate and ran all the way up to the main road. Then I just walked about for a bit, had a drink. I was scared stiff, I didn't know what to do. I went back home after about an hour, I suppose. I wanted to see what was happening. But it was all quiet. I watched from my bedroom for ages. Then about eleven o'clock, the police came, to Mr Connon's house, I mean. I couldn't understand why they'd taken so long. I mean, I thought it was about me, you see. I didn't find out about Mrs Connon till the next morning.'

'Why didn't you come and tell us all this, Stanley?'

The boy wrinkled his nose as if at the stupidity of the question.

'I was scared. I was so frightened I was sick. I

281

couldn't go to work for most of that week. I just hoped that things would get quiet, that it would all blow over. But it didn't.'

His shoulders sagged hopelessly.

Pascoe leaned forward and spoke sympathetically.

'Just one more thing, Stanley,' he said. 'What was it you threw at Mrs Connon?'

Stanley stopped sagging and looked alert, uneasy.

'Why, nothing,' he said. 'Just something I picked up, I suppose. I don't know.'

'Wasn't it something you took into the house with you, Stanley? Wasn't it something belonging to you?'

A look of stubborn obstinacy came over the youth's face. Dalziel stood up and moved swiftly behind him. His hands came down like a pair of great clamps on his shoulders.

'Listen, my lad,' he hissed close to his ear. 'When Sergeant Pascoe asks you a question, he deserves an answer. He's bloody well going to get an answer, isn't he?'

Stanley twisted free.

'What's it matter anyway?' he cried. 'All right. It was a gun. Not a gun really, a pistol, an air-pistol. It was just an old thing. I hadn't used it for years. It was old when I got it as well. I just took it along for . . . I don't know why I took it! I wouldn't have used it, I mean, it didn't work anyway, did it?'

'How should we know, Stanley?' said Pascoe. 'Where is it now?'

'I don't know. I left it. I didn't go back and ask for it.'

The boy crumpled again. Pascoe stood up and went to the door.

'Excuse me a second, sir,' he said.

'Go ahead,' said Dalziel, gloomily looking down at Stanley.

'You're in trouble, lad,' he said. 'Even if you're telling the truth, you're in trouble. You know that. But if you're not, then you're really in it. Just have a think. A long, long think and see if there's anything else you haven't told us.'

They were both still bowed in contemplative silence when Pascoe returned. He was carrying a box.

'Stanley,' he said. 'Open the box.'

The youth reached forward and took the lid off, one-handed, then froze as he saw what was inside.

'Stanley, is that yours?' asked Pascoe.

The boy peered closer, then nodded.

'Yes, that's it. That's mine. But look at it. It's old and rusty. It couldn't hurt anyone, that.'

Pascoe reached into the box and took out the pistol.

'You're right,' he said. 'I don't suppose it could.'

He looked at Dalziel and raised his eyebrows.

Dalziel shook his head.

Pascoe went to the door again.

'Constable,' he said to the uniformed man outside, 'take Mr Curtis along to the interview room, will you? Both his parents are there now. He can talk to them, but be present all the time. And watch him. He's a nippy runner.'

He smiled cheerfully at Stanley as he left the room and the boy managed a wan grin in reply.

'You managed that quite well, Sergeant,' said the superintendent.

'Thank you, sir.'

'Now suppose you let me into your confidence and tell me where you've been hiding this.'

A great paw was waved at the pistol. Pascoe held it up and squinted along the barrel. It was, as Stanley had said, old and rusty, but it still looked formidably solid, eight inches of steel tube pointing menacingly at Dalziel.

'I haven't been hiding it. It was hidden though, in a pond up on the Common. It was brought back to daylight only yesterday, when they were looking for Mickey Annan. I noticed it on the list.'

'But didn't connect it with the Connon case at the time I hope?'

'Of course not, sir. I'd have mentioned it, wouldn't I? But there was a connection there for us to see, if we'd known. In the chair.'

'The chair.'

'The chair she was killed on. There was a list of things they found in it. Ordinary things, money and the like. It's all back with Connon now.'

'I saw it. Wait. Of course, there was a pellet.'

'That's right, one air-gun pellet.'

'But what's this leading to, Sergeant? You're not suggesting she was clubbed to death with the barrel of that thing? How the hell would you hold it if you were trying to produce something like that effect?'

'Like this,' said Pascoe.

He held the pistol up between them twisting his hand so they both had a side view.

And he pressed the trigger.

A six-inch cylinder of steel crashed out of the barrel, extending its length to over a foot.

'Now we load it,' said Pascoe, putting the end against the wall and forcing the internal cylinder back into the shorter barrel.

'Then we fire it again.'

This time he held it close to the frame of the window.

'Hell,' he said, nursing his wrist.

There was a circular dent nearly half-an-inch deep in the wood.

'That's public property,' observed Dalziel. 'Also you're making forensic's job more difficult.'

Pascoe returned the gun to the box.

'I've told them it'll be coming down.'

'That's a nasty bit of machinery,' said Dalziel.

'It's an old-fashioned bit. I don't know if they make them like that any more. It's years since I had an air-pistol. What now, sir?'

Dalziel scratched his navel.

'I think we'd better have another talk with Connon.'

'Do you believe young Curtis?'

'Yes,' said Dalziel, and added surprisingly, 'and I sympathize with him a bit. When you're that age, it's all sex, isn't it? I've seen him hanging around Gwen Evans at the Club too, wishing he dared. He does like 'em big, doesn't he? I think we all discovered the comic-obscene possibilities of the telephone in our teens, didn't we? If Mary Connon had shouted at him, told her husband, started drawing her curtains, that would have been an end to it. But she wasn't like that, Mary. She always liked to be controlling people.'

'What about this other man? Lover? Or what?'

'How the hell should I know? But you're not the only one who's been out detecting today, Sergeant. I had a long talk with Evans, remember?'

I think he's really hurt I didn't ask, thought Pascoe.

'What did he say?'

'He said he met Mary Connon at her invitation. He said she wanted to discuss with him the relationship between his wife and her husband which was causing her considerable distress.'

Pascoe shook his head in amazement.

'That woman. I'm beginning to be glad I didn't know her.'

'Not much chance of that now anyway, lad. It's the living we're after. I've got a man sitting outside Evans's door. He won't go far. But there's a few questions Mr Connon's got to answer first of all. Let's hope he's co-operative or we'll never get to Jacko's party.'

The television was on in Connon's lounge when

286

they arrived. It was Christmas Eve fare, a selection from the old silent film comedies. Antony had turned the sound down to cut out the nauseating superimposed American commentary and the only sound for the past half hour had been his and Jenny's chuckles.

Even Connon had smiled from time to time, Jenny had observed with pleasure.

The doorbell's chime was an unwelcome interruption. Nor were the visitors it harbingered any the more welcome.

'Privately, please,' said Dalziel. 'We'd like to see you alone, Mr Connon. Perhaps we can leave these two young people to their television.'

Jenny rolled her eyes at the unctuous condescension of Dalziel's tone. Pascoe laughed as the Keystone police-waggon lost another half dozen incumbents.

'Come into the dining-room,' said Connon.

He and Pascoe sat opposite each other at the dining-table. Dalziel stood in the bay, blocking out the light.

'Superintendent,' said Connon.

'Yes?'

'Stan Curtis. We saw what happened earlier. What has he got to do with my wife's death?'

'Should he have anything?'

'I cannot imagine so for one moment. Where is he?'

'He's at the station at the moment, sir, helping us with our enquiries.'

'How?'

'He has admitted being illegally present in your house on the night of your wife's death. More serious charges against him are at present under review.'

Nasty old Dalziel, thought Pascoe. What a little liar he is.

'No,' said Connon. 'No. Not Stanley. It was Stanley who was here?'

He sounded amazed.

'That's right. Why not?'

'I didn't think . . .'

Connon tailed off.

'Didn't think what? Never mind. There'll be time for that later.'

Connon was rubbing the side of his head. Dalziel suddenly wheeled round, sat down beside Connon and began speaking urgently, in a low voice to him.

'Come on, Connie. Tell us about it. Make it easy, boy. It's got to come out now. Got to. Just fill in the gaps.'

Connon sat silent. He looked really ill.

'For God's sake!' exploded Dalziel. 'Don't you believe us? We don't know it all, but we know enough. All we want are the little things. Why did you clean up the bathroom windowsill and close the window, for instance? And drop the pistol into the pond on the Common? What were they doing when you came downstairs? What were they up to? Making love?'

Tut, tut, thought Pascoe. He's at it again. He read the pathologist's report as closely as I did.

'Come on, Mr Connon,' he said. 'It'll help everyone to get it out in the open. You. And Jenny. Who was it downstairs? Arthur Evans?'

Connon sat looking blankly ahead. Outside the telephone rang. The door opened and Jenny came in.

'It's for you,' she said to Pascoe. 'Daddy, are you all right? What's going on anyway?'

Pascoe went out to the phone.

It was the desk-sergeant down town.

'Pete?' he said. 'Alan here. Sorry to interrupt whatever I'm interrupting but you did say you wanted anything new at once. Well, it's probably nothing, but a chap called Johnson just rang up for you. Landlord of a boozer, the Blue Bell. He said you'd been asking about Gwen Evans, whether she'd been in on the sixth. None of his lot could remember her, he said, and then it had gone out of his mind, till they started talking about her leaving her husband. News gets round. Then he mentioned it again and one of his women, a temp, only comes in at weekends, says she was definitely in that night, for at least an hour. She served her twice. She remembers clearly she says, because she went sick on the Sunday after and was laid up for the next two weekends.'

'What's she doing there now then? It's not a weekend.'

'It's Christmas Eve. Remember? Lots of people

actually go out and enjoy themselves. Big crowds in pubs. Merry Christmas.'

'You too, Alan. Thanks.'

So Gwen had been in the Blue Bell that night as she said at first, not lying spread out on the counterpane as she was willing to admit later. Later, when Dalziel had had a go at . . .

He went quickly back into the lounge. He'd been dimly aware of background noises as he took his call. Now they stopped, but the little tableau that greeted him – Jenny, flushed, standing with her hands on her father's shoulders; Antony, concerned, just behind her; Connon, blank, staring at the empty rose-bowl in the centre of the table; and Dalziel, hands spread out in front of him, with his injured, professional footballer's what-have-I-done expression on his large face – this was enough to tell him there had been some kind of row.

He didn't need to be a detective to guess the details. But he was a detective, and he was too near the truth now to be deterred by considerations of health, feeling, or sentiment.

'Tell me, Mr Connon,' he said harshly. 'Tell me, why had Mr Felstead come to see your wife that night?'

The tableau remained the same. Only the expressions changed.

But it was Connon's alone that he watched. For a second it froze into an even greater withdrawal, a kind of desperation. Then slowly it dissolved, the life and movement came back and something very like relief rose to the surface of the eyes.

He let out a long sigh and glanced round at his daughter and Antony.

'May they stay?' he asked.

'If you wish it,' said Dalziel.

'Yes. It's best. I'll do my best to be brief.'

'No need to hurry, Mr Connon,' said Pascoe.

He smiled.

'Once you decide to have a tooth out, Sergeant, don't you want to run to the dentist? It's not all that complicated really, not any more than human beings are, anyway. Though that's enough I suppose. What happened was this. Everything I told you about my going home and passing out was true. Only I woke up again much earlier. Shortly after eight I should think. I went out on to the landing. There seemed to be some kind of disturbance downstairs, but I was still too dazed to pay much attention. I went into the bathroom and bathed my face in cold water. That woke me up a little. I noticed the window was wide open and the fresh air helped clear my head as well. Then I set off downstairs.'

'How long had this taken?' asked Dalziel. Jenny looked at him angrily.

'Five minutes. Longer. I don't know. Anyway, I came downstairs and opened the lounge door. The television was still on, no other lights. Mary was still in the chair with its back to me. In front of her stood Marcus. He had this pistol in his hand. I could hear Mary laughing, it was as if something very funny had happened. The pistol was sort of hanging loose. Now Marcus raised it up. Mary stretched out her hand and seemed to pull it towards her. I couldn't see properly because of the chair.'

'What did Mr Felstead look like?' asked Pascoe.

'Like?'

'Angry? Puzzled? Or was he joining in the joke?'

'He looked . . . annoyed. Not in a rage, but annoyed.'

'What happened then?'

'There was a kind of crash and an odd kind of splintering noise. Marcus stepped back. He said something like, "Oh Christ!" And he went deadly pale. Then he looked up and saw me. I came into the room and walked round the chair so I could see Mary.'

He glanced up at Jenny who took his hand and held it hard.

'Her forehead was crushed in. Not much, it seemed, but I could tell she was dead. She still had a cigarette in her hand. I took it out and put it in the ash-tray. Then Marcus started to talk.'

'This is very important,' said Pascoe urgently. 'What did he say?'

'The exact words? I can't remember. He was very very upset. So was I. But he told me he didn't mean it, it was an accident. He kept on saying this. He said over and over again that it was an accident. He begged me to believe him. He became almost hysterical.'

'And you, Mr Connon.'

'I felt numb at first. Then my head began to ache again and I felt sick and faint, just like before. But Marcus was in a worse state, I think, and this seemed to help me. I had to help him out of the room. I got him a drink. Then I went to the telephone. I suppose I was going to phone McManus, or the police. I don't really know. It just seemed necessary to phone someone.'

'And did you?'

Connon shook his head regretfully.

'No. No, I didn't. He stopped me. He begged me not to, till I'd heard him out. Then he told me his story. He told me about him and Gwen Evans to start with.'

'Didn't you know before?'

'Not a thing. He'd kept it very dark. I knew Arthur was very jealous and reckoned that something was going on. Now and then I got the impression he even suspected me.'

He laughed shortly.

'I even told Mary. She was very amused.'

Pascoe glanced at Dalziel who shook his head almost imperceptibly.

'But he certainly never gave Marcus a thought,' went on Connon. 'Nor did I. But according to Marcus, Mary had somehow found out. I don't know how, nor did he.'

He glanced anxiously at his daughter.

'Don't think badly of your mother, dear. I'm sorry you've got to hear this at all, but it's better now than later.'

He looked at Dalziel and added, very clearly, 'In court.'

'What was Mrs Connon up to, sir?' asked Pascoe. 'Some kind of blackmail?'

He kept his gaze firmly away from Jenny.

'Not in the real sense of the word, not in any criminal sense,' said Connon urgently. 'Believe that. No, according to Marcus, she was just entertaining herself, if that's the word, by ringing Gwen up from time to time. She seemed to have a keen instinct for when they were together. She'd just chatter about this or that, ordinary everyday things, but just slanted so that all the time Gwen knew she knew. When they met, it was the same. Conspiratorial glances behind Arthur's back, that kind of thing. Nothing else though. No threats.'

'You believed what Mr Felstead told you.'

Another quick glance at Jenny.

'Yes,' he said slowly. 'I could believe it.'

I bet you could, thought Pascoe. I never met your wife and I could believe it.

'Let's get back to that Saturday night,' said Dalziel.

Connon pulled out a packet of cigarettes and began to light one, then pulled himself up as at an unconscious discourtesy and offered them round.

They all refused. Pascoe was reminded of Stanley Curtis.

'Marcus said that the previous day, Friday, in the morning, Mary had telephoned Gwen to say that she was going to have a drink with Arthur at lunch time. She said it casually, but made it sound full of significance. Gwen was worried sick. She said that Arthur was very strange that night. I don't know whether Mary had seen him or not, or if she had, what she had said.'

Again the glance between Pascoe and Dalziel. This time, Pascoe realized, Antony had caught it too.

'But the following night, Saturday, when Marcus called on Gwen just to see her briefly before she went down to the Club, he found her near breaking point. Mary had been on the phone again earlier in the evening. She'd asked if Arthur had mentioned their meeting. Gwen had started to scream at her down the phone, but Mary had just laughed. She'd kept on listening and laughing. She was capable of great cruelty at times.'

Times we shall never hear of, thought Pascoe. Is the girl old enough to understand? I hope to God she is for both their sakes.

'So Marcus headed round here?' said Dalziel.

'Yes.'

'In a rage? To have a showdown?'

'Yes. I expect so. He told me he came determined to see us both. He'd been tempted to talk to me for some time, he said. But when he asked where I was, Mary told him I was sleeping it off upstairs. She said I was drunk. She must have been up to see where I was earlier and found me on the bed. She'd undone my collar, I think,' he added, as though in irritation.

'Anyway they had a row; or rather, Marcus told me, he yelled and threatened while she just sat and smiled at him. Finally there was a pause and they heard a movement upstairs. I don't know whether it was me or Stanley.'

'Stanley?' said Jenny in surprise. 'Stanley who?'

'I'll explain later, love,' he said. 'She got up then and said it was time I came down to hear what my so-called best friend thought of her. She went to the door and opened it, then screamed. Marcus went after her just in time to see someone scuttle across the hall and out of the front door. He'd thrown something down. It was an airpistol. Marcus picked it up and was going after the intruder, but she stopped him. He said he had a feeling that she thought she knew who it was. If it was Stanley, he was probably right. Well, to cut things short, it all started again. Things got very nasty from the sound of it. Mary suggested they should ring Arthur and ask him what he thought about the affair. Marcus said he was still waving the pistol around. She laughed at him and asked him if he imagined he was a gangster or something. He told me he thought of firing it at her then, but as he lifted it up, he said that the slug came trickling out of the barrel and dropped on the chair beside her. It must have looked a bit absurd. Mary thought it was hilarious. According to Marcus she made a big thing of it, saying things like, "Was he going to kill me, then? With his little toy gun?" that kind of thing. She reached out, he said, and lifted the gun up till it rested against her forehead. That's when I must have come down. Then, Marcus said, still laughing she pressed his finger where it was over the trigger.'

He ran his hand over his face nervously.

'I'm glad you know,' he said.

'But I don't understand,' said Jenny. 'What happened? If there was no pellet in it . . .'

'The pistol was of a type that worked by pressing an inner cylinder into the outer one against a very strong spring as well as the resulting air pressure. Even unloaded, the inner cylinder is jerked out with very great force to an extent of about six inches. Pressed hard against someone's head which in turn was resting hard up against the back of a chair . . .'

Pascoe didn't finish, Jenny sat down, her face pale. Antony hovered anxiously over her.

'Why didn't you ring the police, Mr Connon?' asked Dalziel. 'You still haven't told us.'

Connon shrugged hopelessly.

'I don't know. I wish to God I had. He swore it was an accident, but he asked me how it would sound to the police. Would they believe him? I couldn't say they would. I . . .'

'Go on.'

'I half didn't believe him myself. He was my friend, but it was my wife sitting there, dead. I was lost, quite lost. I couldn't see what to do.'

'Do you believe him now?'

'Yes. Yes, I think I do. The pellet helped. I thought of it later, but I couldn't find it anywhere. Then I doubted him very much. But it turned up among those objects your people found down the chair. I was overjoyed to find it. It makes a difference, doesn't it?'

'Yes, it does,' said Pascoe, more reassuringly than he felt Dalziel would approve.

'Marcus said if I changed my mind later, he'd be ready to tell you everything. But he begged me not to involve him now. He wanted us to let the burglar, Stanley that is, be blamed. But I refused to do that. I said we couldn't do that. I wouldn't risk anyone else being blamed. I suppose once I started arguing on those lines, I'd really agreed to help him. He agreed in the end and in fact it was Marcus who suggested that we should cover up any traces of the intruder.'

'He must have realized that if we got on to the burglar there'd be even more chance of us getting on to him,' observed Dalziel drily.

Connon ignored him.

'I remembered the bathroom window. We cleaned up the sill and closed the window. Marcus put the gun in his pocket and said he'd get rid of it. I could hardly think straight at all, he had to think of everything.'

'The prospect of a murder charge concentrates the mind wonderfully,' said Dalziel.

This time Connon answered.

'No, I don't think it was that, I think it was the thought of Arthur Evans more than anything else. Arthur is potentially a violent man. Marcus isn't. He's a terrible tackler, always was. Not frightened for himself, so much as frightened of causing damage. I think he was thinking of Gwen as much as himself.'

'He's let it all come out in the open now,' said Pascoe.

'I know,' said Connon. 'I had a letter.'

'Where? Where from?' snapped Dalziel eagerly.

'Posted in town, Superintendent. So it's no help, I'm afraid. Oh, you're welcome to see it. He just says they're going. Tells me to tell it all if I have to, not to worry, but says he and Gwen want a time alone, together, without having to worry and lie.'

'He needs to worry,' said Dalziel. 'We'll find him.'

Connon gave a sudden smile which lit up his face.

'I doubt it, Superintendent. Marcus'll see the papers and read between the lines and, in his own time, he'll find you. What happens now? To me I mean. I suppose I've committed any number of offences.'

Dalziel loomed menacingly over him.

'You've been bloody stupid, Connie. No, it's no good giving me those nasty looks, Jennifer! He has and he knows it. He's not a stupid man. He just acts stupid sometimes.'

'I did it for friendship,' said Connon. 'Mary was dead. It seemed to serve no purpose letting my friend be dragged through the courts. But you're right, Dalziel. I knew you were right the next morning. I was even more certain when that letter came to Jenny. I think another week of it would have broken me down, friendship or none. I'm glad you know.'

'So am I,' said Dalziel. 'Don't worry, there'll be no more letters.'

'What happens next isn't up to me,' Dalziel went on. 'You know that. We'll need your statement first. Then a full account of the case will have to be studied by the decision-makers. I hope for your sake they're not soccer men.'

He glowered at Pascoe who said, 'Whatever happens, Mr Connon, you'll be here for Christmas if that's any consolation.'

Connon looked round at Jenny and Antony, who smiled reassuringly at him.

'Yes. Yes,' he said. 'I think it is.'

The Fernies watched the police-car drive away with Connon in it.

'If you say "I told you so",' said Alice, 'I'll hit you so hard you won't be able to sup beer tomorrow, let alone chew turkey.'

'No, no,' said Fernie. 'It's not that. They haven't arrested him. Look at those two, Jenny and that lad. They're looking far too pleased with each other for that.'

'Now you're a long-distance psychiatrist too,' said Alice. 'Hey, get off! What do you think you're on? I've got work to do.'

'Mine when, as and how I cared to use it. That's what you told that policeman, wasn't it? You wouldn't like to be got for perjury, would you?'

'Oh God. This'll ruin the stuffing.'

'But you're right. You've as much as she ever had. And it is noticeably younger.'

'He looks so much happier,' said Jenny as she drove her father's car after the police-car towards town. 'No wonder he was cracking up, with all that on his mind.'

Antony observed her curiously from the passenger seat.

'What about you, love? All that about your mother, I mean, didn't it come as a shock?'

'Not really. I don't mean I approve or defend her, but whatever she was like, she was like that when I knew her, so I don't see why I should suddenly change towards her now.'

She accelerated to cross a light at amber while Antony stood on an imaginary brake.

'I think that she was just jealous. Women do strange things when they're jealous. You'll find out when we get back to college. I want a ring, I don't care if it's expensive or not, but it's got to be bloody big! No, she was jealous of Gwen, that's all. Wanted to control her somehow. She made a friend of Alice Fernie, you see; condescended to her, could control her that way. But with Gwen it had to be something different. Do I sound very cold?'

Antony looked at her face. Her eyes were brimful of tears.

'No, love,' he said. 'Not at all. But if you're going

to cry, pull in to the kerb before you give us all something to cry about.'

Her face broke apart into the Connon grin as the tears overflowed and, glinting in the Christmas lights strung across the streets, rolled down the curve of her cheeks.

'She was a bitch. Thank God I didn't know her,' said Pascoe thickly.

Connon's statement had taken some time. They had got to Jacko's party very late, but had quickly made up for lost time.

'She wasn't that bad,' said Dalziel, more clearly, though Pascoe knew he'd taken twice as much drink as himself. 'Not when I knew her. It depends how you look at them. At least they stayed together.'

He had shown a surprising desire to stick in his sergeant's company at the party. Pascoe wondered if his inferior rank made him a more desirable auditor of drunken ramblings.

'Not like the Evanses. She left him a letter. Hey, talking of letters, what did you mean when you said to Connon, there'd be no more?'

'That letter,' said Dalziel solemnly. 'That letter to Jenny Connon. It was written in green ink.'

'Oh yes?' said Pascoe puzzled. 'What's that sig-nify?'

'It signifies Arthur Evans wrote it. My copy was in black ink. That signified he didn't.'

Pascoe digested this in silence for a while.

'I see,' he said finally. 'What does all that signify?'

'It signifies,' said Dalziel, 'that men do bloody stupid things when they're worried about their wives. I spoke to him. He listened to me. He listened to the advice of experience.'

'His wife still left him.'

'He's still in the Club.'

'I suppose that's some compensation,' said Pascoe doubtfully. 'Better than her being in it, eh, sir?'

They laughed raucously.

'Was she a bitch? She left him. Connon's wife seemed a bigger bitch, but she didn't leave him. Are those the bigger bitches, do you think? Isn't it better to get a letter?'

'My wife,' said Dalziel slowly, 'my wife sent me a telegram.'

Pascoe shifted uneasily, suddenly rather more sober. He wasn't at all sure he wanted to be cast in the role of Dalziel's confidant. Christmas comes but once a year, the jingle tripped incessantly through his mind.

He tried to divert the conversation on to fresh tracks.

'There's a silly game called "Telegram",' he said brightly. (Christ! my brightness is more hammy than even his performances!) But neither his brightness nor his attempts at diversion seemed to be noticed. They would be registered, however; that he was certain of. Dalziel's mind might get as soggy as a damp brantub, but sometime, somehow, he would grope around in the clart and come up with these moments clear and sharp as a policeman's whistle.

'Words too harsh to be spoken,' said Dalziel. 'Words too bloody violent to be heard. Things she couldn't say to me, face to face. Me. Her husband. She wrote them down. On a bit of paper. Gave them to a counter-clerk to count.'

(Which of course is what a counter-clerk ought to be doing, thought Pascoe. Or he might have said it. He couldn't tell which one second later.)

'A stranger read them. They were copied. Printed out. Despatched. All those people knowing what I didn't know.'

Please God, prayed Pascoe, let him stop. I'm an ambitious man. I don't want to hear him. Besides I'm sure Noolan's wife fancies me. Not so old either. But if I don't move soon I'll have to join a queue.

Somewhere in the house a clock chimed midnight. For a moment everyone was still. Most of the Rugby Club lot, the elders at least, were there. He saw them all it seemed as he glanced round the room. He felt almost fond of them.

He fumbled in his pocket and produced a small cylinder of gay Christmas paper. He hadn't known till now whether he would dare give it.

'Merry Christmas, sir.'

'What the hell's this? Apple for teacher?'

That was better.

'Just a little gift. Christmas. And end of case.'

Dalziel carefully unwrapped the large expensive cigar and sniffed it appraisingly.

'It's not ended yet,' he said. 'We've still got to find Felstead.'

'What'll happen?'

'God knows. Manslaughter? At least, I should think. But let's catch him first.'

'Tomorrow, Boxing Day. He's an amateur. And he's got Gwen Evans to attract attention. Five bob they have him in forty-eight hours.'

Dalziel shook his head gloomily.

'I won't take your money, lad. Thanks for this, though.'

He put the cigar in his mouth and lit it.

'Not a bad party,' he said. 'Hey, Willie. Where've you been hiding? Take me to Jacko's brandy bottle.'

Kids, thought Pascoe. Big kids. Like Jenny Connon, and Antony, and Stanley, and Sheila. Little kids.

He started to cut an efficient path through the crowd towards the ample, mature charms of Mrs Willie Noolan.

Envoi

It was a cold, hard January day, the last Saturday in the month. The weather delighted the hearts of thousands who by car, foot, and train were making their way towards Twickenham.

Connon let himself be swept out of the station by the steady onward flow of the crowd. A loudspeaker warned him that the official programme was on sale only in the ground.

As usual, the police seemed to have invented a new system of pedestrian diversion since his last visit and the route they followed afforded him several tantalizing glimpses of the stands before the final approach.

Even so, there was still half an hour to go before kick-off when he reached the ground. He joined a small queue for an official programme, another for an official cushion. Then he joined a larger queue winding its way into the urinal, and smiled to hear someone say, 'Someone's pissing in my pocket.' He always smiled at that.

Outside again he paused, buffeted by the purposeful swirl of people all around him. On an impulse he did not head round to the West Bar where he usually met up with old friends, but made his way directly to his seat. It was high in the East Stand. Round and round he climbed, finally emerging into the bright sunlight and almost frightening spaciousness of the stand itself. A man in a sheepskin jacket and Robin Hood hat looked at his ticket and directed him to his row. He found he was sitting next but one to the aisle.

Far below, an unreal distance it seemed, lay the ground. From up here there was nothing to mar the perfection of the white-edged rectangles of bright green. A military band stood in the middle playing fitfully into the gusty wind. Clusters of notes rose up to the top of the stand and he pieced together a melody from *Oklahoma*. Two boys suddenly ran in from the ringside seats. They carried between them a banner which had painted on it in large red letters 'WALES'. Boos and cheers rose in almost solid blocks from different parts of the ground. Another group of boys climbed over the fence as the banner was brought beneath the West Stand. The Welsh boys recognized the enemy and ran, but found themselves cut off. There was a brief skirmish and the banner was torn. Around the ground the boos and cheers changed places.

'There's a lot more of this nowadays,' said a grey-haired man in front of Connon.

'Too bloody much if you ask me,' said his neighbour.

The ground was very full now. Connon looked along his row. Every seat was taken except the one next to the aisle. Down below the band was on the move. It left the playing area and came to a halt on the touch-line. There was a momentary hush from the crowd. Connon leaned forward expectantly. Then out of the tunnel beneath the West Stand came trotting the red-shirted Welshmen. A great scream of welcome went up from the crowd. The red-rosetted man next to Connon waved his arms so violently that Connon felt in some danger. The noise still had not died down when it was overtaken and swallowed by the great trumpeting cry which announced the appearance of the English.

Clapping enthusiastically, Connon thought, the Celts make more noise, perhaps, but there's a touch of hysteria about it. It's partly a threat. *We* roar for love.

They also sing better, he had to acknowledge a few moments later. But then so do canaries.

England kicked off. The wind caught the ball, held it in the air, then dropped it just short of the ten-yard line. The Welsh took the scrum and won the ball. But the English back row were round like lightning and the ball was despatched to touch. It didn't bounce.

Someone took the seat next to Connon.

'Hello Marcus,' he said.

The English fly-half had the ball. He sent the defence moving the wrong way with a dummy scissors, but not enough. Kick through! urged Connon mentally. He didn't and was dragged down by a Welsh centre.

'Well Connie,' said Marcus. 'What are our chances?'

'Fair, if we use the wind properly. That full-back of theirs has got a big bum. He's slow on the turn. How are you?'

'Very well,' said Marcus.

The Welsh had the ball from the ruck and were developing an attack down the middle. But the cover was good and too quick to allow a break. Play finally came to a halt ten yards behind the English twenty-five.

'They'll be watching for you, Marcus,' said Connon.

'They've found me already,' said Marcus with a laugh.

Now Connon looked round. Standing at the entrance to the stairs about ten feet back were Dalziel and Pascoe.

'I think they were disappointed that I came, in a way. They hoped to see more of the match.'

'Why did you come, Marcus?'

The English full-back took the ball almost on his own line and found touch near half way.

'I couldn't hide forever, could I? I just wanted a few weeks with Gwen. That's all. In case it goes badly. You never know, do you?'

'You kept well out of the way.'

'A cottage in the Lakes. We've been snowed up most of the time. The local bobby actually ploughed his way through to check if we needed help.'

'Did you?'

'It's been the happiest month of my life,' replied Marcus quietly.

The Welsh had the ball again. This time their fly-half had room to move and side-stepped the over-impetuous approach of the wing-forward with ease. This took him back towards the packs but he went on happily with an arrogant certainty that his pack would retrieve the ball from any ruck which made Connon's heart sink. They did, but only with a helping hand from the floor. The English full-back indicated he was going to have a kick at goal.

'You've changed, Connie. I don't know how, but somehow,' said Marcus as preparations for the kick were undertaken. 'You don't believe that I . . . that what happened to Mary wasn't an accident now, do you?'

'No,' said Connon. 'But what I did, or what I didn't do, when I found out what happened, later I knew I couldn't have acted like that if somewhere deep I hadn't been glad Mary was dead. I was glad then, Marcus, glad in some dead, secret way. That stopped it from being a real accident. Volition and result, they don't make an accident.'

Marcus was aghast.

'Listen, Connie,' he urged, 'it was nothing to do with you that it happened. You can't blame yourself . . .'

'Oh, I don't,' said Connon. 'Not now. Because I found I quickly stopped being glad in any way. Mary wasn't a good woman, I know, and often not a very pleasant person. I'd often wished I could escape her. Get far far away from her, from everyone.'

He laughed at himself.

'I got away. To my desert. I got to my desert, and it was just what you'd expect a desert to be. Hot, dusty, empty, killing.'

The full-back stabbed at the ball and sliced it badly. An ironic cheer went up. A Welshman gathered it on his own line and shaped to kick for touch.

'I'm sorry, Connie,' said Marcus quietly. 'I suppose because I knew, about you and Mary I mean, I suppose I thought it didn't matter as much somehow.'

'It always matters. To all of us it matters. It matters to me, it matters to Arthur Evans. I suppose it even mattered to him.'

He jerked his head back to where Dalziel was still standing pointing out some feature of the game to Pascoe.

'Now I can mourn properly. Goodbye Marcus. I shall see you again. I'm in a little bit of trouble myself, you know.'

'I'm sorry,' said Marcus again, standing up. 'Goodbye.'

He went back up the steps to the policemen.

'Well, I got some use out of my ticket,' he said. 'Thanks. Why don't you stay, Bruiser, and see the rest of the game? The sergeant here's more than capable of dealing with me, I'm sure.'

Dalziel looked tempted for a moment, but shook his head.

'Can't be done,' he said. 'Would look bad on my report. Anyway we've got a great deal to ask you, Mr Felstead.'

'So formal,' murmured Marcus. He moved forward, but Dalziel restrained him.

'Wait a mo',' he said.

The Welsh kick had found touch. Now the ball had come back badly on the English side, but the scrum-half got to it. He was pounced on before he could move and the best he could do was to throw out a slow lobbing pass to his fly-half, who had to take it standing still. But miraculously with a simple twist of his hips, he opened a gap between the two Welsh forwards bearing furiously down on him, stepped through it and suddenly accelerated straight ahead.

'Run! Run!' screamed Dalziel.

'Go now!' yelled Pascoe, not quite sure why he felt so excited by this alien game.

'Nothing can stop him,' said Marcus with certainty.

He was right. The cover was far too slow in coming across. Head high, ball held lightly before him, beautifully balanced, he rounded the full-back as though he were rooted and touched down gently, undramatically, between the posts.

'Oh, you beauty!' breathed Dalziel. 'You beauty!'

He sighed and shook his head as though coming back to reality.

'Right,' he said. 'Let's go.'

'The kick?' suggested Marcus.

'To hell with the kick. He might miss it. Let's go now,' said Dalziel.

Marcus took a last glance back at Connon before going through the exit, but he wasn't looking. He was slowly sitting down again after the leap of jubilation which had taken him and thousands of others to their feet.

There were tears in his eyes. He rubbed one away.

The Welshman next to him nudged his neighbour and surreptitiously pointed to Connon.

'The buggers have got feelings after all, boy,' he said.